desert autumn

NOVELS BY MICHAEL CRAFT

Rehearsing

The Mark Manning Series
Flight Dreams
Eye Contact
Body Language
Name Games
Boy Toy

The Claire Gray Series
Desert Autumn

www.michaelcraft.com

MICHAEL CRAFT

desert autumn

 st. martin's minotaur ♏ new york

www.minotaurbooks.com

Design by Michael Collica

ISBN 0-312-28034-3

First Edition: December 2001

10   9   8   7   6   5   4   3   2   1

Mon septième livre,
il commence encore
pour Léon

acknowledgments

The author thanks Gregory Baer, Jack Ellison, L. Joane Garcia-Colson, and Helen Lee for their generous assistance with various plot details. Special notes of gratitude are offered to Teresa Theophano, who makes things happen, and to Mitchell Waters and Keith Kahla, whose efforts, trust, and enthusiasm have helped bring this new series to print.

PART ONE

dust devils

Why, I wondered, would a woman of my age even flirt with the notion of starting over, much less do it? At fifty-four, most of us are resigned to the course of our lives, and if success has deigned to smile upon the efforts of our chosen work, we dare to think ourselves content. Why, then, would I uproot myself from Manhattan, where I have spent my entire adult life, and move some three thousand miles southwest to California, to the Sonoran Desert? Why would I forsake the seedy glamour of Broadway, where my career as a director—

A dust devil skipped across the road, nipping my bout of introspection as I swerved the car to avoid hitting the child-size whirlwind of sand, an oddity of this arid region that still seemed new and unnatural and thrilling to me. Equally new, unnatural, and thrilling was the experience of driving a car, a skill that had never been required during my many years in cab-clogged New York, a skill that I had just recently mastered.

Punching the brake of my days-old Beetle, lurching to a stop a yard or two into the intersection, I realized that "mastered" was a tad generous. Fortunately, traffic was light on that Saturday morning in early September as I drove northwest (up valley, as the locals would phrase it) along Highway 111, leaving Palm Desert, passing through Rancho Mirage, headed toward Palm Springs.

My mission that morning was to meet a plane, or rather a colleague on a plane arriving from Dallas. It was strange to think of Paul Huron as a colleague. Until a few weeks ago, I would have applied that term to a fellow director, a playwright, or even an actor. Paul, though, had nothing to do with theater. He was a sculptor, the newly appointed chairman of the plastic-arts division at Desert Arts College. He was now my colleague because I had accepted an appointment as chair of the school's theater department.

To my left lay the ocher foothills of the Santa Rosa Mountains. Beyond them and ahead, Mount San Jacinto poked a crystalline blue sky with its dusty slopes, sage in the sunlight, mauve in the shadows. The urban canyons I'd left back east bore no resemblance to the real canyons that now surrounded me. Though I have long prided myself as articulate (dramatically so, I daresay), words fail me in attempting to describe the vistas encountered at every turn in the Coachella Valley. All the gushy adjectives readily apply, yet they are rendered pale and threadbare by the actual happenstance of geography: *majestic, serene, breathtaking, galvanizing, gorgeous, humbling, hot.*

Heat. To someone not accustomed to life in the desert, heat is surely its most pronounced and obvious feature. During winter, I'm told, daytime highs typically hover around seventy, with chilly nights in the forties. During summer, locals say it's "getting hot" at 110. As I had never visited the area before embarking on my career change several weeks ago, I have not yet experienced these seasonal extremes. Now, during the first week of September, the afternoons still nudge 100, but the heat, as they say, is dry, and the starry nights are perfect.

At nine in the morning, tooling through paradise in a silver Volkswagen with a freshly plucked bract of bougainvillea in its bud vase, I could not imagine that I'd balked at the offer to make this move. Picking up speed, I touched the button that would raise my window, but stopped, returning my hand to the wheel. The dry, warm wind whorled through the car and mussed my hair. Brushing a stray wisp from my forehead, I caught a glimpse of myself in the mirror and was startled by the smile that beamed back at me. Happiness—it's not only elusive but *complicated.* When it pays an unexpected visit, why question it?

Whisking past the gatehouses of various walled communities— security-conscious developments inhabited mainly by part-time residents, snowbirds who may leave their lavish desert homes for months on end—I glanced at the clock and noted that Paul's 9:20 plane would be landing within fifteen minutes. I had been to the airport only once, when I myself had arrived, so I was less than certain of my route and my timing. I sensed, though, that I was headed in the right direction, and my destination wasn't far. Still, fearing I might be late, I pressed my toe harder against the accelerator. Gaining speed, the car itself pressed harder against my back. The whir of the engine grew louder as the wind grew more playful. I laughed through the noise, feeling exhilarated and powerful. Then, up ahead, the traffic light at the next intersection turned red. Grudgingly, I stopped.

I was at a bend in the highway where a mountain rose from the flat valley floor and elbowed within inches of the road's left shoulder. Drumming my fingers on the wheel, I noted that there was no traffic on the cross street—my movement had been hampered by the arbitrary dictates of a light on a pole. Grousing at this injustice, I realized that I had not yet entirely shaken my innate New York contentiousness. So I closed my eyes, took a deep breath, and tried to focus on adopting the less-stressed mind-set of a happy Californian. You're an actor playing a role, I told myself. Get into character.

When I opened my eyes, I discovered that this impromptu bit of Stanislavski, tinged with Zen, had produced its intended effect—I was feeling downright herbal. I also discovered that the cross street before me led directly up the steep mountainside to Nirvana.

No, I had not wigged out. I had recognized the gatehouse to Nirvana, a development of mountaintop estates where bighorn sheep freely roam. Munching manicured hedges of laurel, they eye the wealthy who sip their morning coffee on their poolside terraces while skimming the pages of the *Desert Sun*. To dub such a place Nirvana, I learned, was truly more descriptive than pretentious. If bliss could be subdivided into half-acre parcels and bought by the highest bidder, it was here. Among the select few who owned these elysian tracts was D. Glenn Yeats, the computer magnate of software renown. And it was he who had lured me to the desert.

Waiting for the stoplight to turn green, I recalled the Wednesday evening, three days earlier, when I had first climbed the mountain to Nirvana.

Kiki was in the car with me. "Claire, dear," she said through a gasp, punching her foot on an imaginary passenger's brake, "there's a steel gate blocking the road. I suggest you stop the car."

Having picked up the car that very afternoon, I was still getting the feel of its controls. Smirking sidelong at Kiki, I managed to stop at the gatehouse with barely a skid.

An elderly guard who looked more avuncular than intimidating, even behind a badge, stepped to the car and leaned to the window. "Evening, ladies."

I nodded, smiled. "Mr. Yeats is expecting us."

"Mm-hm." He held a clipboard at arm's length. "Names, please?"

"I'm Claire Gray, and this is Kiki Jasper-Plunkett."

His tongue clucked in his mouth as he squinted at the list. "Yup, here we are. Say, now"—he turned to focus on my face—"you're that theater lady, aren't you?"

My celebrity status was surely minor compared to that of others he had admitted to these grounds, so I wondered if he'd been coached. Still, the recognition was an ego boost, a friendly portent for the evening to come. Sharing the moment with Kiki, I told him, "Actually, we're both 'theater ladies.' "

He stood aside, pushed a gadget on his belt, and told us, "Welcome to Nirvana." The gate slid silently open.

Before pulling away, I asked, "How do I find Mr. Yeats's house?"

He suppressed a laugh. "It's the big one at the top, Miss Gray."

I should have guessed. Nodding my thanks, I drove through the gateway and started up the winding road. From below, none of the homes were visible, secluded on a private mesa, but the drive itself hinted at the tasteful opulence ahead. Native grasses lined the road, with fountains and clusters of palms at every turn, suggesting an oasis in the wilderness. The evening sky bled orange beyond the distant peaks, glaring across my windshield. The sound of the car's engine seemed lost in a vast silence.

Then Kiki said, "Theater ladies." I turned to see her lips curl in a crooked grin. "We sound ancient. Ancient and single—there's a term for that."

"Fifty-four is hardly ancient." My reassuring words were colored with defensiveness, as we shared the same age. We also shared a friendship that stretched back to our school days together at Evans College, where we both had studied theater in the green foothills of the Berkshires—

worn, old mountains that seemed soft and tame in comparison to the craggy granite slopes that now surrounded us. I returned her grin, asking, "Did you ever think we'd end up back together after all these years?"

"Never a moment's doubt," she lied convincingly (she was acting).

Though we'd been best of friends in school, our professional paths had parted upon graduation. I pursued a career as a director, never losing sight of my ultimate goal to establish a reputation on Broadway. Kiki's interest was behind the scenes, in costuming, which led her to an academic career—right there at Evans College, where she rose through the ranks to become chair of its esteemed theater department.

Over the years, Kiki had made frequent visits to New York, always as my houseguest. We traded homes for a year while she was on sabbatical, allowing me to return to Evans as a visiting professor, writing my first play. I premiered *Traders* at the school with a local cast, then took it home to New York, where it was lavished with both critical and popular acclaim. Later, when the movie appeared, the name Claire Gray became a household word—at least within theatrical circles.

How does any of this relate to Palm Springs and D. Glenn Yeats?

"He did *not* build the Regal Palms," Kiki joked as we passed the entrance to the posh Regal Palms Hotel, about halfway up the mountain. With supreme understatement, she added, ". . . not that he *couldn't* have built it."

Indeed. Glenn Yeats was a builder. He'd built a software empire out of nothing more than a good idea, some technical know-how, and raw ambition. He'd built a string of homes for two wives (now pampered exes) in San Jose, Santa Barbara, and Los Angeles, and another for himself here in the Palm Springs area, in Rancho Mirage. Sensing the need to "give back" to society, he'd built, from the sand up, Desert Arts College, which would open its doors to its first students in less than two weeks. This philanthropic impulse, it was rumored, set him back several hundred million dollars—barely a dent in his total resources. The project was three years in the making, and during the last year or so, he'd focused his corporate-raiding skills upon building a top-notch faculty, securing talent wherever he found it, cherrypicking the staffs of other schools.

That's how he got Kiki, who readily accepted a generous offer to leave Evans and become head costumer for DAC's theater department. All along, he had saved the position of department chair for me, but I just wasn't interested, at least not at first. Eventually, though, he got to me—through Kiki. When it came to setting goals, Glenn Yeats had a knack for building, buying, or inveigling whatever he wanted.

One of the things he was building was a theater, a state-of-the-art playhouse, on his new campus. During the last of several trips he made to New York in an attempt to recruit me, he crowned his efforts with the promise that this theater would be "mine," and he invited me to assist in its design, sending architects and engineers to meet with me. I would have total control over the fledgling theater department and its repertoire. I would be welcome to pursue my skills as a playwright and to premiere any new works in my theater. I would have a budget to bring in guest directors if I ever needed to suspend my duties at the school in order to keep my feet wet professionally in nearby Los Angeles. Altogether, it was an offer I couldn't refuse. So, about a year ago, I had agreed to join the faculty. Two weeks ago, after wrapping up the last of my commitments in New York, I made the actual move.

Rounding a final bend in the steep roadway, we entered Nirvana proper. "Holy shit," I mumbled.

Kiki laughed, reminding me, "I *said* you'd be wowed." Because Kiki had moved to the desert a month or so before I had, she'd paid an earlier visit to Yeats's mountaintop lair. This evening's faculty reception, hosted by the founder and president of the college where I would soon begin teaching, was my first opportunity to enter his lofty sanctum.

Most would describe my background as worldly, and in recent years, I'd come to enjoy a certain level of affluence. Tonight, though, I caught my first glimpse of a lifestyle I'd never before encountered, and Kiki was right—I was wowed. Sprawling single-story houses of inventive, modern design perched on ever-higher plateaus, their glass walls sparkling in the sunset while invisible inhabitants lolled with their cocktails, enjoying serene vistas of neighboring mountains and the valley below. Everywhere, lush plantings softened the slopes like hanging gardens. Cruising past the entrances to some of these homes, I saw tranquil courtyards, walls of polished granite or rough-hewn limestone, meticulous rows of dwarf palms and riotous beds of flowers, all of it washed with discreet lighting from sources unseen. This secluded haven was a palpable, tangible fantasy of wealth, nature, and style.

"The best is yet to come," said Kiki, her gaze aimed up the last stretch of Nirvana Circle.

There, beyond a parapet, rose a wall of glass and stone, crisp and angular, like a dramatic sculpture, a whimsy, reflecting the sunset's glow of burnt sienna, casting its long blue shadow on the roadway. Driving through the momentary darkness, I blinked, then blinked again as I pulled around the side of the house and into its entry court, where a valet stood ready to whisk away arriving cars. Where he disposed of the vehicles was not apparent. This service, I would later learn, was provided not simply to convenience the guests, but to ensure that the pristine streets of Nirvana were not cluttered with parked cars, which would mar the other residents' views.

"Spectacular," I said to no one as I stepped out of the Beetle, which looked decidedly cartoonish in these sleek surroundings. The valet scurried to assist Kiki from the passenger's seat, then bobbed his head at me as he returned to the driver's side, slipped behind the wheel, and puttered away.

A breeze tumbled through the slopes and a slanting shaft of sunlight warmed my face as I crossed the courtyard with Kiki. Though longtime friends, and psychologically in sync, we bore no physical resemblance to each other. Anyone watching us approach the house would find us very much the odd couple.

Kiki is a woman of dramatic bearing, with theatrical tastes to match. Her passion for costuming is not merely an academic interest but an aspect of her everyday life. Back in Evanstown, she'd built a house for the purpose of storing her own sizable collection of period costumes. Some of this will now become the foundation of DAC's costume vault, but Kiki will continue to think of it as her personal wardrobe, raiding it at whim. These whims strike often; Kiki changes clothes several times a day. That evening, she'd finally settled on a flowing gauze tunic worn over a peacock blue jumpsuit. Spangled and bangled from ears to ankles, she sounded like a human wind chime crossing the courtyard. Her hair (it was red that week) was piled high and wrapped in a long silk scarf that looked like a turban with a tail.

I, as usual, wore my hair short and serviceable; I have never tampered with its encroaching silver. I'm a bit shorter than Kiki, leaner too, doubtless due to a lifelong smoking habit that I finally resolved to kick during the summer, while preparing to move west and start over. So far so good. My voice has long carried a touch of telltale tobacco huskiness, which I rather like. I assume that it is now too late for my utterances to revert to Kiki's higher, more mellifluous register.

While I can safely claim that my commitment to theater is every bit as strong as Kiki's, the dramatic mind-set has never surfaced in my dress or bearing. I dress simply, usually in slacks, with little jewelry or other hoo-ha. My sole sartorial flourish is an affection for red, not just any shade but bloody, virile scarlet. I don't wear it often, saving it for special occasions—openings of my plays, for instance, or events that carry the prospect of a sexual encounter, or evenings like that first visit to Nirvana, when I wore a loose-fitting scarlet silk blouse, black linen pants, and a nice pair of Italian sandals. A slinky gold chain hung from my neck, completing the ensemble.

Walking toward the house with Kiki, I didn't speak, busy absorbing details. The front door stood wide open, and as we drew nearer, I realized that there seemed to *be* no door—the house simply opened up to us. Inside, guests mingled, silhouetted against the golden daylight of a terrace beyond. Their party babble was overlaid by the soft, flowing phrases of a piano.

Stepping indoors (we had crossed something of a threshold in the slate paving, but I still saw no door), we were greeted by a tall, ferocious-looking black woman—really tall, well over six feet, and really black, with hair pruned to a perfect cube. Her features were severe; her dress was tight and minimal; her long, muscular legs were gorgeous. She carried a clipboard, but didn't look at it. "Ms. Gray," she said without expression, her soft voice at odds with her hard appearance. She added, "Ms. Jasper-Plunkett." Then she vanished.

I turned to Kiki to comment on this strange encounter, but found that she had already wandered several steps into the fray, where she'd nabbed a waiter with a tray. I heard her tell him, ". . . with just a few drops of cassis," and I knew that she'd ordered my usual kir, plus whatever concoction caught her fancy that night.

"Claire! Welcome!"

Glancing over my shoulder, I saw D. Glenn Yeats, the amiable billionaire himself, rushing toward me from a side hall. Heads turned. The other guests were curious, no doubt, as to why I had been singled out.

Stepping toward our host, I offered my hand. "Thank you, Glenn." Stupidly, I added, "Nice place."

He clasped my hand with both of his. "So then." Big smile. "You're here. At last." He laughed. "You drove a hard bargain, Claire, and even then, I was afraid you'd back out."

"My word is my bond," I assured him.

"But a contract is better," he joshed, winking.

"Well"—I shrugged—"you've got both."

Our small talk moseyed on, but I was barely conscious of our words. Rather, I studied the man. During my decades as a theatrical director, I've learned that the key to a successful production is a keen interpretation of character. Life itself may be thought of as an ongoing drama, with shifting plot and a changing cast. Glenn Yeats had just entered the action of my life. He now had a role in my future and had stepped to center stage. So I asked myself the same two questions I would ask if I'd just encountered him in a script: Who is he? And what makes him tick?

Who is D. Glenn Yeats? Superficial questions are easy ones, with superficial answers. Yeats is a widely known computer genius who founded a software empire. It's a matter of public record that the *D* stands for Dwight and that he is fifty-one years old (three years younger than I), vastly wealthy, twice divorced, with two adult children (one from each marriage) who live in Los Angeles. As Yeats stood there in front of me, nattering about the imminent opening of Desert Arts College, I observed his average height and build—he seemed healthy, but no gym hound. His clothes were casual, but tasteful and expensive, as one would expect—silk shirt with massive cuff links and open collar, alligator slip-ons with no socks. His features were plain, and his hair looked as if he'd cut it himself. The whole package was, in a word, unremarkable. He didn't look like a titan of technology, a captain of industry. Noting this, a recent cover story in *Newsweek* had lauded his "unassuming personality." Nice words. Truth is, he struck me as a bit of a dweeb.

What makes Glenn Yeats tick? That's a far more complicated question, and I still have no definitive answers. But I have some promising theories, which began to develop that evening at his home.

"Let me show you around," he said, gently clutching my elbow. "Introductions are in order."

When he offered to show me around, I assumed he was referring to the house—a private tour would have been dandy. But when he mentioned introductions, I realized that his intentions leaned more toward showing me *off* than around. He'd made it clear, from the first time he'd visited me in New York, that I would be the "crown jewel" (his words) in the DAC faculty. Now he'd snagged me—literally, by the elbow—a trophy to be paraded among his minions.

"Uh," I quavered, "I think I have a drink coming."

"Go ahead," Kiki offered, having witnessed all this. "I'll catch up with you."

"Thanks," I told her dryly.

She asked, "Can I get you something, Glenn?"

"Not just yet, thanks." And he whisked me from the little crowd in the entry hall toward the main room of the house.

As expected, the interior of Yeats's home was spectacular, designed to take full advantage of its setting and its views. The main room was huge, with a ceiling some twenty feet high and a polished stone floor that descended several steps toward an open wall. While this expansive "wall" was nonexistent (I assumed that mechanized panels had been retracted to the sides), the large indoor space was broken up by other walls that seemed more decorative than functional. Thick planes of stone or plaster, all of them strictly rectilinear, intersected the space at varying heights, directing the eye toward the view beyond the terrace. The decorating palette of the room was largely neutral—earth tones hinting at the smoky green and purple of the receding mountains—but one of the decorative walls was a deep, rusty red plaster. Another, black granite. I liked it.

After surveying the room, I began to study the crowd. Presumably the entire faculty of the new college was assembled here, and it struck me that their numbers were on the scant side. Was the group merely dwarfed by the space? Calling on my experience at quick head counts (in half-empty theaters during the early days of my career), I estimated no more than fifty people present. If half were spouses, could the remainder constitute a credible faculty? Were we yet to be joined by an onslaught of late arrivals?

I shooed these questions from my mind as Kiki appeared with my glass of kir and I savored the first few sips.

Glenn proved himself a cordial host, and I chided myself for questioning his motives in introducing me to my new colleagues. Predictably, most of these people had an arty edge—painters, potters, poets, dancers, musicians—to say nothing of the theater contingent. Meeting these artists, learning of their impressive credentials, realizing that I would soon be working with them on a daily basis, I knew that I had made the right decision in accepting Glenn's invitation to join his school, and I silently thanked him for his persistence.

I found myself laughing, chatting, making an earnest effort to remember the slew of new names I learned that night. Many of my colleagues had been drawn from academia, but a fair number of us, myself included, had come directly from real-world professions. Everyone I met, it seemed, had a story, and I marveled at the diversity of the faculty's background, their struggles and triumphs, and our common decision to congregate here, now, embarking on an experiment in education and in life.

Glenn glanced about the living room. Satisfied that he'd missed no introductions, he suggested, "Let's go out to the terrace. There are still a few people you *must* meet, and the view at dusk is extraordinary."

At that moment, a waiter appeared with a fresh kir for me, then disappeared with my empty glass. "Onward," I said, lifting my drink to Glenn as he led me toward the open wall. Kiki followed.

While preparing to cross the invisible boundary between indoors and out, I paused to scrutinize the means of hiding the retractable panels. Were there pockets in the side walls? Tracks on the floor? Perhaps a compartment in the ceiling? The architect had achieved a splendid bit of stagecraft.

"Claire—there you are. I wondered if you'd arrived yet."

The familiar voice nipped my thoughts about the missing wall. Turning, I was surprised to see Grant Knoll walk in from the terrace. Through a confused smile, I said, "Good evening, Grant. What a coincidence." He was my neighbor at Villa Paseo, the small condominium complex in Palm Desert where Kiki and I had recently settled into our new homes. He was a real estate broker and happened to be president of our homeowners' association, so he had handled the transactions for both Kiki and me. He was one of the few locals I'd come to know socially since arriving in the desert. I was delighted to see him at the party that night, but why was he there? Something wasn't clicking.

Kiki helped me piece it together. Laughing, she reminded me, "Grant is head of the sales office here at Nirvana."

Glenn Yeats further explained, "You have me to thank, ladies, for your initial contact with Grant. I told him that the valley was acquiring two special new residents this season and asked him to assist you in finding housing."

Grant added, "We happened to have a couple of units going on the market in my own complex, and I'm always on the lookout for 'special' neighbors, so the rest is history."

"And I can't thank you enough," I told him. "The sale, the move-in, everything went without a hitch. I'm still getting settled, though. I hope you can give me some decorating tips." I assumed Grant was gay.

"Gladly." He did nothing to dispel my notion.

I'd known the man barely two weeks, so my knowledge of his background was sketchy, but everything I did know fit. It wasn't just a matter of flair, which he possessed in abundance—the man could cook, dress, dance, and decorate. I knew his age to be forty-nine, but he looked ten years younger. I found him unquestionably attractive, but instincts told me he was off-limits "that way." I had quickly deduced that there were no women in his life (for that matter, I was aware of no men in his life). I knew of no ex-wife or children. His only mention of family was a brother, who had some connection to the local police. Grant was witty and genial, a consummate professional, a perfect neighbor, and a budding friend.

My brow wrinkled. It *still* wasn't clear why he was there at the faculty party. With a singular lack of discretion, I asked, "You've, uh, made a career switch—to teaching?"

He shook his head patiently. "No, Claire. The sales office at Nirvana assists residents in booking special events with the Regal Palms. The hotel's services are available to homeowners, everything from laundry to catering. I coordinated Glenn's party tonight, and I'm here to keep an eye on things."

I lifted my glass. "Everything's perfect, Grant."

He nodded, satisfied. "In a setting like *this*"—a sweeping gesture encompassed the whole house—"it's hard to go wrong. Have you seen the terrace yet? The night view is remarkable."

Our host told him, "I was just escorting the ladies out for a look."

Kiki gasped, peering past the small throng of partygoers who mingled outdoors. "My God, what a sky," she marveled. At that moment, the pianist segued from his bouncy cocktail music to a gentle rendition of some old tune, nameless and lovely. Kiki added through a purr, "How terribly romantic."

"Oh, *my*," said Grant, feigning demure reproof of Kiki's remark. "Good thing it's just us singles tonight. It'd be a shame to tempt the attached."

As we laughed at his words, it occurred to me that Grant's observation, "just us singles," was not only glib but accurate. He, Glenn Yeats, Kiki, and I were all unattached, presumably available. And I realized that the truth of Grant's words ran even deeper. When I'd arrived, I'd thought the party crowd seemed too small to include all of DAC's faculty, dismissing half of them as spouses. Then Glenn assiduously introduced me to everyone in the room. I now recalled that there'd been barely a spouse or two in the bunch.

This struck me as too unlikely for coincidence—and suddenly disconcerting. I was no longer laughing; my smile fell. I needed some explanation, if there was one, so I turned to Glenn, telling him, "Grant's right. It seems that an inordinate number of us here tonight are unmarried. I mean, we're *more* than old enough. That's curious, isn't it?"

"Hardly," Glenn answered without hesitating. Through a smile, he quipped, "I want nothing but the best for Desert Arts College, and over the years, I've found that the truly talented are wed first to their careers."

His jocular tone acknowledged an outrageous generalization, but I couldn't help noticing that he'd delivered these words while wagging a finger, as if lecturing us. I got the impression that he meant exactly what he said—that he'd consciously, deliberately hired only unmarried people to staff his new school. He was free, in my opinion, to hire his faculty on the basis of any criteria that pleased him. Still, I wondered, did this particular prejudice reveal something at the very core of D. Glenn Yeats? Did he find it easier to manipulate the lives of the unattached? Did he need to *control* people? Is that what made this philanthropic billionaire tick?

Through these disturbing thoughts, I heard the others engaged in some good-natured prattle. Grant excused himself, needing to check on things in the kitchen. Kiki went off to find the powder room. Glenn insisted that now, at last, he would show me the terrace. Once again, he grasped my elbow, then guided me outdoors.

Emerging from the house to the expansive terrace, I banished my vexing suspicions, awed by the spectacle of the desert night. With instant insight, I understood that Glenn's house, indeed all of Nirvana, had been built for the sole purpose of witnessing *this*. The stone terrace, the blackened pool with its infinity edge, the trickle of fountains, the subtle lighting—all was perfect, but man-made. It was merely a frame, a proscenium, for the vast sky beyond. Night had fallen. The dark forms of distant mountains hunkered under the vault of the heavens, which was pinpricked with a dazzling array of stars. It looked like a cyclorama behind a stage setting, the whimsical artifice of some gushing, romantic set designer—reality be damned.

Yet there it was.

Glenn and I had arrived at the far edge of the terrace; my toes touched the stone parapet that separated civilization from the night. Others stood at the low wall with us, gazing reverently at the slow, placid clockwork of the firmament. Below, lights shimmered from the valley floor. A plane raced along the main runway of the airport and slid silently into the vast, black sky. A warm breeze swelled up the slopes and washed over us. Glenn raised a finger to his lips and whispered into my ear, "Do you hear them?"

I strained to filter out the noise from the house—the chatter, the piano, the clink of glasses. "No," I answered. "What?"

"Coyotes."

I held my breath, listening. Then, smiling into the night, I whispered, "There they are. They sound a million miles away."

"Not nearly so far." Glenn chuckled. "They're in the arroyos," he explained, resting one hand on my shoulder, pointing with the other, "in the gullies of the canyons that surround us."

Suddenly, nearby, another coyote picked up the call and chorused loudly with his brothers. I wasn't the only one to jump, and the group of us standing at the parapet broke into laughter.

"Welcome to the desert, Claire," said Glenn, giving my shoulder a hug.

Someone stepped over to us. "Claire Gray?"

"Ah, Paul!" said Glenn, clapping the man's back. "I've been looking for you." Glenn turned to tell me, "Claire, I'd like you to meet Paul Huron, a highly talented sculptor and head of DAC's plastic-arts division—"

I interrupted, "Plastic arts?"

Paul explained, "In other words, sculpture, as opposed to the graphic arts—three dimensions versus two."

"Ah."

Glenn continued, "Paul, this is none other than the renowned Claire Gray, first lady of the directing world and now chair of DAC's theater department."

Paul shook my hand. "It's an honor, Miss Gray."

"Tut-tut," I told him. "First names, Paul."

A woman appeared from the darkness behind him. He brought her forward, saying, "Claire, please meet my wife, Jodie Metz-Huron."

Jodie and I shook hands, and she spoke a few pleasantries that I couldn't quite catch because Glenn had leaned to whisper in my ear, "There now. You can set your mind at ease—a wife. I'm not so closed-minded as you feared."

I laughed at his comment, and in fact I did feel relieved. Trying to bring my focus back to Jodie, I asked, "You're on the faculty as well?"

She shook her head. "I'm a nurse. Fortunately, my career's a lot more 'portable' than Paul's, so when Glenn made the offer, we had no trouble relocating. The desert's *full* of medical centers."

From the corner of his mouth, Paul added, "Plenty of retired folks, too."

Jodie stifled a laugh and admonished Paul for his comment. While the two of them bantered, I studied their interaction and formed initial impressions of each.

They were both thirty or so, with Paul perhaps a few years the elder. His build verged toward burly, but his manner and speech displayed great sensitivity—it was easy to imagine him sweating away with hammer and chisel, liberating from raw stone the delicate beauty of a figure hidden within. He wore all black that night, as did many of our arty colleagues, so his clothing seemed unremarkable, except that he wore it so naturally, with no pretense of jaded, urban sophistication. His hair was short and dark, his complexion ruddy, his hands huge.

Jodie was of course smaller, but in no sense petite. Blond and pretty, she offered a pleasing visual counterpoint to her husband's dark ruggedness. Her conversation confirmed that she was both smart and practical; her words also had a wistful edge, leaving the impression that she was less than happy with their move. Her manner was poised and friendly, but confidently irreverent; her hyphenated last name suggested an independent streak. She dressed smartly in a summery cream-colored outfit, a nice contrast to her husband in black. Assured of her own comeliness, she adorned herself with a few bits of good, modern jewelry that appeared to be of original design. Most notable was the ring on her left hand.

Paul caught my glance as it rested on his wife's finger. Smiling, he asked me, "It *is* beautiful, isn't it?"

Before I could answer, Jodie proudly lifted her hand and displayed the ring a few inches from my face. She explained, "It's actually two rings, interlocking—one for our engagement, the other for the wedding. Paul commissioned it from a fellow faculty member at Rhode Island." Each of the two rings was topped with a pearl, one black, the other white.

This prompted some discussion of Paul's former career at the prestigious Rhode Island School of Design. I learned that the Hurons had moved to the desert back in June, immediately after Paul's teaching duties had ended there.

"And he's been a godsend," Glenn assured me. "Quickly after Paul's arrival, I discovered that he's not only one of the finest sculptors in the field, but an able administrator as well. DAC opens its doors in— what?—twelve days now. We'll be ready. But I swear, without Paul's skillful assistance during the school's crucial summer preparations, we wouldn't have made it on schedule."

Paul hedged modestly, "I enjoy a challenge, that's all."

Glenn touched Paul's arm. "I'm highly grateful. Trust me, Paul— once we're up and running, you'll find yourself on the fast track to an administrative position in the central office, *my* office."

This prediction brought a momentary lull to the discussion.

Jodie smiled, squeezing her husband's arm.

Paul stammered, "But . . . I'm . . . a teacher, an artist."

"You're the best of many worlds," Glenn assured him. "At DAC, you'll have it all. I want to see my people rise to their full potential."

Paul laughed self-consciously, at a loss for words. "Thank you, Glenn. I'll help in any capacity where I'm needed."

This love-in was getting a bit soppy for comfort, so I was relieved to spot Kiki headed toward us with a waiter in tow, his tray laden with an assortment of drinks. "Make way," she commanded, bracelets jangling as she hurried the tuxedoed young man into our midst. "I wasn't sure what everyone was drinking, so we brought a bit of everything."

Laughing, we made our selections from the tray, which the waiter left on a table near the pool before skittering back indoors.

Glenn introduced Kiki to the Hurons, concluding, "Paul's become invaluable to me—putting out fires, shepherding the last phase of construction, generally helping out with all the odd details."

"Some of which," Paul told us with a wink, "have been *exceedingly* odd."

Glenn's tone turned businesslike. "If you're up for another assignment, I have an extremely important little mission for you." He grinned. "This isn't 'dirty work,' Paul. I think you'll find it most gratifying."

How else could Paul answer? "Sure."

Glenn said simply, "Dane Carmichael."

The name was familiar, but I couldn't place it.

Paul's brows arched. "Glass. Seattle."

It clicked—they were speaking of a prominent glass sculptor based near Seattle. His work had largely redefined the medium of art glass, and his studio had become mecca to a new generation of student sculptors who revered the quirky Carmichael as an art god. Several recent large-scale installations of his work in new hotels had brought him a flood of publicity.

Glenn told Paul, "I want him. He *belongs* at DAC."

"But you've already tried. He's not interested."

"We'll try again. I'm nothing if not persistent."

The words slipped out of my mouth: *"I'll* tell the world."

Glenn laughed with the others, then explained, "I talked with Dane again by phone today. Upping the ante, I finally caught his attention. He's going to Dallas for this weekend's opening of an important one-man show. He agreed to spend some time with me there on Friday."

"That's wonderful," said Paul. "If anyone can land him, it's you."

Glenn smiled. "Paul, I'd like *you* to do it."

Through an uncertain laugh, Paul started to say, "I don't think—"

"No, listen," Glenn continued. "You're an *artist,* Paul, and a damned good one. You and Dane speak the same language; you know how to connect. I'm just a money guy. He needs to hear from you why DAC is so important. He needs to be sold on what it can do for *him.* And you're the man to deliver that message."

"I'm flattered, Glenn. I can't promise results, but I'm willing to try."

"That's all I ask. You can fly there tomorrow, meet with him on Friday, and return early Saturday. There are lots of Dallas flights—it's an AirWest commuter route. The trip will hardly put a crimp in your weekend."

Paul turned to Jodie. "Do you mind, honey? A well-timed announcement regarding Dane Carmichael would really put DAC on the map—before it even opens."

She sighed, then laughed. "I'd like to make you feel guilty for abandoning me, but truth is, I'm working that odd night shift at the medical center this weekend. It comes up every few weeks. So my Friday night is shot." She clasped Paul's fingers, kissed his cheek. "Sure, go to Dallas."

"Excellent," said Glenn, rubbing his hands. He told Paul, "I'll have Tide book your flights tonight, then I'll brief you in my office tomorrow before you leave." Turning to the rest of us, he said, "If you'll all excuse me, I'd like to get this taken care of." After a round of quick farewells, he went indoors.

The party had begun to thin out, and we now had the terrace to ourselves. Kiki gestured toward the tray of drinks near the pool. "We have our work cut out for us." Then she added, "Unless you'd rather leave, Claire."

"Not at all." I breathed a happy sigh. "God, what a night. Let's just enjoy it." So Kiki, the Hurons, and I got comfortable, taking seats near the drinks by the pool. Paul and Jodie sat side by side on a chaise longue, Kiki lolled dramatically in an armchair, and I sat between them on an ottoman.

We gabbed and drank, getting better acquainted. I learned that the Hurons lived in Palm Desert, not far from my condominium. We spoke of our various backgrounds, the opening of the new school, and of course the inscrutable Mr. Yeats. Eventually the conversation returned to the Dallas trip, with Paul and Jodie discussing logistics.

She said, "I'm off tomorrow, so I can drive you to your flight anytime."

He nodded. "Thanks, that'll work. I'd drive myself and leave the car at the airport—"

Jodie finished his thought, "But your car's in the shop."

He explained to Kiki and me, "Just a fender bender, nothing serious." His features twisted, as though he'd forgotten something. He asked his wife, "When do I get it back?"

"Friday," she reminded him. "But you won't be here."

With a laugh of mild exasperation, he said, "Details, details. This trip only adds to the confusion."

Jodie told me, "Our cars seem to be a constant source of confusion. We have identical Hondas."

With mock defensiveness, Paul said, "They're good, dependable cars. I was so impressed by Jodie's, I got one of my own. Besides, they're not *identical*—mine's blue, hers is green."

Jodie amplified, "Dusty-metallic blue and dusty-metallic green. Pretty darn close."

Paul nodded, conceding the point. "Anyway, with me out of town on Friday, and you working that goofy shift, how do we get the car back?"

"I'll figure it out," she assured him. "You just go to Dallas and concentrate on Dane Whatsisname, and I'll take care of jockeying the cars—as usual." Then she leaned toward Kiki and me, telling us, "I've found the most *marvelous* mechanic." She winked slyly. "He's *very* accommodating."

What did that mean? The comment slid past Paul.

Jodie told him, "The body shop is up in Palm Springs. Maybe they could drop the car at the airport on Friday, then you'd have it to drive home on Saturday morning. I'll still be at the hospital, so I can't pick you up."

Paul considered this, nodding. Then, "Nah. How would I find *my* dusty-metallic Honda among the *hundreds* at the airport? And what about parking stubs or whatever? Way too complicated. I'll just take a cab home."

"Fine," said Jodie. "That's the plan."

This discussion had grown more mundane than scintillating. I had no desire to prolong the topic, but at that moment, I had a flash of inspiration. *"I'll* pick you up."

All heads turned to me.

"I have nothing scheduled for Saturday. I have a brand-new car. I could use some more experience behind the wheel. I'll pick you up, Paul."

"That's too kind of you, Claire, but I can't expect you to—"

"Nonsense. Besides, a cab from Palm Springs to Palm Desert is expensive. Save the fare. I insist."

He tossed his hands in the air, knowing the issue was settled. "Thanks, Claire. I'll give you my flight information tomorrow." As he said this, a plane rumbled overhead, gliding low on its approach to the airport.

A plane rumbled overhead, gliding low on its approach to the airport, snapping me back to the moment, reminding me of my mission that morning. Zipping along Highway 111, which had become Palm Canyon Drive, I glanced at the Beetle's overhead clock and saw that some eight minutes had passed since my stop near the gatehouse to Nirvana. Chiding myself for daydreaming at the wheel, I tried to get my bearings and saw that I had entered Palm Springs.

The plane overhead—was it Paul's?—had veered sharply to my right, so I figured it was time to turn. The next intersection lay just ahead. I pushed the brake pedal and skidded onto Gene Autry Trail. The maneuver, while clumsy, endangered no one but myself, and it achieved the goal of pointing me toward the airport. The plane, ever lower in the sky, was now in front of me.

By the time I reached Ramon Road, I could see the airport to my left, so I turned. By the time the plane's tires hit the tarmac, blowing puffs of white smoke, I'd found the entrance road to the airport and was speeding toward the terminal, hoping to beat the plane to the gate.

With my mind on the race and my grip on the wheel, I failed to notice the small, dark figure at the roadside until it wandered onto the asphalt, directly in my path. With a wave of panic and no trust in my skills, I was terrified by the options that faced me. Should I brake hard, possibly losing control? Should I swerve to the other lane, risking collision? Should I pull off the road, risking a rollover?

Then, in the moment before I would make this dreadful decision, I was astonished to realize that the child-size figure dancing on the roadway was merely a dust devil, a whirlwind of dirt whipped up by gusts from the runway. With immeasurable relief, I decided that no evasive action was called for, and I plowed right through the little dervish.

A cloud of grime gushed through the open windows of my car. Laughing, blinking, I tasted sand in my teeth.

2

Palm Springs Airport had in recent years undergone an ambitious expansion, adding *International* to its moniker, where it had once been humbly tagged *Regional*. Previously, passengers walked outdoors to their planes, which doubtless had its charms, but now a new terminal building, equipped with the usual Jetways, rose like a huge, festive white tent from the desert floor.

By the time I careened past the graceful, tiered Mexican fountain near the main entrance, I saw that the plane I'd followed was already at its gate, snuggled to its passenger bridge. It was now a minute past 9:20. Since I saw no other planes moving on the ground or in the air, I knew that Paul Huron had arrived. I had planned to meet him at the gate, but now I'd be hard-pressed to beat him to the luggage-claim area.

The airport was still small enough that both arriving and departing passengers used the ground-level doors, so I encountered no tangle of ramps as I drove to the front of the terminal. Saturday-morning travel was light, and I had no trouble finding a prime parking spot (illegal, of course) at the curb outside the baggage area. After some groping around, I figured out how to turn on the Beetle's flashers (just in case), then I left the car, raced to the main entrance, and dashed inside.

Pausing in a central concourse, I spun my head in all directions, trying to recall the layout of the building from my one previous visit. There wasn't much activity, except for a languid stream of people who came from glass doors that led to the gates. Most of them turned toward the far end of the building, where I had parked. I assumed that these were Paul's fellow passengers, headed toward the baggage carousels.

"May I help? You look confused."

Startled, I turned. A young Asian woman stood at my side. She lugged a heavy carry-on bag and was headed toward the taxi stand, but had paused to offer assistance. She even smiled. Back in New York, I'd have clutched my purse, assuming she was up to something. Here in southern California, things were different. People were just . . . well, *nice*. Friendly. They actually seemed to celebrate their diversity of races, languages, and lifestyles. I was used to a culture that greeted such differences with guarded suspicion. This touchy-feely mind-set would take some getting used to.

Taking a moment to breathe, I returned the woman's smile. "Uh," I asked stupidly, "the AirWest flight from Dallas?"

"Yes"—she stretched her smile even wider, nodding toward the flow of people—"right there. We're here."

"Baggage?" (I'd somehow adopted her succinct syntax.)

"Got mine." She was smiling so earnestly now, I feared her face would crack. "Others down there." With her eyes, she pointed in the direction of the carousels.

"Thank you, dear."

"Thank *you*, dear. Good luck." And she headed toward the door.

Marveling at this encounter, I felt ebb from me the anxiety that had risen during the morning's drive. I'd gotten myself to the airport in one piece, and though I'd arrived too late to meet Paul's plane, I'd have no difficulty finding Paul. He knew to look for me, and he couldn't have gone far. He was somewhere in that line of passengers, or he was already at the carousel. So I fell in line with the others and strolled the concourse at an easy pace, eavesdropping as others gabbed. Everyone seemed happy to be here, and I understood why.

Passing several car-rental counters, I saw the carousels ahead of us, with a knot of passengers clumped near the end of one of them. The belt had just started moving, and everyone jockeyed to get near. Then I saw Paul, who stood a few yards back from the crowd, waving at me. There was a wadded handkerchief in his hand, and as I waved back at him, he sneezed, turning to blow his nose. Two pieces of luggage, a garment bag and a Pullman, were there at his feet. He wore black slacks and a black T-shirt, similar to the outfit he'd worn to Wednesday's party.

Draped over one arm was a raw-linen sport coat, well wrinkled from the rigors of travel. As I stepped up to him, he tucked the handkerchief into a hip pocket.

"Welcome back," I told him, offering a hug.

"Morning, Claire." He wrapped his sculptor's arms around me (Jodie, I mused, was one lucky woman). "You really didn't have to do this. How was the drive?"

"A snap," I lied. "Perfectly uneventful." Stepping out of our friendly embrace, I noticed that his eyes were red and puffy. And his nose needed another wipe. I asked, "Catch a cold?"

He shook his head. "Don't worry. Nothing contagious, just allergies. This dry, windy weather really churns up the pollen. Or maybe it's the recirculated jet air—those things are flying petri dishes!" Laughing, he excused himself, turned away from me, pulled out his handkerchief, and indulged in a hearty honk.

When he'd tidied up, he hefted his bags, asking, "Where's the car?"

I nodded toward the nearest door. "Right at the curb. Let me take one of those."

"Nonsense. They're heavy, Claire."

As we started toward the door, I noted, "You don't exactly travel light, do you?"

"I do—usually. But Glenn loaded me up with reports to study, plus heaps of material for Dane Carmichael. It adds up."

I was about to ask him if he'd succeeded in his mission to recruit the glass artist, when my attention shifted to one of the car-rental counters near the door. As we passed by, someone working there, a nice-looking young man, East Indian or Pakistani, looked up from his computer terminal and gave us a smile and a nod, reinforcing my notion that Californians were almost eerily friendly. Paul hadn't noticed the young man's greeting; he was saying something about his luggage, looking down at it, brows furrowed. So I turned back to the clerk, got into the spirit of things, and gave him a big smile and a lascivious wink. He was truly attractive, with a fetching mole on one cheek. Blushing, he swiped a lock of blue-black hair from his brow and resumed typing.

The glass doors slid open in front of Paul and me. As we stepped outdoors, a gust of wind slammed past us, and I blinked at the sand in the air. There at the curb, my car awaited, blinkers still flashing. Noticing a cop working his way in our direction, I told Paul, "Not a moment to spare."

"Hm?" asked Paul. He was preoccupied with his bags again, looking down at them, frowning. "I hate the way the airlines gunk up your luggage with those tags."

I had never found this particularly vexing. In fact, I felt that the stubborn, sticky remnants of old tags made my luggage look well traveled. But Paul's bags looked new, and he apparently wanted to keep them that way. Setting them at the curb near my car, he leaned over and ripped the adhesive, bar-coded strips from the handle of each bag. When he'd crumpled them in his hand, the wind grabbed the wadded labels and carried them away.

Turning our attention to loading the luggage in the Beetle, I saw that we'd have a tight squeeze. The Pullman was clearly too bulky to fit into the backseat through the side door. Paul asked, "The back opens, right?"

"Right. And I think there's a way to fold down the seat."

It took some experimentation with the seat, but we finally managed to hoist the bags through the back. Before I closed the hatch, Paul said, "Just a sec. I need to find my garage-door opener. That's how I generally enter the house—through the garage." I recalled that his car was in the shop for repairs when Paul had left town on Thursday, so he'd apparently held on to the opener, using it as his house key. He zipped open one of the bags, reached inside, and pulled out the transmitter. "All set," he told me, closing the bag. Then, with a sturdy thwack, he shut the rear hatch of my car.

When we'd settled into our seats, I started the engine and pulled away from the curb. I noted that it was now twenty-five past nine; I intended to time the drive back to Palm Desert, as I would surely have future airport excursions.

Paul knew his way around by now, and he guided me away from the terminal, past the fountain, and back toward Palm Canyon Drive. Along the way, he pointed out Bob Hope's house in the foothills of a nearby mountain. It looked like a flying saucer perched up there—a huge one at that.

When we turned southeast onto Palm Canyon, the midmorning sun hung directly ahead. Using one hand as a visor, I squinted to see through the windshield, telling Paul, "Time to invest in a decent pair of sunglasses."

He laughed. "You'll get used to it. Eventually, you'll get bored with the sunshine, welcoming the rare cloudy day."

"I doubt that." I'd slogged through too many cloudy days already.

"Actually"—his tone was now earnest—"the Beetle has a lot of glass, so you might consider getting its windows tinted. Lots of folks do that here. It helps save the car's interior, and you're not always groping for sunglasses."

"Sounds like a good idea."

The scenery was glorious and the company cheerful as we left Palm Springs and tooled through the commercial section of Cathedral City, headed toward Rancho Mirage and Palm Desert beyond. We conversed in fits and starts, getting better acquainted, speaking over the rush of air that streamed through the car's open windows.

At one point, when we were comparing notes about our cross-country moves to the desert, he mentioned with a laugh, "In some ways, Jodie has adapted more quickly than I have," implying that he'd expected the opposite.

I recalled that at Wednesday night's party, there was something wistful in Jodie's tone, suggesting that her heart was still back in Rhode Island. I felt that I now knew Paul well enough to ask, "Jodie isn't happy?"

He hesitated. "She's getting there. When Glenn first offered to bring me out here, both Jodie and I recognized that it was the opportunity of a lifetime—for me. In terms of her own career, she was already where she wanted to be, so this move was a step back for her. On top of which, we came in June, right at the onset of the summer heat. It was not an auspicious start."

I mused, "But cooler weather has warmed her heart."

"In fact, it has. Plus, she's warmed to the new job at the medical center. She's gotten used to the routine, the new set of faces, and things are looking better for her, I can tell. Especially in the last few weeks, her whole outlook has improved. She's got her spunk back—like the woman I married."

Glancing at him, I asked, "When *did* you marry?"

"Five years ago. She was twenty-five; I was twenty-seven. First time for both of us. We were still busy career-building—still are, I guess— so we put off having kids." With a chuckle, he added, "Getting to be about that time, though." Then he turned the tables: "Were you ever married, Claire?"

"No," I said quietly, eyes on the road. "It's a long story."

He could tell I didn't care to pursue this, not now. So he dropped the question of my partnering, or lack of it, and amplified on his own. "I know it sounds cliché, but Jodie is the best thing that ever happened to me. In so many ways, we're entirely different people, but it seems to work well that way; we complement each other, make each other complete. She's beautiful, of course, but just as important, she's an intellectual equal. From the start, we've recognized total equality in our relationship, and that seems to mean a lot to her. Which sort of compensates for *me*. I mean, I can't be the easiest person to live with. You know—us arty types."

With a snort, I confirmed, "Do I ever." After a moment's thought, I added, "We're lucky, Paul. Both you and I have achieved enviable success. Sad to say, we're the exception in the arts. It's a risky field. Fame can be fleeting, if it visits at all. From a coldly practical standpoint, it just makes *sense* to have some backup. You have that in Jodie. She's a proven, dedicated professional in a rock-solid career."

"Oh, it's *solid*," he agreed with a tone of understatement. "Sometimes I wish that her career—to say nothing of her schedule—was a little more flexible."

With a gentle laugh, I reminded him, "She works in the real world, Paul. A life-or-death world."

He nodded, smiling. "Sure. I know. Still, that crazy schedule—it often keeps us apart at odd hours, like right now, when I'm chomping at the proverbial bit to see her again." He winked.

"Down, boy. It's the middle of the morning."

We shared a hearty laugh as I stopped the car at the next intersection. Wryly, I noted that I'd been thwarted again by the same pesky traffic light at the foot of the mountain where the crossroad led up to Nirvana. I was now headed down valley, so the gatehouse was to my right, on

Paul's side of the car. Waiting for the light, I again began to muse about the party three nights prior.

"Oh!" I said as the light turned and I stepped on the gas. "I nearly forgot. Your mission. What happened in Texas?"

He paused. "Nothing."

"Huh?"

"It was the damnedest thing, Claire. I met Dane Carmichael yesterday afternoon at the gallery while they were setting up for the opening of his one-man show. Naturally, he had a lot on his mind, so he wasn't exactly thrilled to see me—I felt that I was intruding. So I decided to return in the evening, take in the exhibit, and try talking to him after things calmed down. He gave me a few minutes, and I presented an honest, enthusiastic pitch for the school, but I knew I wasn't getting through to him. And frankly, I don't blame him. He's got a good gig going, at the peak of his career. What does Desert Arts College have to offer him?"

I suggested, "Money?"

"Sure, Glenn is extremely generous, especially when he sets his sights on something—or someone. He authorized me to up the offer substantially if it came down to a bidding war, but I never got that far with Carmichael. Money was never even mentioned. He just wasn't interested."

"That's curious. Wednesday night, Glenn said that Carmichael finally *was* interested. Did Carmichael tell Glenn what he wanted to hear in order to get Glenn off his back for a while, or was Glenn off base in his interpretation of their phone conversation?"

"Beats me," said Paul with a shake of his head. "Bottom line: my mission to Dallas felt like a wild-goose chase." His words carried a note of annoyance.

"Well," I said soothingly, "you're back now. And nine days from now, DAC will open its doors to its first students—with or without Dane Carmichael. Exciting stuff. I'm proud to be a part of it."

Paul agreed, sloughing off his momentary funk. The stretch of highway leading from Rancho Mirage into Palm Desert seemed especially scenic—there was no room for melancholy on such a sensational morning. We spoke with eager anticipation of the tasks that awaited us during the coming week.

Paul needed to oversee completion of the school's sculpture studios; a kiln and other equipment were still to be installed. He also had to deal with a growing list of administrative chores that Glenn was dreaming up for him.

Having busied myself since my arrival with transforming my vacant condominium into a home, I now needed to get my campus office in order. A more daunting and infinitely more exciting project was the completion of DAC's new theater, "my" theater. During a brief campus visit, I'd seen that the building itself was finished, but the race was on to install lighting, electronics, and stage mechanics in time for the opening of school. While there was little I could contribute to this process hands-on, I was needed to guide the technicians in their tweaking of these systems, and Glenn had insisted that the final okays would rest with me. I couldn't wait to get to campus on Monday morning and roll up my sleeves.

Entering Palm Desert, I asked Paul for directions to his house. I knew that he lived in the vicinity of Villa Paseo, my condo complex, but I was not yet familiar with street names (other than those named after desert celebrities—Gene Autry, Gerald Ford, Bob Hope, Dinah Shore, Frank Sinatra, Fred Waring—would D. Glenn Yeats join their ranks one day?). Paul told me to turn from the highway onto El Paseo (*the* fashionable shopping street, a scaled-down version of Rodeo Drive), then we climbed a hill that seemed to lead away from town. "The next left," Paul told me, and we turned onto a quiet side street.

We were indeed on the outskirts of town. One side of the street was edged by virgin desert; the other bordered a development of newer homes, pleasant but not lavish, all of vaguely southwestern design, some still under construction. "Left again," said Paul, directing me onto a short street that ended in a cul-de-sac. "Fourth driveway. You can pull right in."

Doing so, I stopped the car and glanced at the clock. It was 9:50; the drive from the airport had taken twenty-five minutes. I figured that the drive from my own home, not this far out, would take closer to twenty.

Paul pressed the button on his transmitter, and the garage door lifted open in front of us. "Why don't you come in?" he suggested. "I'll make some coffee."

"Thanks, but it's a bit warm for coffee." I had some errands to run and was itching to roll.

"Iced tea, then. There's always a pitcher in the fridge."

I hesitated. There was no graceful way to turn him down twice. "Sure. Sounds good." I switched off the engine, and we got out of the car.

As Paul extracted his baggage, I surveyed my surroundings. The neighborhood was quiet, still largely uninhabited. The Hurons' house seemed to be one of only two or three that were occupied on that street. The house was clad with sand-colored stucco, conspicuously tidy, lacking the construction rubble that rimmed many neighboring homes. The Hurons had already cultivated a small green plot of turf. Petunias and other annuals had been planted along the driveway in anticipation of autumn (the start, not the end, of the desert's growing season). Queen palms flanked the archway of the front porch. Several species of cactus adorned a rocky bed along the foundation of the house, as shrubbery would in more temperate climes. "This is charming," I told him.

"We're starting to feel settled. It's comfortable." He closed the Beetle's hatch, draped his linen jacket over one shoulder, and lifted his two bags. "I'll show you the place."

Following him into the garage, I paused, letting my eyes adjust to the shade within. Paul set his bags near a door leading into the house, tried the knob, found it locked, then zipped open a pocket on his garment bag, retrieving a key ring. As he did this, we gabbed, and I idly looked about the inside of the garage. Clearly, the Hurons had not lived here long—the garage was far too clean and orderly. There was space for two cars; predictably, only one of the two Hondas was parked there. I recalled that Paul's car was due back from repairs on Friday, and there it was, the dusty-green metallic one. Jodie was at work, and there was her empty parking space. All was well.

I should have suspected on that sunny morning that I was due for an emotional fall. I should have remembered that even in paradise, serpents lurk.

Judging from Paul's chipper small talk, he too had forgotten that life could, without warning, take an ugly turn. Glad to be home, he unlocked the door, swung it open, and heaved his bags past the threshold. Stepping inside, he tossed his jacket onto a nearby chair and switched off a light that had been left on. "Come on in, Claire."

I entered a hall that opened to the kitchen, bright with sunlight from a pair of sliding patio doors. Paul closed the door to the garage, carried his bags across the kitchen, and left them in an arched doorway leading to the rest of the house. He asked, "Iced tea, right?"

"Perfect." I sat on a stool at the kitchen's center island, which contained the sink.

On the opposite side of the island, Paul set out tall glasses on the glazed tile countertop. He opened the refrigerator and pulled out a pitcher of tea, half full, and a saucer that held lemon wedges. Setting this on the counter, he offered sugar, which I declined. He added ice to the glasses, then poured the tea, squeezing lemons for both of us. Handing me one of the glasses, he raised his own, saying, "Thanks, Claire."

"For what?" I tasted the tea. I'd had better.

"For your friendship—and the ride from the airport."

I laughed. "You were putting your life in my hands, you know."

"Never for a moment did I worry." His tone had a theatrical ring, impassioned but less than serious. "We're *here* now, on the brink of something wonderful, leading charmed lives."

I touched my glass to his. "To starting over, Paul."

"To starting over." (His words would soon prove prophetic.) He drank.

Setting down his glass, he asked, "Mind if I leave you alone for a minute? I'd like to show you the house, but let me take my bags to the bedroom first. Jodie wasn't expecting visitors, so I want to make sure everything's . . . presentable." He shrugged an apology.

"Take all the time you like. But please—no fussing on my account."

Grabbing his jacket from the chair where he'd left it, he told me, "Agreed—no serious housekeeping." Then he crossed the kitchen to the archway, picked up his bags, and disappeared farther into the house.

Lazily propping my elbow on the counter, I traced a fingernail along the edge of a row of tile, scraping the grout. I swirled the ice in my glass and swallowed some more tea, wishing I'd asked for sugar. Glancing around the kitchen, I noted the wall clock—five minutes till ten. Then my eyes focused on the coffeemaker, and I noticed an inch or two of coffee in the glass pot. Jodie had worked a night shift, so how long had the coffee sat there—since Friday morning? With a chuckle, I recalled Paul's last words, "no serious housekeeping."

Deciding to make myself useful, I stood, moved to the other side of the island, and removed the carafe from the coffeemaker, intending to give it a good rinse. Swirling the dark liquid in the pot, touching the glass, I was surprised to discover that it was still barely warm. Curious, I sniffed inside the pot. There was no rancid tang; this was not day-old coffee.

Then I heard a thud from the far end of the house, as if Paul had dropped his luggage. He screamed, "My God! *Jodie!* Oh, Jesus . . ."

The pot slipped from my hands, shattering on the edge of the ceramic sink. Most of the mess fell inside the sink, but I felt a hefty slosh of tepid black coffee soak through the front of my white shirt.

Not that I cared. I'd already torn out of the kitchen and was headed through the living room toward the opposite hall. Guided now by Paul's incoherent words—he seemed to be speaking, shrieking, and sobbing all at once—I ran through the hall, turned a corner, and burst into the bedroom, Paul and Jodie's bedroom.

Just inside the doorway, I stopped.

Paul's luggage was there near my feet, where he'd dropped it. The king-sized bed was a tangle of disheveled sheets. And in the middle of the room, Jodie lay sprawled on the floor, wearing a nightshirt that now failed to cover her hips.

Paul squatted next to her, shaking her head, crying her name, kissing her hands, begging her to respond. Through his tears, he sneezed, wiping the snot from his face with his bare arm. He crouched there pitiably, a dark hulk of a man, weaving his sculptor's fingers through the woman's pale hair. "What's wrong, Jodie?" he whimpered. "What happened?"

I had no idea what had happened. To my layman's eye, there was no apparent cause for the woman's condition. There was no blood, no gaping wound, no telltale scar, note, or weapon.

But I had no doubt whatever that Jodie Metz-Huron was dead.

3

Paul was so distraught that my immediate concern for him stole my attention from the riddle of the corpse on the floor.

A big man, fit and self-assured, Paul was now crying, sneezing, rubbing his eyes with his fists, conjuring the bizarre image of a baby in a muscle-tight black T-shirt. "No . . . ," he wailed. "She can't be gone. Jodie, *talk* to me," he insisted, shaking her again. Her sagging jaw wiggled, but she remained stubbornly mute.

Her lack of response intensified Paul's grief. "It's not *fair,*" he moaned, stroking her limp hands. "How could this—"

With a gasp, he'd fallen silent. "Huh?" He was looking at her left hand, holding it near his face.

I had never until that morning encountered a dead person anywhere but in the sanitized setting of a funeral parlor, so this business of a body in the bedroom was wholly unsettling. I felt queasy, and every instinct told me to distance myself from this death. Still, Paul's scrutiny of his wife's hand was irresistibly intriguing. With my curiosity now stronger than my qualms, I stepped to Jodie's side, across from Paul. My knees cracked as I knelt, then sat on the floor. Paul looked up at me, still holding Jodie's hand.

"What?" I asked, seeing nothing.

"Don't you see?" he said. "It's *gone.* Jodie's ring is missing."

Her finger still bore the imprint of the ring I'd seen Wednesday night, the custom-designed wedding ring with two pearls, black and white. I told Paul, "Maybe she took it off. Did she normally wear it to bed?"

"She *never* took it off, not once since we were married. Oh, *God,*" he wailed. "She was robbed. Robbed and killed."

And he was off again. "Look at this place," he said, standing as he waved his arms around the room. Several dresser drawers were open; one had fallen, spilling a few pairs of rolled socks. "We were ransacked! There must have been a burglary. But Jodie was here, and she, and she . . ." Paul didn't bother finishing the thought. Instead, he did a bit of ransacking himself, sifting through the clothes on the floor, opening and closing drawers, generally making a mess.

By now my focus had shifted from Paul to the body that lay spread before me. Far more shocking than the dead woman, I realized, was my own fascination with her remains. Don't get me wrong—nothing kinky—I simply wondered what had happened. Assuming that the answer was hidden there in front of me, I lifted Jodie's hand and studied the mark left on her finger by the missing ring. Though I had no working knowledge of forensics, it struck me that she could not have been dead very long. She looked pale and waxy, but not ghastly, and she had not yet begun to stiffen. Surprised by my composure under these unprecedented circumstances, I wobbled Jodie's lifeless hand, intrigued by its flaccid movement, its total lack of reflex.

Sitting there by the body, touching it, I noticed something else—a distinctive, pungent smell. It was not putrid, not the smell of death, but spicy and familiar. It was vaguely reminiscent of marijuana, but unless I was mistaken, it was perfume, one of those classic scents I'd smelled so often I'd barely noticed it. Leaning close, I sniffed Jodie, her face, her neck, then her wrists, trying to locate any dabs of perfume. But the scent didn't emanate from her flesh. It was subtle, but it seemed to permeate the room.

Lost in the little mystery of the spicy perfume, I'd momentarily wandered from the looming, larger questions: Who killed Jodie? And why?

Paul, however, had not lost his focus for a second. He still thrashed about the room and the adjacent bathroom, rifling drawers, lifting and tossing aside rugs, ripping sheets from the bed and shaking them. All the while, he muttered oaths against the unknown perpetrator, spitting epithets, making threats—the empty invective of sudden, unimaginable loss.

"Paul"—I stood—"what are you *doing?*"

He turned at the sound of my voice, as if he'd forgotten I was there.

"This is a crime scene," I reminded him.

Lamely, he explained, "I'm looking for clues."

"You're not supposed to touch *anything.*" I'd directed enough murder mysteries to know the stock dialogue.

"But I—" Then he flumped himself on the edge of the bed, dropped his head into his hands, and wept, simply wept, beginning the slow, healing process of grief.

His burst of activity and subsequent venting of raw emotion had transpired quickly. Not two minutes had passed since I'd first entered the bedroom. I was certain, though, that during that brief time, Paul had managed to thoroughly contaminate the crime scene. The mystery of Jodie's demise would now be all the more difficult to unravel.

"What'll we do?" murmured Paul. "What'll we do?"

Shaken as I was, I had sufficient wits to pick up the bedside telephone and dial 911. I told the dispatcher who I was, where I was, and why I was calling. "Mrs. Huron is clearly dead," I concluded. "There's no need for an ambulance."

"Don't touch *anything*" were the next words out of the dispatcher's mouth.

I explained to her that it was already too late for that admonition, due to Paul's emotional reaction to his wife's death. "But he's calmed down some. No, I don't think he's in need of immediate medical attention."

She told me to remain with him. Help would be arriving within minutes.

Hanging up the phone, I had a thought, lifted the receiver again, and listened for the dial tone. Hoping I could remember the number correctly, I dialed. It was ten o'clock on a Saturday morning. I assumed that my neighbor, Grant Knoll, would be going to work at the Nirvana sales office that day, and I'd noticed his habit of leaving home around ten. When the fourth ring was cut short, I held my breath, waiting for his answering machine. But no.

"Hello?"

"Hi, Grant. It's Claire Gray. Thank God I caught you."

Within fifteen minutes, the dark, somber silence of the Hurons' bedroom was replaced by the efficient bustle of a murder investigation.

Outside the house, the quiet cul-de-sac had become a makeshift parking lot for an array of police vehicles—squads from the Palm Desert police and Riverside County sheriff's departments, vans for the evidence technicians and medical examiner, and an unmarked county-plated sedan for the investigator in charge, Detective Larry Knoll.

I had phoned Grant, my neighbor, because I recalled that he had a brother on the police force, figuring that any connection, however loose, was better than none. Grant agreed. When he heard what had happened, he immediately offered to phone his brother, calling him "the best detective on the force." Further, Grant asked for the Hurons' address so that he himself could drive over, concerned for my own well-being. I assured him that I was fine, that I didn't want to wrench his busy Saturday, but he insisted, "That's what neighbors are for."

So I now stood in the Hurons' living room talking in hushed tones with Grant while the medical examiner and evidence techs did their duties in the bedroom. Paul was with us, sitting at the end of a black leather sofa, head propped in his hands. Crying quietly, he occasionally raised his head for a gulp of air, or a sob, or a swipe of his damp, knotted handkerchief.

Conversing with Grant, I watched his brother in the bedroom hall, who compared notes with several uniformed police officers and sheriff's deputies. I had not yet met Larry Knoll, but I knew he was Grant's brother the moment he'd entered the house. They shared the same height (not quite six feet), nice build, and kind, blue eyes. I knew Grant was forty-nine, and I guessed Larry to be a few years younger, though Grant wore his years better—reinforcing my assumption that Grant was gay and Larry was not.

Grant dressed better too. He wore tropical-weight charcoal wool slacks, good loafers (tasseled, naturally), a cream-colored knit pullover (probably vicuna), and he carried a nubby, neutral silk sport coat, its breast pocket adorned with a jaunty yellow silk kerchief—all perfectly tasteful, handsome, and gentlemanly. Larry's attire was not nearly so fashionable. True, he was a working police officer, but of the plain-clothes variety, with the emphasis on *plain*. His navy blue suit was neat and well tailored but otherwise workaday. The white oxford shirt was

laundry fresh but predictable. The necktie looked downright uncom-
fortable; I'd seen very few businessmen wearing ties in the desert. Already the morning seemed too warm for the jacket, which he did not
remove. Contemplating this, I wondered if he carried a gun or had
other menacing paraphernalia stowed beneath the jacket. Was it worn
to make him look more like a fellow citizen and less like a cop?

"Yup," Grant told me, "a nice wife, two kids, and a dog."

I'd been ballsy enough to ask if Grant's brother was a family man.
Plunging ahead, I asked, "Larry's older, right?" Though I suspected the
opposite, I assumed Grant would find the question flattering.

"No." Grant didn't gloat in the least. "Larry's three years younger.
He's forty-six." With a gentle smile, Grant added, "His line of work
can be rough sometimes."

I nodded knowingly, but in truth, my knowledge of Larry's work—
or any detective's work—was little more than intuitive. More precisely,
it was nil.

Larry's meeting with the other officers was breaking up, one of them
going into the bedroom, the others heading out of the house. With his
eyes on his notes, Larry stepped back into the living room.

Grant told me, "Let me introduce you," and he crossed the room,
grabbed his brother, and brought him forward. I met them halfway.

"Claire," said Grant, "I'd like you to meet my younger brother, Larry
Knoll of the Riverside County sheriff's department. Larry, this is none
other than Claire Gray, the esteemed Broadway director, one of Palm
Desert's newest residents."

We shook hands. Larry said, "It's an honor, Miss Gray. My brother
speaks very highly of you, both as an artist and as a neighbor."

"The pleasure's mine, Detective. But I insist, do call me Claire."

"Thanks, I will. And you can drop the 'Detective.' To any friend of
Grant's, I'm just Larry." He struck a satisfied pose, hands on hips, pushing back the flaps of his jacket.

I saw the gun. "I'm curious about something, Larry. You work for
the sheriff's department, right? Why aren't the local police handling
this?"

He exhaled a breathy laugh. "Fact is, there *is* no Palm Desert police force. Some of the smaller desert communities contract with Riverside County for police services. You'll see Palm Desert police cars around, but the officers inside are sheriff's deputies. It's a matter of efficiency; in most of these towns, crime rates are extremely low."

At that moment, two deputies from the morgue wheeled a gurney through the front door, passed us in the living room, and clattered through the hall toward the bedroom. Paul looked up from his sniffles long enough to absorb the scene, then broke into another full-blown crying jag.

"Uh," said Larry, scratching behind one ear, "circumstances notwithstanding, homicides are rare here. I'm sorry, Claire, to have something like this darken your arrival to the valley."

I reminded him, "This is far harder on Paul—the dead woman's husband—than it is on me."

"Of course. I haven't spoken to Mr. Huron yet. I thought he could use a little time to pull himself together."

I nodded. "It was a terrible shock. He took it very badly."

Paul's sobs underlaid this entire exchange. Noting this, Grant went over to the sofa and sat next to Paul, offering a fresh linen handkerchief from his hip pocket. Paul accepted it with a nod, dropping his own. The wet wad landed on the terra-cotta floor with a tired splat.

"Larry," I said, speaking low, moving a step or two away from the sofa, "you mentioned that homicides are rare here. That's it, then? You're treating this as a murder?"

He shook his head. "Not officially, not yet. Neither the cause nor the manner of death is apparent. Clearly, the circumstances are suspicious, which warrants a complete medical-legal autopsy. The report shouldn't take long; then we'll have something to go on."

Thinking aloud, I said, "Jodie didn't *look* as though she'd met a violent end. She was just . . . dead. Could she have died of natural causes?"

Though I'd asked the question rhetorically, Larry answered it. "She *could* have, certainly. Or she may have succumbed to drugs or poison or any number of insidious agents. Still, my best bet is that Mrs. Huron was accosted and killed violently, in a struggle."

"Why do you say that?"

"Isn't it obvious? Just take one look at that room, and—"

"Uh . . . ," I interrupted. Fidgeting with my hair, I informed him, "That's not *exactly* the condition in which we found the room."

Larry's kindly blue eyes widened in a cold stare. "What?" he asked flatly.

He shook his head in disbelief as I explained how Paul had discovered the body, gone a bit bonkers, and trashed the crime scene. "He was looking for Jodie's ring, or clues, or whatever."

Larry exhaled a loud, disgusted sigh. He asked, "Were you in the room when he did this?"

"Not when he found the body."

"Where were you?"

"In the kitchen. I was about to rinse out the coffeemaker—and I thought it odd that the coffee smelled fresh—when I heard Paul scream something about Jodie. I dropped and broke the pot." I displayed the front of my shirt, still damp and hopelessly stained.

He grinned. "I was wondering."

"You thought I *dressed* like this?"

Suppressing a laugh, he told me, "No, of course not."

I related the whole chain of events, taking time to be exacting. I concluded, "It all happened so fast. That's when I phoned nine-one-one."

He nodded, finished a few notes, then walked over to the sofa, saying, "Mr. Huron? I'm Detective Larry Knoll." Paul stood. After the expected exchange of introductions, condolences, and thank-yous, the detective told him, "If you feel up to it, I'd like for you to come into the bedroom with me. I have a few routine questions, and you can tell me what happened."

Paul nodded. "This won't be easy. I doubt if I'll ever sleep in there again."

Larry assured him, "I understand." He turned to me, "Why don't you come in as well, Claire? That might make it a bit easier for Mr. Huron, and frankly, I'm impressed by your recollection of detail."

Naturally, I agreed to accompany them.

Grant caught his brother's eye, then stepped him away from Paul to ask, "Would it be okay if I went in there too? Paul's not in good shape. I'd just like to 'be there' for him."

As they were speaking within earshot of me, I closed our circle and, in a facetious tone, told Grant, "I thought you came over this morning to keep an eye on *me.*"

"You seem to be doing just *fine,* Claire."

Larry raised an eyebrow, a silent agreement with his brother's assessment of my mental state.

I realized, with considerable dismay, that I had indeed gotten past the initial shock of finding Jodie's body. And though I was still concerned for Paul and felt sympathy for his loss, my overwhelming emotion just then was raw curiosity: How had this happened?

Pondering this question, I heard Larry tell his brother, "Sure, Grant, keep an eye on Paul for us. I'm sure he'll appreciate having you in there with him."

So I stepped over to Paul, took his hand, and suggested softly, "Come on. Let's get this over with."

He nodded, and we joined Larry and Grant, walking the hall to the bedroom.

At the doorway, Larry asked the investigating crew inside if they could vacate the bedroom for a few minutes—it would be crowded enough with the four of us (plus Jodie) in there. They complied, filing past us in the narrow hall. When the medical examiner appeared, Larry asked, "Any theories?"

He shook his head. "Sorry, just time of death. She hasn't been dead more than an hour or two—that's easy. But how'd it happen? No trauma, no evidence of poisoning, no signs of asphyxiation—in short, not a clue."

Larry thanked him, turned to the rest of us, and said, "Let's have a look."

I followed on his heels, eager to observe the scene again, this time more objectively. Paul, needless to say, was far more reluctant. Behind me, I could hear his choked sobs and Grant's gentle prodding.

When we were all inside the doorway, Larry told us, "Don't touch *anything.*"

I'd been hearing that a lot, like a line from a bad movie, and I had to stifle the impulse to laugh. My glib manner faded fast, though, when my eyes tripped on Jodie's corpse. Her flesh was no longer merely pale but gray. Where her body touched the floor, her skin had taken on an ugly purplish cast. What's more, the room's strange, spicy scent—it reminded me of incense—was now overpowered by the distinct odor of urine.

Paul absorbed all this at the same moment I did; his sobs grew louder, punctuated by a sneeze or two. I turned to see Grant stretch an arm around Paul's shoulders while taking the handkerchief from Paul's clenched hand and dabbing his face with it.

I also saw that the room was now in even greater disarray than when Paul had trashed it. The body and the scene had been thoroughly photographed, a process that left its own debris. Drawers, bed linens, rugs, curtains—everything—had been turned, shaken, emptied, examined. Adding to the room's eerie shambles, every surface that might conceivably have been touched was now powdered in the hunt for fingerprints.

Something occurred to me. I told Larry, "I touched the phone when I called to report this. Sorry."

"No problem. We'll take a set of your prints before you leave. Mr. Huron's too. We already have Mrs. Huron's. We simply need to eliminate the known prints before trying to trace any others that show up."

Paul asked, "Can I sit down?" He sounded weak.

"Of course," Larry told him.

Paul slumped on the edge of the bed, looking down at his dead wife, whose rock-steady stare was now fixed on the sun-filled south window. Without hesitating, Grant sat down next to Paul and patted his back, clucking motherly reassurances. I was glad Grant was there for these duties; otherwise, they would doubtless have fallen to me. I already had enough on my mind, making an inventory of everything I saw:

The bedroom, like the rest of the house, had been tastefully decorated in a spare, modern style with a few southwestern touches—the rough-hewn bed frame, the Indian rug hanging on one of the off-white walls, the bold turquoise paint chosen for closet and bathroom doors. There was something unmistakably artistic about the decor, and I presumed this was influenced by Paul the sculptor rather than Jodie the nurse, who had struck me as more the pragmatic sort.

I glanced through their closets, which the police had left wide open.

On one side was Paul's lean wardrobe of slacks and shirts, both dressy and casual, plus shoes and a few jackets; almost everything was black. On the other side was Jodie's, dominated by her nursing uniforms and casual, athletic attire—though naturally pretty, she didn't dress up much. This observation was reinforced by my perusal of her vanity table, if it could be called that.

Not a frilly-skirted dressing table with curlicued gilt mirror, but a simple white Parsons table with matching stool, Jodie's vanity told me that she was a woman in a hurry who didn't primp or fuss. I saw two tubes of lipstick, face powder, a compact of eye shadow, but no mascara or liner. There was a nail clipper, file, and buffer, but no polish. She had been experimenting with several brands of moisturizer and sunscreen, as I myself had done since moving to the desert. Her jewelry box was just a lidded dish, its contents now spread on the table—a few simple, modern pieces, as I'd observed on Wednesday night, probably custom-crafted by associates of Paul.

Seeing nothing on the table for her hair, I stepped to the bathroom and looked inside. The contents of the drawers on her side of the sink were now arrayed on the counter. I noted a hair dryer, styling brush, and setting gel, but no mousse, spray, or rollers—she couldn't be bothered. I saw her toothbrush, toothpaste, mouthwash, and floss. She had a few prescriptions in orange-plastic pill bottles, plus vitamins, aspirin, antacids, and Ex-Lax. Rounding out this collection were spray deodorant, eye drops, and the expected assortment of "feminine-care" products. Taken as a whole, these sundry remnants of Jodie's daily routine gave the impression of a healthy young woman, active and self-assured—downed in her prime.

Meanwhile, Larry had begun a standard questioning of Paul, taking notes as he went along. "Your wife's name and age, Mr. Huron?"

"Jodie Metz-Huron. She was just thirty, two years younger than me."

"Is Jodie a nickname?"

"No, her given name was Jodie Katherine Metz."

"Where was she from?"

"Michigan, one of the better suburbs of Detroit. Her nursing studies took her east. We met in New Haven—I did my MFA at Yale. When I landed my teaching appointment at Rhode Island, she moved with me, and a couple of years later, we married. That was five years ago. We moved out here together this past June."

"So you've lived together how long?"

Paul paused, counting on his fingers. "Over eight years." A flood of memories forced his face into his hands as a fresh spring of tears rose within him.

After an appropriate silence, Larry asked, "Where did Jodie work?"

Paul composed himself. "Coachella Medical Center. She worked in their cardiac unit. Her skills were highly specialized. She was *so* dedicated—sometimes I'd kid her that her patients meant more to her than I did. Oh, God"—Paul shook his head—"I shouldn't have done that."

Grant patted Paul's knee, telling him softly, "That's okay. You're the man she came home to every night."

Larry dropped out of his cop mode long enough to tell Paul, "She sounds like a wonderful woman."

"She was."

Larry turned to a fresh page of his notebook. "This morning, Paul, it was you who first discovered the body, correct?"

He nodded. "I had just flown in from Dallas and was bringing my bags into the bedroom. When I walked through the door, there she was."

Larry turned to me. "That's when you heard him, from the kitchen?"

"Yes. It was five minutes till ten. I'd just noticed the wall clock in the kitchen."

Larry made note of the time, then asked Paul, "Why were you in Dallas?"

"Glenn Yeats sent me." Paul explained the purpose of the trip and told of his frustrating encounter with Dane Carmichael on Friday night.

"How long were you away?"

"Uh, just two nights. I left Thursday afternoon around three, and arrived back this morning at nine-twenty."

"Do you have the specific flight information?"

Grant told his brother, "Easy, Larry. He's been through enough this morning."

"Exactly," said the detective. "The sooner we can place Paul above suspicion, the easier this investigation will be for him—and for us."

That made sense to me, and it seemed to satisfy both Grant and Paul. "Jeez," said Paul, fingers pronged to his forehead, "I flew on AirWest, but I don't remember the flight numbers. If I kept the boarding passes, they'd be in my jacket." He gestured toward his linen sport coat, piled with his luggage near the door, where he'd dropped everything.

As I was standing nearest the door, I said, "I'll check."

"Thanks, Claire. Try the inside breast pocket."

Picking up the jacket, I looked inside, and, yes, the pocket contained some paperwork in a ticket folder. "No boarding passes," I told Larry, "but here's the printed itinerary." I read it first—it verified the schedule Paul had described—then passed it to the detective, who recorded details of the itinerary in his notebook.

"May I keep this?" Larry asked.

Paul shrugged. "Sure."

Larry turned to me, looking suddenly baffled. "How did *you* happen to be here when Paul arrived home?"

I explained, "I *drove* him here. Paul's car was being repaired last week, so Jodie drove him to the airport on Thursday, and I picked him up this morning."

"So you met Paul's nine-twenty flight at the airport this morning. You drove him from Palm Springs. And that's your Beetle in the driveway, correct?"

"Yes, sir. Correct," I answered with precision, mimicking his no-nonsense tone.

Larry flipped back through some of his notes, then surveyed the room—and the mess that Paul had made, which had now been worsened by his own investigation. He said to Paul, "Claire mentioned that after you found the body, you began searching for a ring. What was that all about?"

"Jodie's wedding ring," Paul explained. "It's missing."

"Are you sure she was wearing it?"

"She *always* wore it. I could still see the mark on her finger."

Larry knelt at Jodie's side and bent to peer closely at her left hand. Satisfied, he rose, asking Paul, "You looked for the ring, and you didn't find it?"

Paul shook his head.

"Is anything else missing?"

Paul hesitated. "I couldn't tell. I mean, nothing obvious is missing, nothing like the TV or computer, but if he was after little stuff like jewelry, it may take a while to realize that something's gone."

I said, *"He* was after little stuff? Who's 'he'?"

Larry glanced at me with arched brows.

Paul answered, "The thief, of course."

Larry asked, "So you assume this was a robbery?"

Paul stood. "Well, *sure.* What *else* could it be?" His tone was now analytical, and he seemed as intrigued by the puzzle as I was. For the moment, at least, he had set aside the shock of losing Jodie. "After all," he said, "Jodie was scheduled for an oddball shift at the hospital last night—they come up every few weeks. Lots of people knew about it, and lots of people knew that I would be out of town."

I told the detective, "He's right. Just Wednesday night, it was discussed at a crowded party. I was there."

Paul continued, "So it must have seemed like a perfect opportunity to rob the place. Except, for some reason, Jodie was here this morning—and she caught the intruder in the act."

Grant rose from the bed, telling his brother, "Sounds reasonable to me."

Larry scratched his temple. "Yeah, maybe. If so, we don't have much to go on. The thief took a diamond ring—needle in a haystack, I'm afraid."

"No, Larry," I said, "it was *not* an everyday diamond wedding ring. It was truly unique, commissioned by Paul from a fellow artist."

Paul described in detail the sculpted, intertwining rings, each topped with a pearl, one white, the other black. "I can probably find a good photo of it, if that would be helpful."

Larry assured him, "That would be *very* helpful. If it was stolen, the thief may try to sell it. A ring that distinctive should be easy to identify."

"There," said Grant, trying to lighten Paul's stress, "a bit of progress already. Larry'll get to the bottom of this."

"I can't promise results," Larry told all of us, "but I can promise my best effort. This case is now my highest priority, an apparent homicide, possibly linked to theft. The desert communities are historically a low-crime area; residents will expect nothing less than quick, decisive action." Then he told Paul, "I can't bring Jodie back, but with any luck, we'll bring her killer to justice."

Paul offered his hand, "Thank you, Detective. I'll help any way I can."

Larry shook Paul's hand, sealing their pact of cooperation. Then he turned to a fresh page in his notebook, asking, "To get my investigation started, are there any names you can give me—people who may have been inside your home, people who are familiar with both Jodie's schedule and your own?"

Paul thought. "No, we haven't been here long enough to nurture many friendships. The only person who fits your question is Oralia."

Larry, Grant, and I focused a collective gaze on Paul that asked, Who?

"Oralia Alvarez, our housekeeper. She's here two afternoons a week, Tuesdays and Thursdays. She knows our schedules. And she has a key."

"Any reason to suspect her?"

"God, I *hope* not. I don't see her that often, but she *seems* honest."

"Still," said Larry, "I'll need to check her out."

Paul told him how to reach his housekeeper.

Larry had no more questions, so Grant offered to take Paul to the kitchen and brew a pot of coffee.

"You'll have to settle for instant," I reminded them, attempting to cover my stained shirt with crossed arms.

Grant assured me, "We'll make do. Come on, Paul." And he led the recent widower out of the bedroom, away from his wife's body.

After a few quiet moments, Larry closed his notes and squatted near Jodie's side, looking down at her, perplexed.

I did likewise, facing the detective from the other side of the body. Thinking aloud, I told him, "She'd be alive and well now, if only she'd been at the hospital, as planned."

"Yup."

I added, "But why, in fact, was Jodie home this morning?"

"Good question."

4

When we'd finished at the Hurons' house, we left Paul and the investigation in the capable hands of Grant's brother. Walking to our cars, Grant suggested, "Let's have lunch. I'll throw together a salad or something. We need to decompress. Maybe Kiki could join us."

The events of that morning had rattled both of us. I was in no mood to dash off and run errands, and Grant decided he'd be useless at the Nirvana sales office. His suggestion sounded wonderful, and I accepted the invitation at once.

After parking in our respective garages at Villa Paseo, he called to me from the courtyard, "Take your time, Claire. Come on over whenever you're ready. The door's open."

I spent a few minutes changing out of my coffee-stained clothes, donning a fresh pair of khakis, an oversize white shirt, and an old pair of Keds—very Saturday. I checked for mail and messages, found neither, then left a brief phone message for Kiki, telling her what had happened and inviting her to join us at Grant's. With these duties done, I stepped outdoors, closing the front door behind me. Crossing the courtyard on my way to my neighbor's, I paused to appreciate my new home.

Villa Paseo is neither lavish in scale nor glamorous in style, but it's comfortable and charming, suiting my needs exactly. When I first saw it, I said, "My God, it looks a bit like Melrose Place." The six condominiums are arrayed around a tile-paved courtyard with a central fountain. The white stucco houses are built on two levels, each with two bedrooms, a fireplace, and French doors leading to small but private outdoor areas. Roofs are terra-cotta; trim is wrought iron. Date palms give dappled shade; bougainvillea climbs the balconies. It looks like a set for some merry operetta, with mountains rimming a backdrop of sky behind the staggered chimneys. If, a year ago, I had been asked to describe what my first California home might look like, I'd have been hard-pressed to concoct an architectural fantasy more pleasingly cliché.

Some ten years earlier, Grant Knoll had worked with a couple of other investors to develop the property. He'd staked out the prime location, adjacent to the common pool, for himself, selling off the other five units to buyers of his choosing. There was never a doubt among the half dozen homeowners that Grant should preside over their condominium association, collecting the fees, contracting the common services, keeping everything picture perfect. In the decade since, the landscaping had matured, the new construction had weathered to a graceful patina, and from time to time, an owner had moved on. That past summer, Kiki and I had lucked into two such openings.

Holding my fingers now under the fountain's cold trickle, I dropped my head back to feel the penetrating warmth of a midday sun in the boundless, dry, autumn-blue sky. A mockingbird sang some ecstatic ditty from the limbs of a nearby peppertree. Breathing deeply, I could not imagine greater peace. I had left behind the day-to-day turmoil of my past, and the daily rigors of my new life had not yet begun. There I was, somewhere between limbo and paradise.

Except, murder had intruded. The most mortal of sins had darkened my day and forever changed a colleague's life. The full emotional impact of that morning's grim discovery had not yet fully registered. Barely two hours had passed since I'd heard Paul's scream and raced to witness his vain attempt to revive his downed wife.

My stomach rumbled, reminding me that I was expected for lunch at the home of my gracious neighbor. So I flicked the fountain's water from my fingers and strolled the few remaining steps to Grant's entry court.

As promised, his door was flung wide open. A recording of soft, soothing jazz played low from within, drifting on the air with the twitter from the peppertree. I knocked on the doorjamb and poked my head inside.

Grant was in the kitchen, fussing with something at the counter, with a cordless telephone nested between his shoulder and ear. Seeing me, he smiled, waving me in. With the fingers of one hand, he mimed a clacking beak—someone was gabbing at him and was slow to wrap it up. He motioned that I should sit at a little breakfast table, where a fat crystal wineglass stood ready but empty; the glass in front of him on the counter was half-empty.

While making accommodating grunts on the phone (the other party was doing most of the talking), Grant opened the fridge, extracted an open bottle of good Chardonnay, stepped over to the breakfast table, and poured a hefty glassful for me. I made no move to curtail his pouring, mouthing a thank-you when he had finished.

He said into the phone, "Tell Arlene I'm sorry, but it'll have to wait. I won't be in the office at all today. I need to be with a friend who's suffered a tragic loss." He winked at me, touching his glass to mine in a silent toast.

I tasted the wine, found it cool and refreshing, then took a larger swallow. When Grant finally said good-bye and turned off the phone (it bleeped as he punched a button on the handset), I told him, "I hope I haven't fouled up your whole day. It sounds as if you're busy."

"I'm *always* busy. There's no routine; it's always some crisis, at least in the eyes of my clients. Would you believe it? Arlene Harris, a dear gal and a good client, phoned my office a few minutes ago, needing an appointment to see me on some 'urgent real estate matter'—those were her words."

I grimaced. "What could be urgent about real estate?"

"You tell *me.*" He laughed. "By its nature, land stays put. Not two years ago, I set up Arlene and her husband, Henry, in a *wonderful* home at Sunhaven. He's retired; she shops. What could be 'urgent'? It'll keep till Monday." Grant returned his attentions to the huge, elegant salad he was preparing for us, picking stems from a bowl of raspberries that would soon infuse his vinaigrette.

I offered, "Can I help?"

He shook his head.

Thinking over what he'd told me about Arlene Harris, I told him, "I'm confused. I know you run the sales office at Nirvana, but how do the Harrises fit in—at Sunhaven?"

While he whisked, he explained, "Aside from my duties at Nirvana, which are relatively recent, I'm an independent broker—have been for years. Hate to sound immodest, but I have a long-established reputation as broker to some of the desert's wealthiest clientele. That's why Nirvana wanted me. I'm highly connected, as they say. On the job, I run in an elite social circle, catering to their changing housing needs in times of both joy and crisis."

I chortled. "So you know the dirt on everyone."

He rolled his eyes. "Oh, honey—the things I could tell." Setting down his whisk, he added, "But of course my lips are sealed." Then he let out a hearty peal of laughter. He continued working on the salad, chopping cilantro, slicing strips of chicken, adding various types of lettuce from a strainer in the sink.

"I hope Kiki gets my message," I told him. "Your salad, while beautiful, looks a bit ambitious for the two of us."

" 'Make no little plans,' " he lectured. Then he named the quote's source: "Daniel H. Burnham, the beaux arts architect who developed the master plan for Chicago after the Great Fire."

"An interesting credo."

With a humble bow of his head, he acknowledged, "It has served me well."

Gabbing in this manner, avoiding the topic that would doubtless dominate our conversation once we settled down to lunch, I rose from the breakfast table with my glass and wandered toward the living room. "Mind if I snoop?"

"Please do. Sorry to be such a lousy host. Kitchen duty—Greta has weekends off," he quipped.

Stepping into the living room, I called back to him, "You seem fairly adept at culinary matters. Does Greta suffer from an inferiority complex?"

"God, no! She's a dominatrix—a *domestic* dominatrix—a shrew in uniform."

Our banter ebbed and flowed as Grant prepared lunch and I surveyed his quarters. Since my move-in, I'd seen his home several times, but I'd not had the opportunity to indulge in a leisurely look at the furnishings, pictures, books, and bric-a-brac that collectively define both a house and its occupant. Grant's surroundings spoke volumes.

His decorating was tasteful, stylish, impeccable—that goes without saying. But his space had the imprint of his own personality, and the trait most clearly conveyed was confidence. He had the confidence, for instance, to decorate in darker colors, choosing charcoal carpeting and sage-colored walls, while everyone else in the desert, it seemed, was on a white-and-beige kick.

He also had the confidence to mix radically different styles with aplomb. Nothing matched, but everything worked together: contemporary sofa, Louis Seize side chairs, glass-and-iron coffee table, silver-leafed bombé sideboard, and the room's focal point, a tall palm tree sculpted of galvanized metal, its fronds spreading wide in the upper reaches of the sloping ceiling. Books were everywhere: novels and current events and philosophy, not to mention art, architecture, decorating, landscaping, and flowers. A collection of old mercury glass was scattered throughout the room, lending sparkle: vases, candlesticks, urns, compotes, saltcellars, probably fifty in all, with some of the larger pieces clustered in front of the fireplace on the hearth.

The room's windows, as well as the French doors leading to the terrace, were curtained with a heavy, nubby vintage fabric featuring a riotous design of ginger flowers and banana leaves. One windowless wall was covered with framed artwork: large architectural photographs, several drawings of nudes (mostly male), a huge collage of paper and torn fabric, a faded blueprint of a Romanesque church, another of Villa Paseo, a David Hockney swimming-pool scene, and an oil portrait that might have been Grant during his college days.

Smaller framed photos stood propped on the mantel, cabinets, tables, and floor. Some of these showed Grant posing with socialites at charity balls and other formal functions. Others, smaller still, were mere snapshots, more personal, his souvenirs of travel: Grant in Paris, in Rome, in the marketplace of some rustic fishing village, on board a cruise ship. These slices of his private life rarely included anyone else. In all but the older photos, he was alone, and with the exception of the smiling celebrities in evening gowns (Carol Channing, Betty Ford, Jane Wyman, Loretta Young), he was never with a woman.

The music had stopped, and I could hear the clatter of cutlery and plates. I stepped to the kitchen doorway. Feeling at ease, I asked quietly, "Where's the man in your life, Grant?"

He looked up at me from the tray he was arranging, neither expecting the question nor shying from it. "You're looking at him."

I strolled into the kitchen, thinking, fingering my wineglass, which was now nearly empty. "How come? You're attractive, talented, affluent. You could have any man you want." Then, realizing I'd probed more deeply than planned, I told him, "Sorry, it's none of my business."

"No, that's okay," he assured me. "The problem, if it *is* a problem, is that I don't know *what* I want."

I raised an eyebrow. Was he still struggling with his sexual identity?

Reading my mind, he laughed, saying, "Don't get me wrong—if there were a someone, it would definitely be a man—I've known that since I was six. Of course, I didn't get active till college. Since then, I've had my share of experience. I've played the field. I've even attempted a few relationships, one of which lasted, gosh, it seemed like a *year*—but it was only ten months. When *that* Mr. Right walked out of my life fifteen years ago, I pretty much stopped trying. I was nearly thirty-five, feeling suddenly middle-aged and scared shitless by AIDS, which had rolled into our lives like a wave of panic. The sane thing, the *safe* thing, I decided, was to go it alone for a while."

"It's been quite a while."

He nodded. "Guess I lost track. Or maybe I got sidetracked by other priorities."

I reminded him, " 'Make no little plans,' Grant."

"Touché." He turned, opened the refrigerator, pulled out the wine, and refilled both of our glasses. Setting the bottle on the counter with a decisive clack, he asked, "So, Claire, where's the man in *your* life?"

I suddenly regretted having broached this topic. Grant had been forthright when I questioned him, so he had every right to expect nothing less from me. The lump in my throat felt like a glass grape. Lamely, I told him, "Guess I've been busy." He stared at me skeptically. I elaborated, "The career, I mean—it's been a full-time job."

He set down his glass, sliding it a few inches aside on the counter, signaling that I was not to be let off the hook that easily. Grinning, he told me, "We all have careers; that excuse doesn't wash. You do 'like men,' don't you? That's not the issue."

"Correct. That's not the issue. I have healthy heterosexual appetites." Then, thinking that Grant might read my choice of the word *healthy* the wrong way, I added, "No offense."

"None taken. Anyway, I knew you were straight."

"And I knew you were gay."

"How?" With a laugh, he added, ". . . aside from *everything.*"

I slurped some wine and let it rest in my mouth, thinking about his question. With a bent smile, I swallowed. "Because you never look at my tits."

He blinked.

Raising a hand, I explained, "I'm the first to acknowledge that my endowment is average at best; I'm no sweater girl. That's not the point. The point is, I do have the basic equipment, like any woman. And most men—straight men—always look at them. During a conversation, their eyes invariably wander down to the tits. They can't help themselves."

With mock sympathy, Grant commiserated, "They're pigs, aren't they?"

"And another thing." I was laughing now. "I knew you were gay because you always look me in the eye when we're talking. I don't know what it is—it must be a 'guy thing'—but straight men never make eye contact."

"They're busy ogling your boobs," Grant reminded me, "wallowing in their lurid, piggish fantasies."

"Of course," I said, thumping my forehead, suddenly enlightened, "it all fits."

Grant finished stacking tableware on the tray. Pensively, he said, "The reason I knew you were straight . . . well, it wasn't nearly so analytical. To be honest, I'd simply never read or heard anything that questioned your sexuality. You're *famous,* Claire, and over the years, I've read any number of news stories and interviews featuring you. Let's face it, you're a major success in a field dominated by men, so suspicions naturally arise. If you were into women, it would be a matter of public record by now. But it's not. And in fact, the name that usually popped up as a romantic connection was Hector Bosch."

"Hector." I shook my head slowly. "He still can't believe I've done this—moved here. We haven't spoken since I left New York."

We were referring to the esteemed, and sometimes caustic, theater critic for the *New York Weekly Review.* Hector Bosch and I were longtime friends and mutual admirers who had occasionally awoken in each other's bed. From his perspective, that was romance; he'd suggested marriage more than once. From my perspective, that was friendship and recreation; I'd never once been tempted to weigh his proposals seriously.

I told Grant, "Hector and I—it's hard to say who was fooling whom. Hector's at least ten years older than I, well into his sixties. He remembers Pearl Harbor. His mind-set is old. I'm just not there yet—and I never want to be."

"Good for you, Claire. I'm with you." Grant paused in thought. "There's been some public speculation about Hector over the years, regarding which way he swings. I mean, he's so—" Grant whirled a hand, at a loss for words.

I suggested, "Glib? Affected? Yes, Hector does indeed leave people guessing, but I can assure you—from *experience*—that his bedtime proclivities are decidedly heterosexual."

"So then," Grant summed up our conversation, "you occasionally enjoy the company of men and the pleasures of the boudoir. Hector, however, is not to be the man in your life. No other possibilities?"

"Not at the moment, Grant. Can we leave it at that?"

"Sure." He gave me a wink and a warm smile. Referring to the bounty he'd arranged on the tray before him, he said, "Luncheon is served. If we hear from Kiki, the more the merrier. I thought we'd eat poolside, if you can stand the heat."

"I'm learning to deal with it. Sounds marvelous."

So I carried the heaping, pink ceramic salad bowl, while Grant hefted the tray containing everything else. Parading out of the kitchen, we crossed the living room and passed through the open French doors to Grant's terrace, which adjoined the pool deck. A round, glass-topped dining table sat in the shade of a latticework arbor, and though the temperature was by now near ninety, the dry heat felt oddly comfortable, almost therapeutic. The tall glass pitcher of iced tea, I noticed, did not sweat. I squinted as sunlight danced lazily on the surface of the pool.

A roadrunner scampered across the far side of the terrace. Overhead, a hummingbird methodically needle-nosed red blooms on the vines that twined the arbor.

Grant began arranging our lunch before me, pouring tea as I lolled in a canvas chair, enjoying the tranquil day and affable company.

"Murder?" shrilled a familiar voice just as a door slammed.

Deadpan, I told Grant, "Kiki's back."

"She must've gotten your message."

We heard Kiki's footfalls race through Villa Paseo, past the fountain, and up to Grant's front door, where they stopped. "Claire, darling!" she hollered. "If this is your idea of a joke . . ."

"We're in back," Grant called to her. "Join us!"

She hesitated, uncertain whether to wander through the house or to use the back gate to the pool. The grating of her footsteps on sandy tile told us she had opted for the back. A moment later, the iron gate creaked open and banged shut as she appeared near the end of the pool and dashed toward the table, looking pale. "You can't be *serious,"* she told me through a breathless, dramatic gasp.

I nodded matter-of-factly. "Afraid so. Sorry."

Speechless, she turned to Grant for confirmation.

He assured her, "Yes, Jodie Metz-Huron was found dead at home this morning, and it appears to be a homicide. Her husband, Paul, discovered the body in their bedroom right after Claire drove him home from the airport. Sit down, Kiki." He rose for a few seconds to help her settle into a chair at the table.

"Good God," she said, looking through us, wagging her head, "what a terrible shock, a terrible tragedy. Poor Paul. He must be devastated."

"He is," I acknowledged. "Would you like some iced tea?"

Grant offered, "Or wine? It's indoors, but I'll get it. Care for more, Claire?"

"No, thanks. I've had two already. It's the middle of the day—that's plenty."

"How on *earth,"* Kiki asked us, practicing her gasp, "can you two pother over *beverages* at a time like *this*?"

Tentatively, Grant asked, "Tea, then? No wine?"

With a jaded sigh, she splayed her fingers over her bosom (which is considerably more ample than mine, even when not accentuated by the perky green sundress she wore that afternoon—an orange chiffon scarf and huge, yellow enameled earrings completed the ensemble, making her look a bit like a parrot). Reconsidering, Kiki admitted, "Some wine would be lovely."

Grant grinned. "If you'll excuse me, ladies, I'll fetch madam's vino." He pushed back his chair, rose, and walked indoors.

Kiki leaned forward, elbows on the table, and took one of my hands into hers. "You poor thing. Such a grisly welcome to our new home. I'm amazed you're so calm about it."

"So am I." My shoulders slumped. "I'm just so relieved that it's *over*— I mean the ordeal at the Hurons' house—I'm probably kidding myself about being so strong. Chances are, the true magnitude of what's happened hasn't quite sunk in yet. I may have a rough night."

From the side of her mouth, in a throaty stage whisper, Kiki advised me, "Take a pill." Then she leaned closer and broke into laughter.

I laughed with her, patting her hand, glad she was there for me, just like old times. She chattered about that morning's events, asking questions, braced for gorier details than I was able to provide. I could tell from her reactions to my tale that she found it insufficiently dramatic. After all, beyond the discovery of the corpse, there was no dagger to the heart, no message scrawled in blood, no missing body parts. Fishing for *something* that might satisfy her blood lust, I mentioned, "The room smelled of urine. After Jodie died, I guess she lost it."

"Oh, ish!"

My pronouncement had not produced its intended effect. Instead of arching her brows and begging for more, Kiki leaned back in her chair, fished a small bottle from her bag, and began spritzing her face and the surrounding atmosphere with a flowery perfume. She dispensed it so heavily, it was too much even for the hummingbird, which darted from the arbor as if it had been gassed, then disappeared over a rooftop.

"Careful with that stuff," I warned her, waving a hand under my nose. "You'll draw bugs."

"Don't be ridiculous, dear. There are no insects in paradise."

This exchange triggered several thoughts that played through my head while we continued to gabble:

First, I realized that Kiki's exaggeration was only slight—I had in fact encountered virtually no insects (perhaps a lone fly now and then) since my arrival in the desert, and this explained the common indulgence here of flinging doors and windows open without screens.

Second, I mused that Kiki was almost as fond of fragrances as she was of clothes. Her dressing table was laden with a prodigious array of flacons and atomizers containing scents that she switched, and even mixed, at will.

Third, I acknowledged that my own affection for fragrances was even less pronounced than my interest in clothes. Many years ago, probably while I was still in college, a matronly aunt had given me a bottle of Chanel. It took me so long to use it, the fragrance had become "mine." To this day, even though I use Chanel sparingly and infrequently, Number Five is the only perfume that I can identify by smell.

Fourth, I still wondered about that distinctive, spicy fragrance that I'd noticed hanging in the Hurons' bedroom. Recalling Jodie's dressing table, I realized there were no perfume bottles among her few cosmetics.

Kiki was comparing the circumstances of Jodie's death to a contemporary three-act mystery she had recently costumed, but I interrupted her. "Kiki, there's a classic perfume—"

But I myself was interrupted by Grant, who appeared just then. "Here we are. I decided to open something decent." In one hand, he managed to carry three pristinely polished wineglasses; in the other, a bottle of Far Niente, an exceptional Chardonnay with an ornate label that even I could recognize.

My eyes widened with interest. "You're going to spoil us, Grant."

"You *will* join us, then?" He set the glasses on the table and began pouring.

I pushed my tea aside; the ice had melted. "Of course."

Soon, the three of us had toasted and settled into lunch, mumbling appreciation for our friendship, the wine, and Grant's abundant salad—an inspired creation, it suited the day, the setting, and my appetite perfectly. This camaraderie was underlaid, though, by our knowledge that Jodie was dead, Paul was grieving, and in a sense, the entire community had been victimized. Invariably, our conversation kept returning to the crime.

Kiki plucked a piece of chicken with her fork and dragged it through a puddle of the raspberry vinaigrette. She told Grant, "It sounds as if your brother has exceedingly little to work with. How does one even *begin* such an investigation?"

"Routine questioning, I guess. Since Jodie's wedding ring seems to be missing, Larry will probably explore the bungled-theft angle first. And there's at least one possible lead."

I asked, "The housekeeper?"

He nodded. "I forget her name."

"Oralia Alvarez."

Both Grant and Kiki looked up at me from their plates. With a laugh, Grant asked, "Were you taking notes?"

"I was tempted."

Grant recalled, "Paul said that Oralia had access to the house and knew both his and Jodie's schedules—"

"In other words," I lectured, "Oralia had the opportunity to commit this crime."

"Right," Grant continued, "but Paul also felt that Oralia is basically honest."

"In other words, she probably lacked the motive of a thief."

Grant nodded. "You need both: motive *and* opportunity."

"You need more than that." I wiped my mouth and set my napkin on the table. "There are three classic criteria for building a case against a suspect: motive, means, and opportunity. In Jodie's case, we can speculate about motive and opportunity—as we already have—but since we don't yet know *how* Jodie died, we can't begin to speculate who might have had the *means* to kill her."

Kiki sat back, blinking. "Very good, Claire. I'm impressed."

"I'm *astounded,*" said Grant, pouring himself another splash of wine. "You sound like a veteran sleuth. Where'd you pick up the mumbo jumbo?"

"Theater," I told him flatly. "And it's not mumbo jumbo. It's logic."

"I didn't realize you'd directed that many mysteries."

"Over the years, my fair share, I guess. But *all* of theater, not just the mystery genre, teaches these lessons. Consider: Every play, every novel, every story that's *about* something is concerned with some conflict, be it murder or war or infidelity or simply some inner psychological turmoil. Once that conflict is established, everything in the play points toward its resolution, like solving a puzzle. Good theater, gripping theater, reflects and distills real life while solving the puzzle, inventing a new, condensed reality onstage.

"That process begins when the script is written; it ends when the script is enacted before an audience. The middle of that process, the meat of the process, is the interpretation of the script by the actors and director. As a director, I've spent decades striving to develop an insight into human nature, plotting, and motivation—much as your brother has, Grant. So in a sense, I *am* a veteran sleuth."

Kiki burst into applause. "Bravo, Claire. Well said!"

Grant added his own applause. "An enlightened performance."

"Thanks." With a shrug, I picked up my fork and attempted to focus less on murder and more on lunch.

But it was not to be. Grant sat back in his chair, swirling his wine, thinking. "There *is* no script—not with Jodie's murder. So there's nothing to 'interpret.' Is there?"

I peered at him from over a forkful of oily greens. "The script is there," I assured him. "It's all in order, carefully plotted, scene by scene, line by line. We just haven't discovered it yet. I'm reasonably certain, though, that the key"—I paused for effect—"the key is motivation."

Grant and Kiki digested these words as I attempted to ingest lettuce.

Again, it was not to be. Grant said, "The killer's motive appears to have been theft. Paul certainly thinks so."

I snorted sarcastically. "This community is brimming with truly wealthy households, but some daunting cat burglar chooses to invade the Hurons' home instead. Then, surprised by the unexpected presence of a woman in a nightshirt, the thief kills Jodie without leaving a mark and absconds with her easily identifiable wedding ring, leaving behind all manner of other valuables that could quickly be turned to cash." I set down my fork. "What kind of scenario is *that*?"

Kiki's features twisted in thought. "It doesn't sound likely, I admit. But if the motive wasn't theft, what was it?" She leaned forward in her seat. "We're all ears, Claire."

Drinking a bit of wine first, I said, "To my way of thinking, motives for murder can be reduced to two: greed and passion. If the motive was theft, insurance, inheritance, or advancement, we have a crime of greed. But if the motive was love, hate, revenge, or lust, we have a crime of passion. Jodie was killed in her bedroom, remember, wearing little more than a T-shirt and a conspicuously bare ring finger. What do *those* circumstances suggest—greed or passion?"

Grant drained his glass and set it on the table. "Claire," he quipped, "maybe you should've been a cop."

5

Although my quarters at Villa Paseo were structurally similar to Grant Knoll's—a mirror image of the same space, in fact—our two homes bore no resemblance in terms of furnishings or decoration. Having lived there only two weeks, I had not yet fully settled in, but even allowing for that, my nest-feathering skills were simply no match for Grant's.

When I crossed the terrace and returned home after lunch that Saturday, my surroundings struck me as especially spartan, compared to my neighbor's highly refined decor. I was tempted to assure myself that, with time, I'd "grow into" my new home, but I knew such reasoning was faulty. I'd had more than twenty years to "grow into" my rent-controlled apartment back in New York; on the day I began packing for my move to California, it still looked as stark and anonymous as it had looked on the day when Reagan first packed for Washington.

I wish I could say that my white walls, miniblinds, and sparse furnishings represented a conscious devotion to the tenets of modern minimalism—less is more—but in truth, I just wasn't very good at decorating. This lack of talent had, over the years, translated itself into a defensive lack of interest, as if attention to one's comfort and surroundings was somehow unseemly, tantamount to unbridled materialism. I knew better, of course, and always insisted upon budgeting top talent to design the sets for my plays, but for some reason I had steadfastly denied my manifest need for help with hearth and home.

It wasn't a matter of money, nor was there a scarcity of first-rate interior designers in either New York or Palm Springs. My resistance was entirely emotional; to acknowledge my lack of the decorating gene seemed equivalent to baring some mortal flaw of character. What self-respecting woman would hire a man to assist with matters that seemed to fall so naturally within her own domain? Christ, I'd spent my entire career proving that a woman could achieve success as a professional theatrical director—there are still damn few of us. Having struggled to place myself upon this lofty pedestal, how could I climb down, step back, and ask a man to pick out my drapes?

Grant had no idea how difficult it had been for me to casually solicit his decorating tips when I'd encountered him the previous Wednesday at Glenn Yeats's party. I knew, though, that this signaled something of a sea change in my attitudes, and once again, I marveled at the many new directions my life was taking. Truly, I was starting over.

Despite these energizing thoughts, that Saturday afternoon seemed suited for nothing more rigorous than a nap. That very morning, I'd stumbled into the scene of a murder, met with the police, and comforted a grieving friend. That day at lunch, I'd discussed these troubling events in numbing detail while indulging in several glasses of good wine. At home now, alone, I was presented with several options: I could hop in the car and dispatch the several errands that I had intended to run that morning. Or I could crack open the school files I'd let amass on my dining-room table, saving myself some effort during the next week when I would organize my office on campus. Or I could succumb to the lure of the sofa.

Kicking off my Keds (the sofa had easily outweighed my other options), I opened a window that looked out onto the courtyard, admitting a gust of afternoon heat that carried with it the fountain's mesmerizing chatter. Padding across the room, I sat on the edge of the couch, which now seemed designed for one purpose, then lifted my legs and reclined, stretching. The wine, the heat, the fountain, the unscheduled afternoon—it would not take long to clear my mind and slip into the indulgent slumber of a weekend nap. As my eyes drifted shut, the room blurred, then darkened.

And the phone rang.

My eyes crackled as they blinked open to an assault of light. My ears rattled as they absorbed the phone's second ring, which sounded magnified and distorted. I could get up and answer it, or I could lie there and wait for my machine to deal with it. Either way, I was awake now. So I sat up, then stood, then stepped to the kitchen. The tile floor felt cold on my feet as I reached for the phone. "Yes?"

"Claire. It's me. You're in."

"Yes, Gwyn. I'm in."

"Well? Can't you say hello?"

"I was napping, Mother. Hello."

"Napping? It's the middle of the day out there." She was phoning from her home in Upstate New York, where it was closer to evening. She gave no clue as to what time, in her opinion, was appropriate for a nap. Barely pausing for breath, she asked, "Have you heard from Hector? You'd better call him."

Even if I hadn't been disoriented by being yanked from the onset of sleep, I would have had a rough time keeping up with my mother's fuzzy logic. So I didn't even try. "How are you feeling, dear?"

"Well enough. Considering."

"Did you see Dr. Paxton this week?"

"Twice. I'm fine. Claire, I really think you should reconsider—"

"No, Gwyn. I've committed to the college. I've made my decision. I'm here."

"But there's nothing *there* for you, sweetie."

"You don't know that. Look, all those years I lived in the city, you did nothing but tell me about its dangers, and now that I'm here—"

"At least you had Hector in the city."

"Forget Hector. I have."

"How can you say such a thing?"

"Quite easily," I assured her through a smug laugh.

As she yammered on (the particulars of her monologue weren't important, but the unspoken subtext was marriage and my ever less likely prospects of achieving it), I toyed with the notion of telling her what had happened that morning. Though she would doubtless be distressed to learn that my path had veered perilously close to a perplexing crime, my story would at least be effective in nipping her discourse and changing the topic. Still, the frailty of her years demanded a certain delicacy in the delivery of upsetting news. Perhaps it would be best if she never knew at all.

She was saying, ". . . because it's simply unnatural. You're a hand-some woman, Claire, but time is running out. There must be a man who—"

"Oh," I interrupted, "did I tell you about the murder?"

There was a predictable silence. Then she asked flatly, "What?"

"A new colleague of mine, a sculptor at the college, found his wife dead in their bedroom this morning, victim of an apparent homicide. Charming couple—Paul and Jodie—I met them just three days ago."

Mother mumbled, "That's . . . terrible. How did you find out about it?"

"I was *with* Paul at the house when he found the body. Suffice it to say, the discovery shook him badly. We spent much of the morning with the police. Everything's under control, at least for now."

"Claire, dear, I tried to warn you that no good could come of this ridiculous notion to pull up your roots and . . ."

I let her prattle onward, wondering how I might add to this conversation a recounting of my luncheon with Grant Knoll—Gwyn had often warned me not to "keep company with homosexuals," as she put it. Even if I had been inclined to heed her narrow-minded admonition, it would have been impossible to do so while living in New York and working in the theater. She was convinced, of course, that rubbing elbows with gay men was at least partially responsible for setting me down that lonesome trail to spinsterhood.

". . . and *when* will I ever see you, now that you're way out there?"

"Let me give that some thought after I'm better settled." Though I would never say it, she could easily guess that part of California's allure for me was its sheer distance from Upstate New York.

". . . and I wish you'd call more often. You're all I have now."

"Yes, dear, I know. I will, I promise." Leaning near the phone, I prepared to hang up, telling her, "Well, it was so nice of you to call. We don't have enough of these little chats."

She started to say something—

"You too, dear. B'bye."

Quickly, I replaced the receiver, then gripped the edge of the counter, catching my breath. My mouth felt suddenly dry—funny, I'd done little of the talking—perhaps it was the residual effect of the wine. I took a glass from the cupboard, opened the refrigerator, and poured some chilled water, drinking it as I nudged the door closed with my hip.

Conversations with Gwyn invariably upset me, and that afternoon's call was all the more disquieting. Was it simply because she had interrupted my nap, or was I nettled by something else? I'd invoked Jodie's murder to intentionally upset my mother, glibly recounting the tragedy as if it were rather ho-hum. I'd spent the latter part of the morning congratulating myself on how well I'd handled such a terrible turn of events, but perhaps I wasn't so strong as I wanted to believe. At lunch, I'd wondered aloud to Kiki whether I was headed for a rough night. Had it already begun, at barely three in the afternoon?

The first pangs of a headache picked at my brain like the tines of a tiny silver fork. Perhaps it was merely the effect of the cold water I'd gulped. Whatever the cause of my malaise, lying down seemed a reasonable remedy, so I retreated to the living room and settled again on the sofa.

Plumping a throw pillow under my head, I closed my eyes and listened to the fountain's playful burble, shooing from my thoughts the phone call and the murder. My mind began to drift toward nothing—little more than pleasant images of my lunch next door—when I realized that Grant Knoll had parked in my subconsciousness. My affable neighbor again sat across from me, poolside, laughing and chatting, offering wine and friendship.

His conversation was engaging, if indistinct, and I got caught up in it, silently contributing to the dialogue. I wasn't sleeping, not that I could tell, and though the encounter had a dreamlike quality, it seemed to have no point, no hidden message—I couldn't even understand the words we spoke. Lying there, I smiled as I watched him, and he smiled back at me, across the table where we sat. Our sentences, our gestures, were all without focus. Only Grant himself, my gay neighbor, was sharply defined.

There are many things I have never understood, but the proclivities of men like Grant are not among the mysteries that vex me. Gay men are so much a part of my profession—I have dealt with them for so long and in so many ways related to my work—I often feel more comfortable with them than with men I have slept with. Now, *there's* a mystery: Is it because I find them witty and charming and talented, or is it a matter of finding them physically and emotionally unthreatening? Either possibility is plausible.

I am certain, though, that my attraction to gay men is not physical, not in the sexual sense. Without question, many gay men are physically attractive; Grant is a good example. To some extent, this may be a matter of luck in the gene pool. To a larger extent, this is simply a matter of grooming, dress, and deportment—they wrote the book, after all. Unlike some women, I don't make the mistake of confusing cosmetics with lust. I appreciate Grant as a neighbor, and I want him as a friend, but my desire to sleep with him is no greater than his craving to bed me, which is nil. He's a man who loves men. He's not a girlfriend with a penis, a sister with balls who—

I opened my eyes, shaking my head, which was pounding. Dismayed by the turn my thoughts had taken, I couldn't tell if these graphic notions had been spun by my conscious mind or if they had surfaced in a dream. Did they spring from cold, brutal logic or from the slippery depths of sleep? Again the pounding.

As my eyes as well as my ears finally focused on my surroundings, I realized, with amused relief, that the sound I had heard was merely a polite knock at the door, a gentle rapping. Sitting up, I explained to myself, Yes, you fell asleep, and some visitor has roused you from a dream. Standing, I glanced at my watch. It was four o'clock; I had been adrift in my miasmic nap for more than an hour.

Once again the gentle rapping.

"Yes?" I said groggily. "Coming."

"Claire? Are you there? Sorry to disturb you."

With a start, I recognized Paul Huron's voice. *He* was apologizing? God, what that poor man had already been through that day. I hurried toward the door; my bare nap-damp feet made gummy sounds when they left the carpeting of the living room and kissed the tile floor of the entry hall. "Paul"—I opened wide the door—"do come in. Gosh, how long have you been there? I was scarcely sure I heard you."

He shrugged. "A minute. Is this a bad time?" He wore black, as usual, but was looking dressier than he had that morning—a collared shirt had replaced his basic T, and his pleated slacks were a silky gabardine.

I blinked away the image of a sleek, handsome raven. "The fact is, I was napping."

"I'm really sorry, Claire. I just wanted to thank you for all your help today. Look, I'll leave and let you get some rest."

"Don't be nuts." Tugging his arm, I brought him inside and closed the door. Then I gave him a hug, feeling suddenly small next to him. Into his chest, I asked, "How's . . . everything?" The question sounded absurd, but under the circumstances, I could invent no better way to phrase it.

He understood both my predicament and my concern. Holding my shoulders at arm's length, he said softly, "My world's been turned upside down." His sad, uncertain words offered a fitting summary of his day from hell, but their tone also suggested that the brunt of the crisis had passed. Though his emotional recovery would surely be lengthy—and might never be complete—he did not, at the moment, teeter at the brink of tears. Perhaps he'd cried enough for one day.

"I'm glad you stopped by," I told him, patting his hand. "Let's sit down. Can I get you some—" I was about to offer iced tea, but stopped short, recalling that our grim discovery that morning had been preceded by the same offer. I rephrased, "Would you like . . . water or anything? Maybe a drink?"

His brows arched at my allusion to alcohol, but then he shook his head. "Nah, thanks, a bit early. Besides, I took a couple of Jodie's Zolofts this afternoon. They calmed me down, thank God, but booze might be risky."

"Fine. Let's just visit." Zoloft, if I recalled correctly, was a long-term antidepressant, not a short-term tranquilizer, so it seemed unlikely that it would have the calming effect Paul described, except as a placebo— a highly plausible explanation. With a smile, I led him the few steps into the living room and gestured toward a pair of chairs near the fireplace.

"This place is great," he said, looking around.

"I haven't quite made it mine yet, but I was lucky to find it." Sitting down, I noted that the two upholstered chairs were all wrong for southern California. Their quaint styling, vaguely colonial, would have looked much more at home in my mother's place, back East. I really did need a few decorating tips.

Paul sat also. "Did Glenn Yeats help you out? I mean, finding the place?"

The question took me by surprise. "As a matter of fact, he did. Glenn asked Grant Knoll, the sales director at Nirvana, to help get me situated. Now I'm Grant's neighbor."

Paul laughed softly, shaking his head. "Same with Jodie and me. As soon as I signed on at DAC, Glenn couldn't have been nicer about putting us in touch with the right people. We found the house fast—at a good price too. In fact, I've wondered if Glenn didn't secretly underwrite part of the sale. He's been great."

I nodded. "He's extremely generous." Spotting my yellowed canvas tennis shoes lumped where I'd left them, near the end of the sofa, I reached from my chair and retrieved them.

Paul's smile fell. "Now this."

Our chitchat had screeched to a neck-snapping halt as the gravity of that morning's events swept over Paul. I asked, "After Grant and I left your house this morning, how did everything go with Grant's brother?"

"Who?"

"The detective—Larry Knoll." I leaned forward, slipped on my Keds, and retied their frayed, sloppy laces.

"Ohhh," he said, swiping a few stray hairs from his forehead, "now I get it. I must have been really out of it this morning—I couldn't fathom who was who. I thought I recognized Grant from Wednesday's party, and he seemed nice and all, but I couldn't imagine what he was doing there with the police. So Grant and Larry are *brothers*. They do sorta look alike."

I explained, "I phoned Grant right there in the bedroom. I recalled that he had a brother connected with the police, and I figured, if there were any strings to be pulled, pull 'em. You weren't . . . quite yourself while I made those calls." As I spoke, I realized that I felt dry-mouthed. The surprise call from my mother, the dream-teased nap, the rehash of that morning's events—there were any number of possible reasons for my sudden thirst.

"Whatever you did," said Paul, "I'm grateful for it. Deputy Knoll struck me as a concerned and dedicated professional. He was the last to leave, and though he frankly admitted he was stumped, he also assured me that the investigation had barely begun. He said he'd devote his full attention to it."

"Then I'm sure he will." My tongue felt sticky against my palate.

"He hasn't wasted any time. He's already visited Oralia. He phoned me when he left her, just before I drove over here."

"He *is* moving fast," I noted, impressed.

"As awful as this has been, at least it's good to know that something's being done, that someone cares."

"We all care," I reminded him softly.

"I know. Thanks, Claire."

I swallowed, with difficulty, then stood. "Excuse me, Paul. I don't mean to be rude, but I'm terribly thirsty. Can't I get you something?"

He stood and followed me toward the kitchen. "Sure, just water. When you first come to the desert, you have to keep reminding yourself to drink plenty of water. This dry heat dehydrates you quickly."

I paused at the refrigerator and turned to him. "So *that's* it. I thought it was a *mental* condition." We both laughed as I took out the bottle of chilled water and poured a glass for each of us. After swallowing a sip or two, feeling instantly revived, I asked, "Did Larry draw any conclusions from his visit with your housekeeper?"

Paul set his half-emptied glass on the counter. "Larry stressed that it was far too early for conclusions, but he did say that Oralia seemed to have a firm alibi." He paused, looking at the ceiling. "God, I can't believe it. Yesterday, alibis were the furthest thing from my mind, as remote and unreal as a cheap TV cop series. Now the word 'alibi' has entered my working vocabulary." His eyes began to look watery.

Trying to keep the conversation objective and unemotional, I asked, "Where *was* Oralia this morning?" I drank more water. Though no longer thirsty, I thought it wise to stoke up, like a camel at an oasis.

"Larry didn't go into detail—Oralia had been working. He said she seemed credible. The news about Jodie stunned her, I guess, and she really broke down. She even offered to come to the house tomorrow morning, on a Sunday, to clean up after the investigation. Larry thought that would be a good idea and accepted her offer on my behalf."

Nodding, I told Paul, "That seems to confirm what you told us about her this morning."

He nodded thoughtfully, fingered his glass, then drank. "Actually, now I'm not so sure."

My brows arched. "Oh? Why the new doubts?"

"Do you remember that Larry asked me if anything other than Jodie's wedding ring was missing?"

"Yes, and I recall your answer: nothing obvious was missing."

"Exactly. Well, sometime after Larry left, after I'd calmed down a bit, I got curious about the possibility of other stuff having been taken."

"I've been curious about that myself. It bears heavily on the probable motive for the crime."

"Right. And it just *seemed* that this must have been a burglary, foiled by Jodie's presence. I mean, why *else* would anyone kill her? But the theory doesn't hold up if the thief took only the wedding ring, so I began a thorough search."

"And?" Feeling bloated by the water I'd been guzzling, I dumped the remainder of the glass in the sink.

"And I discovered a number of things—missing. Several smaller, valuable, inconspicuous items that had been put away were suddenly nowhere to be found. At least I couldn't find them. For instance, our good silver. We rarely use it, and it's stored in a cabinet in the dining room. Most of it's still there, except for several tiny sets of salt and pepper shakers. Also, I have a few wristwatches, which I keep on a shelf in the back closet by the kitchen door. That's where I keep my keys and wallet as well, so I always know where they are when I'm leaving the house. My parents gave me a Rolex when I got my degree from Yale, and to tell the truth, I've never much liked it—a bit too Miami for my tastes. I hardly ever wear it, but I've always kept it with the other watches. On a hunch, I checked for it this afternoon, and sure enough, *nada.*"

"Hm. Was it engraved?"

"I wish. But sorry, 'fraid not."

"What else was missing?"

"I'm not so sure of the rest—little things that aren't where I expected to find them. But we've lived there barely three months, so I could be mistaken; they might turn up. I'm *certain* about those little salt and pepper shakers, though, and the watch is a no-brainer. I can hardly believe it, but these missing items seem to point to Oralia."

"She knew where everything was kept?"

"Well, *sure*. She helped put the stuff away. Then she went back and cleaned everything. She knows the lay of that house better than I do."

I ran the fingers of one hand through my hair, then paused to rub the back of my neck. "I presume you've reported this to Larry."

"Of course. Again, he drew no conclusions, but he assured me that he'd 'look into it.' Point is, Oralia's coming over tomorrow morning at ten to clean up that mess in the bedroom, and to be perfectly honest"—he hesitated, took a breath—"I'm not comfortable with the idea of being alone in the house with her."

I blurted, "You're *afraid* of her? How big is she?" But as soon as I said it, I realized that my flippant comment, intended to be witty, was insensitive. Paul's best theory, in fact his only theory at this point, was that his wife had been killed by Oralia, and for all I knew, he was right.

"Oralia is, uh, not very big at all, but I just meant that . . . well, I'm afraid I might say something to her that's, you know, *inappropriate.*" His words made perfect sense, but his stammering suggested that the surface logic of his explanation glossed over some deeper, more emotional reaction to my question. The cadence of his delivery carried the slightest hint of defensiveness, and I got the impression that he found my comment emasculating.

I gently assured him, "I didn't mean to be rude, Paul. I was trying to inject a note of humor into a grim situation. Forgive my poor judgment—we've all been stressed."

He smiled, looking calmer. "Stressed—that's putting it mildly." He drank the last of his water, then set the glass in the sink.

"If there's any way I can help, don't hesitate to ask."

He paused. "That's why I dropped by—besides needing to thank you for being so supportive this morning. If you're not busy tomorrow, Claire, would you mind coming over to the house around ten? Like I said, Oralia will be there, and I'd just, uh, rather not be with her . . . alone."

"I'd be *happy* to come over," I answered too brightly. I agreed to his request not only out of friendship but mainly out of curiosity. I wanted to get a look at this Oralia character, perhaps even question her, and draw conclusions of my own.

"Thanks. That'll be great. Do you remember how to get there?"

How could I forget? "I'll figure it out."

Paul moved toward the front hall. "I'll see you tomorrow then—and sorry to intrude on your nap time."

Nap time? His well-meaning apology made me feel like a doddering invalid. At fifty-four, I felt ready to begin my best years. At thirty-two, he doubtless thought of me in the same context as his shawled mother. With a show of vigor, I squared my shoulders, opened the front door, and offered, "Let me walk you to the car."

As we emerged from the house together and crossed the courtyard, my vigor was quickly sapped by the sun. The day's heat had just begun to wane, but the thermometer had again nudged the hundred mark, and I was not yet acclimatized to my new desert habitat—it was *hot*.

Paul, dressed neck to toe in black, seemed unfazed by the temperature as he chatted about the investigation. "And talk about lousy timing, with the college opening in a week."

I reminded him, "There's no good timing for what happened today."

"That's for sure."

Stepping through the front gate of Villa Paseo and walking toward the curb where Paul had parked, I realized that he would have a rough evening, and a rougher night, ahead of him. With no family and still few friends in California, who would be there for him as this tragic day drew to a close? And how could he possibly face that empty house tonight, let alone sleep there?

"Paul," I said, placing my fingertips on his forearm. We stood on the parkway in the shade of a palm. "If you'd care to come back later, I'll fix dinner. Nothing fancy—I'm a dreadful cook—but I'm sure you could use some company tonight."

"Aww"—he hugged me (God, it was hot)—"that's so sweet of you, Claire. But I already have plans."

"Oh?" I wasn't jealous, merely curious.

"Yeah. Glenn Yeats phoned this afternoon, wanting to know how everything went in Dallas, but that topic was dropped, of course, as soon as I told him the news about Jodie. He was so *supportive,* Claire, so genuine. He insisted on canceling some other engagement and asked me up to his home this evening. I'm going there now. I'll be spending the night and can stay as long as I need to."

I smiled, relieved to know that Paul would be well cared for. "Chances are, your dinner will be far better than anything I could concoct."

"I'm sure that's not true."

"Don't kid yourself."

He moved to the driver's door of his car. "I need to get going, Claire. But thanks for everything. And I'll meet you tomorrow morning at the house."

"Tomorrow at ten," I confirmed as he got into the car and started the engine.

Stepping back toward the gate, I turned, waved, and watched the green Honda tootle off toward Nirvana.

6

Mornings, like evenings, are glorious in the desert. The air is cool, and the lighting of mountains and sky is dramatic, sliding through a palette of unexpected colors—golds, greens, pinks, and purples—before your very eyes.

Immediately after my move from the East Coast, due to the three-hour time difference, I awoke each day much earlier than was my habit. To my surprise, this jet lag benignly lingered. Now ensconced two weeks in my new home, I still rose with the sun, around 6:30 in early September, with the consequence that I tucked myself in each night well before eleven. We denizens of the theater world are notorious night owls, so this shift of my sleeping pattern was all the more remarkable. I found, though, that I missed none of the whirl of my former nightlife, which was more than compensated for by the intoxicating rewards of sunrise.

That Sunday, like most mornings, dawned pristine and cloudless. French doors from my bedroom, on the upper level of the building, open onto a private terrace perched atop a neighbor's garage. The view, predominantly eastward, includes palms, pines, flowering vines, a cactus or two, a slice of the common swimming pool, and of course, mountains. Opening both doors wide to admit the cool air and warm light, I padded downstairs in a comfortable old robe to switch on the coffeemaker and retrieve the *Desert Sun* from inside my front gate.

While the coffee brewed, I unfurled the paper on the kitchen counter, and as expected, it carried a page-one treatment of Jodie's murder. VALLEY NURSE SLAIN, announced the headline, followed by an italic subhead, "Palm Desert Resident Victim of Apparent Home Invasion." The story contained a few tight-lipped quotes from Detective Larry Knoll, but no information beyond what I already knew. There were also quotes of dismay from some bigwig doctor at Coachella Medical Center, where Jodie worked, and from D. Glenn Yeats, Paul's employer at Desert Arts College. There was a one-column mug shot of Jodie, supplied by the hospital. I was relieved to note that there were no additional photos of the crime scene, the slain victim, or the bereaved widower—nothing sensational, just the facts.

Flipping through the rest of the paper, I reduced its Sunday bulk by disposing of the sports section, the classifieds, and an assortment of circulars, then poured myself a huge ceramic mug of coffee. Thus equipped, I headed upstairs and settled at a table on the terrace, greeting the morning and easing into my day.

The birds were up and at it, but otherwise, nothing stirred. There was barely a sound from the highway a few blocks away. No dogs were walked, no radios played, no church bells rang—yet. I slurped my coffee and rustled the pages of newsprint, still getting acquainted with the names and places and issues that mattered in the community that was now my home. After several trips downstairs to pour more coffee and dispose of successive sections of the paper (the real estate section was an eye-opener, even for a jaded New Yorker), I had lolled away more than two hours. The terrace was getting hot, my neighbors were puttering about, and I felt in need of my morning ablutions.

Tending to my daily ritual, I began to speculate about my ten o'clock meeting with Paul and his suspect housekeeper, the nefarious Oralia Alvarez. Till then, I had not given the woman much thought—I knew only that she had full access to the Hurons' home and that she seemed to have an alibi for the time of the murder. Still, it was impossible not to spin imaginative theories that would allow the woman to be in two places at once. By the time I was showered, dressed, and backing my Beetle out of the garage, I had concocted the bone-chilling portrait of a flagitious chambermaid from Gehenna.

There was virtually no traffic as I drove through Palm Desert, and I easily retraced the route to the quiet side street that led to the Hurons' house. Checking the car clock, I saw that I was five minutes early and hoped that Paul had returned by then from his overnight stay at Glenn

Yeats's estate. If Paul was reluctant to be stuck alone with the treacherous Oralia, then so was I.

Turning into the cul-de-sac, I noted with relief that the Hurons' garage door was open, with Paul's Honda parked in one of the two spaces, just as it had been twenty-four hours earlier when I drove him home from the airport. As I pulled to the curb and cut my engine, I wondered about Jodie's car. Was it still at the hospital? Of course, Paul had been dealing with far graver matters since yesterday's shattering discovery. Besides, he couldn't jockey the second car on his own; two drivers would be needed. I'd offer to help him with this when it seemed appropriate to diddle with such mundane tasks—surely not today.

Walking up the driveway, I debated whether I should use the front door, but decided on the back door to the kitchen. Paul and I had entered the house that way the day before, and now the garage door was left open, presumably in anticipation of my arrival. I entered the cool shade of the garage, stepped up to the kitchen door, and seeing no bell button, knocked.

Paul must have been standing in the kitchen, as his voice instantly answered, "Coming." Footsteps approached the door, which opened within seconds.

"Morning, Paul." My tone carried an odd mix of cheer and sympathy, as I could not yet analyze his mental state.

"Morning, Claire." His tone was similarly ambiguous, but his smile was welcoming. He stood there for a moment, as if wondering what I wanted. Then he stepped aside, opening the door wider. "Well, gee, come on in. Thanks for letting me intrude on your Sunday. I know how lame this must seem."

"Not at all." I gave his arm a squeeze as I entered the kitchen and placed my keys and wallet on the breakfast table.

"I just got back myself. Sorry for the mess."

The room looked much as it had when I'd left around noon the day before. I'd cleaned up what I could of the broken glass coffeepot, but the splashed coffee still stained the tile countertop and streaked the cabinet under the sink. Several water glasses and soda cans, offered to investigators at the scene, now littered the kitchen island. Otherwise, the place looked fine—after all, no one had eaten dinner or breakfast there.

I quickly went to work. "Let me just stow some of this in the dishwasher. Those coffee stains may take a bit of scouring, but I'm sure—"

"*Claire,*" Paul stopped me, "I don't expect you to clean up after me."

I reminded him, "The coffee mess was my own doing. I'll replace that carafe as soon as—"

"You'll do no such thing." He escorted me to a chair with a gentle but decisive grip. "I just wanted your *company* this morning, not your domestic services."

Wryly, I noted, "You've got Oralia for that."

With a nod and a soft laugh, he sat across from me at the table.

"I hate to ask—the question sounds so inadequate—but how's it going, Paul?"

"You mean, am I dealing with it?" He exhaled a sigh. "Yeah. Sure. I have to, right? It was a terrible night for me, but it could have been much worse. Glenn was helpful—he tried to get my mind off the emotional crisis by concentrating on solving the crime. That won't bring Jodie back, but at least it gives me some sense of purpose."

"Exactly." Our conversation was predictable—he tried to remain philosophical about the tragedy that had befallen Jodie and him, and I agreed with everything he said, trying to buck him up without sounding condescending.

As we spoke, I noticed that he'd changed shirts that morning—a basic black T had replaced the collared variety—but he wore the same dressy gabardine slacks as yesterday, only they now showed the wrinkles of a second wearing. A leather duffle sat on the floor near the doorway to the living room. It was a functional but handsome bag, perhaps intended for tennis, and it struck me that Paul had a thing for good luggage—I recalled his fussing at the airport. I assumed that the duffle had served as his overnight bag at Nirvana, and I found it telling that neither the duffle nor Paul had ventured farther into the house than the kitchen.

At a lull, I asked, "Will you be going back to Glenn's place again tonight?"

"Not sure yet. Glenn made it clear that I'm welcome to stay there as long as I like, but I need to start coping with—not avoiding—the situation here at the house."

I reached across the table and patted his hand. "Give yourself time. You can't rush your feelings or your instincts. If the memories here are just too much for you, stay at Glenn's for a while."

"We'll see." He nodded. "I will say this: The accommodations up there aren't too shabby."

Laughing at this understatement, neither of us heard footsteps approaching through the garage, so when the knocking sounded at the door, Paul caught his breath and I let out a gasp. The three knocks were slow, measured, and in the context of our surprise, thoroughly menacing.

"Yes?" said Paul, his voice suddenly weak. "It's open."

The door cracked open, and a woman's head leaned through, barely above the knob. "Mr. Huron?" she asked. Then, seeing Paul at the table, she opened the door wide and rushed inside. Setting down a big carryall brimming with sprays, rags, brushes, and cleansers, the little woman ran up to Paul, who stood as she flung her arms around him, offering a comforting, motherly hug. Her head did not reach his chin as she looked up, brushing aside a tear, to tell him, "I am so very sorry, Mr. Huron. Miss Jodie was such a wonderful woman. What terrible news. I have been offering my prayers for her." Paul leaned down to kiss her forehead, and she clung to his neck, kissing his cheek.

So much for my visualization of the predatory hellhound in maid's clothing.

"Oralia?" I asked, offering my hand. "I'm Claire Gray. It was so thoughtful of you to offer to come over today."

She shook my hand lightly. Paul told her, "Miss Gray is on the faculty of Desert Arts College with me. She's a famous theatrical director."

Oralia's head bobbed back to me as I explained, "I was here with Paul yesterday when he discovered what had happened."

"Ah." She nodded. "Thank God you were here for him, Miss Gray. And again, you are here for him now." She still held my hand, patting it before dropping her own hands, folded together at her waist. "Such a kind friend you must be."

"I'm just glad I was able to help." I failed to mention that I was there that morning because Paul had expressed fear of being alone with her.

Nor did I add that I had eagerly obliged him because I wanted to sound her out as a possible murder suspect, the likelihood of which now dwindled by the second.

Oralia turned to Paul. "Before I, uh . . . start in the bedroom, is there anything I can get for you here? Maybe I should make coffee?"

"I don't think so."

I fessed up, "Sorry, Oralia. During the confusion yesterday, I'm afraid I broke the pot." Her eyes slid toward the sink, widening momentarily upon seeing the mess I'd left. "I think I got all the glass cleaned up. At least I tried."

"Do not worry about it, Miss Gray. Everything will be taken care of." She turned to Paul. "No coffee, then." She shrugged. "I can make iced tea. It will not take long."

Paul answered, "I think there's plenty in the refrigerator already. Claire? Care for some?"

"Thank you, yes," I answered brightly, faking enthusiasm for the mediocre brew. At least it was cold.

"Oralia, have some yourself—you're the one working this morning."

She considered this offer for a moment, answering, "Thank you, Mr. Huron. I will." Then she quietly set about her brief kitchen duties before she would tackle the grim job of cleaning up the shambles of the crime scene in the bedroom.

Paul and I avoided discussing the investigation in front of Oralia (who was, after all, a suspect), making chitchat about the college while she loaded the dishwasher and set out three fresh glasses. When she removed the pitcher of tea from the refrigerator, I noticed her sniff it. She hesitated. Without comment, she added a bit of sugar, a hefty squeeze of lemon, and a long strip of orange peel, stirring the pitcher with quick swirls of a big spoon. Then she added ice to the glasses, poured the tea, and garnished it with more lemon.

"Thanks, Oralia," Paul said as he stood to retrieve two of the glasses.

As I was now the only one seated, I also rose, joining Paul and his housekeeper around the kitchen island. At some unspoken signal, we all paused to lift our glasses and drink. Taking my first sip, I realized that Oralia had transformed yesterday's stale tea into one of the most delicious and refreshing infusions I'd ever tasted. How did she *do* that?

She and Paul briefly discussed her future work schedule, with Paul deciding that nothing should change. Since Jodie was now gone, he'd need all the household help he could get. As they spoke, I studied Oralia and formed a picture of the woman that was considerably more objective than the imaginary demon I'd patched together earlier.

Oralia was a short woman, shorter than I, but she was sturdy for her size and no stranger to physical work. Her tight black hair showed streaks of gray, and though she wore a bit of makeup that morning (had she been to church?), the creases near her eyes confirmed that midlife was approaching. I guessed her age to be in the midthirties. She wore not a maid's costume but slacks, white Nikes, and a tailored gray-green blouse that might have been part of a typical housekeeping uniform. She spoke with care and precision; though English was clearly not her native tongue, she had studied hard and learned it well. I imagined that her children (she made some reference to her sons) spoke with no accent at all. She wore a wedding ring and matching engagement ring with its small diamond barely larger than a chip.

Sidling into the conversation, I said, "Did you mention that you have children, Oralia? How many?"

"Three." She smiled with quiet pride. "Two boys and a girl, aged ten to sixteen. As you can imagine, Miss Gray, I have my hands full."

I chuckled. "You certainly do."

"At least, they are getting to the age now where they can take care of each other. That was not the case when my husband died."

"Oh, Oralia . . . I'm so sorry."

"Thank you, Miss Gray." She nodded. "Hernan was killed in a construction accident just over five years ago. He was so healthy, far too young. He loved the outdoors. It was such a shock."

Paul choked on his thoughts. "Same with Jodie."

Oralia looked into his eyes. "You never truly get over such a loss, Mr. Huron. But with time, you will build your life again."

Which was worse: losing a spouse, as Oralia had, and being left with three small children, or losing a spouse, as Paul had, and being left with none? Oralia and Paul doubtless pitied each other all the more, taking some measure of comfort in their own circumstances—Oralia grateful to watch her children grow, Paul grateful to escape the burdens of single parenthood.

Oralia was explaining to me, ". . . the insurance helped, of course, but there was no question—I *had* to work."

I told her, "You've been a good provider," though in truth, I had no idea how well her children had been clothed or fed. I could only speculate that she'd slaved and scrimped to assure them a happy, comfortable upbringing.

Her tone turned wistful. "I have never complained about work—we all must expect to be useful. What I regret, though, is the years I have missed with my little ones." With a wistful smile, she added, "They are not so little anymore. *Los años vuelan.*"

I took another swallow of tea and realized I had drained the whole glass. "This was wonderful. May I have some more?"

With a bob of her head, she refilled my glass from the pitcher.

Paul asked for some more as well, then told Oralia, "It was so kind of you to come over today. I know you have better things to do." He probably assumed, in light of our discussion, that she'd rather be home with her kids.

"No, no, no." She shook her head. "How could I leave you to take care of the house today, knowing how you must feel? When the detective came to see me yesterday, I could not believe what he told me, not at first. It seemed like a bad joke or a dream. But when I knew, at last, that it was true about Miss Jodie, I also knew that I was needed here."

Since she had conveniently opened the door to a touchy topic, I stepped right in. "We met Detective Knoll here at the house yesterday morning. He seems very concerned, very dedicated—"

"Very thorough," added Oralia.

"Yes, he mentioned that he planned to speak to you. He acted quickly."

"It was fortunate that he arrived at my house when he did. It was early afternoon. I had just returned from a busy morning."

Paul said, "He mentioned that you'd been . . . working?"

She nodded. "I have no regular duties on Saturday, but one of my seasonal clients, Mrs. Warhanik and her husband, will be returning to the desert this week from their summer home in Montana. Their house here in Indian Wells had been closed since Easter, so I spent yesterday morning there, preparing for their arrival."

I asked, "What needed to be done?"

Eyes to the ceiling, she recited from a mental checklist, "Dusting and cleaning, of course. The toilets needed to be checked and scoured—sometimes they dry out. I had to remove the summer panels from the skylights. Also, many fragile items had been placed on the floor, in case there was a bad earthquake, so everything had to be put back. And I always do a little shopping for the kitchen so they will have milk and bread on their first morning. Most important, the air-conditioning had to be checked and reset. The Warhaniks hate coming home to a hot house. And it *was* hot when I arrived."

Nonchalantly, I asked, "And when was that?"

"I worked there from about eight-thirty till noon. The house had been closed for months, so even at that early hour, it was hot inside."

I recalled the previous morning, when the medical examiner told Larry Knoll that Jodie had been dead for no more than an hour or two. By my calculation, that meant sometime after 8:30, which would put Oralia in the clear.

Paul asked her, "You were working at the Warhaniks' alone, right?"

With a grin, she reminded him, "I do not have help, Mr. Huron. I *am* the help." She rinsed her glass, put it in the dishwasher, then stepped near the table, where she'd set her cleaning supplies on the floor. Lifting the carryall, she said, "I must get busy now. Do you want me to put your things away, Mr. Huron?" She gestured toward his duffle.

"Uh." He rubbed the back of his neck. "I'm not sure where I'll be staying tonight, so just leave it there. Thanks, Oralia."

And she left the kitchen, heading through the living room toward the bedroom where Jodie Metz-Huron had died an untimely and mysterious death.

Paul turned to me. "If Oralia was working alone yesterday morning, what kind of alibi is that?"

Though I'd asked myself the very same question, I told Paul, "That's for Larry to decide. He seemed satisfied, didn't he?"

"As far as I could tell. He didn't say much."

"He's surely dealing with more information than we have. Let him do his job. He'll get things sorted out." In truth, though, I'd become every bit as obsessed with the puzzle as had the detective and the victim's husband.

Paul breathed an exasperated sigh, dumping the rest of his tea in the sink. The ice clanked as it hit the drain. "Clearly, Jodie died because of her unexpected presence during a burglary—her own ring was stolen, as well as my Rolex, those silver salt and peppers, and God knows *what* else. That points to Oralia as the obvious suspect. She has a key, knows our schedules, and knows the lay of the house better than I do. If she didn't do it, who could have?" Again he sighed, concluding, "But my gut tells me that Oralia had nothing to do with this."

My own gut told me something altogether different. While I agreed that Oralia probably had nothing to do with Jodie's death, I felt all the more strongly that Jodie's death had nothing to do with burglary.

"Paul—" I began, but stopped, as I didn't judge him prepared to hear what was running through my mind. He had neatly decided that his wife had died as the tragic consequence of interrupting a home invasion. In other words, Paul found a measure of comfort in viewing her death as simply a stroke of bad luck, horrendously bad luck, the accidental adjunct to thievery, a crime motivated by someone's base greed. If Oralia had fit my imaginary profile of a treacherous, cunning domestic, I might have bought into Paul's thinking. The burglary angle appealed to him because he *wanted* to believe it, but my instincts now told me otherwise. More and more, I was convinced that Jodie's death was not a crime of greed but a crime of passion. Which logically led me to wonder if someone had shared Jodie's bed with her on Friday night while Paul was in Dallas.

"Yes?" Paul had been waiting for me to finish my sentence.

Slowly whirling a hand in thought, I asked with a breezy air, as if fishing for nothing in particular, "Did Jodie have many friends? I mean, here, since moving?"

"I went over most of that with Detective Knoll yesterday afternoon after you and Grant left. Sure, Jodie had friends. She was an outgoing, pretty, perky sort of gal." Having sketched these characteristics of his wife, Paul paused with the memory of her. His face looked suddenly pained; he rubbed his eyes. I thought he might be due for another crying jag, but no, he took a deep breath and began telling me about Jodie's friends. He named five or six, which, from his narrative, struck me as mere acquaintances, most of them fellow nurses from the hospital, all of them women.

"Any men?" As I said this, the heaving whine of Oralia's vacuum cleaner shot from the far end of the house as she tore into the bedroom carpet.

Paul winced slightly. I wasn't sure if he recognized my query as a loaded question or if he was simply annoyed by the noise. He shook his head. "Male friends? Not really. Well, there's Dr. Blair, of course."

The name was familiar. "Who?"

"Dr. Percy Blair, head of the cardiac unit at Coachella Medical Center. He's one of the most eminent surgeons in his field, and in fact, it was the opportunity to work with him that convinced Jodie to make the move out here."

It clicked. "Dr. Blair was quoted in this morning's paper, wasn't he? He paid eloquent tribute to Jodie, and his words reflected real loss. Did you see the story?"

Paul nodded. "He's a wonderful man, not only a healer but a visionary. He readily took Jodie under his wing."

"Oh?" It was now impossible to hide my suspicions. "In what sense?" Mercifully, the distant roar of the vacuum ceased.

Paul gave me an admonishing grin. Quietly, he explained, "Percy took Jodie under his wing in the *professional* sense, okay? He assumed the role of a mentor to her, allowing her to learn cutting-edge techniques—at the feet of the master, as it were. Their friendship was related to their work, nothing more."

I had to ask: "You're certain?"

"I'm certain, Claire. I've met Percy Blair; he's not 'that' kind of man. As for Jodie, well, she never once gave me reason to suspect . . . anything. Besides, if something like that were going on, I'd know, wouldn't I? I'd just *know.*"

Figuring I'd pushed this far enough (at least for now), I agreed, "Of course—you'd be the first to suspect if something were wrong. Sorry to even hint at the possibility."

"Exactly, Claire. It was a perfect marriage." He smiled. "More tea?"

I'd somehow emptied my glass again—a subliminal fear of dehydration, I guess. "No, thanks." I raised both hands. "Enough."

Walking around the island and returning the pitcher to the refrigerator, he said offhandedly, "I suppose I ought to be making funeral arrangements. I've never been faced with this."

Though the topic was morbid, it was also practical, objective, and unemotional. I took it as a good sign that Paul was now dealing with the busyness of death, the ritual of closure. As if discussing nothing more significant than a mislaid pack of gum, I asked, "Where is the . . . uh, body?"

"At the county morgue, way out in Riverside."

I nodded, recalling, "Detective Knoll said there'd be a complete medical-legal autopsy. He didn't seem to think it would take very long to get the coroner's report. Then they'll release the body, I imagine. So you've got a bit of time to plan things. Did Jodie belong to a church?"

Paul shook his head. "I think she was raised Lutheran, but she kissed it off long before we met."

I mused, "That simplifies things—perhaps a quiet, tasteful memorial service, then burial."

"Cremation." He turned to me from the refrigerator. "That much I'm sure of—Jodie would want to be cremated. Whenever we went to a funeral, she said it was 'barbaric' to have the body lying there in front of everyone."

"Well then," I further mused, "that makes things even simpler."

Oralia trudged into the kitchen lugging a big, black garbage bag. Her brow and upper lip were beaded with sweat. "The police," she said with an air of exasperation, pausing on her way to the garage, "they were not very tidy."

"Sorry," said Paul. "Much of that mess was my own doing. I must have gone a little nuts when I first found Jodie."

"It is not a problem," Oralia assured him with a nod of understanding. "Oh"—she reached into a pocket of her slacks—"I found under the bed one of your cuff links, but I do not know where you keep them." She held it up to the light from the patio doors. A goodly chunk of gold, it was adorned with a sizable diamond, easily a full carat. Perhaps it was just a showy rhinestone or zircon, but it sparkled with the best of them. "It is very beautiful, Mr. Huron. I hope you were not worried that it was lost." And she placed it in his palm.

Looking down at it, he answered vacantly, "Thank you, Oralia."

Without further comment, Oralia hauled the trash bag to the garage.

Watching this exchange, I became all the more convinced that Oralia had no complicity in Jodie's death. Our earlier conversation had proven her a hard worker, uncomplaining, dedicated to her family. Now, by returning Paul's cuff link, she had proven her basic honesty. And I admired her no-nonsense efficiency. An idea popped into my head; my eyes widened as if to make room for it.

When Oralia returned from the garage and headed back toward the bedroom to resume her cleansing of the crime scene, I stepped in her direction. "Just a moment, Oralia."

She turned. "Yes, Miss Gray?"

"I've just recently moved to the desert, and I'm still getting settled in my new home—it's a smallish condominium, really—and I've begun to feel that I could use some help. I was wondering if you might be interested in doing some cleaning for me—on a regular basis, of course." I smiled expectantly, feeling as if I were begging.

Neither her features nor her tone tipped me to her thinking as she answered flatly, "I would like to see the place first, if you do not mind."

"Certainly," I gushed. As she had a full schedule on Monday, we agreed to meet at Villa Paseo on Tuesday morning at eight.

When Oralia had disappeared through the living room, Paul asked, "You're not trying to steal my housekeeper, are you?" The tone was accusing, but his smile softened the question with jest. "That's the modern equivalent of horse theft, you know. People have been run out of town for less."

Under my breath, I confided, "If I have to steal her from someone, I'll do it—but not from you, I promise." I winked.

He returned the wink, sealing an inviolable pact.

I glanced at the clock, thinking I could spend the rest of the morning catching up on yesterday's suspended errands.

Paul noticed the path of my eyes and easily decoded my readiness to leave. "Claire," he said, pocketing the cuff link that was still in his hand,

"I can't thank you enough for coming over this morning. Truth is, I'm feeling pretty foolish now—about Oralia."

I grinned. "I think you're safe alone in the house with her."

"I'm sure you're right." He offered me a parting hug.

I gladly accepted, cooing hang-in-theres and call-anytimes. Then I took my keys and wallet from the table and moved toward the back door.

But the keys jangling in my hand reminded me of something. Still wondering about the whereabouts of Jodie's car, I turned and said, "I've been meaning to ask about your two Hondas."

"Not in the market for another car already, are you?"

"No, I'm enjoying the Beetle, thanks. I meant that I was curious about the logistics of the two cars. If you need any help, I'd be happy—"

"Ahh. That's kind of you, Claire, but I'll get it worked out. Jodie always seemed to manage taking care of them both. So will I. Maybe I'll get rid of one of them. I just haven't thought it through yet."

He pattered on about the cars, but I wasn't quite listening, having stuck on his comment that Jodie had previously taken responsibility for both cars. This brought to mind the recent repairs to Paul's car, and I recalled how Jodie had winked at me at the party when she told me about finding "the most *marvelous* mechanic." She'd also stressed, "He's *very* accommodating." In light of my evolving crime-of-passion theory, this was definitely worth exploring.

"I *knew* there was something else," I said through a lamebrained laugh as I stepped back to the center of the kitchen. "Window tinting."

His blank stare wondered what planet I was from.

I reminded him, "In the Beetle yesterday morning, driving back from the airport, you suggested that I get the car's windows tinted. It's a good idea; I'd like to follow through. Jodie mentioned being especially pleased with the work that was being done on *your* car. Do you happen to know the name of the shop?"

"Ohhh." He laughed softly, having forgotten his own recommendation. "Gosh, I don't know it offhand, but let's see, I'm sure there's some paperwork." He stepped to the end of the counter, where a flat basket bulged with coupons, utility bills, old greeting cards, and junk mail. "It ought to be near the top," he mumbled, flipping through the pile. "Here we are." He held up a multicolored bundle of estimates, work orders, invoices, and receipts, held together with an oversize paperclip. As I leaned close to have a look, he said, "The shop is Desert Detail. They're in north Palm Springs."

Reading the list of services imprinted on one of the forms, I said, "How 'bout that—they do window tinting."

"Out here, most of the shops do."

Clipped to the top of the paperwork was a business card. "May I see that?"

"Sure." Paul removed the card and handed it to me.

Centered under the Desert Detail logo was the name TANNER GRIFFIN. Underneath the name, in cursive letters, were the words *Customer Service*. I asked Paul, "May I keep this?"

He shrugged. "Be my guest. And happy hunting."

There was no point in visiting Desert Detail on a Sunday, but I decided to drive out there the next morning. Monday. Early.

7

Later on Sunday, I spotted Grant Knoll in the courtyard at Villa Paseo, using a plastic kitchen colander to skim leaves from the surface of the fountain. On a whim, I asked if I could take him to dinner that evening, at any restaurant of his choice. I wanted to repay my neighbor's courtesy in hosting Saturday's impromptu poolside luncheon. More to the point, Grant was my conduit to his brother, the detective, so when Grant accepted my invitation, I offhandedly suggested, "Maybe Larry could join us. I'd like to thank him for taking such an interest in the Huron case."

"That's his job," Grant reminded me. Eyeing me askance, he had found my purpose transparent.

"All right," I conceded, "I need to pick his brain a bit."

Grant crossed his arms. "Why, doll? Why such an interest in the case?"

Good question. For my own benefit as well as Grant's, I tried to explain, "Though I have no stake in the outcome of the mystery sur- rounding Jodie's death, I saw firsthand how Paul was devastated by his discovery of the tragedy. He's a new colleague of mine, and he deserves my friendship and support. For his sake, I hope to see justice done."

"How very noble." There was a tinge of sarcasm to Grant's tone, and I knew he hadn't bought my explanation.

Nor did I myself buy it. "Okay. My interest in Jodie's demise is not entirely high-minded. I'm a director, Grant, and a playwright to boot. It may sound cliché, but theater is my life. Let's just say I can't resist the whiff of a nicely tangled plot."

That he bought (so did I). Chortling as he flicked a wad of wet leaves from the colander, he told me, "Just trying to keep you honest. As for Larry, you're in luck. His wife took the kids, *and* the dog, on an extended weekend visit to her parents' place in San Diego. So my baby brother the cop is baching it tonight. I'm sure he'd love to join us." Grant cupped a hand over his mouth, adding in a stage whisper, "Little could the intrepid detective suspect that it is he, not the meat, that will be grilled this evening."

With the motive behind my hospitality thus bared, there was nothing else to discuss, save time and place. "Many of the desert's better restaurants are still closed for the summer," Grant told me. "The season doesn't get into full swing till October. But I've heard some great buzz about a new place in downtown Palm Springs called Fusión." He pronounced it with a Castilian lisp: foothy-*own*.

"Sounds . . . interesting. Think we can get in?"

Lifting a hand to examine the clip of his nails, he assured me, "We'll get in. How about seven-thirty? I'll ask Larry to meet us there."

So at seven-thirty, Grant roared up Indian Canyon Drive in the silver Beetle with me in the passenger seat—he had asked to drive, claiming the car brought back nostalgic memories of a brief, experimental fling he'd had during the summer after high school. "He was a football jock," recalled Grant, "named, believe it or not, Butch. Or was it Bruce? A total lunkhead, but *Lord* was he good in the sack. Wonder what happened to Brucie. Married, I suppose. Ten or twenty kids, I imagine. Haven't thought of him in years."

I wasn't at all certain if Bruce—or Butch—had ever existed, but I enjoyed Grant's wistful prattle. As he swung the car onto a crowded side street between Indian Canyon and Palm Canyon, I asked, "Have you ever felt cheated, not having kids?"

He blew a low, pensive whistle. "I used to. Sort of. But not anymore." Glancing over, he asked, "How about you?"

I paused, chiding myself for inviting the question, when I noticed the restaurant just a few doors ahead. "Oh," I chirped, "we're here."

Grant grunted—I'd gotten off the hook too easily. Gliding to the curb and coasting to a stop at the valet stand, he told me, "Eventually, dear lady, you *will* open up to me."

I smiled. "Perhaps. But not tonight. I have other things on my mind."

"Like murder." He shook his head, laughing.

A pair of parking attendants flanked the Beetle and opened the doors. Both were handsome, tan, and collegiate, wearing tennis shorts. From my vantage point in the car, I got a good look at some great legs. Grant noticed too, turning to me with a devilish glance and a discreet growl before we got out of the car.

The sun had set, but the street felt hot, even in twilight. Grant bantered for a moment with one of the guys, protracting an exchange of tickets and tips, looking radiant as he basked in the younger man's attention. Grant always dressed well, but tonight he'd outdone himself in a loose-fitting pewter-colored silk suit that would make any woman, and most men, take notice. As for me, though on a mission, I'd already weathered a trying weekend and felt in a festive mood, so I'd donned a red dress for the evening. My hair was perfect, and I'd even indulged in a dab of Chanel. As Grant turned from the curb and escorted me to the door, I decided I was up to snuff—he could do a *lot* worse.

Entering the dark, cool foyer of the restaurant, we paused to take in our surroundings, which were starkly minimal—black carpeting, black leather upholstery, and sand-etched glass, accented with chrome trim, narrow-beamed spotlights, and eye-searing arrangements of red tropical flowers. The hostess—young, pretty, but gaunt, in a shiny black bodysuit that made her look like a scuba diver—approached us with a smile and a hushed "Welcome to Fusión." She forwent the Castilian: foo-see-*own*.

Grant instantly adapted to the drop-dead chic, coaxing from the woman not only a blush but a promise of the room's best table.

She added, "Your brother has already arrived, Mr. Knoll. You'll find him in the bar." With a barely perceptible turn of her head, she pointed us to the doorway.

The bar was a tiny room, more of a hallway, that led to the rest rooms. Four or five stools faced the mirror-backed bar, where a muscular bald man wearing a black leather vest and nipple rings shook the bejesus out of someone's martini. Larry Knoll, looking miles out of his element, was perched on one of the stools, sipping something dark (on the rocks with a cherry) while perusing a menu. Looking up as we entered, he stood and greeted us with a feeble smile that begged for rescue.

Grant clapped him on the back, squeezed a shoulder. "So. You found it, Larry."

Warily, he answered, "Uh-huh." Then, turning to me: "Evening, Claire. Thanks for the invitation—really thoughtful of you."

"My pleasure," I assured him, leaning in for a little hug. I added, in a whisper, "Grant picked it," as if to say, Don't blame me.

He whispered back, "You won't *believe* the menu."

That was ominous. Anyone would assume the place was expensive, but I got the impression he wasn't referring to prices.

He stepped back, taking a studied look at Grant and me. "Hey, you guys look *great* tonight." We thanked him, returning the compliment, which he self-effacingly dismissed. While he was naturally good-looking, and perfectly presentable in a dark suit and nice knit shirt, he simply hadn't attained his brother's fashion proficiency. On a scale of Grant-to-Larry, I'd rank my own sense of style smack in the middle.

Within a few minutes we were seated in the dining room and ordered our drinks, still waiting for menus. The hostess had made good on her promise; we occupied a spacious table that surveyed all of the small but comfortable room. Though it was filled to capacity, it was not, like most trendy spots, noisy. In fact, the whole ambience seemed calm and genteel, which struck me as refreshingly civil.

Our drinks arrived: a second bourbon for Larry, my usual kir (I'd consider moving up to hard stuff later, unless we had wine), and a martini for Grant, perfectly served in an oversize birdbath, adrift with chipped ice and the cool scent of lemon.

Our waitress, another twiggy figure gloved in black spandex, who identified herself as Karissa, waited while we skoaled and sipped; then she presented the menus. "Let me tell you about tonight's specials," her spiel began. "As an appetizer, we're offering a delicate cucumber-infused granité atop a lone Wellfleet oyster. Our fresh fish this evening includes wild black bass served with a confit of heirloom tomatoes, chorizo, and a subtle basil emulsion. If you prefer meat, we have a rack of Australian lamb presented with sautéed artichokes and brioche bread pudding. And for dessert, I highly recommend our chocolate soufflé cake with prune and armagnac ice cream."

Larry caught my eye during this, and I struggled to maintain a straight face. Finally, when our server backed away and disappeared, Larry leaned and whispered, "Welcome to California."

Don't, I silently pleaded through a grin.

Oblivious to this interplay, Grant studied his menu, cooing his approval and calling it "imaginative."

Food dominated our conversation, naturally, until we had ordered. Grant followed all of our server's recommendations, choosing the lamb over the bass. Larry ordered the pickled-ginger Caesar, then stewed beef with whole roasted papaya.

My own choices were embarrassingly tame, at least by comparison— baby-tomato tart lined with goat cheese and herbs, followed by seared monkfish on a potato cake infused with lemon confit. "And a martini like Mr. Knoll's," I added.

With the decisions and details of our dinner thus dispatched, our conversation hit a momentary lull. So I swallowed the last of my kir, set the glass aside, and got down to business. "Larry," I began, "I saw Paul Huron this morning, and—"

"How's he getting along?" asked the detective.

"Better, thanks. He's still sorting through his emotions, naturally, but the shock of yesterday seems to have passed, and he's back in touch with reality—he mentioned funeral plans."

Larry nodded. "Poor guy. I reached him at home this afternoon to give him a progress report on the medical examiner's findings. The coroner's office will probably release Jodie's body on Tuesday, so I let Paul know that he could start making plans."

Fingering the rim of my empty glass, I mustered an air of indifference to ask, "And, uh, what were the results of the autopsy?"

Larry glanced at his brother; the two shared a grin; then Larry's eyes returned to me. "When Grant phoned to invite me here tonight, he mentioned that—just maybe—you had an ulterior motive behind hosting this soirée. It seems you've developed an inordinate interest in the Huron case. Why do I have an inkling that you intend to wheedle out of me the inside track on the police investigation?" Planting an elbow on the table, he leaned toward me and raised a single brow, a facial expression that was at once inquisitive, accusing, and comical.

Squirming, I admitted, "You got me, Larry. Maybe it was the emotional impact of being there when Paul discovered the body. Or maybe it's a desire to help a friend and colleague during a time of crisis. Or maybe it's nothing more than base, blatant snoopiness and the lure of an intriguing plot. Whatever its root, my puzzling over Jodie's death has indeed grown some, from simple curiosity to mild obsession. I'd like to help. And at the risk of sounding presumptuous, Larry, I think my . . . 'theatrical' perspective of this tragedy could be useful to you."

Larry had listened stone-faced, and I was unable to gauge how he might react to my words. He leaned back in his chair, then allowed a soft smile. "I'm reluctant to admit this, Claire, but I think you *could* be useful on this case. I have no idea whether your theatrical background can translate into crime solving, but I do know this: You were acquainted with both Jodie and her husband before she died, while I was not. You seem genuinely motivated to solve the mystery of Jodie's death, without emotional connections to cloud your objectivity. And most important, I was impressed by your recall and your attention to detail yesterday at the crime scene. You've *already* been helpful."

He leaned forward again, crossing his forearms on the table, concluding, "We're dealing with a murder case, and I have no active suspects. I'll tell you what I know, and I'll welcome anything you can offer. *But:* you must agree to keep me in the loop and not to venture off on theories of your own. We're trying to unmask a killer, and that's inherently dangerous."

"I agree." I nodded eagerly, leaning toward him. "I understand."

Grant flumped back in his chair, laughing, causing diners at nearby tables to glance over at us. "Good God," he said, "my neighbor gets a new hobby, and my brother gets a sidekick."

Both Larry and I turned to him with disapproving stares.

"Fine," he told us, raising his hands in defeat, "I'll back off. If milady wants to dabble in a bit a sleuthing, far be it from me to thwart her."

"Not that you could," I admonished him.

He leaned forward, tightening our circle around the table. "Mind if I listen in? Or is this strictly confidential?"

Larry told his brother, "This *is* confidential, but of course you can listen."

Just as we were about to get down to it, Karissa appeared with my martini. Grant and Larry signaled that they were ready for fresh drinks as well, and the waitress left the table.

I sipped from the surface of the gin while it was still icy cold, savoring the first swallow. "Now, then," I said to Larry, "what were the results of that autopsy?"

He nodded. "The results are not yet conclusive; the coroner's final report will still take a while. What's more, tissue and fluid samples are being sent out for toxicology tests, which can take weeks."

I asked, "Is poisoning suspected?"

"Not at all. Toxicology is a routine part of the forensic examination of any suspicious death. In this case, I'm reasonably certain it will merely confirm that Jodie was *not* a victim of poisoning—or drugs."

Grant said, "It sounds as if you already know quite a bit."

"Not enough to point to a suspected killer, but we've pinned down some of the basics. For starters, the time of death is now firmly established between eight-thirty and nine on Saturday morning."

I said, "That puts Oralia in the clear, right?" (There was more at stake here than solving a murder—I needed a good housekeeper.)

"Seemingly," replied Larry. "We're working on that."

"Whoa," said Grant. "What'd I miss?"

He'd been at the crime scene when the Hurons' housekeeper was first mentioned as a possible suspect in the bungled-burglary premise, but Grant knew none of the follow-up, so we filled him in regarding Larry's visit with her on Saturday afternoon and my own encounter with her when she came to the Hurons' to clean the ransacked bedroom.

"Paul had expressed fear of being alone in the house with her," I explained, "but when I met her this morning, she struck me as neither physically nor emotionally capable of having killed Jodie. What's more, she has an alibi—she was opening a house for some out-of-towners on Saturday morning. She told me she worked there 'from about eight-thirty till noon.' "

Larry said, "That's exactly what she told me. The house is in a gated community in Indian Wells, so I checked with the security guard at the gatehouse. He'd been on duty that morning and easily recalled Oralia's coming and going. They keep a pencil log of every in and out, which clearly showed Oralia leaving at ten past twelve. Her arrival time was sketchy, though—the guard said he'd gotten busy with something and waited till later to log several arrivals from memory. He listed her entering at eight-fifty, but wasn't confident of his accuracy. I'd like to clear Oralia and move in another direction, but if she did in fact arrive that late, she could have conceivably killed Jodie in Palm Desert at eight-thirty or so and arrived in Indian Wells by eight-fifty—the drive doesn't take ten minutes."

Grant wondered, "Is there a security camera at the gatehouse?"

"No, unfortunately. A time-stamped videotape would have been ideal. Lacking that, I still have a few options to explore."

I felt that Larry was simply on the wrong track, but the moment didn't seem right for voicing my crime-of-passion theory. So I asked, "What else did the autopsy reveal?"

Larry paused for effect. "Cause of death."

Grant and I leaned closer, hungry for details.

"Cardiac arrest," Larry told us. Responding to my quizzical stare, he continued, "But this was no ordinary heart attack. It was a rare but well-known phenomenon, termed *commotio cordis* by the pathologist: a perfectly healthy person can sometimes drop dead after sustaining a minor but direct blow to the center of the chest. The impact, in freakish instances, can upset the electrical circuit of nerves controlling rhythmic contraction of the heart, which stops, causing almost instant death. It leaves no visible damage to the heart or the interior chest wall."

"How awful," said Grant, shaking his head.

I asked, "Haven't I heard of kids dying that way in softball games?"

"Exactly the same phenomenon," said Larry. "It wasn't apparent at the crime scene, due to Jodie's rumpled nightshirt, but she did develop a slight bruise on her chest, between and just below the breasts. It could have been inflicted by a fist or an elbow or even a knee. One thing's clear though—it wasn't accidental. We're treating this as a homicide."

"Ironic," I muttered, "that Jodie was a cardiac nurse, with a healthy heart—and died of heart failure."

Larry nodded. "That crossed my mind as well. It's terrible."

Karissa appeared at the table, bearing the Knoll brothers' fresh cocktails. "I apologize," she said, "for the delay on your appetizers. Chef wasn't pleased with the granité and had to start over."

Grant told us, "Sorry, gang." The pesky order was his.

"No problem whatever," I assured him. Then, turning to Karissa, I said, "We're not rushed—we're enjoying some good conversation." And the girl disappeared.

We raised our glasses in a perfunctory toast, then returned our attention to Jodie's demise. Grant said, "This seems so obvious, but did anyone check with the neighbors? If Jodie was the victim of a home invader—at eight-thirty on a Saturday morning—*someone* must have heard or seen something."

"We had deputies check as soon as we arrived at the scene," Larry answered. "No soap. The house is in a developing neighborhood, not densely settled yet, and the few people living there, including Paul and Jodie, had moved in recently. Since the neighbors aren't aware of each other's routines yet, they wouldn't recognize 'suspicious' activity if they saw it. Screeching tires or bloodcurdling screams might have caught someone's attention, but no one saw or heard anything the least unusual. It was just a quiet Saturday morning."

I swirled the gin in my glass, thinking aloud, "A quiet Saturday morning. What *was* Jodie doing at home? She was supposed to be working at the hospital. I heard her say so last Wednesday at Glenn Yeats's party. That's why I picked up Paul at the airport."

Larry hesitated. The plot was about to thicken. He told us, "A simple check with the medical center revealed that Jodie had never been scheduled to work that oddball shift on Friday night and Saturday morning. It doesn't seem likely that she'd be mistaken about her own schedule, so I can only conclude that she lied about it to you and Paul."

Grant raised his brows—and his glass. "*Well*, now, Claire. I salute your astuteness." With a wink, he sipped.

"Huh?" asked Larry.

The moment had arrived to float my theory. I told Larry, "While lunching with Grant yesterday, I explained that motives for murder—at least on the stage—can generally be reduced to either greed or passion. If Jodie died as the result of a bungled burglary, she was a victim of greed. That's what Paul wants to believe; perhaps he *needs* to believe that. From the beginning, though, I felt that the circumstances of Jodie's death suggested otherwise.

"Consider: She was killed in her own bedroom. She was wearing little more than a T-shirt. And conspicuously, her wedding ring was taken. Now we've learned that she had lied to her husband about working an overnight shift during his absence on a business trip. Does that suggest greed? Or passion? In short, I think that Jodie was involved with another man. And chances are, her clandestine love affair soured."

"Big-time," agreed Grant. He turned to his brother. "It's a reasonable theory."

"It's speculative," said the detective, "but I admit, it fits."

I rewarded myself with a hefty slurp of my martini.

Larry grinned. "You were a step ahead of me, Claire, if you were focusing on a crime of passion as early as yesterday. My own thinking didn't turn in that direction till this morning, when I got word of the hospital schedule."

"You're a pro," I reminded him. "You're not supposed to jump to conclusions. I, however, as a rank amateur, can indulge in the luxury of sloppy procedure."

Pressing onward, Larry said, "This afternoon, when I talked to the medical examiner, his reported findings did indeed bolster the case for a crime of passion." He lowered his voice, leaning forward a few inches. "Jodie had recently had sex, as evidenced by mild inflammation of her genital area. What's more, we've verified that Paul met with Dane Carmichael, the glass artist, in Dallas on Friday night. It was after the last flight from Dallas to Palm Springs, so we *know* that Jodie had sex with someone other than Paul overnight. If her partner used a condom, we found no evidence of it, and unfortunately, the examination revealed that Jodie had thoroughly showered and cleansed herself—inside and out—leaving no trace of semen or any stray, *dark* pubic hairs."

I nodded. "Jodie was blond."

"Right. But most of the population is not, so there's a good chance that her sex partner would have dark pubic hair. Dark hair samples were collected from the bed and from the shower drain, which could simply be Paul's, but DNA testing will be required to determine this, and the testing is complicated and lengthy."

I asked, "Is there any other way to prove that someone else had been in Jodie's bedroom?"

"Sure. Fingerprints. The place had been badly contaminated by Paul's madcap search for 'clues' when he found the body, but still, we were able to pull five clean sets of prints from the scene: Jodie's and Paul's, as would be expected; Oralia's, which is not surprising; yours, Claire, on the phone, just as you had predicted; and a fifth set, which we cannot identify."

Perking up, Grant asked, "The secret lover?"

"Seems like a good bet. The mystery prints were clean, fresh, and *everywhere*—light switches, doorknobs, the shower, one of the sinks, both nightstands, and all over the wall near the bed, where we even found a few footprints."

"How energetic of them," I noted.

"And limber," Grant added.

"Yeah," Larry continued, "we're trying to trace the prints, but that's a dead end unless our Romeo has a past. He's probably just some guy who had the hots for Jodie—and trust me, lots of guys would find her plenty desirable."

Straight-faced, Grant told his brother, "I'll have to take your word on that."

I told Larry, "This morning at Paul's house, I asked him—as tactfully as possible, of course—about the possibility of Jodie's involvement with other men."

Larry's brows arched with interest. "And?"

"And he flat-out denied it. He went so far as to call their relationship 'perfect,' which only heightened my skepticism. I sensed that I'd scratched the surface of an issue that was highly emotional—and possibly volatile."

Larry nodded, then took another swallow of his bourbon. "Thanks for the warning. I'd planned, first thing tomorrow, to confront Paul with these findings and question him about Jodie's fidelity. Since you've already broached the topic and found that he's unwilling to open up, I won't push it—not just yet. I need to work on tracing those prints, if possible, and establishing Oralia's alibi. Meanwhile, Paul's supposed to find a photo of the missing ring."

"He told me that he's since discovered a few other items missing."

"Yeah, a Rolex, some silverware, and such. Virtually impossible to find and identify, I'm afraid. Definitely, the ring's our best bet. He thinks the photo is with some boxed files that are stored in his new office at the college. He's planning to look for it tomorrow."

As if sensing that we'd wrapped up our sleuthing for the evening, Karissa appeared from the kitchen, accompanied by a strapping young hulk of a busboy who carried a tray bearing our appetizers. His "uniform" included tight black bicycling shorts, and as luck would have it, he stationed himself at Grant's side while Karissa removed the plates from the tray and positioned them in front of us. Though the food was indeed beautifully presented, Grant's eyes were otherwise occupied, examining the plump crotch that had so fortuitously landed near his shoulder. In truth, I myself was pleasantly mesmerized by this unexpected spectacle, and it wasn't until Larry said, "Wow, this is amazing," that I blinked, cleared my brain of a salacious thought or two, and focused on the first course of our dinner.

What a whirl—in the span of thirty seconds, my attention had shifted from murder to a well-endowed busboy to the tomato tart with goat cheese. My martini (not to mention the busboy) had stimulated great appetite, and I ate hungrily, marveling at the delicate fusion of flavors that had been concocted for both my pleasure and my nourishment. We were soon sharing tastes from each other's plates, eagerly speculating about the culinary magic that would accompany our main course. By the time we finished dessert, we all agreed that the meal had lived up to the buzz, forcing me to wonder aloud how the world had taken so long to discover armagnac ice cream.

At meal's end, the Knolls each tried to wrestle the check from Karissa, but I had taken preemptory action during a foray to the ladies' room, when I had cornered the waitress in a hall, giving her my credit card and inviolable woman-to-woman instructions.

Leaving the restaurant, we thanked the black-garbed hostess for a wonderful evening, promising to return. The three of us then passed through the door and emerged onto the busy street, where the parking valets took stubs from both Grant and Larry, trotting off into the night to fetch our cars.

Grant checked his watch. "Gosh, after ten already."

Larry said, "The time really flew—what a meal."

Grant told me, "I was meaning to phone Arlene Harris this evening. She's been leaving messages all weekend about that 'urgent' bit of real-estate business, but I haven't been able to track her down." Tapping his watch, he decided, "It can wait till morning."

Larry asked, "What could be 'urgent' about real estate?"

I told him, "That's what Grant and I were wondering."

"Speaking of urgent business," said Larry, pulling his wallet from a hip pocket, "let me give you my card, in case something comes up and you need to reach me." He pointed out several numbers—his office at the sheriff's department in Riverside, his home number in Palm Springs, and his pager.

I took the card, telling him, "I don't have a business card from Desert Arts College yet, and I don't even know my office phone number." So I gave him the main number of the college, as well as my home phone, which he noted on the back of one of his own cards. I promised, "If I hear anything, or even think of anything, you'll be the first to know."

He shook a finger but said through a grin, "Be sure of that, Claire." Then his tone turned serious as he reminded me, "This isn't a game; it's not just a puzzle. We're dealing with an unknown opponent, some-one who's capable of murder. Any slipup could prove deadly." His words hung in the warm night air as one of the valets braked his car at the curb. Larry smiled. "Thanks again for dinner, Claire. It was great, and it was good to get to know you better." He gave me a little hug, then also hugged his brother, saying good night before he got into his car and drove away.

Grant turned to me. "Well, you're knee-deep in it now. Hope you're happy."

"I am," I told him, surprised that my words had the ring of sincerity, not defensiveness.

Waiting for my car, we gabbed of nothing in particular, and I snapped open my purse to put away Larry's card. Sliding it into my wallet, I noticed another business card, which I had placed there just that morn-ing. Removing the Desert Detail card, I showed it to Grant, asking, "Do you know where this is?"

With mock umbrage, he reminded me, "I'm a real estate broker—I know where *everything* is. Not that my specialty is body shops, mind you. I tend to specialize in tonier abodes for the well-heeled and discerning few." Then he stopped his patter and looked at me quizzically. "What possible interest does milady have in"—he squinted at the card, which he held gingerly, as if it were dirty—"Desert Detail?"

"I've been told I should have my car windows tinted, and this place comes highly recommended." Coyly, I offered no further explanation, forcing me to wonder if I would be equally secretive with Larry's brother, the cop I'd just promised to keep informed of my every move.

"Ah," said Grant, buying my explanation without question, "this address is on the far northwest side of Palm Springs, on the fringes of town; the area is a mix of commercial and industrial properties. Would you be driving from home?"

"Probably."

"Then I wouldn't bother with Highway One-Eleven. It would get you there, but there's too much stop-and-go. No, from Palm Desert, I'd cross the valley first, probably on Monterey, then catch Interstate Ten, heading west toward Los Angeles. Watch the exits just past Palm Springs; you'll land right at their door. When are you planning to drive out there?"

"I have no idea. Whenever." Why, I wondered, was I being so evasive about this, especially to Grant, of all people? "Actually," I told him, "I thought I might visit Desert Detail first thing in the morning."

The parking valet—the cuter, beefier one, whom Grant had tipped so handsomely when we arrived—drove up to the curb in my Beetle and hopped out, opening both doors. I asked Grant, "Still in the mood to drive?"

"Of *course*," he said, strolling me to the street. "Time for another cruise down memory lane with Brucie—or was it Butch? Or whatever the hell his name was. He's now the father of thirty children, you know, and they all have his adorable eyes—one brown, the other blue, like an odd-eyed cat."

8

Monday morning I awoke even earlier than usual, rested but eager to meet the "marvelous mechanic" whom Jodie Metz-Huron had found so accommodating. I drank coffee, as the day before, on my bedroom terrace, but today I didn't tarry with the *Desert Sun*. Rather, I skimmed the front section in search of developments on the Huron case. Finding nothing, I realized how trusting and informative Larry Knoll had been. I already knew many more intimate details of Jodie's demise than did the local press.

Before long, I had showered and dressed and was driving away from Villa Paseo, turning north onto Monterey Avenue, the route Grant Knoll had recommended. The Beetle's overhead clock flashed seven o'clock, and I calculated that I should reach the far side of Palm Springs promptly by 7:30, when Desert Detail would open for business.

The body shop's card protruded from the edge of the car's sun visor; I had stuck it there so I could refer to the address. TANNER GRIFFIN— the name caught my eye. *Customer Service*—what did that mean? Envisioning a leering grease monkey in whom Jodie had found some odd, lowbrow appeal, I instinctively grimaced. After all, she was not only lovely but intelligent and worldly as well. She had a sensitive, artistic husband and a demanding, rewarding career. Had she indulged some inexplicable drive to escape so many positive realities by getting down and dirty with the likes of Tanner Griffin? Or was I on the wrong track entirely? What interest would a woman like Jodie have in a guy from the garage?

Interstate Ten appeared beyond a rise in the roadway, and a minute or two later, I was zipping along the westbound entrance ramp, pointed toward Los Angeles and the Pacific beyond.

Revving the car to full speed, I was soon streaking through a vast, arid panorama of endless sand under a faultless autumn sky. The wide highway, the steady rush of traffic, and the sandy sameness of the desert landscape blurred into a monotony of sound and vision that was strangely comforting. The noise of the engine was itself a kind of silence—the chattering man-made silence of steel gears engaging spinning axles—accompanied by the droning silence of taut rubber gliding over flat pavement. Though still alert to the chore of driving, I slipped into the silence, fell into its void. My eyes absorbed everything around me, yet saw nothing. I dreamed, but never slept. I cannot say how long I drifted in this peaceful state; it seemed as though hours had been compressed into an instant. And then . . . I thought of Gwyn.

I blinked.

She had sneaked into my mind and yanked me from my reverie. I searched the landscape for familiar features, but found none, save a cluster of white windmills in the distant hills, a vague reminder of church spires in the New England town where I grew up, the town where my mother still lives. Was it the setting that turned my thoughts to her? Or was I still, perhaps, in a subliminal tiff over her phone call of Saturday afternoon?

I'm not openly hostile toward Gwyn. I treat her kindly at best, respectfully at worst. I've learned not to address her criticisms, argue her beliefs, or play her games. My only defense against her loving attacks is a buffer of nonchalance, so I call her "dear" and "darling" as though we were great old chums. I perform the required visits. We gab like schoolgirls until she starts probing my past, questioning my future, harping about marriage—and I announce that the discussion is closed.

I continued to grip the wheel, gazing through the windshield, mulling my thoughts, not reacting to the things I saw, never flinching as other cars swept past me. I was lost again in the whir of the engine, in the soothing vibrations of the vehicle that propelled me forward. I was lulled into another waking dream.

It began as a nagging germ of an idea that throbbed with the overlaid rhythms of the car's mechanical heart. It began as a minor sore, a mere vexation, that would grow within me and burst. But the pain began so gently, the thought nudged my brain so slowly and was born so serenely,

I was taken unawares by the foretaste of my mother's death.

Mystics and dreamers may question death's grip, but I do not. I've long known death as an intellectual reality, but it never once scratched my emotions till I pondered the surety of my own mother's passing. I am fifty-four years old; my mother is past eighty. While healthy and alert, she is living beyond her time. Any day, I could face the task of burying her.

The facts of life and death become apparent to any farsighted person while slipping into middle age. The inescapable is more imminent with each passing year, month, hour. My thoughts on the road that morning were startling not because they were new but because of their clarity. Not that I pictured my mother's death scene in a clairvoyant sense, but I did see what it would mean to me.

I would be free.

It's an uneasy admission—something of a confession—that so grievous a loss can be sweetened by the lure of freedom. I have no reason to wish her dead. She doesn't live with me; she hasn't turned mean or senile; I haven't known the horrors of those who must nurse their failing parents. Yet the thought I could not shake was this:

There is a woman out there, somewhere among the billions, who claims me as hers. I may be fifty-something, but I am hers. No one else can cripple me with such physical ties, such emotional bonds.

I want loose.

I wanted loose that morning in the car. I saw with sudden insight that I would be free, I would be my *self,* only at the moment of my mother's death. Burying her would be my ultimate act of maturity, my last rite of passage into adulthood.

The distant white windmills were now much closer, and I was amazed to discover that there were hundreds of them, perhaps thousands. Arrayed like sentinels along the slopes of the San Gorgonio Pass, the receding rows of sleek white fingers poked the sky, their long delicate blades capturing the energy of winds that were constantly funneled between the San Bernardino and San Jacinto mountains. Most of the blades whirled in unison, facing the winds en masse, but some of the blades spun more slowly, attuned to different breezes, as if confused. Others, even more perplexed, had ceased twirling at all, tensing in the direction of past, forgotten winds.

9

Contemplating the windmills, I wasn't watching the road signs and nearly missed my exit. Fortunately, the sight of the massed windmills, known locally as the energy farms or wind farms, had slowed the speed of my driving. I was plugging along in the outer lane, gawking at this attempt to harness nature—which struck me as both noble and, well, something of a desecration—when I glimpsed the exit sign for Indian Avenue at the north end of Palm Springs. There was no one close behind me, so I applied the brakes, signaled a right turn, and managed to lean into the curve that ramped off the highway.

The ramp led up to the overpass of the crossroad, and I hesitated, needing to turn left or right. I glanced at the address on the business card—as if, miraculously, it would inform me, Turn left at the overpass. Surveying the surrounding landscape, I saw that turning right would lead me farther from town, into virtual wilderness, so I turned left, which angled back through the outskirts of the city.

After I'd crossed some railroad tracks, buildings appeared, and I knew I was headed in the right direction. Grant's description of the area as both industrial and commercial was apt. There were rows of generic-looking corrugated-metal buildings, many as anonymous as warehouses. No-frills signage identified some of these businesses as plumbing suppliers or electrical contractors. Then, at the next corner, I spotted it— Desert Detail.

I had been expecting some run-down garage with a gravel parking lot, where the rusty remains of stripped and abandoned cars could momentarily snag the passing tumbleweeds. To my chagrin, the establishment was slick, tidy, and inviting, at least to the extent that a body shop could be called "inviting." It was obvious that, decades earlier, the place had been a gas station. A stylish renovation now alluded to the property's automotive past while luring a new clientele with neat landscaping, tasteful graphics, and eye-catching accents of chrome and neon. Taken as a whole, the enterprise conveyed an image of precision, cleanliness, and fussy attention to detail. I could well understand why Jodie had been so impressed and effusive. Anyone, myself included, would have nary a qualm about handing over their keys to Desert Detail.

As I crossed the intersection and pulled into the driveway, I saw that the shop was just opening for the day. An immaculate black Jeep (the smaller, open, military-looking variety) was parked near the closed front door, where two rolled newspapers leaned at the jamb. On the door of the Jeep, in pristine gold letters, was the same Desert Detail logo that appeared on the business card. The Jeep's driver had entered the building through one of the garage doors, which gaped open, and I noticed lights blinking on indoors as the proprietor made his way through the shop toward the front office.

Getting out of the Beetle, I crossed the small parking lot toward the building. Through the glare of the windows, I saw a figure in the office raising window shades, switching on signs, but he made no move to unlock the front door. Since he had entered through the garage, it wasn't clear to me if the office door was meant to be used, so I poked my head into the garage and gave a yoo-hoo.

Hearing no response, I stepped a few paces inside, calling, "Anybody home?"

"Can I help you?"

I turned toward the voice—which sounded rich, resonant, and slightly amused—and saw a young man backlit by the morning sun outside the garage. He held the two rolled newspapers under one arm, a sizable ring of keys in his hand. "I was opening the shop," he explained, "and thought I heard someone. Then I saw the Beetle." He jerked his head over his shoulder toward my car. "Cute."

"That's an understatement," I mumbled as I stepped out of the shadows and got a good look at him.

"Beg pardon?" he asked, turning to me with a smile that made my knees weak.

"Nothing," I tried to answer, but choked on the word, covering my muddlement with a cough.

"They were great cars, with lots of character," he was saying, his voice clear and pleasant, almost musical, though wonderfully masculine, "but I like the new ones even better."

For all I knew, he could have been reciting the phone book or reading recipes. Hell, I wasn't listening. I was *looking* at him, studying him, still agog.

Now and then, someone comes along who personifies beauty or vulnerability or animal magnetism or a charming personality, but rarely, if ever, does someone have all those qualities rolled into one squeaky-clean, health-conscious, man-size package. More rarely still, if ever, does such a person answer your yoo-hoo, compliment your car, and pause to engage you in conversation. If *this* was Jodie's leering grease monkey, then her winking, swooning allusion to a "marvelous mechanic" had been fully justified, though her description didn't begin to paint a sufficient picture of the man.

He was in his midtwenties, not a kid, but his face, indeed his whole bearing, had not yet lost its boyish appeal, its illusion of fresh innocence. He was of medium height with a solid build—not intimidating or brutish, just pleasingly muscled. His body was displayed to great advantage that morning in loose-fitting, olive-drab cargo shorts and a tight, spotless white T-shirt. His tan work boots coordinated perfectly with his thick, sand-colored hair—was he vain enough, or clever enough, to have chosen his utilitarian footwear for that reason?

". . . but it looks brand-new," he was saying. "It doesn't seem to be in need of any repairs. So how can I help you?" Again that smile—full lips, perfect teeth, strong chin.

"Well," I began to explain, "I've just recently moved to the desert, and I understand that many drivers here get their car windows—"

"My God," he interrupted, "you're Claire Gray." The smile. "Aren't you?"

I was so flustered—and flattered—by this unexpected recognition, I had to think which way to respond. "Yes," I said, sounding idiotically uncertain, "I am."

"Wow, I can't believe it!" Pocketing his keys, he let the newspapers fall to the ground, then clapped imagined grime from his palms, extending one hand. "What an honor, Miss Gray. And what a surprise—to find *you* standing here."

With a weak laugh, I shook his meaty hand, telling him, "I was thinking much the same thing."

"I'd heard you were joining the faculty at the new college, and I wondered if I'd ever run into you."

Flipping my hands, I announced the obvious: "And here I am."

"And here you are," he repeated, grinning. His tone grew serious when he added, "I've admired your work for years. You're simply the best. The college—the whole community—is lucky to have you here."

While all this adulation was gratifying (I could think of far worse ways to start a Monday morning), it was also weird. Even back in Manhattan, where I'd lived for decades and established my career, my claim to fame, I was never once recognized by a stranger on the street. After all, my role in the theatrical world was behind the scenes, and though I'd been interviewed in print many times over the years, neither my face nor my name was known much beyond Broadway. Now here I stood, three thousand miles away, in the parking lot of a body shop in the middle of the desert, with a hot young fantasy hunk (I was old enough to be his mother) gushing over me as if he were starstruck. What was I missing?

I thanked him for his kind words, then asked, "Uh, have we perhaps met?"

He shook his head. "Never. Well, *now* we have." He offered his hand again. "My name's Tanner Griffin."

"I thought so." Gladly, I indulged in his redundant handshake.

It was now he who seemed perplexed. *"Have* we met?"

"No"—I laughed—"someone gave me your card. Desert Detail comes *highly* recommended." From the lilt of my voice, anyone would have gotten the ridiculous impression that I was flirting. With a casual primp, I asked, "You're the owner?"

"Not exactly. Not yet. I'm sort of a junior partner, with plenty of sweat equity. The real owner is quite a bit older. He retired from another job in the Midwest a few years ago, then moved out here and had this notion to start a body shop. That was about the time I finished college;

I'd just moved here from L.A. and was looking for work. We got to know each other, he hired me, and I pretty much set up the business, hired the crew, made it happen. I'm basically in charge." He laughed. "Which simply means that I'm first to arrive in the morning."

"And last to leave at night?"

"Yeah, most of the time." Picking up the papers he'd dropped, he said, "Come on inside. It's cooler in the office. Let's talk about that Beetle."

Following him (Lord, what a sight, just watching him walk), I wondered aloud, "When you were in college, is this what you thought you'd end up doing?" He turned quizzically, and I added at once, "Don't get me wrong—you've got a great deal to be proud of here. What I meant was, did you always have a dream to start up a business?"

We stepped inside the office, and he sat on a stool, placing the papers on the counter, resting his arm there. His orotund voice was colored with wistfulness as he told me, "No, Miss Gray, though I was a business major in college, it was never my dream to found a body-shop empire. My dream"—the pause, the smile—"was to act."

I beaded him with a sly stare. "Now, *why* doesn't this surprise me?"

"It doesn't?"

I laughed. "God, Tanner—your voice, your presence. What's the story? Waiting to be discovered?"

"I don't *think* so." He shook his head, chuckling.

Then I remembered that he'd been a business major. Sitting on the stool next to his, I said, "Pardon an old snoop, but if acting was your dream, why didn't you pursue it?"

He raised a hand in admonishment. "First, you are *not* old."

"Tanner, you're as gracious as you are handsome." Again, anyone would have reached the preposterous conclusion that I was flirting.

"Second, you may be snooping, but considering the nature of your query, I'm flattered that you'd ask. Why didn't I pursue acting? In a word: parents."

"Aha." During the year I'd spent teaching at Evans College, to say nothing of the four years I'd studied there, I'd rarely met parents of a theater major who were totally comfortable with the career being pursued by their progeny—my mother certainly wasn't. Objections ranged from "too iffy" for the girls to "too effeminate" for the boys. Granted, theater is a chancy vocation at best, so it's difficult to blame parents for being wary of dreams spun by children who simply don't have the maturity to distinguish between the curtain-call rewards of a high-school drama guild and the probable disappointments of a dead-ended career. Still, some of us do weather the transition, beat the odds, and know the supreme privilege of truly loving our work. I asked Tanner, "They threatened to cut you off?"

"At the knees. I wanted to study theater in college, but they wouldn't hear of it. 'It's a wonderful hobby,' they told me, 'but we're not spending tens of thousands of dollars just so you can wait tables for the rest of your life'—or words to that effect."

I nodded. I'd heard it all before.

"So I majored in business. They called that 'sensible.' I called it 'job training,' a wasted education. So after I graduated, I moved out here—the classic quest to find myself. Took a few odd jobs, menial stuff. I've always sort of enjoyed real labor. It's kept me in shape."

"Yes," I observed dryly, "it has."

"Then Desert Detail happened. Things just fell together for me. I'm happy with it—reasonably."

"There's no need to convince *me*, Tanner."

With a soft laugh, he agreed, "Sometimes I need to convince myself that I haven't wasted a gift."

"You're good then?" My tone was businesslike and matter-of-fact. I was asking for an objective assessment of his acting skills.

He understood—no bullshit. "People *said* I was good—not just friends but directors in both high school and college. I usually played leading roles, even in college, and that's really something, since I wasn't a theater major. I heard that the good roles almost always went to majors so they could build their résumés."

I affirmed, "That's how it works. You *must* be good."

"Well, let's just say that I *was*. Haven't done much lately."

"No opportunities here?"

"A few. But it's just that . . . well, I've never *studied* theater. My acting has been essentially intuitive. There's a lot I don't know."

Before I could weigh the implications of what I was saying, I heard the words slip out of me: "Have you ever considered going back to school?"

He paused before answering, "Yes, I've often thought of it."

A long silence followed, as neither of us felt prepared to discuss the next step. The topic of his returning to school had seemingly bubbled up from nowhere, backing us into an awkward corner.

Changing the topic, Tanner said, "Jodie Metz-Huron told me she'd met you. That's how I happened to recognize you—we were just talking about you." With a laugh, he added, "But I had no idea you'd appear in the driveway this morning."

Though I was unprepared to hear Jodie's name at that moment, I was even more surprised by the casual tone with which Tanner invoked it. There was nothing in his voice that conveyed knowledge of Jodie's death. Had he truly not heard? (Or was he—perhaps—acting?)

Matching his casual tone, I mentioned, "Actually, it was Jodie who recommended you. And her husband Paul gave me your card."

"Ahhh," he said, realizing that my visit was less than coincidental. "I haven't met Paul." Tanner got up from the stool and gestured toward the doorway into the garage. "But I have met his Honda."

"So I hear." I stood as well. "Jodie paid you a high compliment on the repairs. She said you were most accommodating."

"Try to be. We do good work at Desert Detail. Our reputation depends on it. That's why we did the paint job over—I just wasn't satisfied the first time. Now it's beautiful. Just needs a final waxing today."

Huh? "You mean . . . Paul's car is . . . still here?" Before I'd finished speaking, I'd stepped to the doorway, and sure enough, there was a gleaming Honda, showroom perfect. Its color was dusty-metallic blue. "I thought the car was being returned on Friday."

"That was the plan," said Tanner, repeating his explanation of the faulty paint job while walking me into the garage for a closer look at Paul's blue car.

As he spoke, my mind raced to recall the particulars of Jodie and Paul's conversation the previous Wednesday night at Glenn Yeats's party: Paul's car was in the shop for repairs, to be returned on Friday. Paul was leaving for Dallas on Thursday, and Jodie would drive him to the airport. Paul was returning on Saturday morning, but since Jodie claimed to be working an overnight shift at the hospital, I volunteered to meet Paul and drive him home. Jodie had mentioned, "Our cars seem to be a constant source of confusion." And yes, Paul had specifically said, "Mine's blue, hers is green."

That solved at least *one* mystery. At the Hurons' house on Sunday morning, I'd seen the green car in the garage and, assuming it was Paul's, I'd wondered if Jodie's car was perhaps at the hospital. I also wondered why Paul hadn't yet retrieved it. Now it made sense: Paul hadn't been concerned about Jodie's car because it was right there. A new question though: Wouldn't Paul have wondered about the whereabouts of his own car?

Tanner was still talking about the need for a paint job to cure properly, when I interrupted to ask, "When did you decide to repaint the car?"

"Friday morning. We were going to wax it and return it that day, but it wasn't up to snuff. So I called Jodie and explained the situation, promising to return the car on Monday—today. She assured me it was no problem at all because her husband was out of town on business and a friend had offered to pick him up at the airport over the weekend. She mentioned that she'd be talking to Paul on the phone later that day and would let him know that his car would be ready Monday."

Satisfied that these loose ends regarding Jodie and Paul were resolved, I again turned my attention to Tanner himself. He had still given no hint of knowledge of Jodie's death. He was far more concerned with the need to get Paul's car waxed, complaining that his crew never seemed to arrive on time on Monday morning. "For some guys, weekends are one long party."

Unsure how to broach this, I asked, "What did *you* do this weekend, Tanner?"

The smile. God, what a face. "Early to bed on Saturday, then up first thing Sunday for an all-day hike in the Indian Canyons. It had been a couple of years since I'd seen them. They're absolutely beautiful, Miss Gray, true desert oases with springs and ponds, incredible vegetation, and all manner of wildlife. I even saw a rattler."

I raised a hand. "You're oversharing, Tanner. I did *not* need to hear that."

"Oh. Sorry."

"Did you happen to see yesterday's paper? Or maybe watch the late news?"

"Hate to sound snobbish, but I never watch TV. Besides, after a full day in the canyons, I was shot. As for newspapers, I don't subscribe, but I always look at the *Desert Sun* here at the shop."

"And that was Sunday's paper, waiting there at the door?"

"Both Sunday's and Monday's—I'll catch up." He cocked his head warily. "Why?"

I hesitated. This was not the sort of news one relished delivering. Complicating my emotions was the suspicion, however remote, that he already knew full well what had happened. I explained somberly, "There's a story on the front page of Sunday's paper. It's about Jodie. I'm afraid she died on Saturday."

He looked at me dumbstruck. "How?" he asked, barely audible.

"That's the worst part, Tanner. Jodie was killed. Murdered at home."

"My . . . God," he mumbled, then raced into the office, opening the larger of the two rolled newspapers that lay on the counter, spreading out the front page. The headline, the photo, told him at a glance that it was all true.

Following him into the office, I elaborated, "The initial police investigation is focusing on the possibility of home invasion, robbery. It seems Jodie was simply in the wrong place at the wrong time." He skimmed the newspaper story, which told him the same thing. I didn't mention that both Larry Knoll, the detective in charge, and I now harbored another theory—a theory that assumed Jodie had indulged in a Friday-night tryst with some unknown man.

Tanner turned to me with sagging shoulders and a sunken expression. "I can't believe it. What a terrible loss. She'd just moved here." Right on cue, a tear slid down his ruddy cheek. He seemed genuinely shocked and grieving. (Or was he acting?) He said through a sigh, "And so beautiful."

"Was she?" I asked, stepping near the counter to study her photo. Feigning female cattiness, I told him, "I hadn't noticed."

"You hadn't?" he asked with dismay. "It's obvious even in that dopey newspaper picture." He wiped an eye with the back of his hand.

"I suppose. She just didn't strike me as . . . well, your 'type.' "

He looked at me with a confused smile. "Why not?"

I crossed my arms. "How old are you, Tanner?"

"Just turned twenty-six."

"Jodie was thirty." I grinned. "Pushing thirty-one."

He suppressed a little laugh. "Miss Gray, what's a few years when the match seems right?"

I couldn't help wondering what, in his view, constituted a few years. More important, I wondered if he felt that the match with Jodie had seemed right.

"Besides," he continued, "I've always been attracted to older women."

Kettle drums. Fanfares. My legs wobbled. "You have?" I asked stupidly, transparently. "*All* older women?"

"Of course not."

That brought me down a notch.

He amplified, "I judge the whole person—her mind, her ideas, her accomplishments. Attraction can stem from lots of hidden sources."

"And you *did* find Jodie attractive?" The question was inflected to convey an academic or philosophical curiosity. I doubt if he understood that I was really asking if he'd slept with her. And I hope to God he didn't understand that I was also wondering where I myself stood in his eyes.

The smile. "I found Jodie *very* attractive. She was pretty, smart, caring. A *nurse*. I hate to admit this"—he hung his head, looking adorably boyish with his sandy blond hair—"but I even came on to her."

"Oh, really?"

"Really." He nodded. "God, was I embarrassed. When she first brought in the Honda for an estimate, I didn't know it was her *husband's* car. I got the impression she was interested in me. And when I asked her out, she *thought* about it before flashing me her ring finger. I apologized—it just didn't look like a wedding ring. Then she laughed, saying, 'It *does* keep people guessing, doesn't it?' "

"Hm. I saw that ring. And it was missing when her body was discovered."

"Whew. That *is* bizarre. Kinda creepy, too."

"Kinda," I agreed. "But the bottom line is, she didn't seem insulted by your advance."

"Not at all. We saw each other again when she brought the car back for us to do the work, and we talked on the phone a couple of times as well. I could hear it in her voice—she wasn't the *least* bit put off by my interest in her. I was tempted to try again, but didn't."

I smiled. "Why not—scruples?"

He hedged. "Maybe. But more than that, I think it was the hopelessness."

"You mean, *you* found it hopeless? A lost cause?"

He shook his head. "*She* had a hopelessness about her—or *something* in her voice, something faraway. I guess it was more of a . . . wistfulness."

"We met only once, but I too noticed that. Paul later told me that she hadn't been thrilled with their move out here."

"Maybe that's all it was." Tanner stretched an arm behind his head and rubbed the base of his neck. "But that's not the impression I got."

I waited for him to elaborate.

Finishing with his neck, he shoved both hands into his pockets, telling me, "Okay, this may sound nutty, and it's based on nothing more than my imagination, but I interpreted her odd tone, her moodiness, as meaning one of two things: I felt that perhaps she was already involved with someone else, not her husband. Or maybe she had some serious health problem, something she was covering up, not dealing with."

Interesting. Tanner's theory that Jodie was involved with another man matched my own thinking dead-on, though he'd come to the notion through entirely different circumstances. At the same time, I had to remind myself that Tanner could just possibly be this "someone else"—he could be floating this theory as a clever means of deflecting suspicion from himself. As to the idea that Jodie had been moodily harboring knowledge of some morbid illness, it seemed far-fetched at best. Yes, Tanner had acknowledged that the poor-health angle was merely an inkling, a lingering instinct, but he might also have invented it on the spot, purely as a means of muddying the waters.

He sat on one of the stools, splayed his knees, propped an elbow on the counter, and ran five strong fingers through his mop of golden hair—quite a picture. Watching him, I admitted to myself with a measure of alarm that, yes, I found him attractive. Not only was he desirable in the physical sense, but I was drawn to the "whole person," as he had put it. He had a mind, sensitivity, strength, and the endearing neediness of an unfulfilled dream. My intellect reminded me, though, that he was off-limits (too young, too awed by my stature within the theatrical world), so I was content simply to enjoy the sight of him, shooing varied and prurient whims from my brain, saving them, perhaps, for some later, older conquest.

Watching Tanner's fingers in his hair, I also realized that the pale strands were nearly the same flaxen color as Jodie's. If there had been any of Tanner's hair at the crime scene, it could easily have been mistaken for hers, and in fact, Larry Knoll had told me that only dark hair samples had been collected for identification.

With his head still in his hand, Tanner said, "I'd arranged with Jodie to deliver the Honda to their house today, but now?" He stood. "Guess I should phone Paul to make new arrangements—and to extend my sympathies. Poor guy." He shook his head slowly, sharing a bit of Paul's grief.

Stepping near, I patted Tanner's arm, told him that Paul would surely appreciate hearing from him, and gave him the phone number for Desert Arts College, where Paul could doubtless be found that day. Tanner thanked me; then I said good-bye and left the office through the front door.

"Oh," said Tanner from the doorway, "I nearly forgot. What can I do for you? I mean, the Beetle?"

"Oh," I echoed. Looking at the car, then back at Tanner, I decided that the window tinting could wait. The topic seemed so frivolous, almost irreverent, as a follow-up to our discussion of Jodie's murder. I told him, "Some other time, okay?"

He understood my mood because he clearly shared it. With a nod and a wave, he retreated into the office of the body shop.

Crossing the pavement toward my car, I noticed the energy farms in the distance. Still conspicuous among the rank and file of whirring white windmills that filled the canted fields, a few random stalwarts gazed lazily toward other, weaker breezes. They seemed so perplexed, I thought. Then I realized that their confusion merely mirrored my own.

10

Driving away from Desert Detail, I decided to take my time returning to Palm Desert. It was still early, barely past eight o'clock, and besides, I was in no mood to encounter my mother in another daydream on the interstate, so I wound through downtown Palm Springs on Palm Canyon Drive, following the turn east that would take me down valley. The morning sun hung squarely in the Beetle's windshield. Squinting, I resolved that I would indeed have the windows tinted. Then I grinned, pleased to have an excuse to encounter Tanner Griffin again—purely in the name of crime solving, of course. The silver glint of a plane glided low into my field of vision, its engines rumbling as it approached the nearby airport.

Traffic was getting heavy that Monday morning, so it was nearly eight-thirty when I drove into Rancho Mirage, passing the gatehouse at the foot of the road leading up to Nirvana. I recalled Glenn Yeats's spectacular home, perched high above on the secluded mesa, and I wondered if Paul Huron had spent a second night there.

After another mile or so, I turned left off Palm Canyon, crossing the valley again. If I kept going, I would return to the interstate, but my destination was not that far. The valley floor is checkered with large tracts of vacant desert land, some reserved for local Indian tribes, others simply undeveloped. One of these huge tracts had been snapped up by Glenn Yeats for an undisclosed price a few years earlier, just before the valley's vigorous recovery from a long real estate slump, and it was here that Glenn's dream, Desert Arts College, now rose resplendent, phoenixlike, from the sands.

Turning into the main entrance, I followed the palm-lined central drive to the campus proper, where signs led me to the shaded faculty parking structure. I easily found my assigned space (a particularly desirable one, I noted) near the pedestrian ramp to College Circle. On more traditional campuses, this central public space would typically be called a quadrangle, but at Desert Arts College, the overall design contained no right angles. In fact, the plan was circular.

Leaving my car, I walked the curved ramp and emerged into full sun. At the edge of an expansive reflecting pool, I paused to admire what Glenn had built, from scratch, in three short years.

There was still plenty of room for expansion, and the current campus felt compact in scale, but its aesthetic impact was stunning. The buildings, all designed by the same renowned architect, each had a distinctive, even idiosyncratic, look, but they were united by a vaguely modern style and a governing sense of proportion. Collectively, these structures constituted an instant landmark, and the final phases of construction had been documented by architectural journals worldwide. The buildings ringed the large paved plaza where I stood, providing a sculptural backdrop for College Circle's lush, oasislike landscaping. Palms, pools, and fountains delighted the eye and tickled the senses; even a scorching afternoon would seem benignly cool in such inviting surroundings.

In a week, the plaza would be bustling with students—its charter enrollment on the first day of classes—but today it was quiet, with a hushed, rushed sense of anticipation. Workmen passed from building to building, where they scurried to meet deadlines with their finishing touches. Faculty sought out their offices, got their bearings, and started to feel at home. A few curious tourists ambled and gawked, awed by the power of one man's wealth.

That man had built me a theater, one of the most prominent structures on his new campus. Theaters are, by their nature, big, and mine was no exception, but its prominence was not only a matter of size. The exterior of the building was fancifully artistic, with soaring curved sidewalls that reminded me of applauding hands. The fly space above the stage was suggestive of a theatrical curtain, drawn but ready to rise, revealing mystery and magic. The gleaming lobby doors opened directly onto College Circle, so that the entire plaza felt like one enormous entryway—the portal to "my" theater.

With classes beginning in a week, I had plenty to do that morning. I needed to set up my office. There were course plans to work on and files to organize. Piles of administrative paperwork beckoned. But none of these duties struck me as urgent; they could wait. Crossing the plaza, I felt my heartbeat quicken as I fished in my purse for my key—the key to my theater. I had met with the head architect, signing off on his plans before the first shovel had tasted earth, and I had visited the theater since my arrival in the desert, confirming that the building itself was finished. But now, during this next week, the race would be on to work with technicians in the tweaking of stage mechanics, electronics, and lighting. These were the systems, the lifeblood, that would transform a gaping hall into a holy place, a place where new realities would be created, where minds would be expanded, tears would be shed, laughter would be laughed. My key turned the lock, the door opened, and I stepped inside.

Instantly, I felt calmer. My breathing eased as I passed through the lobby and into the semidarkness of the auditorium itself.

"Morning, Miss Gray—that you?" said someone from a ladder on-stage, shielding his eyes from the lights, spotting me in the shadows.

"Yes," I said in a well-practiced directorial elocution, projecting my words from the back row of seats, "it is I. Everything on schedule?"

"Morning, Miss Gray," said someone else, appearing from the far left vomitory. "Glad you're here. I have a few questions." He started up the aisle with a sheaf of blueprints.

"Hey, I saw her first," said the guy on the ladder, scampering down.

And they were quickly joined by other workers from backstage, the fly space, the control booth, the catwalks. We ended up clumped around a makeshift worktable between the stage apron and the front row of seats. They had questions; I had answers. It was absolute heaven.

I have often wondered what it is about being in the theater (that is, my physical presence inside a theater) that has such an intoxicating appeal. To be seated expectantly in an audience is amply rewarding, to be sure, but to be at *work* in a theater is a special joy, a privilege, that the layman cannot fathom. Creativity, camaraderie, teamwork, discipline, timing, delivery, applause—all of these aspects of the theatrical process contribute to its allure. But still, the sum is greater than its parts, and as a director, I have found these delights to be all the more heady. The satisfaction is complex and seems to defy analysis. Or do I simply enjoy being boss?

"Whatever you say, Miss Gray," said the lighting foreman with a little salute. "We'll have that up and running by this afternoon."

Maybe it's not so complex.

Reveling in all this, I breathed a happy sigh as everyone got back to work, so eager to please. In the ambient light that spilled from the stage, the entire auditorium, now nearly finished, glowed rich and warm, the perfect setting in which to make theater happen. From my vantage point at the front of the stage, the room was a soft, marshamallowy sea of velvet. The choice of upholstery for the five hundred seats had been left to me, and it didn't take a moment's thought. I knew that on opening night I'd be wearing a red dress, coordinating nicely with the cushy scarlet seats.

The couple of hours I spent in the theater that morning was a pleasant respite from the murder puzzle that had consumed me since Saturday, but after a point, I realized, my time there had become more self-indulgent than productive. The technicians on hand were fully competent professionals, needing me for only a sense of direction and a final thumbs-up; I could contribute nothing to the grunt work, and they were hard at it.

Glancing at my watch around eleven o'clock, I noted that most of the morning had slipped away. It was time to tend to my other duties at the college, so I called a general farewell to the workmen, telling them I'd return later that afternoon.

Exiting through the lobby, I crossed College Circle in the direction of the administration building. The morning had grown hot, and though the azure autumnal sky was still cloudless, the air had taken on a heavy, languid character. The burble of the fountains seemed slower, lacking enthusiasm, as I strolled to the center of campus, ready to find my office.

The circular plan of the campus defined a clear pecking order. Administrative offices were near the middle, with college president D. Glenn Yeats's posh suite at the very epicenter. Department heads, like Paul Huron and me, had individual offices arrayed in a circle around

Glenn's. Other faculty in each department clustered around their respective chairmen like the petals of a flower. Classrooms and studios were located still farther from center.

The concept made sense, and it doubtless looked good on paper, but in practice, the whole setup proved difficult to navigate. When I entered the administration building, I first felt assaulted by the icy breath of air-conditioning (the system was apparently still in need of adjustment), which brought a crop of goose bumps to my bare arms. Hugging myself, I looked left and right down the circular hallway, confused as to which direction would lead to my office. Though I knew the number of the room, its placement seemed arbitrary, as there was no grid to lend logic to the numbering. Was my thinking too stilted and rectilinear? Was the computer genius teaching his minions to think beyond the box?

The only way to find my office was to start exploring, and I decided to travel clockwise. If I overshot the mark, I told myself, I'd end up back where I'd started—except I wouldn't know that I'd returned because there was nothing to give me a visual fix on my position.

I was not alone in this confusion. As I wandered the circular hall, calls of "this way" and "over here" frequently sounded—siren songs of the lost. I encountered fellow faculty roving in the opposite direction; some looked familiar from the party at Nirvana; most wore sweaters; many laughed; others grumbled. Along the curving inner wall, most of the office doors were closed, but some stood open, revealing occupants at work, attempting to personalize these sterile new quarters with pictures, posters, plants, pots—*anything* to overcome the chalky smell and fluorescent glare of freshly painted plaster-white walls.

Having passed the mahogany double doors to Glenn Yeats's suite not once but twice, I was sorely tempted to march inside and ask how the hell I was supposed to find my desk, when I heard Kiki's melodic twitter no more than a few yards away, just beyond the curve. Rushing in the direction of her voice, I saw her standing in an office doorway, speaking to someone within.

"If there's anything we can do for you," she was saying, "don't hesitate to ask. We're *all* your family now, dear."

"Thank you, Kiki. Everyone's been so kind." It was Paul Huron's voice.

I stepped up behind her. "Kiki? Paul? Thank God."

She turned. "Claire—darling—you look dreadful."

"Thanks."

"I was looking for you in your office, but you weren't there."

"I can't *find* it."

Paul stood; he'd been rummaging in a box. "Hi, Claire. Sorry for the confusion. Glenn wanted better signage, so we had to start over with the supplier. It should be installed by the end of the week."

Managing a laugh, I told him, "Glad to hear it."

Kiki said, "Since you seem to be wondering, your office is four doors down." She pointed counterclockwise. "I'm in the same pod, but one rung out."

I pressed my fingers to my forehead. "Thank you."

"Look for me later, 'kay? I simply *must* get back. The costume vault is a shambles, and the cutting room's a *zoo*, dear, a veritable *zoo.*" With a lofty wave, and a considerable jangling of bracelets, she was gone.

Paul chortled. "I love her. Quite a character."

"Yes," I agreed, deadpan, "isn't she."

"Hey," he said, as if something had occurred to him, "glad you happened to find me. Got a minute?" He waved me in.

"Sure, Paul." Stepping inside the bare office, I closed the door a few inches. "How's . . . everything?"

He sighed. "Fine, I guess. Under the circumstances."

"How was last night? Did you sleep?"

"A few hours, maybe, but it's still pretty rough. I was up at Nirvana again, which helped. Tonight, though, I'll stay at the house. Can't put it off forever, so I might as well confront it—the empty house, I mean."

"I know, Paul."

"Meanwhile, it helps to keep busy. There's plenty to do here." He made a gesture encompassing the room.

I laughed at his understatement. "I dread getting started, now that I know where my office is."

Hunkering on the floor, he shoved aside a bulging corrugated box and opened another, brimming with papers, folders, and whatnot. "I've been trying to find those photos of Jodie's wedding ring for Larry Knoll, but so far, no luck." He tried fingering through a file folder that was wedged near the side of the carton.

"Maybe you should modify your approach."

He looked up at me. "I'm open to suggestions."

With a low laugh, I told him, "I'm a fine one to talk, but why not unpack everything and get your whole office organized? The photos are bound to pop up in the process, aren't they?"

He nodded. "I'm reasonably sure they're here somewhere—can't imagine where *else* they'd be. Guess I was hoping the quick approach would save me some trouble. But you're right; the whole job needs to be done anyway. Might as well get at it." And he began lifting armloads of papers out of the box, setting them on the cluttered desk.

As he worked, I began telling him, "I had dinner with Larry Knoll last night—"

"Oh," he turned, interrupting me, "I *knew* there was something I wanted to talk to you about. Larry phoned me yesterday afternoon to say that the medical examiner was finishing with the autopsy. Jodie's body will probably be released by the coroner's office tomorrow."

"Yes," I recalled, "he mentioned that to me as well."

"As I've already told you, Jodie would want to be cremated, so I've arranged for that." Resting his rump on the edge of the desk, he explained, "Since all of Jodie's family is back in Michigan, I thought I'd split the ashes so there can be two memorial services, one at home for the family, and another for everyone who got to know her out here."

Considering this, I nodded. "Sounds like a good idea."

"It's relatively easy on everyone. No one has to travel—except me, of course."

"And half of Jodie's ashes," I added, wishing I hadn't. Though the comment was made purely for the sake of precision, I feared that it had a flippant ring.

Paul took no apparent offense. "The local memorial will probably be the day after tomorrow. I hope you can be there."

"Aww." I stepped to him and hugged his shoulders. "Of *course,* Paul. I'll gladly attend. Do you know the particulars?"

"In fact, I do. Everything still depends on the coroner's office, but if the body is released and cremated tomorrow as planned, the service will be Wednesday morning at eleven—at Nirvana."

I stepped back, brow raised. "Oh?"

"Talking over everything with Glenn last evening, he offered the use of his home for the memorial. Jodie wasn't religious, and it *is* a beautiful setting up there, and it won't cost me a thing, so I thought, Why not?"

"Sure." I nodded. "Why not? Gee, that was thoughtful of Glenn."

"Wasn't it? Generous, too. He's been *so* helpful."

We pattered on about our benevolent boss and some specifics of the service (there would be a catered lunch), but Paul had work to do, and so did I, so I soon excused myself, determined at last to find my office and get my desk in order.

Just as I was stepping out into the hall, though, I remembered something and turned back. "By the way," I told Paul from the doorway, "I met Tanner Griffin this morning."

Paul eyed me with a blank expression. "Who?"

"The gentleman at Desert Detail—you gave me his card yesterday."

"Ohhh, sure. You're, uh, getting the Beetle's windows tinted?"

"We discussed it, yes." In truth we'd never gotten around to it. "He mentioned that he'll be phoning you today. I didn't realize it, but they still have your blue car."

Paul nodded. "It was supposed to be ready on Friday, but there was something they needed to do over. Jodie phoned me in Dallas and said they'd be finished with it today. Frankly, with the events of this past weekend, I'd forgotten."

"Of course—you've had a lot on your mind."

"Like I said yesterday, I'll most likely get rid of one of the Hondas. Why would I need two cars—nearly identical ones, at that? But I *will* be glad to get my own car back. Driving hers since Saturday has really bothered me. What an awful reminder." His shoulders slumped.

I probably should have taken my cue to offer some last words of consolation and leave, but I was compelled to ask, "Have you ever met Tanner Griffin?"

"No," he answered with the slightest shrug. "Jodie took care of the repairs for me—I was busy every day here at DAC. I don't recall that she ever mentioned the guy by name. Why do you ask?"

I couldn't blame him for wondering, nor could I give him a direct answer. I told Paul, "No reason," aping his slight shrug, then said good-bye and headed down the hall, counterclockwise.

As directed by Kiki, I counted four doors to my own office, finding both the room number and my name scrawled in pencil on a piece of masking tape—makeshift signage that I'd easily missed on my previous rounds. Opening the door with my key and switching on the lights in the windowless white room, I found my new quarters to be identical to Paul's office; the only difference was the brand of mover's boxes, mine trucked from New York.

Working through the noon hour, I made a first pass at emptying cartons, arranging files, tidying my desk, and hanging a few old, framed mementos—reviews, playbills, press photos—on the bare walls. Checking my watch, I felt suddenly hungry, still chilled to the bone by the aggressive air-conditioning. It was time for a break, so I decided to rush out to my car, warm up, and find a fast lunch someplace.

Locking my office behind me, I headed down the circular hall, clockwise this time, and as I approached the twin mahogany doors to the presidential suite, who should arrive from the opposite direction but D. Glenn Yeats himself.

"Claire!" he greeted me with outstretched arms. "Getting settled?"

We embraced briefly, then joined all four hands, wiggling them in an odd permutation of a handshake. I told him, "It's been a bit of a challenge finding my way around, but I'm into my office now and starting to get things put away."

"I presume you're keeping an eye on the progress in your theater." He grinned, making a show of affability but not quite overcoming his innate geekiness.

"You bet. The building's *gorgeous,* Glenn, and the tech installation seems to be going smoothly. I'll check again later this afternoon." I rubbed my arms, stunting a shiver.

"What's wrong?" asked the computer genius. (Any lamebrain should have been able to figure out that I was cold.)

"The *air*-conditioning. It's on steroids."

"Oh?" He sniffed the air, as if able to gauge its temperature through his nose. "Let me take care of that. Come on in." And he opened one of the twin doors, stepping into his outer office.

I followed, curious to get a look at the inner sanctum. Expecting to be impressed, I was not disappointed. There was a waiting room, then a secretary's office, and beyond, glimpses of his own domain. The carpeting was like thick, plush velvet, the muted color of champagne. Walls were paneled with some rich, exotic hardwood, polished to a mirrorlike shine. A few oil paintings hung here and there—*real* art of museum quality, perfectly lit by tiny, hidden projector lamps beaming white, white light. All the furnishings were sleekly modern and extravagantly tasteful, the best that money could buy.

He led me past his secretary's desk (there was no one there) and into his own office, where I stopped in my tracks at the sight of his personal work space.

It looked like a command station for rocket launchings, except that everything was so lavishly finished, not starkly utilitarian. The desk itself, raised on a round dais, was huge and semicircular, topped with a thick slab of bullnosed black granite. A fat, unfurled bundle of architect's plans, which Glenn had apparently been studying, covered much of the desk.

The other half of the implied circle, behind Glenn's high-backed swivel chair, was a curved travertine wall inset with television and computer monitors, several dozen of them aflicker with stock charts, scrolling data, or security-camera images (plus one of them tuned to the Cooking Channel, which showed a toqued Asian chef skinning an eel). All of the screens were crisply framed by gunmetal bezels.

Glenn mounted the dais and sat in the big swivel chair, looking like the Wizard of Oz, except that his hair was not white and frizzy but dark, straight, and a tad oily. Glancing over his shoulder and checking one of the monitors, he typed a few strokes on the keyboard at his desk. As he did so, something in the bowels of the building stopped—a rumble so slight I hadn't even noticed it until now that it was gone. In the same instant, the whoosh of glacial air abated. It would be a few minutes before the chill left my fingers, but relief was now imminent.

"Sit down, Claire," he said. "Make yourself comfortable."

Several buttery leather armchairs and a matching sofa were arranged facing his desk, suggesting that he sometimes granted group audiences, lecturing his listeners from on high.

"Thanks, Glenn, but I'll stand if you don't mind. I'm just trying to take everything in. You've certainly—" I stopped. Noticing some detail of the plans on his desk, I asked, "That's the theater, isn't it?"

"Your theater," he corrected me. "Is the technical installation proceeding to your satisfaction?"

"I was over there earlier, and—"

From behind me, a soft, mellow voice interrupted, "I didn't know you'd returned, Mr. Yeats."

I turned, and there in the door stood that amazon of a woman who'd greeted me at Glenn's party the previous week, the one with severe features, skimpy dress, great legs, and an Afro clipped to a perfect cube. It was hard to peg her age. Maybe twenty or so. Maybe thirty.

"Oh," she said without expression, "good afternoon, Ms. Gray." Then to Glenn: "Sorry, Mr. Yeats. I didn't know you were occupied." As at the party, I was struck by her voice—its wispiness was so much at odds with her hard appearance.

Glenn told her, "That's perfectly all right, Tide. Can I presume that you and Miss Gray have already met?"

"Actually," I told him, "we've never been introduced."

"Ah. Forgive me." He stood. "Claire, I'd like you to meet Tide Arden, my special assistant—my executive secretary. Tide is even more efficient and loyal than she is beautiful. I find her absolutely indispensable."

Tide turned to say, "Thank you, Mr. Yeats. Too kind of you." Then she stepped toward me, offering her long hand. "It's an honor, Ms. Gray."

Glenn began, "Claire is the most celebrated—"

"I'm well aware," Tide told both of us. She managed to crack a smile as I shook her hand. Backing to the doorway, she said, "If I'm needed, I'll be at my desk working on arrangements for Wednesday's memorial service." Then she disappeared.

I gave Glenn a warm smile. "I talked to Paul earlier today. He told me about your offer to host Jodie's memorial up at Nirvana. That's *so* kindhearted of you, Glenn. It gives Paul one less thing to worry about."

"Exactly. Paul's had a terrible shock, but I hope he'll soon be able to get beyond this and focus on the school. Our doors open a week from today." He tapped the granite desktop decisively. "We have to be ready."

I winced. Soon get beyond this? Paul's wife had been murdered only two days ago, and Glenn now expected him to move on, to focus on the school? The computer genius, it seemed, still had a few things to learn about human nature. Even though I found his priorities embarrassingly inappropriate, I also realized that owing to his computer savvy, he was in a position to help me solve the puzzle and name Jodie's killer, which would go a long way toward providing Paul with some sense of closure.

Taking a deep breath, I paused, then asked, "Can I tell you something in confidence, Glenn?"

"Of *course*, Claire." Big smile. He sat again, peering at the blueprints of the theater. "What is it?"

Stepping near his desk, I explained, "You're right about Paul. We do need to help him, as you say, get beyond this. As you're aware, Grant Knoll, from the Nirvana sales office, is my neighbor. It happens that his brother, Larry Knoll, is the sheriff's detective in charge of investigating Jodie's murder. Larry, Grant, and I went to dinner last night, and I was made privy to some inside information on the case. I floated a few ideas of my own regarding the murder, and Larry seemed to think I might be able to help—"

"*What?* That's dangerous, Claire. Besides, with school about to—"

"No, listen, Glenn. I have no intention of lurking in phone booths, trailing suspects, or packing a pistol. I'm simply trying to help figure out the puzzle—for Paul's sake."

"Fine." He rolled up the plans and set them aside. "Good luck."

Placing my palms on his desk, I leaned forward, grinning. With my face mere inches from his, I said, "A new angle was raised this morning, and I'll bet you could help me explore it."

"*Me?*" His chair squeaked as he tilted it back from me. "How?"

"Those things." I pointed to the bank of computer monitors behind him.

He glanced at the screens, then turned back to me with an uncertain smile. "You need . . . information?"

"Yes. And you're *good* at that, Glenn—probably the best. Hell, you practically *invented* computers. To me, they're just fancy typewriters."

He laughed heartily, truly amused. "Typewriters, indeed!" When his mirth subsided, he told me, "Okay. I'll help you—maybe—if I can. But just this once. We do *not* want to make a habit of this."

I answered with quick, tiny shakes of my head, "Of course we don't."

He heaved a sigh. "So then. What's this 'angle'?"

Pulling my thoughts together, I told him, "An acquaintance, a friend, has raised the possibility that Jodie may have had some serious health problem. I'm not sure how that would relate to the murder, but it's an intriguing wrinkle. I don't want to needlessly upset Paul with this theory, so I'm wondering if there's some other way for us to get details of Jodie's medical history." I raised a brow.

Glenn rolled his eyes. "God, Claire, I thought you were going to ask me something *hard*. You want to know: Was Jodie hiding some serious health problem? Let's find out."

He picked up the keyboard, which had no cord, placed it in his lap, and swiveled his chair to face the monitors. I perched on the edge of his desk, looking over his shoulder. He began typing as he explained, "If you know what you're doing—and I do—you can have instant access to virtually unlimited data on anyone and anything. In this instance, we don't need to search much further than DAC's own data banks. Access to the health records of a faculty spouse is something of a no-brainer. Jodie's records are linked to Paul's, so we simply start there." His fingers ceased rattling the keys, then he tapped ENTER.

A split second later, one of the larger computer screens at the center of the display came to life, aglow with Paul Huron's detailed medical history. Glenn typed a few more strokes, then tapped ENTER again.

The screen flickered, then Paul's records were replaced by Jodie's. There was a head shot of her (the same hospital-personnel ID photo that had appeared in the paper), some employment information, then detailed medical records stretching back to her grade-school days in

Michigan. I stood, moving closer to the screen. As Glenn scrolled through the history, we both read it all.

Finally, Glenn told me, "Your friend was mistaken. Jodie was perfectly healthy. She had no problems at all, other than a period of psychotherapy a while ago." Glenn tapped BACK, and Jodie's records disappeared, reverting to Paul's.

I paced a few feet, thinking aloud, "Paul mentioned to me that Jodie wasn't happy about the move out here, and it struck me that perhaps the problem ran deeper—like bouts of depression. Her history with the psychologist bears that out, and she'd been taking the antidepressant Zoloft. It all fits, I guess. She was clinically depressed, but dealing with it."

Glenn nodded. "Otherwise, physically, she was in great health."

"So"—I smiled at him—"I can scratch that theory. Thanks, Glenn."

"My pleasure. Sorry our hacking didn't prove more productive."

As he spoke, I noticed the computer monitor behind him, where Paul's medical history was still displayed. Peering closer, I asked, "What's that, highlighted in red?"

Glenn looked over his shoulder at it. "Just allergies," he explained. "Penicillin, fragrances, cats—nothing life-threatening, I should think."

I nodded, recalling that Paul was suffering from allergies when I picked him up at the airport on Saturday morning. I told Glenn, "Don't forget hay fever. Paul is allergic to pollen."

Glenn glanced at the screen again, then logged off. Smugly, he told me, "I think you're mistaken."

Just as smugly, I told the computer genius, "I think your files need updating."

And with a wink of farewell, I left his office, hungry for lunch.

11

Tuesday morning I awoke with a start, feeling anxious and tense. It was not the murder that had nettled my sleeping brain. I had not been vexed by dreams of my mother or by overnight fantasies of a sandy-haired mechanic. Nor did I feel any restless urgency to organize my files, plan my classes, or tweak the acoustics of my theater. No, the root of my discomfiture was Oralia Alvarez. I needed a housekeeper, and Oralia was scheduled to visit my condo at eight that morning. In most job interviews, the employer evaluates the potential employee, but this morning the tables would be turned. I was to be evaluated, my home was to be scrutinized, my entire "situation" was to be assessed by the woman who I hoped would deign to become my cleaning lady.

Coffee didn't help. The first sip brought a knot to my stomach. By the second sip, the knot had discharged something acidic. So I didn't even bother with my ritual of the morning paper on the bedroom terrace. As the sky began to brighten beyond the kitchen window, my shaky hand set the full mug of coffee in the sink. Clad in only a red silk bathrobe, I grabbed a dust cloth and a bottle of Windex, then undertook a manic burst of housekeeping.

By the time I'd hosed the front terrace, dusted the blinds, and made the bed, there were but a few minutes remaining to put *myself* together. After a quick shower, a touch of makeup, and a futile attempt to do something with my hair, I jumped into khakis, blouse, and a pair of thongs—just in time to catch my breath and hear the knock.

"Coming," I lilted pleasantly while flip-flopping down the half-flight of stairs from the bedroom to answer the front door. It was precisely eight o'clock.

"Good morning, Miss Gray." Oralia stood primly on the doormat, hands folded at her waist, as if I'd interrupted a moment of prayer.

"Good morning, Oralia," I replied properly. "So good of you to drop by this morning. Do come in."

She allowed a polite but noneffusive smile while stepping into the little foyer. I noticed that she wore the same style of green uniform-blouse that she'd worn to the Huron house on Sunday; presumably, she was on her way to some other cleaning job this morning.

While I blathered about the diminutive size of the place and assured her that I would be cooking very little, entertaining even less, she glanced about, sizing things up, giving no clue as to what she thought. "It's just a matter of light housekeeping—that and a bit of laundry. I won't even *ask* if you do windows."

Instinctively, her eye had been drawn to the kitchen, and when I paused for a breath during my monologue, she asked, "May I?"

"Of *course.*" My permission for her to enter the kitchen was a needless formality, as she had already stepped past me to begin her inspection.

As if riveted to a radio distress signal, she beelined to the sink, found the cold mug of coffee I'd oafishly left there, and dumped it down the drain. Frozen with fear, I watched as she rinsed the drain, rinsed the cup, and set it on the counter. My heart was sinking fast—one stupid mistake! I was prepared for a stern lecture, when she asked, "Can I make you a fresh pot?"

I paused to breathe again. "If you'll have some with me."

"Thank you, Miss Gray. I would like that."

Before long, we were chatting comfortably, sharing a good pot of coffee—better than mine, in fact, which was a neat trick on her part, considering that she had nothing to work with other than my beans, my coffeemaker, and my tap water. Cup in hand, I gave her the not-so-grand tour, showing her through my little home, which she claimed to find "very pretty."

"It still needs some fixing up, I'm afraid. I'm not quite settled yet."

"All in good time, Miss Gray. *Paciencia.*"

We both agreed that the terrace off the upstairs bedroom was the condo's most appealing feature. I suggested that we sit at the table there to finish our coffee and "talk business."

The warm morning sun felt wonderful, and I shifted the angle of my chair to face it squarely. A mockingbird perched on a chimney across the courtyard, practicing his drill; unseen mourning doves doo-wopped a soulful backup. Oralia and I listened for a few moments without speaking, enjoying the impromptu recital.

I was ready to hire the woman, and her easy manner told me that she was ready to accept. I reminded myself, though, that Larry Knoll still considered her a potential suspect in Jodie's death. If Paul's theory was correct that Jodie had died as the unfortunate consequence of a bungled burglary, then Oralia could indeed be deemed suspicious, since there was some doubt about the timing of her alibi at the Warhaniks' house in Indian Wells. Still, I was satisfied that Paul clung to this theory only because it allowed him to deny that his marriage had been less than perfect. I was beginning to understand that Jodie was a woman of complex character and shifting emotions who also had a wandering eye. The chain of events that led to Jodie's death, I was increasingly convinced, had nothing whatever to do with her housekeeper.

"So then, Oralia"—I set my cup on the table, breaking the lull— "what do you think? Would you like to work for me?" I smiled sweetly, expectantly.

"I think I would like very much to clean for you, Miss Gray."

"Marvelous! Then—"

"But I cannot. At least not now."

I took a moment to clear my head. "But . . . why not?"

She blinked, as if the explanation were self-evident. "My other jobs."

"You mean, you're . . . *overbooked?*"

With a soft laugh, she explained, "Not now, Miss Gray, but if I took you on, I *would* be."

Hm. She was clearly in high demand. "If it's a matter of money—"

"No, Miss Gray. It is a matter of time." She put a finger to her temple, recalling her schedule, "I clean for Mr. Huron on Tuesday and Thursday afternoons. Now that the Warhaniks have returned, they will need me on Monday and Friday mornings. Then, on Wednesdays . . ." The list went on and on. The bottom line? I was screwed.

Unless . . .

I asked, "With Mr. Huron alone now, do you think he'll still need you *two* afternoons each week?"

She shook her head sadly. "If anything, he will need more help, not less."

"Then why," I asked with a measure of exasperation, "did you bother coming over here this morning?"

She gave a consoling grin. "Cleaning jobs come and go. You will be first on my waiting list, Miss Gray. It should not be long. Till then, you can get by." With a nod of approval, she added, "You do keep a *clean* house." Good thing she hadn't arrived an hour earlier.

"Thank you." I let it go at that, thinking it prudent not to disillusion her. Judging our meeting at least half successful, I decided not to stretch my luck by pressing for an estimate of her expected availability. Dropping the topic of her employment, I turned to the *other* topic, the one that had not been broached since her arrival: "Jodie's murder has been a terrible shock to everyone who knew her. It was kind of you to help out at the house on Sunday."

Oralia hung her head. "Miss Jodie was a wonderful woman. I cannot think who would do such a terrible thing."

I stood, needing to stretch. Stepping to the edge of the terrace, I said vacantly, "Paul seems to think it was a thief who did it." I placed my hands on the wrought-iron railing and gazed at the mountains beyond the valley.

"Mr. Huron must deal with his own sadness." Oralia's voice was thin but firm. I turned back to her as she continued, "He will think what he must. But I do not think it was a thief who did this."

With arched brows, I paused to weigh her words, then told her, "Neither do I."

"Oh?" She did not look at me.

Crossing to her chair, I said from behind, "Well, it just doesn't add up, does it? If this thief broke into the Hurons' because he thought the house was empty, then discovered Jodie was there, then killed her, why would he end up stealing, of all things, the wedding ring off her finger? It sounds sick. Sort of deranged. But it does *not* sound like robbery."

Oralia gently shook her head in agreement, but still did not turn to look at me. She balled her hands, wringing them in her lap. Her voice was thin but firm again when she said, "I think Miss Jodie had a visitor."

Ahaaa. I thought so. Larry Knoll thought so. Even Tanner Griffin, who seemed barely to know Jodie, had gotten the impression that she was involved with someone other than her husband. And now her own housekeeper, who was doubtless acquainted with all manner of dirty laundry (both real and figurative), had drawn the conclusion that Jodie had had a "visitor."

I asked, "By 'visitor,' Oralia, do you mean . . . 'boyfriend'?" My word choice was almost as euphemistic as hers, but I didn't know the limits of her sensibilities.

She turned and looked me in the eye. "I think Miss Jodie had a lover."

Now that we were in sync linguistically as well as theoretically, I asked, "Why didn't you tell the police that?"

She stood. "They did not ask me."

"But they did ask where you were at the time of the murder. Don't you understand? You were under suspicion."

"I was *at* the Warhaniks' house—I had nothing to hide, nothing to fear."

There was no reason to mention that Larry Knoll had not yet been able to verify her alibi for the exact time frame of the murder. If she was feeling calmly innocent and cleared of suspicion, why instill jitters that would serve no purpose other than to give her the appearance of guilt? So instead of grilling her about what had not been said to the police, I decided to take a more positive approach: "Why do you think Jodie had a lover?"

She hesitated. "They fought, Miss Gray."

"Who, Oralia?" I walked her to the railing, repeating softly, "Who fought? Jodie and who?"

She looked blankly across the tile rooftops, quietly telling the sky, "Miss Jodie and Mr. Huron sometimes fought."

"You mean . . . he hit her?"

"No, no, no." She quickly turned back to me, jiggling her raised hands. "It was not like that, Miss Gray. They fought sometimes with words. They argued."

"About other men?"

She shook her head with a sad smile. "Nothing that direct. It was complicated. Little things. Many little things. Miss Jodie was a wonderful person—she was always good to me—but she was not happy."

That fit. Jodie had been clinically depressed. "Was Paul happy?"

Oralia had to think before answering, "He was more happy than she was."

This painted a picture of a relationship altogether different from the "perfect marriage" Paul had described. I asked Oralia, "If they never argued about other men in Jodie's life, why do you think she was involved with someone?"

She hesitated. "I never saw Miss Jodie with another man, but sometimes she was home during the day while I was there, and I heard her talking on the telephone. Two or three times, I think. Do not get me wrong, Miss Gray—I was not *trying* to listen. Miss Jodie did not seem to care that I was there. She laughed with this man and sounded happy. And once I heard her make plans to meet him."

"Are you sure it was a man? Did she address him by name?"

Oralia thought for a moment. "I cannot recall if she said his name, but from the sound of her voice, she was talking to a *man.*" She lifted her fingers to her lips, as if she had spoken an indelicacy.

I suggested, "Maybe she was speaking to Paul."

She shook her head decisively. "She mentioned Mr. Huron to the other man on the phone."

"Oralia"—I faced her squarely, placing a hand on her shoulder—"you really must tell this to Detective Knoll. If you don't, I'll have to."

"You may tell him what you wish." Her voice was resolute, yet carried no hint of uppishness. "But I cannot."

Her intention to keep this information from the police had me baffled. As a witness to the Hurons' marital problems, she could help focus the investigation and steer it in a productive direction, away from herself. My perplexity must have registered on my face.

She explained, "Miss Gray, I did not grow up in this country. I am now a citizen, I work hard, I have never been on welfare, and I pay my taxes. I do not fear the law—it is meant to protect us all—but still, I prefer to keep my distance from the police. I may be wrong, but I think it is better if I do not get involved."

"But your story could help solve a murder."

"And it would put both Miss Jodie and Mr. Huron in a bad light. They do not deserve that from me. I have worked for them. When I am paid to be in someone's home, I am like a priest in the confessional. Though I hear many things—" She mimed zipping her lip.

I must admit, her scruples appealed to me, especially since I hoped the day would soon come when she'd have a key to my condo—and ready access to my drawers and closets.

"Besides, I think it would be better for the detective to hear these things from Mr. Huron." Her tone of voice had lightened, and though I may have imagined it, her dark eyes seemed to twinkle.

I was about to tell her, But Paul's in a state of heavy denial.

She continued, "That is why I gave to Mr. Huron the cuff link."

In the silence that followed, she raised a brow, as if to ask, Get it?

I must have been dense. "You mean Paul's cuff link, the one you found while cleaning the bedroom on Sunday? You gave it to him while I was there."

"That is the cuff link, Miss Gray, but it did not belong to Mr. Huron."

Wide-eyed, I whispered, "You mean? . . ."

She nodded. "It was the cuff link of Miss Jodie's visitor."

"How can you be sure?"

"Mr. Huron wears no cuff links; he *has* no cuff links. I would know. I have seen everything, I have cleaned everything in their house." With a little laugh, she added, "Miss *Jodie* wore no cuff links, so it must have belonged to the visitor."

I nodded, enlightened. Her logic seemed rock solid, as far as it went. But I was still confused. "Then why did you give it to Paul?"

"So that he would *know*. I did not want to tell him about Jodie's visitor, and I did not need to—the cuff link told the whole story. Now it is up to Mr. Huron to tell the detective."

Shaking my head, I thought aloud, "He'll never do that. Paul can't admit to himself, much less to the police, that his marriage was rocky. If anything, now that he has tangible proof that Jodie had been unfaithful, he may slip into even deeper denial—perhaps he already has. And that's just not healthy. I'm worried about him."

Oralia breathed an uneasy sigh. "Then I will watch him carefully this afternoon when I go to the house to clean. Maybe he will want to talk."

"I doubt if he'll be home this afternoon. Classes start next week, and he's been busy setting up at the college. I'll probably see him before you do."

"Ah." She nodded. "You can try to look after him, then?"

I smiled. "Yes, I can try."

Though my meeting with Oralia that morning hadn't netted me a housekeeper, at least not yet, our chat had been plenty productive. There was now ample reason to believe that a man other than Paul had shared Jodie's bed, and my crime-of-passion theory seemed more and more solid. Still, I was no closer to identifying Jodie's lover/killer than I had been on Saturday, when my suspicions were first aroused. Needing to let these new morsels of information digest for a while, I sensed that Oralia and I had talked enough business.

"More coffee?" I suggested. Our cups sat on the table, cold and empty.

Oralia checked her watch. "Thank you, Miss Gray, but I must go. I am due at a house in Rancho Mirage at nine, and it is getting late."

"God," I said, checking my own watch, "I nearly forgot. I told Paul that I'd swing past his house this morning and give him a ride to campus." The previous afternoon, he'd heard from Tanner Griffin at Desert Detail, who arranged to deliver the blue Honda to Paul at the college today. Since I'd already offered to assist Paul with the car jockeying, he asked me to give him a ride that morning.

Oralia cleared the table of our coffee things, offering, "Let me rinse these, then we can both be on our way."

I helped, of course, but did not decline her offer, taking it as a sign that she was earnest in her intent to find a slot for me in her work schedule. Within a few minutes, the terrace was tidied and locked, the coffeemaker was clean, the cups were stowed in the dishwasher, and the kitchen was spotless.

After kicking off my thongs and slipping on a decent pair of shoes, I grabbed my keys, telling her, "I'll walk you out." And together we left through the front door.

In the tiled courtyard, near the center fountain, I thanked her for coming over, and we said our good-byes. She left through the gate to the street, where she had parked, and I turned in the direction of my garage.

"Morning, doll," a voice lilted from behind me.

Turning, I broke into a smile. "Morning, Grant. Bit early for *you,* isn't it?" He generally left for his office an hour later, around ten.

"Busy day ahead—that 'urgent business' for Arlene Harris." He winked, then laughed. "And you? How's milady's sleuthing biz?"

"As a matter of fact . . ." And I filled him in on Oralia's visit, culminating with the enticing detail of the cuff link.

"Well, now," he said, having listened to my whole narrative in silence, fingers to chin, "there must be something in the air—an infidelity bug."

"Oh?"

"Yes, indeed. You'll recall that Arlene Harris was trying to reach me all weekend. I met with her yesterday and got an earload. It turns out, her husband, Henry—who's pushing seventy, mind you, and recently recovered from major surgery—has been having an affair. Arlene is livid, of course, and they're separating. Divorce, apparently, would be unwise. In any event, Arlene wants a new home—a big one—and fast."

I shook my head, bemused by the tribulations of the wealthy. "Grant Knoll to the rescue?"

"That's right, doll. Gotta run."

And he did.

12

Around eleven that morning, at the desk in my office at Desert Arts College, I took off my reading glasses, set them down, and rubbed the bridge of my nose. I'd spent a couple of productive hours sorting files and preparing for next week's first classes, deciding that those clerical tasks were more crucial than sprucing up the room's nude walls, one of which was curved (due to the circular hallway), presenting an impossible challenge. Besides, I figured, if I finished the paperwork in short order, I'd be able to leave; then my bleak work cell wouldn't bother me in the least.

The paper pushing, however, took longer than I'd gauged and was far from complete, so escape was not yet in the cards. Not only my eyes but my whole body felt tired, which I attributed to my salvo of early-morning housekeeping, intended to impress my prospective cleaning lady. Now I was slumping, in dire need of another cup of coffee, the one that had been flushed down the drain back at my condo.

Then a thought brightened my disposition. If I recalled correctly from yesterday, during my dizzying exploration of the building's circuitous halls, there was a coffee room, a staff lounge of sorts, just a few doors away. Perfect. I was due for a break anyway, so I rose from the desk, stretched, stepped into the hall, and hesitated, deciding to try the clockwise route.

Before I had wandered far, I realized that I was outside of Paul Huron's office. His door was open, and he was talking on the phone. Though it was not apparent what he was discussing or with whom, his tone was clearly upbeat, even jocular, which made me curious enough to pause at the doorway. After all, the man's wife had been murdered only three days prior. Two days ago, he had learned indirectly from his housekeeper that Jodie had cuckolded him with someone who wore diamond-studded cuff links. The night before, he had spent his first night alone in the very house where both the transgression and the murder had occurred. And then that very morning, when I had picked him up and driven him to campus, he had been in a glum mood, complaining, "The police have done *nothing* yet—not a damn thing— to identify the thief who killed poor Jodie."

Now he was laughing and animated. I had little choice but to eavesdrop. Besides, the door was wide open—his voluble conversation was hardly meant to be secretive.

Paul gabbed into the phone, "And *there* they were, right where I'd left them, naturally." He was sitting at his desk with his back to me. A few empty packing cartons were stacked near the door, but one, half-full, was there at his feet. Fanned out before him on the desk were four or five eight-by-ten glossy photos. I couldn't see them clearly from where I stood, but I now understood that he'd located the pictures of the ring he'd commissioned for Jodie, the ring that was now missing. "That's right, Detective. One of the shots shows it from just the right angle—anyone would recognize the ring if they saw it." Listening, Paul then reached across the desk for a notepad, and as he did so, he noticed me in the doorway. Smiling, he waved me in with a broad gesture.

"Success?" I asked quietly, returning his smile.

He nodded, handing me one of the glossies. Then he grabbed a ballpoint pen and jotted a few notes, presumably from Larry Knoll.

Studying the photo at arm's length (my glasses were still on my desk), I marveled at the unique piece of jewelry I'd seen only once—on Jodie's finger, the Wednesday before at Glenn Yeats's party. Two pearls, one black, the other white, topped two interlocking rings, both of which were intricately sculpted in the form of sensual, abstract figures who leaned over backward with impossible agility, linking their hands to their toes. In the much bigger-than-life enlargement, one of the figures was clearly male, the other female. Did they represent Paul and Jodie, I wondered? Surely they did. The male ring was topped with the black pearl, suggestive of Paul's dark hair; the white pearl atop the female ring could be seen as Jodie's blond hair. The concept was marvelously poetic, its execution masterful. And for the first time, I understood the depth of Paul's consternation. It wasn't just his slain wife's wedding ring that was missing. It was art.

Paul said into the phone, "Thanks, Larry. That's awfully good of you. I'll put the photo in an envelope with your name on it and leave it with the receptionist in the front office." He listened for a moment, replying, "I hope so too. Thanks so much." Then they said their good-byes, and Paul hung up.

"*There*, now," I echoed his cheery tone, hoping to bolster it, "things seem to be looking up. The elusive photos have surfaced, eh?" Obviously—there they were—but I was inviting him to brag some about finding them.

He tossed his hands, letting them drop in his lap. "Haste does indeed make waste. That was one of the first boxes I searched—I *thought* that's where they were—but I was in such a state, such a rush, I didn't find them on the first pass, and I didn't check again till I'd been through everything *else*. Ugh!" His grunt of disgust also carried a happy note of relief.

"Better late than never," I told him, setting the photo back on the desk. "So Larry's sending someone over to pick it up?"

"He said he'd come get it *himself*, and his office is way out in Riverside. I told him I'd be happy to drive it out to him, but he wanted to save me the trouble." Paul stood. "You know, that Larry Knoll is really a decent guy."

"Yes, I *do* know," I assured him with a laugh. "Larry's the best on the force, Paul, and despite what you may have thought, he's been hard at work behind the scenes, mounting an aggressive investigation. He cares."

"I know that," Paul said softly with a contrite bob of his head. "It's just so easy to get self-absorbed at a time like this—to play the victim, to demand sympathy and attention. But *Jodie* was the victim."

Mention of his murdered wife sobered Paul's mood, and I feared he might funk, donning again his cloak of denial, railing that his imaginary thief must be brought to justice.

"Excuse me? Mr. Huron?"

Both Paul and I turned toward the voice in the doorway. The unexpected sight of Tanner Griffin standing there made my jaw sag. My God, what an attractive man. He wore cool, baggy olive-drab shorts, as on the day before, but his T-shirt had been replaced with a dressier polo shirt in pale yellow, which seemed to glow against the desert tan of his skin. Somehow, the polo showed off his torso even better than the T-shirt had; I unabashedly stared at him, drinking in the sight as if mesmerized. And that hair, that thick, sandy hair—*anyone* would be tempted to touch it, to run ten fingers through it, just as—

"Yes?" said Paul, interrupting my fugacious fantasy, one that should have made me blush, but didn't.

Realizing that Paul and Tanner had not yet met, I seized my cue and did my duty. "Good morning, Tanner," I said brightly, trying not to sound giddy, "what a nice surprise. Yes, this is Paul Huron." Turning to Paul, I told him, "This is Tanner Griffin, from Desert Detail."

"Ah. Of course," said Paul. He began to tell Tanner, "Thanks for—"

Tanner stepped forward, cutting him off, shaking his hand. "I'm so sorry, Paul, about Jodie—about everything. I couldn't believe it."

Paul nodded, accepting the condolences with a wan smile. "I can barely believe it myself. It doesn't seem possible that she's really gone. I keep thinking that it's a bad dream, that I just woke up. Then I imagine that Jodie's working at the medical center, that she'll be back home tonight." Paul's words were getting too wistful for comfort—I recalled the ebb and flow of his crying jags on Saturday. Fortunately Paul, too, seemed to realize that his mood was verging near the edge, and he snapped out of it, telling Tanner, "I'm glad you had the chance to meet Jodie. She spoke highly of you."

"She was a lovely woman. I can appreciate your loss."

While they exchanged predictable tributes and platitudes, I pondered Paul's statement that Jodie had spoken highly of Tanner. The previous afternoon, Paul had told me that she'd never mentioned him. Was Paul now merely being polite in complimenting a stranger? Or was he now beginning to surface from his miasma of denial. Perhaps Jodie had indeed mentioned Tanner, making one too many references to her "marvelous mechanic." Perhaps, even as Tanner spoke, Paul was eyeing his work clothes, wondering if the guy ever wore cuff links.

". . . so the Honda's out in the parking lot," Tanner was saying as he placed a folder of papers on the desk, opening it, "and now that we've repainted, it's looking good as new." With a quiet laugh, he added, "Better."

Paul shook his head, staring at the pile of insurance forms, receipts, and faxes. "Who'd think such a minor fender bender could get so involved."

"You should see a *complicated* job." Then Tanner asked Paul to sign an acknowledgment that the repairs were completed as ordered.

Paul scribed his arty signature, grinning. "As you know, I haven't even *seen* the car yet."

Tanner handed him the keys. "When you drive me back to the shop, I'll make sure you're completely satisfied. If you find any problem whatever, we'll start over."

"I'm sure it's fine." Paul signed several other forms. "Oh," he said, thinking of something, "I hope you're not in a big hurry to get back to the Springs. I have to pull a few things together for the police before I leave, and I need to okay a delivery of AV equipment down in the receiving department. I shouldn't need more than a few minutes."

"Take your time." Tanner divvied up the paperwork, leaving some for Paul, keeping most of it in the manila folder, which he flipped shut and lifted from the desk. "Actually, I was hoping I might get a look at the place."

Again, I seized my cue: "I'd be happy to show you around. Besides, I need to talk to you about my Beetle."

"Oh, *yeah*," said Tanner, eyeing me askance. "What's up, Miss Gray?"

Tanner still had no idea that the ostensible purpose of my visit to the body shop on Monday morning was to have my car windows tinted, but I'd later reported to Paul that we'd already discussed it. Whisking Tanner toward the door, I said, "Let's go to my office." As we stepped into the hall together, I turned to tell Paul, "We'll check back in a while."

Paul waved us off. "Give him the Cook's tour. Enjoy." The first sentence was directed to me, the latter to Tanner, but I had an inkling that I'd enjoy our excursion as much as he would.

Walking the curved hall with me, Tanner said, "I had a heck of a time finding Paul's office. The whole layout's sort of disorienting."

"Tell me," I agreed. "Here we are—I think." And I led him into my office, apologizing, "I'm not quite settled in yet."

Tanner surveyed the sterile room. "Well, at least it's new—and clean."

"Have a seat," I offered as I sat, gesturing toward a stiff little chair next to the desk. Donning my glasses, I attempted to do some quick sorting of the papers that littered my blotter, making two stacks, to-do and done. I was distracted, though, by the sight of Tanner as he tried to get comfortable in the side chair, first crossing his bare legs, then uncrossing them, planting both feet on the floor, knees parted. He set his folder at the edge of the desk, then rested an arm there. Its fine nap of sun-bleached hair gleamed warm and golden, even in the cold glare of the room's fluorescent light.

"So, Miss Gray, what can I do for you? I mean, the Beetle."

I sat back, removing my glasses, looking professorial. "First, Tanner, you can stop calling me Miss Gray." With a smile, I added, "Please, it's Claire."

His eyes bugged. "Really?" Then he smiled (God, that smile). "I'm honored—*Claire*. Thank you."

"The pleasure's mine," I assured him. Then I explained, "I didn't mean to seem so . . . *mysterious* about the car. I simply want to have its windows tinted." Sitting forward again, I replaced my glasses and sorted through the last of the stray papers on my desk, completing the two piles.

"Sure," said Tanner, "that's a good idea, especially out here in the desert, especially with all the glass on that car. I'd be happy to handle it for you. You have several options regarding . . ." And he began a discourse on black versus silver, film versus dyes, degree of tint, and so on. "Make the wrong choices"—he laughed—"and you end up looking like a drug dealer."

As he spoke, my eye wandered to an open carton near my chair containing an odd assortment of desk appurtenances that I'd hurriedly packed when leaving New York. I took out a stapler, a tape dispenser, an old paperweight, a bundle of pens and pencils secured by a thick rubber band, and a small covered box containing paper clips, erasers, dried-out ink cartridges, and several decades' worth of grit. Sorting and arranging this miscellany on my desk, I noticed that the spherical blue-glass paperweight was badly smudged from careless handling and hasty packing. Taking a long shred of tissue from the cardboard carton, I used it to polish the paperweight, restoring its lenslike luster. Satisfied, I plopped it atop my stack of finished paperwork, which sat at the end of the desk near Tanner. Then I wadded the tissue and tossed it back into the carton.

"Hey, that's a pretty one," said Tanner of the paperweight, interrupting his dialectic on the variables of window tinting. "May I?" He reached to pick it up.

I shrugged. "Be my guest."

"Cobalt," he said, holding the bauble to the light, peering deep within it as if it havened secrets. "I love that color—so pure and elemental."

"Sometimes at twilight, here in the desert, the sky turns that color. But it lasts only a moment."

He smiled, nodding, then returned the blue globe to the stack of papers. As his hand left the glass orb, I noticed that its slick surface had been smudged by his fingertips. Though tempted to grab another sheet of tissue and restore the pristine shine—like some withered fortune-teller doting over her crystal ball—I decided to forgo this obsessive impulse, at least until later, when I wouldn't appear to be cleaning up after him.

"I'll put together a packet of information, with options and prices," he said.

I blinked, then realized the topic had shifted back to window tinting. "That's very thoughtful, but can't I just leave it up to you? You're the pro."

He laughed softly. "And you're the customer. I'd prefer to leave the choices up to you. If I could have your address, I'll pop something in the mail to you later today. Or would you prefer that I send it here to your office?"

Hm. This extraordinarily fetching young man had just asked for my address, then backed off, sensing that he might have sounded forward. Or was I imagining these dynamics—*wanting* to imagine this interplay?

Get real, I told myself. He was merely being accommodating, exactly as Jodie had said. "It doesn't matter," I told him with easy indifference. "Just send it to my home." And I gave him the address at Villa Paseo. He jotted the information on the back of one of his business cards, which he then returned to his wallet.

"There, now," I said, standing, "we've done our business. If you'd care for a quick tour of the college, I could take you around campus and point out a few highlights, assuming we can find our way out of these offices."

He stood with me. "That would be great, Claire. What I'd *really* like to see, though, is the theater. Any chance?"

I winked at him. "You're in luck. They're installing the tech systems, and I haven't checked in yet today." I jerked my head. "Come on."

Without further conversation, Tanner followed as I led him from my office through the circular hall and out to the plaza of College Circle. Crossing the pavement in the noontide sun, we passed the pools and fountains, approaching the soaring, curved structure of my theater, stepping within its shadow. Our pace slowed as I checked for my key. We stopped at the center door, which I unlocked and heaved open with a whoosh of the dark, cool, quiet air within. We entered the space reverently. The sensation was identical to what I had once felt upon entering a church, back in the days when I still believed.

We paused in the lobby, Tanner at my side, and I knew with certainty that he too felt the awe that was owed this holy place.

These thoughts were far from sacrilegious; they were, in fact, religious.

My bone-deep love of theater has derived from a lifetime's study of its history, its rituals, its taboos, its icons, and its inspired texts. The theatrical tradition stretches back as far as any religion, and indeed, all religions have borrowed heavily from theater's artifice in casting their spells upon minds that are willing to suspend disbelief. It's no accident that churches and theaters bear such an uncanny resemblance. Still, after all these millennia, only theater survives for its own sake, not for the propagation of one god's dogma over another's. Why? At the root of theater's power is its intrinsic *creative* force. Within theater, as in literature and all the arts, resides the spark to create new realities, to mold our perception of the world, and to redefine our very humanity. These same claims may be made by Bible-thumping yahoos, serpent handlers, mystics, or priests, but they are all, to a man, either beguiling or beguiled.

Thoughts such as these leave me cowed by theater's majesty every time I enter a playhouse—and we had not yet crossed the lobby. I told Tanner, "Wait till you see the auditorium."

He answered with a silent look of anticipation that told me, yes, he *belonged* here. I'd never seen him act, I'd never even heard him read a line, but I knew that look, I knew that mood, and I knew that his life would be lacking if he forever sublimated his passion for theater to the more practical goals envisioned by his parents. "You're twenty-six years old," I told him, halting at the double doors to the auditorium, placing my hand over the crack that separated them, barring entry.

He laughed uncertainly at my non sequitur. "What, Claire?"

As if speaking in riddles, I asked, "Isn't it time we all grew up?"

His soft smile conveyed that he understood my admonishment—he was old enough to think for himself and to choose his own destiny. He could not have fathomed, though, that I was chiding myself as well, that I still chafed at the expectations of others, particularly Gwyn. He touched the door handle and gave the slightest tug, asking quietly, "Let me in?"

My hand still guarded the sanctuary, and my thoughts were lost in issues of my past. Tanner stared at me with an odd expression, doubtless wondering what was wrong with me. Snapping back to the moment, I lowered my hand, swung the door open with a grand flourish, and together we entered.

I saw at a glance that progress had been swift since Monday. The glare of bare-bulbed work lights on the stage had been replaced by a full array of lighting instruments; someone in the control booth now ran tests of circuits, flashing banks of lights in sequence, checking the speed of computer-controlled dimmers on each. Sound technicians up in the catwalks ran cables to hidden loudspeakers. Installation of the scenery lifts and hydraulics looked complete; a section of the stage magically lowered, disappearing in the deep pit space, then returned to its original position, blending seamlessly with the floor. There was so much to take in, I wondered which detail Tanner would focus on first.

"Red seats." He laughed his approval. "Now, *that's* theatrical."

"They're scarlet," I corrected him. "I love that color—so pure and elemental."

"Sometimes at twilight, here in the desert, the sky turns that color. But it lasts only a moment."

We had repeated each other's words, verbatim, from our earlier discussion of the cobalt paperweight. The message was clear: not only did Tanner have an ear for dialogue, but he had hung on my every word. And I had hung on his.

"Miss Gray?" called one of the workers, spotting me.

And within seconds, I was surrounded by crew foremen. Besieged by questions, I doled out answers like a monarch tossing coins.

Tanner watched in silence for a few minutes, amused by the pleasure I found in this merry confusion. Then he strolled down the aisle toward the stage, gazing at various aspects of this state-of-the-art performance space, soaking it all in. Finally he took a seat, first row, center. Slouching back, he lolled his head, eyes to the lights. I thought he might have tired—or simply gotten bored.

When the last of the technicians was fully informed and satisfied, I trotted down the aisle and joined Tanner in the front row of seats, sitting next to him. From behind, I had seen no movement and thought he might have fallen asleep. But no, his eyes were wide and alert. A smile turned his parted lips. His mind seemed to race with thoughts behind his face, behind those handsome but disarming features, at once so boyish and so manly.

I began to apologize, "I didn't mean to take so long with—"

"I have a confession," he said, sitting up and facing me with a grin, looking not the least bit penitent.

"Oh?" I mirrored his grin.

"The reason I offered to deliver Paul Huron's car to him here on campus is that I hoped to run into you."

"I'm glad you did." My voice sounded dry, so I coughed and swallowed.

"And I hoped you would show me the theater."

I laughed lamely. "Yet another wish come true."

He touched my wrist. "Claire, since talking to you yesterday, I haven't been able to get your question out of my mind. You asked if I'd ever considered going back to school, to study acting. I'm probably way out of my league, and it's nuts even to ask, but I'm wondering . . . well, I'm wondering if there's any possibility of my enrolling in your program here at DAC."

"Tanner, I—"

"Oh, God," he said, standing, pacing in front of me, thinking aloud, "I didn't mean to put you on the spot. I haven't acted in several years, so I have no real credentials, and with you here, the competition must be incredible. I've never studied acting, but have a degree in business, of all things. This is an undergrad school, and here I am, practically middle-aged, the manager of an auto-body shop. Then there's *tuition*—"

"Tanner." I stood, interrupting his self-effacing monologue. "If you're trying to sell me on this idea, you could use a few lessons."

He stopped pacing and hung his head with a feeble laugh.

"Listen," I told him, "if this is something you want to pursue, you should give it a try. Get an application rolling, and we'll see where it leads. Quite honestly, I think you could be useful to my program here. You've got 'leading man' written all over you, and being a few years older than the 'kids' in the program would be a plus for you, not a disadvantage. If it finally boils down to finances, I have plenty of sway in recommending scholarships. Glenn Yeats wants me to build a department *he* can be proud of, and he's given me the tools to do it. As for the whole rigmarole of applications and transcripts and deadlines and such—sorry, I'm a dunce, I'm new at this. But I'll look into it. Let's see what we can do."

He looked at me dumbstruck. "I . . . I can't believe this is happening."

In truth, neither could I. Though I'd planted the idea in his head on Monday morning, even then, I'd wondered what I was doing. Just now, he'd recited a list of convincing reasons why he should *not* enroll at DAC. And there I was, telling him just the opposite. What exactly were my motives in recruiting him? Had my objectivity been clouded by physical attraction? It was a disturbing notion, the thought that I was already plumping the pillows on the proverbial casting couch. If I were a woman of greater integrity, would I turn my back on him, sending him away—for his own good? Maybe. But that lofty reasoning didn't sway me in the least. The bottom line was, I found Tanner Griffin just too damn hot to let him walk away. I needed to sort out my thoughts and do some soul-searching. I was buying time.

"Can you order a set of your college transcripts?" I asked.

"I'll get right on it."

"And an acting résumé—got one?"

He repeated, "I'll get right on it."

"Good. Meanwhile, I'll find out what I can about the application procedure. Even though classes start next week, I assume it's not too late. Hell, if I want you in the program, you're in—but we need to do this by the book."

He reminded me, "I've, uh . . . never even auditioned for you."

I nodded. "In due time. Let me get the rest in order; then we'll set something up. I'll give you a call at the shop—soon."

"Great. Wow." He ran a hand through his hair, still dizzied by the turn of our conversation. Then he remembered, "Oh, you might have trouble reaching me tomorrow. On Wednesdays, I—"

"It won't be tomorrow," I told him, shaking my head. "The coroner's office is expected to release Jodie's body this afternoon. If all goes as planned, her memorial service will be held tomorrow."

"Ahhh." He slouched, hooking his thumbs through his belt, head bowed.

"I think it's going to be rough on everyone. It always is, when someone dies young."

Jodie's body was indeed released by the coroner's office shortly after noon on Tuesday. Paul had arranged with a local mortuary to pick up the autopsied corpse at the morgue in Riverside, cremate it, split the remains, and deliver them in two urns to Glenn Yeats's estate by mid-morning on Wednesday. Paul told me on the phone Tuesday night that when he had gotten word from the medical examiner that the body could be claimed, he had alerted Glenn, wondering if there would be sufficient time to proceed with the service as planned. Glenn assured Paul that everything was under control, that the Regal Palms catering service was on standby, and that his own secretary, Tide Arden, would spend the rest of the day notifying Jodie's friends and co-workers that the service would take place as scheduled, the next morning at eleven, poolside at Nirvana. "Besides," Glenn told Paul, "we should move this along—out of respect for Jodie, of course, and with an eye toward expediency. School opens next week."

So Wednesday morning, shortly before eleven, my silver Beetle joined the procession of cars that filed past the Nirvana gatehouse and chugged up the winding road to Glenn's home, perched above the arroyos of the granite cliffs. The weather was perfect, the setting spectacular; if not for our morose purpose that morning, it would have been a delightful excursion. Kiki rode with me, dressed for the occasion in black gloves and a big, floppy hat with mourning veil. She carried an oversize black straw purse. Combined with the hat, it made her look gigantic, and in fact, she had trouble getting into my car, rattling her bracelets as she made the tight squeeze. I chose not to wear black, finding it too grim, or red, which was too festive, settling upon a simple gray dress, knee-length and sleeveless. Knotted about my neck was a short silk scarf, rep-striped white and green—white for hope, green for rebirth—wishful thinking, perhaps, but appropriate to the sentiments of the day.

A crew of parking valets met us as we pulled into Glenn's courtyard. The amazonian Tide Arden, as ferocious-looking but delicate-tongued as ever, greeted guests, checking names against a list on her acid-pink acrylic clipboard. Indoors, Grant Knoll directed a crew of caterers, who fussed with the luncheon that would follow. Smartly uniformed waiters offered cocktails to the bereaved, escorting us through the house toward the terrace. Congregating there were Jodie's friends from the medical center, Paul's friends from the college, Paul himself with something like a coffee canister tucked under an arm, a few neighbors and acquaintances, and, watching from the shade of a palm at the far side of the pool, Detective Larry Knoll.

I realized nearly three days had passed since my Sunday night dinner with Larry, when he had invited my participation in his investigation, cautioning me, however, to stay in touch and not to embark on any forays of my own. Since then, I hadn't bothered to phone him, while I had indeed bothered to seek out the victim's auto mechanic and quiz the victim's housekeeper. From across the terrace, Larry eyed me with an accusing stare.

"Kiki," I said, nabbing my friend's sleeve, "could you get me a drink, dear? Grant's brother is standing over there, and—"

"The *law?*" she gushed.

"The same. I need to have a word with him." And I took my leave.

Pecking my way through the crowd, I marveled at the serene vista of sky, clouds, and mountains. It was a flawless desert-autumn day, warm and dry with a cooling breeze that would occasionally gust from the slopes and whorl across the mesa. In the distance, I could see the airport on the valley floor, a plane gliding low on its approach to the main runway. Seated between the swimming pool and the spa, a string quartet, plus harp (a harp quintet?), played something sprightly and baroque, hardly funereal, in fact rather fun. Standing just beyond the harpist was Larry Knoll, fingering a short, icy glass of something brown.

Sidling up to him, I asked, "Bourbon, Detective? Aren't you on duty?"

"It's diet Coke." He raised the fingers of his other hand to his lips and suppressed a belch. "Excuse me."

"Don't mention it. Any . . . uh, progress?"

He stared at me. "I might ask *you* the same. Are you keeping out of trouble?"

I laughed, tossing a shoulder. "I'm *here*. No bullet wounds, no—"

As he leaned close to me, I saw the glint of a polished leather holster beneath his jacket. "Claire, this is no joking matter. Someone, perhaps someone here today, is deadly serious."

"Sorry," I said, dropping my glib air of street savvy. "I *do* seem to forget that we're dealing with murder. I suppose I ought to be more grief-stricken—for Paul's sake, or at least out of respect for Jodie—but mainly I'm perplexed. There are so many pieces that don't seem to fit. I just can't make sense of it."

The detective allowed a smile. "You are *into* it, aren't you? Maybe you should've been a cop."

"Hm. Just last Saturday, your brother said the same thing."

"Despite outward appearances, we do think alike."

"Not *entirely* alike," I reminded Larry as Grant appeared through the open wall of the house, stopping an Adonis of a waiter to pouf the knot of his bow tie and square the shoulders of his tux. "So. Has the crime stopper in the family made any progress he can report to a nosy layman?"

He insisted, "You first. What have you been up to?"

"Well," I hawed, "I did drive out to the body shop where Jodie was having Paul's car repaired. She'd raved about a 'marvelous mechanic,' and I wondered if there was more to it than that."

"Was there?" Fortunately, Larry's curiosity outweighed his annoyance that I had pursued this angle on my own.

I shook my head. "He's a kid—well, he's twenty-six. There may have been a spark of interest between him and Jodie, but that's as far as it went, I'm sure." In truth, I could be sure of no such thing, but I wanted to believe it, and saying it seemed to make it more real.

"Who is he?"

"Tanner Griffin." I recited a few pertinent details about the body shop, showing Larry the business card. "In any event, he has no idea I drove out there to sound him out as a suspect. I'm having my car's windows tinted."

Larry gave me an approving nod. "Shrewd."

I smiled, not mentioning that I *needed* to have the windows tinted—it was hardly a ploy. "As it turns out, Mr. Griffin has an interest in theater and might make a good addition to my program at the new college." Saying this, I was reminded that Tanner was a self-described actor. Had I been too trusting in accepting him at face value? Was my confused infatuation the direct result of his own careful planning?

Larry set down his glass and scratched a note to himself. "I'll run a routine background check on him anyway. Now and then, something pops up."

I nodded knowingly, though I was ignorant of what background they'd check, and I felt certain there was nothing to pop up. Still, it would be good to know if there was something heinous lurking in Tanner's past, since I'd all but promised him tuition-free admission to my theater program.

"Anything else?" Responding to my quizzical look, Larry elaborated, "Have you been exploring any other angles?"

Sheepishly, I admitted, "I had a long talk with Oralia yesterday."

"Oh? I've had a development of my own on that front. It seems—"

"Claire, darling," said Kiki, whisking into our conversation, bearing two glasses, "the lad at the bar was an idiot. I asked for your kir, and he looked at me as if I'd just landed from Mars. I *tried* to explain, and I *think* he spoke English, but I have *no* idea what you ended up with." She handed me the glass.

"Thank you, Kiki. Have you met—?"

"Good *morning,* Detective," she interrupted, pivoting on her black patent heel, extending her hand to Larry. "Such a pleasure. Kiki Jasper-Plunkett, Claire's dearest—well, *oldest*—friend." She threw back her head and laughed, fluttering the gauze veil that hung from her wide-brimmed hat.

Larry dutifully shook her hand, introducing himself. "Can I presume investigation of Jodie's death?"

"She has. She's so excited. And I think it's so *cute:* Claire, a sidekick."

"Kiki"—I yanked her veil—*"*that's enough."

Laughing, Larry told her, "I must admit, your friend has brought a unique perspective to the investigation. And if you don't mind, we were about to discuss a recent development that—"

"Not *now,*" Kiki told him. "I think the service is about to begin. They're shooing everyone out from the bar."

She was right. The terrace had grown more crowded, and more quiet. The strings had stopped playing, but the harpist continued to diddle, as if filling time. Looking about for Paul, I didn't see him, and I then realized that I'd yet to see Glenn Yeats that morning. Guests gabbed and mingled, clumped around the pool or at the parapet, tisking the tragedy. Party dresses flapped in the fitful breeze. The dull roar of another plane approaching the airport brought to mind the same sound I'd heard at the faculty party a week ago, last Wednesday, when I'd met Jodie. Now we'd come to bury her—or whatever.

Leaning to Kiki, I lowered my voice to ask, "What do you suppose they're actually going to do with Jodie's ashes?"

She shrugged. "Beats me, love. But I overheard at the bar that Glenn himself will deliver the eulogy."

"You're kidding. He barely knew the woman."

She shrugged again. "That's what I heard."

Larry said, "If you'll excuse me, ladies, I need to circulate and keep my ears open." Leaning near me, he added, "After the service, let's sit down and compare notes on Oralia."

I nodded, and he left.

Across the swimming pool, in front of the low stone parapet that separated the edge of the terrace from the gullies below, stood a simple white pedestal of the Ionic order, perhaps three feet high. There was nothing atop the volutes of its capital; bunches of white lilies and orchids bracketed its fluted column symmetrically from the sides. A small gold-toned easel in front of the pedestal displayed a framed photo of Jodie. All of this was cordoned off from the rest of the terrace by a blue velvet rope hung from chrome stanchions.

Mourners instinctively began to gather near the rope and around the pool, facing the pedestal and the peaceful vista beyond. Kiki and I stood near the back of the crowd, nearer the house, sipping our cocktails—mine was indeed a mystery concoction, but I liked it, wondering if the formula might be wheedled from the bartender. Smells of our catered luncheon wafted from within the house, then drifted away on the breeze, causing my stomach to rumble.

Kiki nudged me, directing my glance to a side door, where Glenn Yeats and Paul Huron appeared together from within. Pausing while the string quartet revved up and joined the harp, Glenn and Paul then began their solemn walk across the terrace toward the festooned pedestal. It looked for all the world like a gay wedding, an image made all the more vivid by the two men's attire. Paul, true to his usual fashion, wore a simple, unstructured black suit and matching silk shirt, still carrying the canister under his arm. Glenn, by contrast, was all in white, wearing a linen suit and traditional dress shirt, French cuffed, sporting gorgeous, dazzling platinum cuff links. Wedged under one arm was a folded sheaf of papers, doubtless his prepared eulogy.

Bemused by this unlikely paring, certain they had no inkling of the impression they gave, I sipped more of my drink, chortling to myself, sniffing more food smells, getting hungrier by the minute. What, I wondered, were we having for lunch? Sorting through the aromas, I detected a wine sauce (that was easy) and orange (easier still). The palette of smells was underlaid by something heavy, rich, and cheesy (an Alfredo, perhaps?). Curiously, at the same time, it was overlaid by something spicy, pungent, and familiar.

My eyes bugged. My nostrils flared. I realized with a jolt that the spicy smell wasn't food. No, it was perfume, the same heavy perfume that had lingered at the crime scene when Paul and I found Jodie's body. Someone right there, near me, was wearing it.

"Kiki," I whispered urgently, "what's that smell?"

She turned. "What smell?" Some of the nearby bereaved shot us a disapproving look.

Grasping her elbow, I stepped her back a few feet from the crowd. "That perfume, that strong perfume." But even as I said it, the breeze picked up again, and I'd lost the scent.

She made a show of lifting her veil and sniffing the air. "Sorry, dear. I detect nothing but lunch. Which smells delightful, by the way." Her brows arched as she dropped the veil.

Paul stepped forward, placing Jodie's canned remains on top of the pedestal.

The music reached a delicate cadence, ending as Glenn joined Paul amid the profusion of flowers, clearing his throat.

I explained to Kiki, "On the morning Jodie was killed, I noticed the heavy smell of perfume in her bedroom, and just now, I smelled the same scent."

"*Lots* of people wear perfume," Kiki told me. "Maybe it was Jodie's."

"My friends," began Glenn, speaking to the whole crowd, "we gather today to pay tribute to a young woman cut down in her prime, within three months of moving cross-country to her new home in California. Jodie Katherine Metz-Huron was a loving wife to our friend Paul, and a skilled nurse as well, dedicated to . . ."

"No," I told Kiki, "Jodie didn't wear perfume. Last Saturday, I took a good look at her bedroom, her dressing table, and the bathroom. There were no perfume bottles. Then, on Monday morning, I learned from Glenn Yeats that Paul is allergic to fragrances, among other things. So it just makes *sense* that Jodie never wore perfume."

"So?" asked Kiki. "Do you mean to tell me there had been another woman in the bedroom with Jodie that morning?"

I mumbled, "I don't know," now truly confused.

"I first came to know Paul," Glenn was saying, "purely by reputation. At the Rhode Island School of Design, he established himself as a pre-eminent sculptor and educator, among a handful of the most talented and the best. I knew even then . . ."

I was flummoxed. If I'd smelled perfume in Jodie's bedroom, and Jodie wasn't wearing it, what *did* that mean? Had Oralia in fact been there that morning? Or had I been miles off base in my speculation about Jodie's clandestine lover?

"What did it smell like?" asked Kiki, more interested in this new riddle than in Glenn's eulogy, which, beyond the first sentence or two, had barely mentioned Jodie, focusing instead on Paul.

"It was a distinctive smell," I told Kiki. "That's why I noticed it—

it was strong, peculiar, yet familiar, one of those classic scents that's been around forever. It's pungent, like incense. In a way, it reminds me of marijuana."

She eyed me askance. "Are you sure it *wasn't?*"

"It was *not* marijuana, but it had that same heavy, piercing quality."

"How lovely," she cooed sarcastically.

"During these few short months," said Glenn, "we've come to know Paul not only as an esteemed artist but as a trusted friend and a valued co-worker. Thanks in large measure to his efforts, Desert Arts College will open its doors on schedule next week. Gathering today and sharing his loss, we can all prove our friendship to Paul by helping him get beyond this, by focusing on the work that lies ahead at the college. For in the everyday tribulations of work do we find the wellspring of strength that can . . ."

As he yammered on, I marveled at both his words and his sentiments, finding them grossly inappropriate. Pushing again for Paul to "get beyond this," was Glenn simply insensitive, or was he truly that driven and self-absorbed?

The wind shifted again, snapping my attention back to the mystery scent, which now wafted clearly from the knot of people standing in front of us. *"There,"* I told Kiki, tapping a finger to my nose. "There it is again. Surely you smell that."

She lifted her veil and screwed up her eyes, preparing to make a concerted effort of sniffing, but then she blinked, turned, and asked, *"That?"* She laughed. "Why, Claire, that's just patchouli—I'd know it anywhere." Her tone suggested that the smell was so distinctive, it shouldn't stump an eight-year-old.

"I've . . . *heard* of it," I admitted, "but I've never paid much attention to brands of perfume."

"It's not a brand, Claire. Patchouli is a classic generic scent made from an East Indian shrub. It's such a strong, heavy fragrance, it's long been favored by many men as well as women."

Aha. Then the "perfume" that had lingered at the crime scene did not necessarily complicate the puzzle with overtones of lesbianism. My other-man theory was still fully plausible, so long as the other man reeked like a hippie in a head shop. Scanning the backs of the mourners who stood assembled before us, I wondered if there was a redolent killer among them.

"Who's *wearing* that?" I asked Kiki while inching forward, the better to sniff.

She crouched, joining me in the hunt, but the jangle of her bracelets blew our cover. Heads turned, annoyed to find us lurking and appalled to catch us smelling. Besides, the fickle breeze had turned yet again, carrying a whiff of something more akin to pot roast than patchouli.

As there was no present hope of identifying the fragranced mourner, I returned my attention to the parapet, where Glenn had just finished speaking. He moved aside, and Paul stepped forward.

"Thank you, Glenn," said the widower in black silk, turning briefly to the billionaire in white linen, "your friendship and generosity are truly amazing." Then Paul faced the crowd. "Jodie was a loving woman, with virtues too numerous to list. Some of you knew her as a friend, others as a co-worker, others as a caregiver, and some as a casual acquaintance. But every life she touched was better for it—especially my own life, which she touched most closely." Paul paused to brush a tear from his cheek, and a wave of whimpering swept across the terrace.

When he'd composed himself, he continued, "Jodie had simple tastes. She wasn't a fancy dresser or a picky eater. Her goals were clear, her expectations high. She loved nature and had no patience for pretense or ceremony. That's why we decided on this simple memorial to her today—I'm sure she would have approved."

He stepped back, raising his hand and resting it on the canister that sat atop the pedestal. "As you all know, Jodie didn't grow up here. Her family's in Michigan, and I'll be traveling there next week with half of her ashes for a second memorial, one that I hope will . . ."

As he spoke, I noticed that Glenn could barely conceal his dismay. Classes would begin next week. Paul was greatly needed at the college, and here he was announcing plans to traipse off to Michigan for the needless repetition of an exercise that Glenn had already so efficiently dispatched. What's *wrong* with people? wondered Glenn, the thought plainly visible through his astonished gaze.

Paul continued, "Jodie was the classic 'free spirit.' " With a soft laugh, he added, "Anyone who knew her would agree with *that*. So it didn't seem right that she should be buried in a box, covered with earth." He tapped the canister. "And it doesn't seem right that she should rest in an urn on a mantel, like a genie trapped in a bottle. No, Jodie was a child of nature, and she should be free, free for eternity, returning to nature. Though she was new to the desert, new to these mountains, she quickly came to love this majestic setting. I can think of no greater tribute to Jodie than to let her ashes mix with the sands of the desert far below this terrace."

Uh-oh. Did he really intend to—?

"I ask you, then, to join me in a moment of solemn silence as I commit Jodie's remains to the crags of these granite slopes." As all watched, Paul lifted the canister from the pedestal, removed the metal lid, reached over the parapet, and slowly shook his wife's ashes into the jagged arroyos. "Rest in peace, my love."

The round of sobs and sniffles should have brought the service to a poignant close, but Jodie wasn't ready to rest in peace. She had barely left the canister when that pesky wind whirled up the gullies and took hold of her.

Before everyone's astonished eyes, her scattered ashes compressed into a dust devil, a four-foot funnel cloud of ashes and bone dust that rose up from behind the wall, tore through the flower arrangements, and skipped across the swimming pool, pausing to hula over the water for a moment before continuing across the terrace, parting the horrified crowd. With a collective gasp, punctuated by a scream or two and the crash of dropped glassware, the shaken mourners watched as Jodie's dervish circled a palm, then leaped the parapet, disappearing into the crags of an arroyo.

PART TWO

arroyos

Shaken by Jodie's tornadic exit, the crowd of mourners moved indoors to calm their nerves with liquor. Paul remained on the terrace by the parapet, first gazing into the canyons below, then turning to gather the lilies and orchids that had been scattered by the dusty whirlwind.

Kiki asked me, "Are you coming?"

"Maybe Paul could use some company. Go ahead, Kiki. I won't be long."

"Shall I get you another drink?"

"Why not? Same thing, please. Whatever it was, it wasn't bad."

"I'd be surprised if it can be duplicated, but we'll try." She drifted indoors.

Strolling around the pool, I stooped and gathered a few of the flowers that had been thrown farthest; several others floated on the water. Handing a bunch to Paul, keeping one of the lilies for idle sniffing, I told him, "For such a simple ceremony, it had quite a climax." I grinned.

He shook his head, chuckling softly. In spite of his grief, the comic undertones of Jodie's grand exit were all too evident. "That's Jodie for you. I wouldn't expect her to go quietly." He sat on the parapet, laying the flowers aside in a neat clump. "I'm glad I divided the ashes first; otherwise, I'd have lost them all." He explained, "The other canister is out in the car."

"Ah." I nodded, sitting next to him. "How did Jodie's family take the news?"

He stared at his knees. "They were devastated, of course. Parents never expect to outlive a child. Somehow, when they do, they feel . . . guilty. I'm not looking forward to that trip to Michigan next week."

Pointedly, I noted, "Neither is Glenn Yeats."

Paul turned to me. *"He's* not going." Then he understood. "Oh, yeah, I caught that. Glenn seemed a bit perturbed that I'd be leaving town during the first week of class."

I patted Paul's knee. "The timing is never 'right' for tragedy. It's beyond your control, so do what you must. Glenn will survive, and so will the school."

"Thanks, Claire." He talked about some college duties that had to be wrapped up prior to his trip, then began reminiscing about happier days with Jodie.

I listened quietly, but wasn't paying attention. My gaze had crossed the windy parapet and fallen down the craggy mountainside, peering into the arroyos, which seemed to harbor answers to the puzzles that had dominated my waking hours of the past week. The gulches and gullies seemed to mirror my shifting and eroding suspicions. The notion of a bungled burglary had been replaced by my crime-of-passion theory; Jodie's presumptive lover had shifted sexes from male to female and back again; I had varying degrees of suspicion for every man Jodie had come to know since moving to the desert, including Tanner Griffin, who had become yet another source of perplexed confusion.

Paul said, "Too early to tell, but the worst may be over. Today really helped."

I was tempted to ask, Today helped? In spite of Jodie's unscripted curtain call at her own funeral?

Instead, I agreed, "Ceremonies, rituals, they do seem to carry a sense of closure. They can help you get beyond—" I stopped myself, realizing I was about to quote Glenn's exhortation to "help Paul get beyond this."

Paul caught it. "Glenn does seem sort of eager to help me sweep this under the rug, doesn't he?"

Exactly, I thought. But I told Paul, "Glenn marches to a different drummer. I can't say I understand what makes him tick—I doubt if *anyone* does. Maybe that's the secret to his success."

"He's made billions," Paul acknowledged, "but he's known no success in love," referring to the tycoon's failed marriages. "I've one-upped him on that count." Paul smiled with quiet pride.

He was still deluding himself, apparently, with invented recollections of his perfect marriage. Though I felt he was overdue for a stiff dose of reality, this was not the time, in the moments following Jodie's funeral, to confront Paul with my suspicions of her infidelity. Instead, I stood. Dropping my lily on the pile with the others, I asked, "Do you have any plans for breakfast tomorrow?"

He stood as well. "I don't usually 'do' breakfast. And with Jodie gone . . ."

"Precisely—no point in brooding around the house alone tomorrow morning. Why don't you come over to my condo around eight? We can have coffee on the terrace by the pool, share some conversation, then head over to campus together for a productive day's work."

"Great." He flashed me a warm smile. "I'll be there."

At that moment, I noticed Glenn standing at the other end of the terrace, near the open wall of the house. He'd removed the jacket of his white suit, looking comfortable in his shirtsleeves. In one hand, he carried a buffet plate. With the index finger of his other hand, he wiggled a come-hither.

Not sure whether this gesture was directed to me or to Paul, I touched my chest, mouthing, Me?

Glenn nodded, smiling.

"Excuse me," I told Paul, adding under my breath, "bwana beckons."

"Thanks for your friendship, Claire. If I don't catch you later—breakfast at eight."

"At eight," I echoed, leaving him, crossing the terrace toward Glenn.

As I approached the open wall of the house, Glenn hoisted his plate, telling me, "Try the Alfredo. It's wonderful."

"It *smells* wonderful." I'd been smelling it all morning.

Most of the other guests had by now served themselves, so the buffet table was momentarily vacant. Glenn accompanied me as I prepared a plate, taking not only some pasta but salad as well, and a thick slice of rare tenderloin, dolloping it with two sauces, mustard- and wine-based. It was a heftier lunch than I'd normally indulge in, but hell, I'd done a funeral.

"Claire, dear," said Kiki, rustling forward, *"there* you are. Our friend"—she winked, meaning that she was referring to her bartender—"is serving wine now, so I managed to procure your kir." She tendered the glass triumphantly.

"Delightful," I said, taking it. Now, though, I was loaded up with a plate, cutlery, napkin, and wineglass. It was task enough to juggle it all; to eat or drink was impossible. Looking about, I saw that all the seats were occupied. Some guests sat on the floor.

Kiki told me, "I ate in the kitchen." She extracted a compact from her huge black purse and touched up her lips, holding the mirror under her veil.

Glenn laughed. "No need for that, ladies. Care to use my den? It's out of the way, so I'm sure it's not occupied."

"Thanks," I agreed readily.

"I've already finished," said Kiki. "Think I'll just mingle." And she mingled.

"This way then," Glenn told me, leading me through the crowd, past the decorative red wall, back toward the entry hall, where another short hallway led to a set of twin mahogany doors. They reminded me instantly of the doors outside his suite of offices on campus. He fished a key out of his pocket and unlocked one of the doors, swinging it open.

I walked inside and was swept by a sense of déjà vu. Not only did the room resemble his office at the college; it was, in fact, identical to it. There was no waiting room or secretary's desk, but his den here at home exactly replicated the inner sanctum of his office at the college. More precisely, the college office, having just been built, replicated the home office. Point is, they were the same in every respect, most notably the semicircular desk on a dais, backed by the curved travertine wall, inset with banks of computer monitors. A grouping of leather armchairs and matching sofa fronted the desk, just as in the other office.

"Make yourself at home," said Glenn, gesturing toward the chairs. Though his choice of words was cliché, he said them warmly, with the sincere ring of wanting to share his private space with me.

Thanking him, I sat in one of the buttery brown leather chairs. He offered to hold my glass and silver while I spread the big linen napkin over my lap, resting the plate on top of it. Once I was settled, he sat in the adjacent chair, and we began eating quietly. Everything was delicious—after all, the Regal Palms had catered, with Grant Knoll taskmastering. I told Glenn, "You're the perfect host."

"I have plenty of help," he said modestly, almost bashfully—a side of the man's personality I hadn't seen before.

As we continued to eat, our words were few and of little consequence. Finally, though, Glenn set aside his plate and asked with a grin, "Any progress on your caper?"

I returned the grin. "Nothing conclusive, of course, but there *have* been some developments. Why do you ask?"

He hedged, "Just curious." Then he added, "Just want to make sure you're keeping out of trouble."

"Don't be condescending," I told him flatly, meaning it.

He raised his hands. "Never. Not me."

"Are you aware that Larry Knoll, the sheriff's detective in charge of the case, is here today?"

He assured me, "I'm aware of *everyone* who's here today." Then he explained. "Paul pointed him out to me."

"It's eerie, isn't it, to think that Jodie's killer could be right here, among us, mingling with the bereaved."

Glenn crossed his arms. "Somehow, that seems implausibly melodramatic, a murderer lurking at his victim's funeral. I find it highly improbable."

Forking the last of my meat, I reminded him, "Detective Knoll seems to find it a distinct possibility. Why else would he be here?" I chewed the beef.

Glenn speculated, "Just being thorough."

"Maybe," I said, dropping the topic, but in truth, I felt that Larry's presence that day was anything but routine. This impression was bolstered by the whiff of patchouli I'd sniffed on the terrace. Certainly, *anyone* might wear the stuff—Jodie's killer had no exclusive rights to it. Still, the scent was no longer as popular as it had been during the psychedelic seventies. The only other time I'd recently smelled it was at the crime scene.

And there I sat, twirling my fork in a puddle of Alfredo sauce.

"Glenn"—I rose suddenly, gathering my lunch things—"thanks for the bit of privacy, but I think I should get back to the crowd."

He stood, befuddled by my abruptness. "There's no rush, is there?"

"No, but I've sort of 'abandoned' Kiki, and there's, uh, something I need to discuss with the detective."

"Ah." He grinned. "Well, then. You'd better not keep them waiting. I'm going to stay here and do a little work, if you don't mind."

All the better to tend to my own business, I mused. "You'll be missed."

He smiled. "I doubt that. Oh: just leave your dishes. They'll be taken care of."

So I set down everything but my wineglass, exchanged farewells, and took my leave, closing behind me the den's double doors.

Out in the main hall, guests mingled and gabbed. I could tell that the crowd had thinned some, and I chided myself for not having tried to sniff out the patchouli earlier, when all were still present. Some of the guests circled the buffet table, picking at desserts; others cozied up to the bar, waiving the possibility of a productive afternoon. I didn't see Kiki, but I did spot Larry Knoll, who stood near the doorway to the catering kitchen with an empty plate in his hand, talking quietly with his brother, Grant. Beelining toward them, I reminded myself that I had two topics to cover with Larry—Oralia and patchouli.

Grant was first to spot me. *"There* she is. We were about to send out the dogs."

Straight-faced, Larry asked me, "Riffling through drawers in the bedrooms?"

"No," I simpered, "I was having a private chat with a computer genius in his inner sanctum."

"Pardon *me,"* said Grant, arching his brows. La-di-da.

I turned to Larry. "We need to talk."

"Right. Oralia."

Grant said, "Excuse me, kids, but I'm needed in the kitch." Understanding that his brother and I were about to engage in a round of sleuth chat, he obligingly slipped away.

Larry paused, glancing about for potential eavesdroppers. Satisfied, he said, "Out on the terrace, you told me that you had a conversation with Oralia yesterday."

I nodded. "I was interviewing her for a housekeeping job—or *she* was interviewing *me.*"

"Any luck?"

"No, not on the housekeeping front, not yet. But our meeting did give us a chance to talk—about the murder, of course—and the bottom line is that Oralia has strong suspicions that Jodie was seeing another man. She was reluctant, by the way, to tell any of this to you, but she had no problem opening up to me."

The detective nodded. "Too bad. Immigrants often feel that way— no police."

"See? That's why you need me."

He let my comment pass.

I continued, "She also told me that Jodie and Paul had argued in her presence several times. She characterized Jodie as essentially unhappy, which is no surprise—she suffered through some serious bouts of depression. And according to Oralia, Paul didn't seem much happier than his wife. Which confirms my suspicion that his claims of a perfect marriage were inflated, if not downright fantasized."

"Let's back up," Larry told me. "These arguments that Oralia heard, were they about the 'other man'?"

"No. Small stuff. The arguments merely proved there was tension. *But.* Oralia also overheard Jodie on the phone several times, sounding upbeat. She was clearly talking to a man, a man who wasn't Paul, and on one occasion, she made plans to meet this person. Is there a way to check phone records?"

"Sure. And in fact, the Hurons' phone records have already been ordered as a matter of routine. The phone company usually takes several days to comply. We haven't gotten the report yet."

"Then there's also the matter of the cuff link." I sipped my kir.

Larry gave me a blank look.

"On the Sunday morning after the murder, Oralia came over to the Huron house to clean up the mess in the bedroom. I was there; that's when I first met her. While cleaning, she found a large, gold cuff link in the bedroom, then returned it to Paul. Yesterday, though, she told me that it couldn't have been Paul's because he doesn't *have* any cuff links."

Larry was bug-eyed. "Then what the hell did she give it to *him* for? That was *evidence,* for God's sake."

I nodded wearily. "The whole 'police' thing, I guess. If I understood Oralia correctly, she was trying to let Paul know, gently, that Jodie had had a male visitor. Presumably, she expected Paul to see the light and inform you of this angle."

"Which he has *not,*" said Larry, disgusted. "Damn. I can't believe our evidence techs overlooked something so obvious as a cuff link. By now it's been contaminated by both Oralia and Paul handling it. Well, we can't put it off much longer—Paul has to be confronted with the likelihood of Jodie's infidelity."

"I know. But the funeral . . ."

"I know. Not today. But if things don't develop one way or the other by tomorrow, it'll be time for the heart-to-heart with Paul."

I nodded, dreading, on Paul's behalf, the emotional crisis that might be precipitated by baring the very issue he'd been struggling to suppress.

Larry told me, "There's another development regarding Oralia. I'm afraid we've confirmed a disturbing chink in her alibi."

Confused, I said, "I thought you were losing interest in the foiled-robbery theory."

"I *don't* subscribe to it. However, from the outset, Paul *has.* What's more, he named Oralia as a likely suspect, based on her having access to the house, knowledge of its contents, and familiarity with Jodie's schedule. I'd like to dismiss this theory, but I can't unless Oralia has a firm alibi. As you know, she was working at a house in Indian Wells on Saturday morning, but the records at the gatehouse were fuzzy about her arrival time. Like many larger homes out here, the Warhaniks' house has a security system, which is monitored by a service. When Oralia arrived at the house that morning, she used her keypad code to disarm the security system—standard operating procedure. Every change in the system's status is conveyed by phone line to the monitoring service, which keeps a computerized log. We checked. Oralia arrived on the job that morning at eight-fifty precisely."

"And she told us," I recalled, "that she worked there 'from about eight-thirty till noon.' That's a little sloppy at the front end."

Larry nodded. "She doesn't know what *we* know—that Jodie's time of death has been pegged between eight-thirty and nine that morning—unless, of course, she actually *did* kill Jodie. If Jodie was killed at eight-thirty, Oralia could easily have gotten to the house in Indian Wells by eight-fifty."

I shook my head. "But she *couldn't* have killed Jodie. She just couldn't have."

"Stay objective, Claire. We know that Jodie was killed by a blow to the chest, and it needn't have had much force. It could have been the result of a mere shoving match. Oralia—or just about anyone, for that matter—would be physically capable of delivering the death blow."

I had meant, of course, that Oralia couldn't be *emotionally* capable of killing Jodie, but Larry's reasoning made sense, and it was highly disturbing. I couldn't help wondering: During my conversation with Oralia on Tuesday morning, had she *invented* the story about overhearing Jodie on the phone with some unknown "other man" as a deliberate ploy to cast suspicion away from herself?

I told Larry, "If the culprit *was* Oralia, or any other thief, then the surest way to identify the killer is to link him, or her, to the items that Paul said are missing from the house."

"We're working on that. As I told you before, the Rolex and the saltcellars are a dead end—they'd be impossible to identify—so the wedding ring, which is so distinctive, is our best bet."

"Paul found the photo for you. I saw it."

"And I picked it up yesterday afternoon. By the time we got it copied and over to the *Desert Sun,* we'd missed their deadline for this morning's paper, but it should be on page one tomorrow. If theft was the background motive for Jodie's death, things could develop fast, once that photo gets published."

"If not," I suggested, "the crime-of-passion scenario returns to the fore, and—"

"*Claire,*" gushed Kiki, rushing up to me from the crowd in the living room, "I just got another whiff of it."

I'd nearly forgotten—I'd meant to tell Larry about my evolving theory regarding patchouli, but the topic had been sidetracked by news of Oralia's faulty alibi. I asked Kiki, "Where?"

She jerked her head. "Over there, near the fireplace."

I looked. A couple of well-dressed gentlemen—one middle-aged, probably in his late forties, the other looking older, even frail—conversed near the hearth of a huge, two-sided stone fireplace that divided the main room.

"Which one?" I asked.

"The younger one."

"That's a relief. I can't imagine what Jodie would see in the *old* guy."

"We don't *know* that Jodie saw anything in either of them, but—"

"What on earth," Larry interrupted, "are you two blabbering about?"

I told him, "Patchouli."

"God bless you." He smirked.

"Larry, I don't have time to explain, not right now—I need to go smell those two and figure out who they are." I set my empty wineglass on a sideboard near the kitchen door and grabbed Kiki's arm, hustling her away, leaving Larry with a look of blank-faced bewilderment.

"Good work," I told Kiki as we crossed the room together. "Did you hear anything? Who are they?"

She shook her head. "They were talking about the hospital, but half the people here have *some* connection to the medical center. I happened to be drifting by them when I noticed the patchouli—that's when I hightailed it over to you."

We closed the distance to the fireplace without further discussion and fell in near the two men, pretending to appreciate the mountain view as we gazed quietly through the open wall to the terrace.

The older one was saying, "It was a dreadful summer, such an ordeal. But I was well cared for, no question about it." As he spoke, he fussed with the knot of his conservative, striped necktie. He wore a double-breasted blazer, charcoal slacks, and a French-cuffed shirt—with expensive-looking cuff links. He also wore a simple, gold wedding ring.

The younger, taller, better-looking one fingered a nearly empty glass of wine, saying, "I appreciate the compliment, Henry. That's what makes this such a dreadful loss. We all feel it." He wore a light-colored suit, very fashion-forward, with gorgeous Italian oxfords. His necktie, a pattern-on-pattern design in dark neutrals, was clearly Armani. Like Henry, he too wore a French-cuffed shirt—with expensive-looking cuff links. His bulky wedding ring was studded with diamonds.

Both men struck me as overdressed. Neckties had virtually been banished from the desert, even for business; they looked hot, stuffy, and out of place. The cuff links also struck me as passé, but I suppose they still gave men an excuse to indulge in a bit of jewelry without looking gangsterish. After all, even Glenn Yeats regularly wore them, as had Jodie's secret visitor. It seemed that Henry, the older man, was clinging to the conventions of a passing generation; he'd dressed "properly" for a funeral. The younger man was simply a clotheshorse.

Henry said, "During those long weeks—and I mean this sincerely—I truly came to love Jodie."

Hm. *Love* is one of those words that men tend not to drop casually. What, exactly, did Henry mean by that statement?

"Henry!" said a familiar voice. I turned—it was my neighbor, Grant Knoll. "I didn't see you earlier. What a nice surprise."

Henry turned, exchanged a greeting, burbled something.

I wanted an introduction, and I knew I could depend on Grant for it. So I stepped in his direction, smiled, and waited.

"Oh, Claire," Grant obliged, "I'd like you to meet Henry Harris, a good client of mine." Grant fixed me in his gaze meaningfully for a moment, then added, "Arlene's husband."

Ahhh. Arlene Harris was the woman who had wanted to discuss urgent real estate business with Grant the previous weekend. On Tuesday, Grant told me that she was separating from her husband because she'd just learned he was having an affair. Here, in the flesh, was the old philanderer himself, and I'd just heard him say that he loved Jodie. He was wearing cuff links—but not patchouli. Just who *was* that other guy?

After Grant introduced Kiki to Henry, it was Henry's turn to introduce his companion. He told us, "I'd like you all to meet Dr. Percy Blair, head of cardiology at Coachella Medical Center. Dr. Blair is the eminent surgeon who saved my life."

Ahhh. Percy Blair was the bigwig heart doctor who "took Jodie under his wing," as Paul had told me, insisting that their relationship was strictly professional. Here, in the flesh, was Dr. Do-Good himself. He was wearing cuff links—*and* patchouli. In fact, he reeked of it.

I confirmed this by taking a good, close sniff as I leaned forward to shake his hand. He'd doused it on so heavy, it was enough to make my eyes water. "Such a pleasure, Doctor. I'm honored. As I recall, you were quoted in last Sunday's paper, paying Jodie a marvelous tribute. It was eloquently stated—I daresay loving."

"And it was heartfelt," he assured us, tapping the organ beneath his sternum.

"We *all* loved Jodie," Henry told us, muddying the waters.

I asked him, "You knew Jodie from the hospital?"

The old man nodded woefully. "Arlene and I moved out here for my health some years ago, but a lifetime of bad habits finally caught up with me." He patted his ticker. "This summer, I went in for stents, but they collapsed. Then a quadruple bypass, but there were complications. I'm back on my feet now, thank God, but I was bedridden there for *weeks*. At times I didn't think I'd make it. If it weren't for Jodie—and Dr. Blair, or course—I probably *wouldn't* have made it. So I had to be here today, for Jodie. She was such an angel, such a love."

"We *all* loved Jodie," Dr. Do-Good said, echoing Henry's earlier line. With a sigh, he downed the last of his wine and set the glass on the fireplace mantel. In a shaft of sunlight from the terrace, the bowl of the wineglass glowed with greasy smudges from the surgeon's fingers. Apparently I wasn't the only one who'd had difficulty juggling the buffet lunch.

Grant offered, "Can I get you some more wine, Doctor?"

"Thanks, but I'll get it myself, assuming the bar's still open."

"Indeed it is." Grant gestured in its direction.

"Henry?" asked the doctor. "Something to drink?"

The old man cocked his head. "Is it, uh . . . permitted?"

The doctor chuckled. "Yes, Henry, it is indeed permitted." And he ushered his patient away to be medicated.

I'd held my breath during this exchange, hoping the doctor would want a fresh glass and leave the used one on the mantel. He did.

"Kiki," I said, eyeing her big straw handbag, "may I borrow your purse?"

She looked at me quizzically. "Well . . . of course, dear." She handed it to me.

"Grant," I asked while picking up someone's discarded linen napkin, shaking crumbs from it, "is there some way you could arrange for me to meet Arlene Harris—without raising any suspicions?"

He arched a single eyebrow. "Do I detect suspicions of your own?"

I sighed. "I don't know yet. Henry can't seem to stop talking about how much he 'loved' Jodie, and his wife has just told you that he's been unfaithful. Maybe he *was* involved with Jodie. But I'm merely piecing together circumstances, so I'd like to get some more background, preferably from Arlene."

Grant crossed his arms. "As it happens, you're in luck. I'm taking Arlene to dinner tonight."

"Oh?" Reaching up to the mantel, I picked up the doctor's wineglass by its stem. Glancing about to make sure no one noticed, I nonchalantly rolled the glass in the napkin and dropped the bundle into Kiki's gaping purse.

Grinning as he watched my every move, Grant continued, "I'm meeting Arlene at Fusión." (He lisped it.) "Care for a return visit?"

"It *was* wonderful," I recalled. "I won't be intruding?"

"Nonsense." He smiled. "I'll think of *some* excuse to have you there."

I touched his arm. "Thank you, Grant." Looking about the still-crowded room, I asked, "Do you know where your brother is?"

"I was talking to Larry in the front hall just before I spotted Henry over here. I think he was getting ready to leave."

"Oh, gosh." I glanced at the wrapped wineglass in the purse.

"He may still be in the courtyard," Grant told me. "It takes a while to bring the cars up."

I nodded my thanks and took off toward the entry hall.

A few guests mingled in the hall and outdoors in the courtyard, waiting for the valets to fetch their cars. I spotted Larry away from the others, studying the drooping arms of a Joshua tree, a magnificent specimen planted at the far end of the courtyard, near the street. Leaving the house to talk to him, I noted that the day had heated up—it was now early afternoon.

"Larry," I called, "I have something for you." I made a show of lugging Kiki's enormous straw handbag.

He turned to watch me, planting one hand on his hip. Imitating his brother, he camped, "Thanks, doll, but I never carry a purse."

Laughing, I strode up to him. "Not the purse, wise guy—*this.*" I gave him a peek inside. "It's a wineglass. It has a lovely mess of fingerprints all over it, and I think you should have them checked."

His hand was still on his hip. "Why, pray tell?"

I took a deep breath. "It's sort of a long story—the patchouli."

"I'm listening."

"When you were at the crime scene on Saturday, didn't you notice that distinctive smell of perfume in the bedroom?"

"Sorry. No, I didn't."

"By the time you got there, it had dissipated some, and Jodie, uh . . . her bladder had spilled. But earlier, when Paul and I first discovered the body, there was a lingering scent of strong perfume in the room. I assumed it was Jodie's, but then I noticed that she had no perfume bottles, and later I learned that Paul is allergic to fragrances—so, no, it wasn't Jodie's."

"Whose, then?"

"Exactly. Whose was it? I was confused at first because it implied there had been another woman in the bedroom with Jodie."

"Oralia?"

"Maybe. But if we were focusing on a crime of passion, that suggested Jodie might have been involved with a *woman.*"

"Oh, Lord. Here we go."

"But I got a whiff of it again here today on the terrace, and Kiki recognized it. She explained that patchouli, being such a strong and spicy scent, is worn by men as well as women."

"And that's who you tried to sniff out, back in the living room."

"Right. Turns out, it was Dr. Percy Blair, Jodie's 'boss' and mentor."

"Interesting," Larry conceded, "but we can't book him for wearing perfume."

"Of course not." I showed Larry the wrapped wineglass again. "His prints are all over it. Maybe they'll match the unidentified set of prints from the bedroom."

"It's a long shot." He lifted the bundle out of the purse. "But I like your logic. We'll check it out."

"Larry, I'm more and more convinced that Jodie's murder was a crime of passion. There's certainly no shortage of possible suspects. Besides Dr. Do-Good, consider Henry Harris." I told Larry about Henry's lengthy hospital stay that summer, about his professed love of Jodie, his cuff links, and his wife's contention that he'd been having an affair.

I continued, "And then, of course, there's—" But I hesitated, leaving the statement incomplete. I had been thinking of Tanner Griffin, Jodie's "marvelous mechanic." I didn't really believe, though, that Tanner had played a role in Jodie's death, so why raise his name again? Still, if I had any doubts, wouldn't it just make sense to have him investigated, to clear him, and to put those doubts to rest? And with a flash of inspiration, I knew how I could do it. Back in my office, that cobalt-glass paperweight was covered with Tanner's fingerprints, much as the wineglass was covered with Percy Blair's.

I'd been silent with my thoughts too long. Larry prompted me, "And then, of course, there's . . . who?"

"There's . . ." But I couldn't do it. I just couldn't bring myself to use Tanner's fingerprints against him that way. It would be a different matter if I truly suspected him of complicity in the crime, but I did not. Fishing, I told Larry, "And then, of course, there's . . . Paul Huron himself."

Larry frowned. "Why do you say that?"

I shrugged. "If Jodie was having a clandestine love affair, wouldn't her wronged husband have a strong motive for revenge?"

"Well, *sure.*" Larry snorted. "A cuckolded husband always shoots right to the top of my suspect list. But at the time of *this* murder," he reminded me, "Paul was six miles up, somewhere between Dallas and Palm Springs. We know he'd spent the night in Texas, and you yourself met his flight on Saturday morning."

I grinned. "Just keeping you on your toes, Larry."

One of the valets pulled an unmarked county sedan into the courtyard. Larry said, "Here we are," and I walked him to the car. As he opened the back door and set the wrapped wineglass on the seat, he told me, "Stay in touch. I want to hear from you every day—got it?"

I nodded. "Got it."

Then, for the first time, in the heat of the afternoon, I saw him remove his jacket, which he laid on the seat, over the glass. He shut the back door, opened the front, and got in behind the wheel. "Things could develop fast now. Communication is essential."

I nodded again, but I wasn't listening. I was focused on his shoulder holster, intrigued by the glint of gunmetal.

Thumping his door closed, he shifted into gear and drove away.

15

Funerals have a way of putting a crimp in one's day. Even when the deceased is someone not close—I barely knew Jodie and felt no personal loss—the notion of death takes center stage at a funeral, leaving all but the most hardened or cynical of souls to contemplate their own mortality. Such days bode ill for business as usual.

As funerals go, Jodie's memorial service that Wednesday was simple, neat, and civilized—a few kind words, then lunch. There was no body, no burial, no trappings of religion to make a grim matter worse. The event's lone otherworldly aspect was Jodie's surprise resurrection in the form of a dust devil, and even that, after all, was just a fluke of the wind, not a portent from the beyond.

Still, I'd indulged in wishful thinking when I'd planned to spend the rest of that day at my office on campus. Though there was plenty that needed my attention there, my mood was all wrong for the minutiae and inanities of paper pushing. It seemed so pointless against the weightier, more solemn context of a life cut short by tragedy. So when Kiki and I finally got into the Beetle and left Glenn Yeats's house at Nirvana, I drove straight home to Villa Paseo.

After parking in my garage, we exchanged a hug in the courtyard by the fountain. "Get some rest," said one of us.

"Call later," said the other.

We nodded, retreating to our own condominiums.

Though it was the middle of the day, I felt like undressing, as if, by shedding the garb of that morning's ritual, I could distance myself from the mortality issues that had been addressed so baldly. Upstairs in my bedroom, finding it hot, I drew the curtains across the room's south window, shutting out the midday sun. Then I removed my gray dress, hanging it in the closet, and fingered several silk bathrobes that awaited on a row of hooks. Basic black was fine—I assured myself the color had no funereal significance before slipping on the robe and cinching its slinky belt with a big, sloppy bow.

Padding barefoot down to the living room, I noted that the dining table was still cluttered with a loose stack of errant paperwork that had not yet been schlepped to my office. Resolving to accomplish at least some small measure of real work that day, I found a pair of reading glasses and sat at the table, sorting through the pile from the top. At one point, I needed a pen; at another juncture, I had to check information against a document I'd left upstairs in my briefcase. After a while, I'd left the table numerous times, having succeeded at little more than transforming the single heap of papers into three.

Each time I passed through the living room, I eyed the sofa, growing convinced that a short nap would prove more productive than my bumbling attempt at desk work. Besides, I reminded myself, some quiet time would help rest me for that evening—I'd need to be alert at dinner with Grant Knoll and Arlene Harris. Before long, I reasoned that lying down was an essential preparation for the investigative challenges I would later face.

So I plumped a pillow, stretched, and succumbed to the lure of the couch. Curling up on it, I tucked my toes behind the seat cushions, closed my eyes, and slowly cleared my mind. Content with these stolen moments of solitude, I began to drift off.

Predictably, the phone rang.

Sitting up, I didn't even debate whether or not to answer it. The nap spell had been shattered. What's more, I wondered if Larry Knoll was trying to reach me; that very afternoon, he'd lectured me on the importance of open communication. Stumbling to the kitchen, though, I conjectured that my caller was not in Riverside but in Upstate New York—I knew that ring.

I lifted the phone. "Yes?" Even the faint hiss of the long-distance connection sounded familiar and foreboding.

"Claire. It's me. You're in."

"You sound surprised. If you didn't think I was here, Gwyn, why call?"

"I called your office *first*."

"Oh. I was at Jodie's funeral—the young woman I told you about."

"How sad. But now, at least, she's with God."

I wouldn't even *touch* that one. "I needed some time by myself this afternoon. The memorial service sort of weirded me out. And I thought I could use some rest—dinner plans tonight."

Mother paused, tantalized. Coyly, she asked, "With whom?"

"Sorry, Gwyn, it's not a date. I'll be with Grant Knoll, my gay neighbor, and Arlene Harris, whose husband is a possible suspect in the murder case."

Reacting to this double whammy, Mother sputtered, uncertain where to begin. Homicide apparently outweighed homosexuality, as she asked, "Of what conceivable interest is 'the murder case' to *you?*"

The time wasn't right to inform her that I'd taken on a minor role in the investigation. "I already told you, dear: I was with Jodie's husband when he found the body."

"Fine, Claire, I understand that. But why would—?"

"Mother," I explained bluntly, changing my mind, "the detective in charge of the case has invited my participation. He seems to feel I have some unique insights. So I've been following up on a theory or two."

"*Claire,*" she gasped, "it's bad enough that you never had sense enough to settle down with Hector. And it's worse still, even after moving to California, that you continue to keep company with men of a peculiar persuasion. But now *this*. What will people say when . . ."

Gwyn prattled on; I tuned out. Doing so, I recalled the waking dream I'd had on Monday morning while driving on the interstate. Even when I'd dreamed it, the appealing foretaste of Gwyn's death had been unsettling. Now, mere hours after attending a funeral, confronting a *real* death and its doleful aftermath, I found it all the more unsettling that the inevitable passing of my own mother threatened greater logistical problems than emotional ones.

How, I wondered, would I actually tend to the event? As an only child, I would not be able to burden some long-suffering sibling with the dirty work while pleading geographical distance. There would be a service to arrange, a house to sell, an estate to settle. But even that impending commotion could not dampen the lure of liberation. It was overdue, I felt. It was time. I had the *right* not to answer to her. Simply put, it was my turn to be in charge. I'd waited long enough.

I asked, "Have you talked to Dr. Paxton this week?"

"Just this morning." And the litany of woe began.

Was I insensitive to be bored with it? At least I was polite, listening quietly, offering occasional clucks of sympathy, pretending to care, until we got to her report on "daily elimination," as she euphemistically termed it.

"Maybe you should just eat more cheese," I suggested absentmindedly.

"Cheese?" She snorted. "Cheese makes it *worse.*"

"Fruit, then?" Honestly, I couldn't keep track of whether she was trying to push or pull. This point of confusion was soon set straight, however, in graphic, numbing detail. Trying not to sound impatient, I waited for a pause in her disquisition, then said, "I'm sure you'll be tip-top by morning, dear—it's really not worth fretting over. What, by the way, was on your mind when you phoned?"

She sighed. "Now, I know you won't like hearing this, and I don't mean to upset you, but . . ."

But, indeed. I'd heard this preamble before, which always teetered on the *but.* What she was telling me, in effect, was that she knew fully well I would be upset by what she had to say, and she had decided, in spite of this knowledge, to go ahead and upset me anyway. In other words, she was being intentionally malicious. And it was always, of course, for my own good.

". . . but this is something you *need* to hear. It's for your own good, Claire darling." She was lying through her teeth. It was for *her* good, *her* ego, that she tried to retain control, holding on as if for dear life. And maybe it was just that simple: she was scared o' dyin'. "There's a *wisdom* that comes with my years, and you've got to recognize the value of my judgment. Trust me, Claire . . ."

If there's one thing I've learned in my scant fifty-four years on this planet, it is *never* to trust those who demand it. Age alone is no guarantee of wisdom, and position holds no lock on respect. Those who tout their wisdom and lay claim to respect are insecure bullies, baring their own deficiencies. What is the worth of their inflated opinions? Consider the source.

Think for yourself.

But never presume to think for others.

". . . studies prove it, and it's common sense. If a respected medical journal can . . ." She was better read than most doctors when it came to the latest arcane research, particularly when she found it applicable to my circumstances. "Happily married people *live* longer, but the longer you wait to make a commitment . . ."

I wanted to yell, What about *your* marriage?

Instead, I fudged, "Oops, there's the door, Mother. So nice to hear from you, dear. Good luck with the cheese—er, fruit. 'Bye, now." And I replaced the receiver, midsquawk, exhaling a sigh of relief as I savored the silence.

When my pulse had returned to near normal, I considered lying down again, but knew that it would be impossible to nap—I was too keyed up. At least I had the satisfaction of having taken charge of a disagreeable situation. I had, in essence, hung up on Gwyn. I'd only recently begun to do this, and I was getting better at it. True, I'd masked my action behind the fabricated need to answer the door, but my lie was sufficiently transparent to convey my annoyance with her. Perhaps she'd take the hint and her calls would become less critical. If not, perhaps I'd learn to hang up on her without the sugarcoating of pretense.

My falsely stated need to answer the door brought to mind that I had not yet checked for mail that day. Since I'd only recently moved, junk mailers hadn't yet caught up with me, and I'd discovered how refreshing it can be to open the mailbox and find something that matters. Pulling on a pair of sandals that I kept in the entry hall (I'd learned that, in the afternoon, the courtyard's tiles were far too hot for bare feet), I opened the door and strolled outside.

The mailboxes were grouped near the front of the complex, at the street gate, so in the interest of modesty, I tugged the belt of my silk robe a few inches tighter—a precaution against gusty desert breezes. Swinging open the gate of my entry court, I was about to cross the larger common courtyard when I noticed a hefty manila envelope that had been left leaning between my gate's wrought-iron bars. Picking it up, I saw at a glance that the envelope had been hand-delivered, not mailed. My name and address were written on it, and in the upper-left corner was Desert Detail's printed logo.

Catching my breath, I wondered when *he* had been here—this was surely from Tanner Griffin. Had I just now missed him? Had he tiptoed to my door even as I lied to Gwyn about the arrival of some visitor? Why hadn't he knocked?

Perhaps he had, earlier. Checking the sight lines of my entry court, I noted that I would not have seen the envelope when I returned home that afternoon, parking in the garage. Tanner could have dropped by anytime that morning, knocked, then left the envelope behind. The more I thought about it, I was glad he had missed me. Though not by nature a vain person, I didn't want him catching me in a bathrobe— God forbid.

As I stood there in the full afternoon sun, carking over the hows and whens, the black silk robe felt suddenly hot, so I stepped back indoors while slipping my finger under the manila flap and tearing it open.

Yes, it was indeed from Tanner, the information he'd promised regarding tinting of my car windows. His familiar business card was clipped to several brochures. On a sheet of stationery he'd laser-printed prices for the various options, writing at the bottom of the page, "Let me know which way you're leaning. I'll make sure you're completely satisfied! Tanner."

Lord, even his handwriting was gorgeous—confident, solid, clear, and masculine—just like his voice. And was it merely my imagination, or was his message *meant* to convey that seductive double entendre? Certainly, it was easy to read the words that way, and in fact, on the morning we'd met, he'd told me that he was attracted to older women. My judgment, however, was no longer reliable. In light of the fantasies that I no longer bothered to suppress (I now shamelessly conjured, with increased regularity, torrid daydreams featuring the sandy-haired lad), he could have quilled an insipid "Have a nice day" and I'd still have found it risqué.

No, I told myself, his written words carried no suggestive subtext, at least not intentionally. One of Tanner's most endearing qualities was his ingenuousness—he seemed oblivious to the extent and effect of his charms. Which, of course, made him all the more appealing.

My, my, I thought, Jodie was right—what an extraordinarily accommodating young man. Waltzing into the kitchen (yes, I was that giddy), I plopped the brochures onto the tile countertop, plucked the receiver from the phone, peeped at the number on his card, poised my index finger, and punched seven buttons. The phone tones seemed musical—no, *rhapsodic*—as electrical impulses shot across the valley, found their target, and rang bells in Palm Springs.

"Good afternoon. Desert Detail."

"Tanner!" Bring it down a notch, I warned myself. "You're in." Gag me—I sounded like Gwyn.

"Miss Gray? I mean, Claire?" He laughed. "Where'd you *think* I'd be?"

"Well, I *just* found your envelope, and I wasn't sure when you'd stopped by. I thought you might still be out and around."

"Nah. I dropped it off this morning."

"It was *very* thoughtful."

He mimicked my gushy tone: "You're a *very* important customer." Then, strictly business: "Any decisions yet?"

"Beg pardon?"

"Any decisions about tinting your car windows?"

"Oh!" I laughed. "I haven't really studied the information yet. I had no *idea* this could get so *involved.*" Amazed by my own inflections, which made me sound like an airheaded debutante, I cleared my throat, collected my thoughts, and told him calmly, "I just called to thank you. I know this is a piddling job for you. You've been kind to be so helpful."

"My pleasure." His tone was sincere, neither too formal nor vacuous. Again the word *solid* leaped to mind in describing him.

With a groan, I confessed, "I haven't yet had time to compile those enrollment materials for DAC. Jodie's memorial service was this morning, and—"

"Gosh, I'm sorry. Rough day?"

"Rougher than expected. I'd meant to spend the afternoon in the office, and I could have gotten the ball rolling for you, but I ended up here at home." I had a thought: "Why don't I run over to campus, put together that material for you, and drive it over to your shop? I could have it to you in an hour or so. It's the least I could do—you've been so accommodating."

"Claire," he said cheerfully, "don't be silly. There's no rush."

"Actually," I reminded him, "there is. Classes start Monday."

"Look. I'll be running errands down valley tomorrow morning, so I can just swing past the campus and stop at your office to pick up the material. God, that sounds intimidating, like nuclear waste."

"It is, in fact, intimidating," I warned him with a low laugh. "When should I expect you?"

"Is ten sharp okay?"

"Perfect. I'll be there, and I promise, a thick dossier will await."

We exchanged a few more pleasantries, wished each other a nice evening, and said good-bye. Hanging up the phone, I breathed a contented sigh, marveling that the despondency inspired by my mother's call had been completely vanquished.

Checking the wall clock there in the kitchen, I noted that there was still time for a brief nap before getting ready for dinner. But who was I kidding? How could I sleep—now?

My restless mind was awash with thoughts of Tanner Griffin.

Solid, I thought.

Yes, that was the word.

16

Dinner was booked for 7:30 that evening.

Grant was kept longer than expected at Nirvana that day, arriving back at Villa Paseo with barely enough time for a quick shower and change. Around seven, he knocked at my door, freshly blow-dried, carrying a single white rose, raring to hit the road. As he still claimed an affection for my Beetle (not sure why—he owned a beast of a Mercedes), I readily offered to let him drive the Bug again. He helped me into the car, then slid his rose into the bud vase with the sprigs of Japanese plum I'd put there. Moments later, we were on the road.

"Since we're running a tad late," he told me, glancing over from the wheel, "and I don't want to keep Arlene waiting, I think I'll take the interstate. Not scenic, but it's fast." And he turned onto Monterey Avenue, heading across the valley to the highway, just as I had done on Monday morning when I drove to Desert Detail.

Perhaps it was the flat, straight-line monotony of the drive that inspired our silence; neither of us spoke for some minutes. Finally, I asked Grant, "Lost in thoughts of Bruce?

He turned to me. "Who?"

I laughed. "Or was it Butch? I *knew* you were making that up—your high-school crush, the jock with mismatched eyes."

"Guilty," he conceded. "No, if I was lost in thought, it was just business. Plenty on my mind today."

"Ah."

"How 'bout you? Milady is uncharacteristically tight-lipped *ce soir*. Bummed by the funeral?"

It would have been easy to dismiss my taciturn mood with the excuse

Grant had handed me, and I nearly did, but then reconsidered. Grant had become a close friend, and he'd invited me to open up before, but I'd consistently declined. The time felt right.

"It's not Jodie's memorial service," I told him, "which, by the way, was lovely."

He nodded his thanks for my approval of the event he'd arranged.

"I had a call at home this afternoon from my mother."

"Uh-oh." His eyes were focused on the road. "How old is she?"

I had to think about it. "Eighty-two. Well, close enough."

"Close enough, indeed."

"Let's just say we have some . . . issues. I don't even know where to begin. It's a long story."

"We have a few minutes." He grinned. "And I'm *all* ears."

"Oh, God . . . ," I groaned, lolling against the headrest, feeling as if I'd just plopped myself on a psychiatrist's couch. Did I really want to get into this? I began, "This has vexed me since childhood. Simply put, Gwyn Gray, my mother, gave me the idea, when I was very young, that I was *better* than other people."

"You *are* better than other people," Grant insisted. "Good for Gwyn."

Shushing him, I continued, "It was her way, I suppose, of building my self-esteem, as well as her own. God knows, she needed it. She and my father were estranged from the time I was born. They never divorced or even separated, but he just . . ."

"He just wasn't around much?"

I nodded. "When I grew old enough to understand such things, I got the idea that he was keeping a mistress. I wanted to talk to him about it, but the time was never right. I wasn't upset by the idea; I just wanted to know. Truth is, I hope he did have a mistress. He deserved some happiness." Pausing, I recalled, "He died almost twenty years ago."

"Hmm," Grant mulled my story. "Ever discuss your hunch with Maman?"

"God, no. I don't know whether it was the cause or the result of my father's wandering eye, but my mother has always been a woman of 'attitude.' There's no nice way to say it: she's a snob. And she turned *me* into one too. In the countless ways that a mother can influence her child, she taught me to look down on others. Maybe they had less money or less education; maybe they went to the wrong church or even the wrong hairdresser. She could always find something to convince me that they were lacking. It's no wonder, then, that I grew up pretty damned pleased with myself. Lonely, too. Marriage? Who could possibly fill the bill?"

"Hector Bosch?" suggested Grant. His tone was facetious.

There was no need to respond. Instead, I remembered, "Even as a child, I had few friends, precocious interests, and a will of iron. Many little girls dream of blossoming into starlets, but my theatrical goal was different: I would become a director. I had to be the boss. Theater is a risky career for anyone, and directing is especially chancy for a woman. But I have never been afraid of risks, and I've discovered that directing, at least on the surface, is easy. You tell people what to do, they do it, and everyone is rewarded with bouquets and applause. Life certainly doesn't work that way. People don't always do what they're told, nor should they.

"It's ironic that I owe my success to the ambitions and self-confidence that Gwyn gave me. Still, by learning to set myself apart from the rest of the world, I've built a life that has been essentially . . . unhappy. And I've *accepted* this as both necessary and normal."

"Claire," said Grant, turning to me with a look of concern, "there's no reason—"

"Listen, Grant. There's so much I should never have listened to when I was young, but I was in no position then to make meaningful judgments. They teach us such crap—and it has colored and twisted every important encounter of my life, from my mother to Hector Bosch to Tanner Griffin to—"

"Who?"

"He's, uh, he was Jodie's mechanic at Desert Detail."

"And you consider him an 'important encounter'?"

"Never mind Tanner. The point is that it's time for me to slough off this confusion, grow up, and face a simple but elusive reality: adults enter relationships as traders might, expecting to take as well as to give, aware and unashamed that the motive for trade is the taking, not the giving." I paused, exhaling loudly, having rambled far more than intended.

"These ideas," said Grant, "about 'trading.' That's what you developed in your play, in *Traders,* right?"

I nodded feebly. "I tried. But for some reason, the message didn't really sink in—and *I* wrote it."

He reached over and clasped my hand. "Rest assured, dear lady: it sank in for *lots* of people. That play, and the movie that followed, truly 'made a difference.' "

Engrossed in conversation and ideas, we had traveled the interstate farther than necessary; we were approaching the Indian Avenue exit, which would shoot us back toward downtown Palm Springs. As Grant steered off the highway, from the rise of the overpass I could see the energy farm beyond.

As before, most of the windmills faced the same direction, their blades whirling in unison in the last light of dusk. The ones that caught my eye, though, had tensed in the direction of past, forgotten winds. Obstinately, like me, they clung to the notion that they were better than the rest.

Give it up, Claire, I told myself. Grow up. Take charge of your life.

Within a couple of minutes, we had sped into town, negotiated the one-ways, and found ourselves on the crowded little side street that was our destination. Just ahead, not a block away, was Fusión. To my surprise, instead of roaring up to the canopy, Grant braked the car and pulled over to the curb, several doors short.

"We're a minute or two late," I told him, tapping my watch. "What's up?"

"Nothing . . . ," he said vacantly, drumming his fingers on the wheel.

Intrigued, I watched as Grant watched the handsome college-age valet waiting in front of the restaurant. He wore the same studly uniform as before—tennis shorts, knit shirt, and a perfect tan. What, I wondered, was Grant waiting for? Go for it.

A car pulled ahead of us, parking at the restaurant, and the kid stepped forward to do his duty. At that moment, another kid trotted up the sidewalk, having just parked a car. And I recalled: there were *two* valets, and this was the cuter, beefier one whom Grant had overtipped on our previous visit.

Grant revved the engine and pulled forward, sliding up behind the other car as the parker pulled it away. The valet, the pet one, bounded to the Beetle, opening my door first, then circled the front of the car toward Grant. We both watched hungrily as the hunky, tan legs scissored past the windshield. From the side of my mouth, I told Grant, "I admire your taste."

With a suave nod, he acknowledged my compliment, plucking the white rose from the bud vase.

We both got out of the car, and I watched from the curb as he stood chatting in the street for a moment with the object of his affection. He made a show of removing with his thumbnail a thorn or two that protruded from the flower's short stem. Then he slid the rose through a buttonhole in the placket of the boy's shirt, telling him simply, "This is for you."

It was the smoothest act of seduction I had ever witnessed—one of the nerviest as well. I held my breath, thinking the kid might be insulted, or at least embarrassed. But no, he looked cross-eyed down at the flower, then up at Grant. With a drop-dead smile and an acquiescent nod, he said, "Thank you, sir."

"My name's Grant, by the way."

"I'm Kane." They shook hands.

"You'll take good care of the Beetle, won't you, Kane? It belongs to my dear neighbor, and she's very fond of it." Grant gestured to me, telling the kid, in effect, that we weren't a couple.

"I'll keep my eye on it. That's why I'm here." Kane handed Grant the parking stub.

"Thank you so much." Grant smiled, touching his fingertips to the boy's shoulder for a fraction of a second before turning, walking to the curb, and without looking back, escorting me across the sidewalk to the door of the restaurant.

I leaned to tell him, "Wow . . ."

Sotto voce, he assured me, "Just keeping in practice, doll."

We stepped inside the dark, austere foyer. My eyes had not yet adjusted to the lighting, but I heard the hostess greet us, "Welcome to

Fusión." Her eyes seemed to focus as mine did. "Oh, welcome back," she told us, dropping the haughty attitude.

Grant approached her podium. "A Mrs. Harris is joining us. Has she arrived?"

"Ah!" said the girl, tapping her book. "Mrs. Harris phoned a few minutes ago, Mr. Grant. She asked me to let you know that she's running a few minutes late. She is coming, though, and asked me to extend her apologies."

"Thank you. No problem. We'll just have a drink—at table, please."

For whatever reason, the folks at Fusión must have decided that they liked us (was it the trendy gay-man/straight-woman thing?), because we were instantly whisked to the same prime table we'd occupied before. It was the only open table in the room, clearly held for us.

As soon as we were seated, our former waitress in black spandex appeared, reintroducing herself as Karissa and asking if she could bring cocktails. I'd already had a kir that day at the funeral, which was still rife with glum overtones, so I joined Grant in ordering one of those huge, ice-slicked martinis we'd enjoyed on our previous visit. Karissa slipped away.

I told Grant, "Thanks for letting me horn in tonight. I'm sure my interest in the Huron case is starting to look downright nutty."

He crossed his arms, shook his head. "You were *there.* You found the *body.* Of *course* the murder has begun to prey on you. But, uh"—he suppressed a laugh—"Henry Harris? I've known the Harrises for years, Claire. Henry hardly strikes me as fitting the homicidal profile."

"See? You *do* think I'm nutty. And I'm apt to *agree* with you."

Again he shook his head—such a polite, considerate, and gentle man. "Help me with this. At Glenn Yeats's house today, when you hatched this theory, I was torn in umpteen directions with the staff. What led you to suspect Henry?"

"Let's start from the beginning. On Saturday when we found Jodie's body, because her wedding ring was missing Paul was quick to assume that the house had been robbed and that Jodie had somehow gotten killed in a scuffle."

"But *you* never bought in to that, even from the start. You said so at lunch on Saturday."

"Right. The whole setup struck me as a crime of passion, not greed. The case is four days old now, and none of the items reported missing by Paul, including the wedding ring, have turned up. What's more, Paul's insistence on the bungled-burglary angle has seemed more emotional than rational. He *wants* to believe it so that he needn't face the possibility of Jodie's infidelity."

Grant thought for a moment. "So, if you're correct, the murder may have been the result of a soured love affair with some secret Casanova."

"Exactly."

Karissa appeared with a tiny silver tray bearing the two enormous martinis. My mouth watered at the sight of them. She served us, scrunched her face in an odd smile, and hopped away.

We lifted our glasses with care—they were filled to the brim, with flecks of shaken ice still floating, crackling, on the surface. It was inadvisable to clink the glasses, as we'd doubtless spill the best part, so we limited our toast to an air-skoal.

With a twisted grin, I said, "To justice."

Grant seconded, "To truth."

And we sipped.

"Who then," asked Grant, getting back to business, "was the secret lover?"

"That's the big question. As you know, a set of unidentified fingerprints was found all over the crime scene, reinforcing the theory that Jodie had been 'entertaining' in the boudoir. At today's luncheon, a number of factors converged, pointing me in the direction of *both* Henry Harris and Dr. Percy Blair." I detailed for Grant the whole business of the patchouli, the cuff link, Paul's description of Dr. Blair as Jodie's mentor, and Henry's profession of love for his dedicated and caring nurse.

I failed to mention, however, that if one were being entirely objective, there was a third possible candidate, beyond Henry and the doctor, for the role of Jodie's paramour. Tanner Griffin had admitted to me that he had found Jodie attractive and had even made a move. He was also candid about her rebuff, so the case seemed closed. While I knew that Tanner had spent Sunday hiking in the Indian Canyons (that is, I had no reason to question this claim), I still had no idea where he'd been on Saturday morning at the time of the murder. I reminded myself that Tanner was a self-described actor, apparently a skilled one. Had I been duped by a finely crafted, well-rehearsed performance? Again I thought of that cobalt paperweight in my office, bearing a pristine set of Tanner's fingerprints; it could settle the whole question with reasonable certainty.

No, I decided, there was no reason whatever to mention my groundless suspicions either to Grant or to his brother. I had an appointment to see Tanner at my office tomorrow at ten. I'd simply ask him, forthright, without pretense, where he'd been on Saturday morning. I was certain he'd appreciate my candor in asking, and I was equally certain I'd be satisfied with his answer. At least I hoped so.

"I *hope* so," said Grant laughing. For the life of me, I didn't know what he was referring to. I'd been carrying on a conversation with him, but I'd been absorbed by my flip-flopping over Tanner. My martini glass, I noticed, was now half-empty. Grant continued, "If it's a question of 'the other man,' I'd put my money on the doctor, not Henry."

"Or maybe," I mused, fingering the rim of my glass, "we're being too simplistic. Are we overlooking something?"

Grant paused. "Like what?"

I tisked. "If I *knew*, we wouldn't be overlooking it."

"Pardon *me*," he said, mocking the inflection of the affronted. Then, with a smile, he sipped from his glass.

"I mean, we've considered theft, and we've considered soured passions, but might there be some *other* motive for wanting Jodie out of the picture?"

Grant's face turned quizzical. "Why? Was Jodie 'in the way' of something?"

I shook my head as if to clear my thinking. "Not to my knowledge. I can't imagine how." Still, I had the nagging feeling that I'd forgotten something, that some obvious detail had—

"Grant, *dahling!*" gushed a matronly woman, chugging toward our table. A great hound of a thing with big hair, she wore a flounced-up Oscar de la Renta evening dress and carried one of those beaded Judith Leiber purses shaped like an animal. This one looked like a fat little pig.

Grant stood. Big smile. "Good evening, Arlene."

"Sorry to keep you waiting—and I have *so* looked forward to meeting your, uh, friend." Clearly, she didn't have a clue as to who I was or why I was there. Which suited me fine.

Grant introduced us, explaining to Arlene that I was his new neighbor and director of the theater program at Desert Arts College.

Upon hearing my name for the second or third time, Arlene blurted, *"Claire Gray?* Why, I've *heard* of you, Claire!"

I thanked her, willing to assume that her comment was meant as a compliment.

We were soon seated, forming a triangle at the round table. Karissa appeared, offering another round of drinks, to which Grant and I readily assented.

"Martinis," gasped Arlene, eyeing our empty birdbaths, "how *elegant.* Let's keep it simple—make it three, dahling." This last "dahling" was directed to Karissa, who bobbed her understanding and vanished into the darkness beyond our table.

Arlene breathed a heavy sigh, primping her huge coif, which she wore like a helmet. *"What* a week." Though she was presumably referring to the breakup of her marriage, her tone seemed no more genuinely frazzled than if the dry cleaner had botched a delivery.

Grant told her, "For you and Claire *both.* That's why I asked Claire to join us tonight—for some mindless amusement." He winked at me.

"Oh?" Arlene peered over the table at me. "Trouble, hon?"

"The crisis wasn't my own, but one life has been lost, another shattered." Smugly, I noted that my words had tantalized her.

Grant explained, "Claire is the friend I told you about—over the weekend when you were trying to reach me. She and a colleague from the new school discovered his dead wife's body at home on Saturday morning."

"That was *you,* Claire? How awful for you—I'm so sorry. The desert, it seems, is turning into a veritable rat's nest of crime."

Grant reminded her, "There hasn't been a homicide in Palm Desert in nearly a year, Arlene."

"Well, that just makes it all the *worse,* doesn't it?"

Moments later, Karissa returned with our drinks. We shared a quick toast to happier times, then listened to Karissa's recitation of that night's special offerings.

Arlene was palpably wary of the offbeat recipes. "It all sounds *too* mahvelous," she said with a laugh. "Do choose *for* me, Grant dear." He complied, making sure the meal would be memorable—Arlene would reap several weeks' worth of bridge-club fodder from Grant's fearless selections. As for me, I'd learned on my last visit that no dish was apt to disappoint, so my choices were considerably more adventurous this time, built around a saddle of lapin.

With dinner ordered and fresh drinks in front of us, we three could finally settle in for some serious discussion. No point in wasting time, I reasoned, so I got down to the dirt: "I was so sorry, Arlene, to hear from Grant that you and your husband have hit a rough spot."

"'*Rough* spot'? My dear, it's *over.*"

Grant patted her hand. "You were so agitated when we first talked about it, I didn't quite get the whole story. But we're *here* for you, Arlene. You're among friends. We're good listeners. Tell us what happened."

After some preambular throat-clearing and expressions of lament, Arlene told us, "Henry is sixty-seven; I'm three years younger. We moved out to the desert from L.A. some ten years ago for Henry's health. He built a chain of auto malls and made a *fortune,* but he nearly killed himself doing it. So at his doctor's urging, and mine as well, he sold the business and retired early. The weather out here has extended his years, I'm sure, and he loves to golf, so things have been pleasant.

"Until last spring, when he started to have some serious heart problems. This summer, the crisis hit. His doctors became so concerned, he had a number of stents implanted in his arteries, only to have *them* fail. Open-heart surgery was then the only option, and there were problems with *that*—I never understood the technicalities. In all, Henry was hospitalized for over a month this past summer. He's back on his feet now, barely. And if you ask me, he still looks like hell.

"That's not the point though, is it? No, the point is, sometime during all this, Henry became involved with another woman. Can you believe it—a man of his age, in his condition? I don't know how or where they met, and I don't know who she is, but she's *ruined* the life we built together." Arlene paused long enough to take a goodly slurp of her martini. The bitter look that crossed her face may have been a reaction to either the story or the gin.

I asked, "How did you find out? Did the guilt get to Henry? Did he confess?"

"Hell, *no.*" Her nostrils flared. "He didn't *confess.* The tramp *wrote* to me!"

"Uh-oh," said Grant, under his breath.

"Why would she do that?" I asked. "What did she want?"

"She wanted *Henry*, of course. The letter, which arrived in last Friday's mail, simply informed me that she and Henry had been seeing each other for some time. They were in love, it said, and I deserved to know. Period. And it was signed—get this—'The Other Woman.' "

"How original," Grant cooed.

"Clearly, her intent in exposing the affair was to separate Henry and me, freeing him to marry his newfound love. Friday evening, when Henry returned home from the club, I confronted him with the letter. He was *furious* with The Other Woman's ploy—so much so, I thought he might drop dead then and there—and this time, as far as I was concerned, he could damn well do it. But he didn't, of course. He acknowledged that there was indeed another woman, that he may have loved her, but that he never had any intention of marrying her, which she had known from the start. Now, he said, he was through with her; she'd destroyed any affection he'd ever felt for her. Though he was outraged by what she had done, he refused to tell me who she was. So I demanded a separation—and, of course, a comfortable new home— which he contritely agreed to. Hence my urgent calls to you, Grant, the very next morning."

The very next morning was Saturday, the time of the murder. I asked Arlene, "While you were phoning Grant, what was Henry doing? Had he calmed down?"

"I *doubt* it, though I didn't see him that morning. He had a golf game at the club, leaving home at daybreak, not returning till afternoon."

" 'The club'?" I asked. "Which one?" In the desert, country clubs are more common than supermarkets.

"Ugh," she thought aloud, pressing her manicured nails to her forehead, "they all sound alike. He's been a member for years. Oh, Mission Palms, that's it. The clubhouse dining room isn't bad," she conceded. "They do a decent Sunday brunch. Mahvelous quiche."

Suppressing a laugh, Grant gulped from his martini.

I asked Arlene, "This letter—from The Other Woman—it gave no clue as to who she was? Did it perhaps allude to the woman's job?"

Arlene shook her head. "See for yourself." Plopping her pig purse on the table, she snapped it open, extracted a small, girlie-pink envelope, and handed it to me.

As I removed the letter and opened it, the smell of perfume rose to my nostrils. It was sweet and flowery, decidedly feminine—*not* patchouli. Grant leaned to my side and read the letter as I did. The wording was exactly as Arlene had described it, terse and anonymous. It was indeed signed, "The Other Woman."

I studied the letter for a moment before handing it back to Arlene. Grant was telling her, "You may be in luck regarding housing. Just this afternoon, one of the larger homes up at Nirvana went on the market. A last-minute deal—I was almost late getting here tonight because of it. Anyway, it's furnished, it's lovely, it's available, and it's *you,* Arlene. But"—he paused—"it *is* expensive."

Harrumph. "Henry can afford it," she assured him flatly.

Before long, our first course arrived, and our talk shifted from murder and infidelity to monkfish livers and porcini gnocchi. The meal, as before, was a stunning success. Even skeptical Arlene was won over.

As course followed course, I kept an ear to the conversation, contributing from time to time, but my mind was focused on what I'd learned that night.

Before Arlene had arrived, Grant had mentioned that he'd be willing to bet money that Henry had not been involved with Jodie, and I had assumed he was very likely right. Now, though, I wasn't so sure. Physically, Henry was no prize, but he *was* loaded—and practically at death's door—which may have been ample reason for Jodie to take an interest in him. Though the sweetly perfumed letter seemed to distance Henry from the crime (Jodie didn't wear perfume), the timing of the letter's arrival, coupled with Henry's subsequent outrage and his Saturday-morning "golf game," was sufficient to cast him in a suspicious light.

At meal's end, Grant, Arlene, and I left the restaurant together, stepping out to the sidewalk. Having lingered through an enjoyable meal, we were among the last patrons to finish, and it was now late. A cool, still night had descended upon the desert from a velvety black sky. The trendy side street was quieter than I'd seen it, and Grant looked about for a parking valet, preferably the pet.

We were about to step back inside and ask about our cars when Kane, the pet, jogged up the sidewalk toward us. I was surprised to note that he still had the white rose tucked in his shirt; I'd assumed he would pitch it the moment we were out of sight. "Sorry," he said, breathless, "it got slow, so my buddy went home and I'm the only one here. I'll take care of you."

"Ah!" said Grant. "Thank you, Kane. Arlene, do you have your stub?"

She fished it from her pig and handed it to Grant, who handed it with a bill to Kane. "Right back!" said the parker, taking off at a trot.

The three of us chatted for a couple of minutes, just small talk. Grant offered to show Arlene the house at Nirvana, but she declined, trilling, "You've already said it was *perfect* for me. Write it up, dahling."

Kane rumbled to the curb in Arlene's yellow Bentley, got out of the car, and held the door. Grant walked Arlene to the street, wished her well, and kissed her cheek. It took both Grant *and* Kane to help her get comfortably situated behind the wheel—there was a lot of dress to deal with. Then she screeched away, honking, putting all twelve cylinders to the test.

Grant offered Kane an apologetic grin as he began searching his pockets for the other parking stub.

"That's okay. I know, the silver Beetle." The kid scampered off.

Grant joined me on the sidewalk. "I already know that you enjoyed the meal, so there's no need to ask about it. And I can assume what you thought of Arlene, so I won't force a fudged answer. But I *would* like to know: Was the evening useful to you?"

I smiled. "Very. You had nearly convinced me to scratch Henry

Harris off my suspect list. But now? I'm not so sure, Grant."

He stuffed his hands in his pockets. "I admit, the whole business about the letter, especially its timing, raises some serious questions."

"The most pertinent being, was Henry in fact golfing on Saturday morning at the time of the murder?"

"That should be easy to check out."

I nodded. "Could you do me a favor?"

"Anything."

"Phone your brother, tell him what we learned, and ask him to check with Mission Palms Country Club. They surely have a record of Saturday's tee times, and they probably won't flinch at answering questions from a sheriff's detective."

"I'll call Larry at home as soon as we get back."

"I'd do it myself," I continued, "but there's a part two. You could also phone Henry and ask him to meet you tomorrow at the Nirvana sales office—on the pretext of discussing and approving Arlene's purchase plans."

Grant laughed. "That's hardly a 'pretext.' Arlene's new hilltop bungalow is going to set Henry back millions."

"Wonderful—you can talk business. But the point is, your brother Larry and I will just 'happen' to be there, and if Henry's golf alibi hasn't checked out, the questioning can begin."

"Okay," he said, "I get it. You need me to coordinate the meeting with everyone's schedules—mine, Larry's, Henry's, and yours."

"Right. And my day is wide open, by the way." Then I recalled Tanner Griffin. "Oops, sorry, I have a ten o'clock meeting on campus, but otherwise I'm free."

Grant smirked. "I'll make a note of it." Just then, the Beetle pulled up to the curb, putting all four cylinders to the test. "Here we are," said Grant, escorting me across the sidewalk.

Kane hopped out of the car and began to circle around to open my door, but Grant waved him off, telling him with a smile, "Thanks, but I can get it."

The valet returned to the open driver's door, and as I got into the car, I saw him reach in to get something from behind the seat. Grant stepped into the street, rounding the rear of the car. Kane stood holding the door for him. When Grant reached into a pocket for his wallet, the kid stopped him with a gesture.

"No, really, Kane." Grant laughed softly. "You've been especially good to us tonight. I'd like to give you—"

But the kid cut him off again. "This, uh," he stammered, looking suddenly bashful, "this is for you." And from behind his back he produced a rose, a red one. He repeated Grant's earlier show of dulling a thorn with his thumbnail, then he slid the short stem into the breast pocket of Grant's sport coat, pausing to pat it in place.

The tension in their shared gaze was electric—it even gave *me* a tingle.

Grant offered his arms, and Kane stepped into them for a full, slow embrace. With the sides of their heads pressed together, Grant smelled the younger man's sweat. Barely audible, he said, "Thank you, Kane."

The kid laughed quietly. "No, thank *you,* Grant."

When they stepped apart, Grant slid the wallet out of his pocket with resolve, producing a crisp twenty.

"No," Kane said gently but decisively.

Grant paused, shrugged, and put away his money. Cupping his hand behind Kane's head, he squeezed the nape of the young man's sturdy neck before stepping back and getting into the car.

Taking hold of the door, Kane crouched to tell us, "Come back soon." He looked adorable, squatting there in his white shorts and tennis shoes, knees aimed at us.

Watching him, Grant could barely speak. "I . . . I'm sure we will."

Kane smiled, nodded, and thumped the door closed as Grant revved the engine and puttered away from the curb.

"Well, now," I said, *"that* was promising."

Grant shook his head, as if awaking from a dream. "Promising? That was astounding." And he fell silent, eyes fixed on the dark road ahead.

In his mind, I'm sure, his face was still pressed to Kane's damp cheek.

17

Though our evening at Fusión had been both enjoyable and productive, it had also involved a large meal, ample liquor, and a late bedtime. So Thursday morning, I slept nearly an hour later than usual, rising around seven, which didn't give me much time to prepare for Paul Huron's arrival at eight. The previous day, at Jodie's memorial service, I had invited him to come for breakfast, thinking he could use some companionship and quiet chatter after spending the night alone, a night that was surely haunted by images of his late wife. Though my motives had been laudable, I now regretted having extended the invitation, feeling rushed. It was all I could do to make the bed, shower, dress, and get the coffee going. The phone calls didn't help either.

First, Grant called from next door, saying that he'd reached both his brother, Detective Larry Knoll, and Arlene's now-estranged husband, Henry Harris. Larry was now fully apprised of the developments from dinner, and he would get busy checking Henry's story that he'd been golfing on Saturday morning. As for Henry, he now knew only that Arlene had her eye on a rambling house at Nirvana, and he had readily agreed to Grant's suggestion that they meet to discuss the transaction that morning at eleven. Unknown to him, Larry and I would "happen" to be there as well.

My morning was now fully booked: I would have breakfast with Paul at eight, arrive on campus by nine for some desk work, meet with Tanner Griffin at ten to discuss his possible enrollment, then rush over to the Nirvana sales office by eleven. But first, I *had* to do something with my hair. I was still deciding on what to wear—leaning toward a red linen jumpsuit I typically saved for more "special" occasions, but what the hell—when the phone rang a second time.

It was Larry Knoll, calling from his car to compliment me on the plan I'd hatched. He'd already talked to the pro shop at Mission Palms, and sure enough, Henry Harris had *not* been scheduled to play on Saturday morning. In fact, he had missed a tee time that was booked for later that afternoon. "It'll be interesting to hear how the old guy explains *that.*"

"And what about Dr. Blair?" I asked.

The dead silence told me that Larry had forgotten something.

I began to explain, "The wineglass, wrapped in a napkin, that I gave you yesterday at—"

"I know. I know," he assured me, sounding disgusted. "It's here, right here in the car where I left it, still covered with my suit coat. It got hot yesterday afternoon, so I left my jacket in the car, and I forgot what was underneath. Sorry, Claire."

He was far more embarrassed by the slipup than I was annoyed by it. With an understanding laugh, I asked, "Fingerprints 'keep,' don't they?"

"Sure." He allowed himself a chuckle. "I'm out on a call right now, but I'll be going in to the station a bit later, and I'll hand over the glass to the lab. It won't take them long to determine if we've got a match or not."

"I'll see you at eleven?"

"Right, at Nirvana. I should have a report on the prints by then. *And"*—his voice broke off for a tantalizing pause—"I should have a much better idea whether Oralia has been on the level with her alibi."

"I'm intrigued. Tell me more."

"In due time, Claire. Can't talk right now. Later." And he hung up.

Mention of Oralia reminded me that I really *could* use some household help, especially that morning. Glancing in a mirror, I decided that I was more than presentable for the hour (the jumpsuit was a good choice), and I still had five or ten minutes during which I could throw together something resembling breakfast.

Coffee was ready. Juice was easy. I'd thought to pick up some English muffins earlier that week, and I now split a few and put them in the toaster oven. I transferred a couple of tubs of yogurt to sherbet glasses, washed some fruit, and arranged it all on a tray with butter, jams, napkins, and silver. Stepping back, I surveyed my culinary handiwork and found it surprisingly adequate, considering I'd winged it.

Checking the time, I saw that it was just past eight, and I realized that in my rush that morning, I hadn't even cracked open the front door to take in the paper. So I tumbled the dead bolt and stepped outside.

My entry court was still in shade; a trace of the night's chill still clung to the terra-cotta tiles. As I stooped near the gate to pick up the rolled copy of the *Desert Sun,* I heard the slam of a car door out front, so I opened the gate and walked into the main courtyard, stopping at the fountain, where I could glimpse the street. Paul had just arrived; I saw the rear of his blue Honda parked at the curb. A moment later, Paul himself stepped into view, waving as he saw me. He wore his workaday black jeans and black T-shirt; his black hair glistened in the sunlight, still wet from the shower. He was a good-looking man—an artist with a sense of personal style and a sensitive nature as well. There was a bounce to his step that I hadn't seen all week.

"You were *waiting* for me?" he asked from a distance. "Am I late?"

"Just stepped out for the paper, and I happened to hear you."

Arriving at the fountain, he gave me a hug. "Morning, Claire. Thanks for having me over. What a nice idea."

Taking his arm, I strolled him toward my door, warning, "Breakfast isn't much, I'm afraid, but the hospitality is sincere." I patted his hand. "Glad you're here."

Once inside, I closed the front door, set down the paper, and opened the French doors to the back terrace. "It's such lovely morning, let's eat by the pool."

"Sounds great. How can I help?"

There was little left to do other than to carry things, so I put Paul to good use, loading him up with the tray and wedging the newspaper under his arm. I carried the glass pot of coffee, leading him outside, closing the doors behind us, and guiding him to the common terrace by the pool.

It was a glorious morning—ho hum, just another perfect day in paradise—cloudless, dry, and agreeably warm. As we arranged our breakfast things on a glass table in the shade of a few clumped orange trees, a finch broke the stillness with an ecstatic trill, signaling to others to take up the call. By the time we sat, the tiny chorus was in full voice, to which I added my own laughter as I poured coffee for two. "I've been here three weeks, and it still doesn't seem real."

"The place really grows on you, doesn't it?"

"It doesn't take long! If you're not happy *here,* you're not—" I cut myself short, realizing that my giddy proclamation didn't quite apply to a man who'd just scattered his murdered wife's ashes. "Forgive me, Paul. That was insensitive."

He brushed off my apology. "You meant no harm. And you're right. If ever there was a setting that could ease life's bumps, this is it." He buttered a muffin.

I was surprised—and delighted, of course—to see him in such good spirits. He'd just referred to his wife's death as one of "life's bumps," and I'd noticed since his arrival that he seemed well rested, at ease, and almost chipper. Day by day, I reasoned, the immediate shock of Jodie's death became more remote, and apparently the previous day's memorial service had provided that all-important sense of closure. There would still be a long period of mourning with its occasional spasms of grief, but Paul now seemed able to view the tragedy itself from an emotionally safe distance, where he could analyze it, perhaps ponder it, but refuse to be consumed by it.

He offered me the buttered muffin.

"Thanks, Paul." I sighed, contented, while spreading a dab of raspberry preserves over the warm, craggy toast. "I don't mean to sound patronizing, but I'm glad you're beginning to put 'everything' behind you." My air quotes around *everything* signaled that it was a euphemism for *murder.*

He nodded. "I've had a lot of help. Lots of good friends. Not to mention Glenn's campaign to, uh . . . help me 'get beyond this.' "

Licking jam from my fingers, I owned, "He *has* seemed a bit eager, hasn't he?"

"Well"—Paul grinned—"you know *Glenn.* Once he gets focused on something, little can stand in the way."

"*That's* an understatement." I shared a laugh with Paul, knowing that I'd never stood a chance once Glenn had decided to recruit me for his faculty. He needed to build a theater to convince me, but he did it.

Paul tasted the coffee and nodded his approval. "Give me another week, and I should have my feet on the ground again. Yesterday's service was a big help, but as you know, Jodie's memorial is only half complete."

"When is the trip to Michigan?"

"Wednesday. It's all set. I'll fly out Tuesday evening with Jodie's ashes and return Wednesday night—without them. Short and sweet."

Pointedly, I noted, "Then you'll miss only a day of classes. That should keep someone happy." I ate the last bite of the muffin, then asked, "Speaking of classes, is everything on schedule for Monday?"

"Sure." He nodded confidently. "There are bound to be last-minute crises, but the doors will open, students will enter, and classes will begin. It's been an enormous effort, but well coordinated from the outset. Say what you will about Glenn, but he deserves a lot of credit."

With a chortle, I reminded him, "Glenn says the same thing about *you*. He seems to find you indispensable."

"We have a certain affinity," he admitted. "Glenn and I just sort of clicked. I mean, I'm a *sculptor*, not an administrator, but it seems I've been useful."

Offering more coffee, I told him, "Don't be so modest."

Our conversation continued along these lines, relating mostly to the school, covering such details as enrollment figures, direct deposit of paychecks, grading procedures, and all manner of bureaucratic whatnot. Though I could easily have become bored with this talk, I did not. Indeed, discussing the logistics of my new life was oddly invigorating— and considerably less taxing than the mystery of who had killed Jodie Metz-Huron.

Reminding myself that the school, not the investigation, was the purpose of my move, I began to focus again on the new challenges that would await me as I attempted to build, from scratch, a college theater program second to none. Glenn Yeats was a man of very high goals, which he had a habit of meeting, and for this I respected him enormously, having always felt similarly driven. Now he had handed me the opportunity to make a real difference among the next generation of actors, an opportunity to steer the future course of American theater. And this new phase of my life, this mission, would begin in just four days, when Desert Arts College would officially open to its charter enrollment. Suddenly, I was champing at the bit to get over to my office and make it happen.

Our conversation had lapsed, and Paul lolled with his cup of coffee, enjoying the morning. "Did you want your paper?" he asked, offering me the rolled copy of the *Desert Sun,* which he'd set aside when we arranged the table.

"Thanks, sure." I took the newspaper, sensing that I'd been wanting to look at it, though not sure why. As soon as I unrolled it, I had my answer. "My God, Paul. I forgot—here's the story about Jodie's ring."

"Oh, yeah?" he asked brightly.

I held the paper so he could see it. There, above the fold on page one, was a large color photo of Jodie's wedding ring, accompanied by a story that was headlined UNIQUE RING MAY HOLD KEY TO NURSE'S MURDER. Though I hadn't brought my reading glasses outdoors, I found I didn't need them in the full sunlight, and I read the opening of the story to Paul:

> Riverside County Sheriff's Department investigators have released a photo of a unique wedding ring that was reported missing from Jodie Metz-Huron's finger. The thirty-year-old nurse's lifeless body was discovered at home last Saturday in Palm Desert.
>
> The ring was custom-designed and commissioned five years ago by her husband, Paul Huron, who was then on the faculty of the Rhode Island School of Design. The distinctive piece of jewelry is actually two interlocking rings representing male and female figures. Each is topped with a large pearl, one black, the other white.
>
> Detective Larry Knoll, who is leading the homicide investigation, explained, "Due to the ring's unique design, it should be easily identified by anyone who happens to see it. This could supply the single most important clue we need in tracing this crime to the assailant." Detective Knoll is asking all citizens, but particularly jewelers and pawnbrokers, to be on the lookout for the distinctive ring.

The photo itself was found on Tuesday by the victim's husband, who moved to the valley this summer to join the new faculty at Desert Arts College. "The department thanks Mr. Huron," said Detective Knoll, "for his diligence in providing this photograph, which could prove highly valuable to the investigation."

To date, there has been no definitive evidence that . . .

I looked up from the paper, telling Paul, "*Well*, now, they're certainly giving it the full treatment. No lack of cooperation from the press."

He smiled. "That's great. It's good to know that *something*, at last, is being done." He tasted the pink yogurt I'd put out, then licked the spoon, enjoying it.

I reminded him, "Larry's been hard at work behind the scenes since the start. Now that the case is back on page one, maybe something'll shake loose."

"God, I hope so." He took another spoonful of yogurt, telling me, "Larry has mentioned that you've made some valuable contributions to his investigation. I can't thank you enough, Claire."

I opened my mouth, intending to dismiss his thanks, to assure him that I'd been enjoying the challenge. Realizing, however, that his perspective on these events was far different from mine, I simply told him, "Glad to be of help. Let's see, the story goes on to quote Larry about 'several leads that are still under active investigation'—blah, blah, blah. Then it goes back and recaps the whole chronology, starting with the events of Saturday morning. 'Mr. Huron had just flown home from a business trip to Dallas, when . . .'" I paused, needing to flip below the fold.

"*Hey,*" I said, bug-eyed, "congratulations, Paul. You made page one."

"Huh?"

As I held up the paper so he could see the entire page, he leaned closer with a quizzical look. There, just below the fold, was a one-column mug shot of Paul himself. "Very handsome," I assured him.

Standing, he took the paper from my hands. "What the hell . . . ," he muttered, staring at his photo.

Through a soft laugh, I again tried to tell him, "It's a *very* nice picture, and—"

"No"—he shook his head—"they shouldn't have done that."

"Why not? The story refers to you several times. Like it or not, Paul, this is news. This is a legitimate—"

"But it's *Jodie's* story," he explained, folding the paper and setting it on the table. "This story isn't about *me*. I'm not looking for sympathy. How did they even *get* the picture?"

"There was a credit line, I think, but I couldn't read it without my glasses." I handed him the paper again.

He looked at the line of small type. "Figures." Then he tossed the paper back onto the table.

I guessed, " 'Photo courtesy of Desert Arts College'?"

"Naturally. Glenn supplied it, I'll bet. Anything to publicize the school, even in six-point type."

I stood. Our relaxed breakfast was over. "I'm sure he was only trying to help."

Paul scratched behind an ear. "Yeah."

"Uh, look, Paul. If you need to be going, I can clean up here." I assumed he'd insist on helping me haul everything indoors.

"In fact"—his tone was apologetic—"if you really don't mind, I've got tons of work waiting in my office, and I haven't checked on progress in the studios for days, and I hear there was a major problem installing one of the kilns, and—"

I laughed. "Paul, say no more. It won't take me a minute to clear everything. Hop along now."

"Thanks, Claire." He hugged me. "This was wonderful."

"I enjoyed your company," I told him, returning the hug. "I'll be driving over to campus shortly. See you at the office?"

"I'll be there."

We said our farewells.

Then I pointed the way to the front courtyard, and he left.

18

An hour later, I was seated at the desk in my campus office at Desert Arts College. I had arrived from home shortly after nine and had been pulling files, making phone calls, and searching my own soul in preparation for Tanner Griffin's visit, scheduled for ten o'clock, now but a few minutes away. I had found, as expected, that I held complete authority to admit to the theater program any student I wished, regardless of his or her academic background, age, or finances. Glenn Yeats had granted me carte blanche in building the best program possible, however I saw fit.

Which left but one hurdle to cross, an obstacle that seemed simultaneously simple and impossible. I had to answer but one question: Was I truly prepared to recommend that Tanner enroll in my program? The answer would necessarily be predicated on another, underlying, question: Was I motivated by his best interests—or by my own irresponsible fantasies?

I was heading into dangerous territory, and I knew it. Several thick files on my desk contained nearly a year's worth of correspondence from students who had applied from all over the country. Some were high-schoolers, ready to embark on their college careers and willing to take a chance on a new school—simply because I had agreed to be there. Others were already in college, seeking to transfer to a school still under construction—again, because I had agreed to be there. I could afford to be highly selective, and I was; the files bulging with the rejected were far heftier than the tidy stack of applications from the elite, the accepted.

All of these kids were committed and talented. They had hoped and sweated and scrimped and probably cried during the months I'd pondered my decisions. And now here I was, getting fickle with my own standards, itching to roll out the welcome mat to a mechanic with a business degree who'd bent to his parents' wishes that he not follow his dream.

Mulling these matters at my desk, struggling with a decision that seemed emotionally appealing but intellectually untenable, I set the question aside for a moment as my eye came to rest on the stack of the accepted, the chosen. What had set *them* apart? I had never met most of them, though I'd watched videotapes of their work. They had all demonstrated competence at the basics of stagecraft; for that matter, so had most of the rejected. Beyond that, there were intangibles at work— vibes, for lack of a better term—that had emerged from between the lines of their applications and hinted at the potential for achievement, perhaps even greatness.

The documents at the top of the pile were a good example. A young man from Wisconsin, Thad Quatrain, had discovered the lure of theater during his junior year of high school. When he first submitted his application to DAC, he'd had only a year's involvement with theater, experience in only four plays. But there was a passion to his writing and a spark to his taped audition that had caught my eye and set him apart. What had clinched Thad's acceptance, though, had little to do with his objective merits.

One of the letters in support of Thad's application had been written by his uncle, one Mark Manning—I recognized the name at once. Mark had been a Chicago newspaper reporter with a national reputation for his high-profile stories. I'd met him a few years earlier while I was in that city for an important festival of arts and sciences. I'd found him to be a warm and charming man as well as a coldly rational thinker and a top-notch writer. Through a set of circumstances that still baffled me, he had moved from Chicago to a small town in central Wisconsin, where he now served as publisher of the local paper and as surrogate parent to his recently orphaned nephew.

If Mark Manning told me that some kid from Wisconsin would work his butt off to excel in my program at DAC, that was good enough for me. Though I'd never met Thad Quatrain, I knew someone who knew him well, someone I trusted. I felt sufficiently "connected" to have confidence in the boy.

Tanner Griffin represented the other side of the coin. I *had* met him. I'd seen his face, heard his voice, and felt a sheer magnetism that could easily translate to a powerful stage presence. I had not, however, seen him act, not even on tape, and though he claimed to be good at it, I was considering him without references or recommendations. If I admitted him and he fell short, would I have the ability to bring him up to speed? For that matter, would he have the drive to work at it? After all, he'd given it up before.

The bottom line, I knew, was that I found him achingly attractive— not a good basis for a teacher's choice of students. Still, if I reacted to him that way, there was a fair chance that audiences would as well. If at some point he beat the odds and was catapulted to stardom, he would add immeasurable luster to the school, its program, and my own reputation.

I had all but decided: there would be three tests. If Tanner arrived promptly for our meeting, if he still showed the passion to commit to a new venture in his life, and if I still felt the spark that told me he was that rarest of talents, a "natural," then I would admit him to my program.

"Claire?" his soft tone apologized for interrupting my thoughts.

I turned from my desk to find Tanner standing just inside the door, which I'd left open a few inches. He wore the same style of cargo shorts I'd seen him wear before, only these were stone colored, not olive, which made him look bronzer and hunkier than ever. He wore the same tan work shoes that seemed to match his sandy hair. This morning he wore not a knit shirt but an oversize white cotton camp-style shirt, perfectly clean and freshly pressed. Tucked into his shorts, it bloused a bit above his belt, accentuating his thin waist and broad chest. Good God, I felt like a bobby-soxer ogling the senior quarterback in homeroom.

I rose, greeting him with a smile, "Morning, Tanner. Come in." Glancing at my watch, I noted that he'd passed the first and easiest of my tests. It was a minute before ten.

Walking into the room (ah, the sight of him in motion), he told me,

"That's a neat, uh . . . outfit." He wasn't sure what to call my jumpsuit.

Flustered, I was tempted to ask, This old thing? but had sense enough not to.

"You look good in red."

"Thank you, Tanner." I nodded my appreciation, adding objectively, "I've always thought so too. Care to sit down?"

"Uh-oh." He grinned. "Sounds like bad news." He sat, as before, in the chair next to my desk.

"Not at all." I sat facing him. "I just thought we should talk a bit."

"Great." He exhaled. "I didn't sleep very well last night."

Under my breath, I told him, "It doesn't show."

"Oh?" He laughed (that smile—save me). "How *could* I sleep? I mean, today's a turning point, maybe. I was dumb enough, or weak enough, not to follow my instincts when I was in college. Not many people are lucky enough to get a second chance to pursue . . . what, a dream, a passion? I'm older now, only four years, but they were important ones. I'm not a kid anymore who has the luxury of flitting from major to major, trying things out, hoping for a match. This is life, this is me, this is it. *If* in fact there's an opportunity for me to return to school—here, with you, Claire—I've decided to go for it. I'll do whatever it takes to make it happen, and this time, there'll be no turning back. *That's* what kept me up last night."

My, I thought, he was skimming through my tests rather quickly, having just passed the second with his willingness to make a commitment. All that remained was for me to feel the spark confirming his natural talents. We could then wrap this up, and I'd process his paperwork.

Not that I was in a rush to be rid of him. Hardly. "I'm glad to hear you taking this so seriously. If we go through with this, I'll be taking a real chance on you."

He nodded. "I know that. You barely know me. You have no idea who I am." He rested his arm on the desk and leaned toward me. "If you end up going to bat for me, that only doubles my commitment—I owe it to *you* as well as to *me*."

He was saying all the right things, but one of his sentences stuck in my mind. "You have no idea who I am," he'd said, and he was right.

The only reason that we had happened to meet, just three days ago, was that a murdered woman's words had raised my suspicions of him. Though my theories regarding Jodie's nameless killer were now focused in other directions, I had no objective proof that Tanner had not been with her on Saturday morning.

My eye drifted toward the cobalt paperweight that still sat atop a pile of documents at the corner of the desk, exactly where Tanner had placed it on Tuesday. The glass was still smudged with his fingerprints—instinctively, I had not touched it. If I felt so certain that Tanner could not possibly be Jodie's killer, why hadn't I cleaned the paperweight? Did I still harbor suspicions about him? Or had I simply been so confident of his innocence that I'd deliberately kept the fingerprints as testament to my faith that there was nothing to hide?

I recalled that at dinner the previous night I'd resolved to ask Tanner today about where he'd been on Saturday morning. What's more, I'd resolved to ask him this question outright, without subterfuge. As we sat there at my desk, however, talking in abstractions about commitment to goals, passion for the arts, and love of learning, I found it all but impossible to segue to the topic of his whereabouts at the time of Jodie's death.

After a lull in our discussion, Tanner provided the opening I needed. "Oh," he asked, "have you reached any decisions about tinting your Beetle's windows?"

"Sorry." I laughed. "I *still* haven't studied the material you left for me."

He nodded. "Guess you've had a lot on your mind this week—school and all."

"School, yes, but mostly, I've been perplexed about Jodie Huron."

"Ahhh." He nodded. "Yeah, it's awful."

"As a matter of fact, Tanner, when I met you Monday morning at Desert Detail, there was an ulterior motive for my visit."

He paused before telling me, "You know, that did strike me as . . . 'off' somehow. You told me that you needed something done with the Beetle, but you never got around to saying what. We spent most of our time talking about Jodie."

I nodded, feeling guilty. Swallowing, I explained, "I met Jodie only once, just a few days before she was killed. During our conversation that evening, she mentioned you, not by name but in the context of having Paul's car repaired. She told me, 'I've found the most *marvelous* mechanic.' Then she winked, adding, 'He's *very* accommodating.' "

Tanner slapped a hand to his forehead. "Oh, God," he moaned. "No *wonder* you seemed to think I'd been involved with her."

"Exactly. And one of the theories we're working on—"

" 'We'?"

Did I really want to go into this? Tanner revered me as a living legend of the American theater. He'd professed a profound desire to study, as it were, at my feet. Would he see me as a total ditz if he discovered that those feet were now shod with gumshoes?

I told him, "When Paul Huron found Jodie's body on Saturday morning, I was with him; I'd just driven him home from the airport. Naturally, the police questioned me about what had happened, and I helped in any way I could. I've stayed in touch with the detective, and we've weighed a few ideas together."

"Wow. I'm impressed."

"Originally, it seemed that Jodie might have been the innocent casualty of a bungled home invasion, but now, a far stronger theory suggests that Jodie had been having an affair with someone—and something went wrong."

Tanner sat back in his chair, stonefaced, as my point became clear. "In other words," he said, "you thought I might have done it."

Leaning forward, I touched my fingers to his bare knee. "At first, it struck me as a possibility. I just didn't know."

"And you *still* don't, right?"

"Tanner, you've never given me reason to doubt you. So humor me. Tell me outright: Where were you last Saturday morning between eight-thirty and nine?" I pulled back, holding my breath, wary of his reaction to so blunt a question.

To my great relief, he smiled. "That's easy: I was at the shop. I'm there *every* Saturday morning."

I returned his smile. "Thank God. That *is* easy." If necessary, Tanner's alibi could later be corroborated by other workers at Desert Detail.

Now it was his turn to lean forward. His features fell as he asked quietly, "Is that what this is all about? This meeting—it's about Jodie's murder?" Though he didn't elaborate, he was asking if our discussion of his enrollment had been merely a stratagem to sound out a suspect.

"No," I assured him flatly. "From the moment when I first suggested that you consider returning to school—it was Monday at the shop—I was thinking that you might be valuable to my program here. Certainly, I feel the program could be valuable to you as well. It has to work both ways, a fair exchange."

He grinned. "Traders?" He was referring both to a concept and to the title of the play I'd written, which was thematically based on that concept.

Nodding, I smiled, flattered that he was so familiar with my work, grateful that he had the intellectual maturity to grasp it. Heartened by his understanding, I added, "My original suspicions that linked you to Jodie have had no bearing on our discussions of your enrollment at DAC. If I had any ulterior motive in asking you to come here today"—I hesitated, then decided, yes, honesty is best—"it is simply that I enjoy your company." Sitting back in my chair, I offered a wan smile that was meant to ask, Have I sufficiently disillusioned you?

He had watched me with a blank expression, fearsome in its lack of emotion, but then the corners of his mouth began to turn—upward. He spoke softly and precisely, without ambiguity: "I am honored beyond measure. And I, too, enjoy *your* company."

I may have blushed, but I didn't care; we had just stepped beyond pretense or coyness. If the blood rising to my flesh revealed the excitement generated by his mere presence, so be it. "Well, then," I told him, opening a folder on my desk, "it seems the admiration is mutual."

Cautiously, he asked, "Are we still talking about . . . school?"

"I *hope* so. Are you still interested in enrolling?"

He stood, stepped to the front of my desk. "Well . . . *yes.*"

Putting my glasses on, I perused the documents I'd gathered for him, explaining, "There are formalities to the application procedure, and the tuition waiver involves jumping through a few hoops, but basically Glenn Yeats has left to my discretion any decisions pertaining to the theater department."

"Must be nice." Tanner turned to me with a smile. He was skimming the framed copy of a *New Yorker* interview that hung near my desk. It had been published shortly after *Traders* closed on Broadway and went into film production.

"It beats having to beg," I admitted, "but right now, getting started, it can be overwhelming. See this?" I tapped another document, a computer printout that I'd shoved to the side of the desk. "It's a checklist I found under my office door this morning. Installation of the theater's tech systems is nearly complete, but Glenn won't make payment to any of the contractors till I've signed off on their work—and there are always those last-minute glitches." Intrigued by some detail, I placed the list in front of me and began studying it.

Tanner was saying, "When you showed me the theater on Tuesday, they seemed to be having some trouble with one of the pinrails."

"Hm?" I looked up from the checklist.

Tanner had just pulled a white handkerchief out of his hip pocket. "The fly lines to the fire curtain kept tangling."

"Really? I hadn't noticed. *That* won't do." Though concerned about the problem, I was delighted to discover the extent of Tanner's technical knowledge as well as his attention to detail.

"I was watching from the front row while you were talking with the sound guy in back." Tanner picked up the blue paperweight and began polishing it with his handkerchief. "If it's not on your checklist, they must've figured it out."

"What are you doing?" Dumbfounded, I stared as he removed his fingerprints from the glass.

Replacing the paperweight where he'd found it, handling it with the cloth, he explained with a laugh, "Someone left paw marks all over it. Much better now, though." And he stuffed the handkerchief back into his pocket.

The cobalt glass shone beautifully, casting a pool of blue light on the white paper beneath it. I smiled, thanking Tanner for his attention to detail, dismissing the notion that his tidiness had been motivated by something sinister. But a frown wrinkled my brow.

"What's wrong?" he asked.

"That fire curtain—it has me worried." I stood. "Do you mind if we continue this discussion in the theater?"

He beamed. "Not at all."

"I wasn't on campus at all yesterday, and I haven't checked the theater yet this morning. You can point out the problem you saw. And we can wrap up our meeting in far more pleasant surroundings."

"Great."

Gathering up a few files and my keys from the desk, I paused, looking about. With a shudder, I asked Tanner, "Is it just me, or does this office leave you cold?"

He glanced around, then nodded without comment.

Out in the curved hallway, I pulled my door closed, then jiggled the knob, confirming that it was locked. Tanner and I exchanged a few predictable, derisive comments about the circular layout of the building as we passed several doors. "Oh," I said, "Paul's office is just around the bend. I'd like to pop in. We had breakfast this morning, and I neglected to ask him—"

But Paul's door was closed, with a pile of morning mail shoved under the crack. Clearly, he wasn't in, so I didn't bother knocking. I told Tanner, "He must be over in the sculpture studios—problems with a kiln."

"Ah," said Tanner, and we continued down the hall. After a moment, he added, "Don't take this the wrong way, but I'm sort of glad we missed him."

"Paul? How come?"

Tanner hedged, "Well, don't you find it sort of . . . awkward? I mean, his *wife* just died. I never know what to say."

I laughed quietly. Tanner was young. Year by year, the abstraction of death would become more real, almost tangible, to him; he would become far better practiced in greeting and consoling the bereaved. I told him, "You simply extend your sympathies, then get on with the business of living. When I saw Paul this morning, I could tell he was starting to cope, focusing on today and even next week, instead of last Saturday."

Tanner nodded, looking pensive. "It's just that, well, I *knew* Jodie, and there *was* some attraction between us. Nothing ever happened, but I can't help wondering if Paul picked up on the chemistry."

He had a point. I'd learned from previous discussions that Paul had never known of Tanner by name, but he'd been well aware of Jodie's enthusiasm for her accommodating mechanic. Paul finally met Tanner when he returned the blue Honda on Tuesday; one look should have been sufficient for Paul to understand why his wife had gotten giddy over car repairs. I'd determined that Paul was in a state of serious denial over Jodie's apparent infidelities, but in his heart of hearts, he surely "knew." Had he also come to suspect Tanner as the other man?

Dismissing this concern, I told Tanner, "You have nothing to be ashamed of, so don't get paranoid." With a sly laugh, I added, "It only fosters an aura of guilt."

He returned the laugh. "We wouldn't want *that,* would we?"

"Claire! There you are. I just tried phoning your office." It was Glenn Yeats, standing ahead of us in the hall, near the mahogany doors to his office suite.

"Hi, Glenn," I returned the greeting, approaching him with Tanner. "Glad we ran into you. I'd like you to meet someone."

"My pleasure, I'm sure." He smiled, waiting.

"Glenn, this is Tanner Griffin, who's thinking of applying to our theater program. He could be a valuable asset to the school."

Glenn shook Tanner's hand. "Listen to this lady. If Claire Gray thinks you're right for DAC, then you *belong* here." He beamed.

Almost as an afterthought, I said, "Tanner, this is D. Glenn Yeats."

Tanner's jaw dropped. "Good, uh, *morning,* Mr. Yeats. Gosh . . . it's an honor, sir." Glenn's celebrity far outweighed my own, even to Tanner, an avowed theater buff. After all, Glenn was one of the nation's wealthiest men, and his name was a household word, virtually synonymous with personal computing. Seeing him in the flesh, Tanner simply hadn't recognized him; few would, as Glenn's face was far less memorable than his name. Yet there he stood, the multibillionaire titan of e-industry.

Glenn turned to me. "Claire, I know it's short notice, but I wonder if you're free tomorrow evening."

"Friday?" I asked, as if to say, You've *got* to be kidding. "Truth is, my social life is something less than a whirl. Nothing's booked, Glenn. Why?"

"I'm still concerned about Paul. There's so *much* going on next week. We've all got to help him get beyond this."

Lord, he was back on *that* kick. I told him, "Paul seems to be doing just fine. I had breakfast with him today, and he was quite chipper."

"Wonderful." Glenn nodded. "With the weekend looming, though, I'm afraid he might slip emotionally. Saturday morning marks a week since the tragedy, and he could easily relive it. He needs to be with friends as much as possible."

It hadn't occurred to me that the one-week milestone was approaching fast. "What do you have in mind?"

He blinked. "A party! Tomorrow night, seven o'clock, my place. Just a small gathering, a group of friends to help Paul get beyond this."

I wanted to blurt, *Stop saying that!* I told him, "Sounds lovely."

"Cocktails. Late buffet dinner on the terrace. The usual."

"I'll be there."

Stepping close, Glenn told me in a stage whisper, as if divulging a secret scheme, "The party will run late; the booze will flow. I'm hoping to convince Paul to spend the night at Nirvana so he won't be anywhere near that house on Saturday morning." He winked.

It sounded sort of screwy, Glenn attempting to liquor up the grieving widower and keep him in a cloistered stupor to avoid painful memories, but at the same time, I had to admit, it made perfect sense. At least Glenn was thinking ahead. Wryly, I told him, "And to think there are those who say your legendary genius is inflated."

"Who? I want names." He was kidding, of course—I think. He turned to Tanner. "Well, then, young man, have you seen the campus yet?"

"Much of it, sir. It's beautiful. Congratulations."

"And how about that *theater*?" Glenn glanced at me, grinning.

"That," said Tanner, "is beyond belief. Sincerely, thank you for everything you've done for the community."

Glenn gave a gracious bow of his head, looking downright humble.

"As a matter of fact," I told him, "we were just on our way over there. Tanner noticed some problems with the fly rigging the other day, and I thought we'd better check it out."

"Then by all means," said Glenn, gesturing with a flourish toward the door, "don't let me keep you from such *very* important work." With a smile, he took his leave, walking down the hallway and disappearing around the curve.

I turned to Tanner. "He's a bit of an enigma." My breezy inflection was heavy with understatement.

A minute or two later, around 10:15, we had crossed College Circle under the midmorning sun and entered the hushed, dark lobby of my theater. The thick pile of the plush wool carpeting felt new, smelled new, even *sounded* new as our feet squished its silky, velvety nap. I pulled open one of the auditorium doors, and a shaft of light cut across us. "Good," I told Tanner, "the crew's still here. I wouldn't know how to find the lights."

Walking down the aisle, I checked one of the folders under my arm, making sure I'd brought the checklist. Before Tanner and I had reached the middle row of seats, a workman named Morgan spotted us. "Howdy, Miss Gray. You're just in time to answer a few questions."

Today the questions were, in fact, few. Only two workers remained on the job, doing some final tweaking of the stage lifts; the other contractors had finished, needing only my final inspection. My theater was nearing completion.

When I had dealt with Morgan the foreman's immediate concerns, I told him, "I understand there was a problem with the fire curtain, something to do with the pinrail?"

"It's all taken care of, Miss Gray. Care to look?"

Indeed I did. Tanner and I followed Morgan onstage as he explained, "The counterbalance was off. With a brand-new system, it takes some trial and error to get everything right, but now she's spinning like a top." He then demonstrated several applications of the fly apparatus, including the fire curtain, which sealed the proscenium from the auditorium. While none of it, to my mind, resembled a spinning top, it all worked flawlessly, silently, precisely on cue.

"Bravo," I told him as the fire curtain disappeared again in the heights above the stage.

Focused as I was on the machinery, I hadn't noticed that someone, feeling whimsical, had tried his hand at set decorating. Center stage, an armless Edwardian lolling couch anchored an arrangement of furniture that also included a stuffed chair, a spindled side chair, and a small writing table. A large potted fern and a dusty, stuffed bird—a mangy parrot on a corroded brass perch—completed the grouping, an island of antiquities in the middle of an otherwise bare stage. A stark, white cyclorama swept across the back wall; rigging hung above; all manner of equipment was stacked in the wings.

"Oh, dear," I said, contemplating the frumpy decor, frowning. "Are we doing Chekhov this season?"

Tanner laughed.

"No, Miss Gray, sorry," said Morgan. "One of the consignment stores delivered a truckload of donated furniture for the prop room while the lighting guys were testing circuits. So they did some improvising. I guess they wanted a scene to light."

I chortled. "Well, they got one."

He offered, "Care to see how this works? I mean, the rehearsal panel."

As I didn't know what he meant, I thought it best to accept his offer. I soon learned that he was referring to a secondary set of lighting controls. The main controls were in the tech booth at the back of the auditorium, where, with the aid of computers, circuits could be set, dim rates could be established, and complex cross-fades could be timed exactly to the needs of the script. The secondary panel, located in the wing, offstage right, allowed many of these preset functions to be controlled during rehearsal without a full tech crew; the stage manager, for example, might run lights during a particular scene, giving the actors a better sense of its mood and timing.

Morgan demonstrated several presets that the lighting crew had designed for their improvised Chekhovian parlor. I was enthralled; they had done beautiful work. And to my amazement, operation of the rehearsal panel was simple and intuitive. Even I quickly had it spinning like a top.

"Do you plan on staying for a while?" Morgan asked.

I didn't need to leave for my eleven o'clock meeting at Nirvana for another twenty minutes or so. "I think so, yes. Why?"

"We need to pick up a special socket wrench down in Indio before we can finish here." He was referring to himself and his helper, who'd puttered backstage without saying a word since our arrival. "By the time we drive there and return, it'll be time for lunch, so we won't be back here till about one. Don't worry, though. Everything'll be wrapped up by tomorrow."

"Glad to hear it."

"So anyway, before you leave, if you could shut down everything but the work lights"—he pointed to a row of switches—"I'd appreciate it."

"Sure, Morgan. I think I can handle that."

"Thank you, Miss Gray." He gave me a little salute and summoned his helper. Then they disappeared through a stage door, which closed with a reverberant thud.

Tanner and I were still standing onstage. Turning to him, I put a finger to my lips, pausing for several long seconds. I whispered, "Hear that?"

He scrunched his features. "What?"

"Nothing! Isn't it marvelous?"

He nodded. "For such a large space, it *is* amazingly quiet."

"I insisted that I wanted a quiet theater with first-rate acoustics, and Glenn spared no expense. All the noisy mechanicals—ventilation, air-conditioning, and whatnot—are located about a half block away, connected by tunnel." I arched my brows, impressed by my own ability to demand such fussing.

Tanner fell to one knee. "I genuflect before the power and wisdom of the first lady of American theater." He swooshed an arm, mimicking an elaborate Muslim bow that brought his head to the floor.

"Flattery will get you everywhere, Tanner. If you're ready to commit to the program, you're in. Classes start Monday."

His head turned up to me. "Really?"

I laughed softly. "Sure. I'm reasonably satisfied that you could benefit from the school—and vice versa."

He stood. "That's all there is to it? What do I have to do? I mean, applications, scheduling, and all."

"Well, let's see," I said, crossing the stage to the writing table and setting down my folders. Handing him a pile of forms, I explained,

"This is all a formality now—Glenn all but *ordered* you to enroll—but fill out the paperwork over the weekend and have it ready for me by Monday morning. Get your transcripts ordered—"

"That's already done."

"—and I'll work up your schedule for the fall semester. I assume you'd like to be in both my workshop and my seminar."

"A fair assumption." He grinned. Then he paused, touching my shoulder. "Hey, thanks, Claire. This has happened so fast. It's beyond my wildest expectations." He shook his head. "And to think, you've never even seen me act. I feel that I should at least *read* for you."

As he said this, I realized that I'd set three tests for him that morning, two of which he'd easily passed. The clincher was to be my gut assessment of his acting talent. I wanted to feel that spark, that "wow factor," not merely as a result of his animal presence (there was no shortage of that) but in reaction to his natural ability to *become* another character and deliver the role. A tall order.

He continued, "Here we are, in a theater. May I read you a scene?"

I closed the folder of admission forms. "Yes, I'd like that. Did you bring a script?"

"Uh, no." Sheepish shrug.

I returned the shrug. "I have nothing with me. If I'd known, I could've—"

"What if I do a scene from memory?"

"Better yet." I smiled as if to challenge him, Are you man enough?

"It'll have to be a monologue."

"Logical enough. Shakespeare?"

"If you like. I could muddle through some Lear or Hamlet. I have a particular passion, though, for a soliloquy from a newer masterpiece."

"Don't tell me." I guessed knowingly, "Salieri, from *Amadeus,* end of act one." It was a favorite for open auditions, and with good reason.

He shook his head. "Both the play and its setting are contemporary."

"Hm. Williams, Miller, O'Neill?"

"Newer still."

"Albee!" Certain I was on the mark, I declared, "George, from *Virginia Woolf.*"

"Nope. Jerome, from *Traders.*"

I froze, unaccustomed to hearing my play's title in the context of such lofty company. Tanner Griffin was either very discerning or very calculating. I asked, "You've *played* Jerome?"

"No—I *wish*. But I do have the script, and I've read it often. And like everyone else, I've seen the movie—several times over."

I grumbled, "Hollywood has a way of chopping up soliloquies."

"I noticed. Anyway, I spent some time last night working up Jerome's long speech from act two. I'd be honored to recite it for the esteemed playwright."

Flattered beyond measure, I blustered, "Don't 'recite' it, Tanner. Interpret it, emote it, *act* it." And I left the stage, stepping down the movable rehearsal stairs from the apron to the auditorium, where I slipped into the shadows and sat in a row near the back, wanting to judge his projection. "Whenever you're ready . . . ," I prompted him.

He stood center stage, amid the Edwardian furniture, appealingly anachronistic in his butch Desert Detail getup. With his head bowed in concentration as he assumed the character of Jerome, his sun-streaked hair fell forward, radiant in the multicolored beams of stage light. Then he lifted his face to the unseen crowd. And he spoke.

That voice. Instinctively, my hand rose to my lips as I suspended disbelief and let that voice wash over me. His normal speaking voice, disarmingly seductive in its own right, had not prepared me for the powerful effect of his stage voice—perfectly projected without the edge of shouting, clearly enunciated without apparent artifice, it conveyed both strength and warmth. Again, the word *solid* sprang to mind in describing everything about him.

He was more than a body, more than a voice. His delivery reached deep into the structure of the scripted words as he interpreted their overlapping shades of meaning and spoke them as if newly thought. Though the words were mine—I knew them well—he made them his, as though they'd never before been spoken.

The speech moved forward, propelled by its own dynamics as well as by Tanner's acting. I'd hoped for a spark, and I'd gotten it, but good. No question—Tanner was a born actor, a natural talent. I congratulated myself for my instincts and knew without doubt that I would be lauded for "discovering" him. And there I sat, an audience of one, listening to my own words spoken by this hunky young heartthrob who sorta wanted to act.

The monologue would continue for several minutes yet, so I rose and began to move about the theater, listening to his voice from varying distances, watching him from different angles. If he was aware of my movement, he showed no signs of distraction, so focused was his concentration on the role. So I decided to do some experimenting with the lighting, even as he spoke, to see if I could better set the mood for the soliloquy's end.

Mounting the rehearsal stairs to stage right, I stepped off to the wing and made a few adjustments to the control panel. At my touch, the stage lighting changed hue from cool to warm—it was pink, a particular pink known in the trade as bastard amber—and began a long, slow fade as Jerome's words coursed to their end. Moving out to the stage apron, I watched and listened at close range as Tanner continued to bring new meaning to his lines, finding an interpretation that had not been apparent even to me.

Spellbound by his articulation, I had not been paying attention to his movements, when I realized that he was taking off his shirt. Just as suddenly, I realized that this bit of stage business had been motivated by a subtext he'd found in his lines. It seemed not only natural and intuitive, but essential to the meaning of the script. I was stunned. I'd directed this play twice—Christ, I *wrote* it—and I'd never even thought of that angle.

His shirt lay like a white puddle on the black stage floor. That spark I was looking for? It was more like fireworks. It wasn't just the high drama, of course. It wasn't just the aesthetic depth of Tanner's interpretation. It was the sight of him there in front of me, buffed and bronzed in the fading pink light. Hooking one thumb under his belt, raking his other hand through his hair, he delivered the closing phrases of Jerome's long speech, carving out their meaning with surgical precision, and then, exhaling, he stopped.

I paused, stunned. The lights had completed their slow, programmed fade. Now they brightened slightly, still pink. "Tanner—"

He looked at me, snapping back to the moment, as if unaware that I'd been there. He smiled (God, that smile). "Well? Was it . . . all right?"

Taking a few tentative steps forward, I told him, "It was far better than 'all right.' In fact, I've never seen it performed better."

Stooping to pick up his shirt, he paused before rising. With a modest laugh, he said, "I'm sure that's an exaggeration. But thank you."

Stepping next to him, standing over him, I touched his head, felt his hair. "No, Tanner, I mean it—that was superb. You found meaning in my words that I'd never heard before."

He rose, standing in front of me. Smiling, he suggested, "Then I must have been way off base." Our faces were inches apart.

Anything I might have said just then would have sounded inane, so I said nothing. And it wasn't my imagination—it wasn't a mere fantasy playing through my mind. No, we were caught in each other's wondering stare. I felt as if I were struggling for breath.

I raised a hand, wanting to touch his face, but I stopped as a flood of conflicting emotions raced through me: Our age difference made this evolving scene ludicrous. Our teacher-student relationship raised monumental issues of propriety. And even now, there was still that lingering suspicion that Tanner Griffin could possibly be a killer. (Was he acting? He'd proven he had the skill.) My hand was still raised, near his face.

"What? . . ." He laughed softly, with heavy breath.

"May I?"

"Of course." He smiled (God, that smile). "Go ahead. Touch me."

I felt his face, first with one hand, then with both.

"You look good in red," he told me, bringing his whole body against mine.

Dry-mouthed, I told him, "You'd look good in anything."

Grinning, he asked, "May I?"

Though I didn't know precisely the object of his query, a cursory review of the possibilities turned up nothing I was inclined to deny him. "Of course."

A moment later, his cargo shorts dropped to the floor with a clunk, weighted by his heavy belt. Stepping free of them, he rubbed against me, then kissed me deeply. Glancing at my wrist over his shoulder, I saw that I still had a few minutes before I was due at Nirvana. No hurry—this would be time well spent.

Dragging his tongue across my ear, he asked, "Would you care to get comfortable?" It wasn't clear whether he meant "get undressed" or "lie down."

"Yes," I answered, amenable to either, and he helped me unzip the jumpsuit while making our way to Mr. Chekhov's lolling couch.

There, under a warm shaft of dim, pink light, Tanner got a little crazy, and so did I. It was impossible to say who was seducing whom or what interplay of motives may have been at work. Tanner's arousal was genuine enough—guys can't fake it—but I had no way of knowing what he was thinking or feeling.

For whatever it's worth, it felt a bit like love.

(Or was he acting?)

At that particular moment, I didn't much care.

19

Dazed, sated, and running a few minutes late, I sped my Beetle up the mountainside road from the Nirvana gatehouse, passing the entrance to the Regal Palms Hotel and parking in one of the spaces at the sales office. Grant Knoll's white Mercedes was there, as expected, and so was his brother Larry's anonymous-looking county sedan. There were no other cars, so I reasoned that Henry Harris had not yet arrived; I could still, as planned, just "happen" to be there when he showed up for his meeting with Grant.

Parking next to the Mercedes, I set my brake and got out of the car. The mesa was some ten degrees cooler than the valley floor, so the breezy, late-morning air felt barely warm. A few stray clouds appeared snagged on the distant peak of Mount San Jacinto; another cloud, high and thin, drifted overhead but cast no shadow. A bighorn sheep, a fat ram, grazed lazily a few yards from my car, paying no heed, seemingly too content, or bored, to bother looking at me. A pair of quail skittered from the grass to the asphalt, disappearing behind the low fronds of a sago palm in the courtyard.

The sales office bore no resemblance to the typical contractor's trailer often seen at developing building sites. It was more akin to a rambling mountain home, every bit as dramatic and tasteful as the "real" houses within Nirvana's guarded walls. Walking through the meticulously landscaped entry court toward the beveled-glass doors, I mused that I could easily be happy *living* in such an office.

I found that the building's residential, noncommercial flavor also marked its interior. A wall of glass at the far side of the structure looked out on a craggy promontory and a view of the valley beyond.

"Miss Gray?" said a receptionist, poking her head out from a hallway. "Mr. Knoll and his brother are waiting for you in the conference room." With a practiced smile, she led me past a media room, through the main room (which looked for all the world like a living room) to the conference room (which looked like a dining room). Grant and Larry were seated there, deep in discussion.

"Gentlemen," I greeted them. They stood.

Grant checked his watch. "My, my. The lady in red has arrived." He paused, studying me. "If I may say so, doll, you're looking positively radiant this morning. If I didn't know better, I'd swear you'd stopped off for a quickie on the way over."

I mused, "When opportunity knocks . . ." He assumed I was joking.

"Hi, Claire," said the other brother, the one with a gun holstered beneath his jacket, "glad you're here." He got right down to business. "Since Harris seems to be running late, let me bring you up to date on Oralia."

I took a chair at the long, oval table; its granite top felt cool beneath the sleeves of my jumpsuit. "Any luck with her alibi?"

As the brothers sat again, Larry told me, "Yes. You'll recall that she disarmed the security system in Indian Wells at eight-fifty on Saturday morning, when she entered the Warhanik house."

"Right. And she'd said earlier that she'd worked 'from about eight-thirty till noon.' Since Jodie's death has been pegged as early as eight-thirty that morning, Oralia's story was too loose to be conclusive."

The detective nodded. "Yesterday afternoon, after the memorial service, I caught up with Oralia and questioned her on this discrepancy, and she explained that she'd done some grocery shopping at Vons for the Warhaniks before arriving at their house."

"Aha. She mentioned to me earlier that shopping was among her usual duties when opening a house for seasonal residents."

Again he nodded. "She'd left the Vons receipt for the Warhaniks to reimburse her, and fortunately, they still had it. I drove out there earlier this morning and saw it myself. It was time-stamped by the cash register at eight-forty that morning. So everything fits: Oralia went to the supermarket around eight-thirty, went through the checkout line about ten minutes later, and arrived at the house some ten minutes after that."

"Then she *couldn't* have been at the Hurons' house in Palm Desert anytime between eight-thirty and nine, the time of death."

"Correct. She's clear. Which greatly diminishes the likelihood of theft as motive for the murder. Your crime-of-passion theory seems more and more likely, Claire."

Grant chirped in, "Milady's had her mind on sex since the very start of these sordid doings."

"Shush, Grant." Returning my attention to Larry, I said, "I saw this morning's page-one article on the ring—great coverage. Maybe it'll jog someone's memory and—"

"Wait a minute," Grant butted in again. "If you've dismissed theft as a motive, why stew over the missing ring?"

"Because it's so *symbolic,*" I explained. "People don't steal a wedding ring from a corpse because they need something to hock. They do it out of anger—to make a point or send a message."

"Mr. Knoll?" said the receptionist, popping into the room. "Sorry to interrupt. Mr. Harris just drove up."

"Thank you, Tracie," Grant told her. "Give me a minute to get ready for him. Offer him something to drink." Tracie slipped through a doorway to another room that looked like a kitchen.

We all rose. Grant gathered some paperwork and blueprints from a credenza along the wall, presumably relevant to the house that Henry Harris was to purchase for his peeved wife, Arlene. Larry and I pushed our chairs neatly to the table and gathered a few notes he'd spread there. I asked Grant, "Where do you want us?"

He looked about. "Why don't you just follow Tracie? Get comfortable in one of the offices, or just mosey out to the main room after Henry and I get settled here. Then, whenever you're ready, jump in."

Larry and I nodded to each other, leaving the conference room.

We found Tracie in the next room. Now that I got a better look at it, I could tell that it had been designed not as a residential kitchen but more as a caterer's prep area. There were no windows, and the room's general finish, as well as its appliances, seemed strictly utilitarian, not intended to impress. Tracie stood at the counter, loading a tray with glasses, iced tea, and bottled water. She told us over her shoulder, "I need to get this out front before Mr. Harris wanders in." Laughing, she added, "He takes his time."

Larry offered, "Can I carry anything?"

She hefted the tray. "No, thanks, I can get it. Follow me?"

She led us from the kitchen toward the front of the building, passing a file room and a few offices. They'd make dandy bedrooms, I thought as I continued my mental move-in. We ended up in a reception area near the beveled-glass front doors. "Make yourselves at home," she told us while setting the tray on a sideboard. Henry Harris was just reaching for the door, having doddered from his car.

Larry and I strolled into the media room, which contained a topographic model of the development, complete with tiny-scale replicas of the houses already built. I had no trouble spotting Glenn Yeats's sprawling abode near the top of the road.

"Good morning, Mr. Harris," said Tracie as the old man entered. "It's a lovely day, isn't it?"

He mustered a smile. "I suppose so, yes." He was a man with much on his mind, matters far graver than the weather. He wore full, conservative business attire—dark suit, striped tie, and cuff links—all very proper but stuffy, similar to his outfit at yesterday's memorial service. I watched as he paused for a breather after his short trek through the courtyard.

Tracie asked, "Would you like something to drink—iced tea, maybe?"

He glanced at the tray. "Some water would be nice, thank you. Just water."

She screwed the lid off one of the plastic bottles, which bore the custom label of the Regal Palms Hotel, and plucked up a short-stemmed water glass. "Mr. Knoll asked me to have you join him in the conference room," she explained, then began leading Henry toward the back of the building. Judging from Henry's pace, this excursion would take a while.

Eyeing Larry, I jerked my head, and he followed as I sauntered out to the main room. The purported object of my interest was another topographic model displayed there—a much larger one, depicting the entire mountainside, the hotel, and a terraced golf course still in the planning stages. The model, I discovered, was interesting enough, but my true purpose was to position Larry and myself where we could keep an eye on the conference room. Grant was unfurling some floor plans on the granite table as Henry plodded past us with Tracie in tow, bearing his water. As they neared, I turned, leaned, and peered closely at the model, mumbling something to Larry about the golf course.

"The plan is controversial," he mumbled back. "Environmentalists are afraid it'll endanger the bighorns."

"Oh puh-leeze," I tittered. "You're making that up, aren't you, honey?"

If Henry noticed us at all, he paid no mind, chugging stalwartly onward. He showed no sign of recognizing us from Jodie's service.

"Henry!" said Grant, pretending to notice his arrival just then. Stepping around the table, he met the old man in the wide doorway and shook his hand. "Thanks for driving up on such short notice."

Henry nodded. "I appreciated the call, Grant. You've been a great help ever since we first moved out here to the desert. Arlene needs you now. Thanks for taking care of her."

Tracie zipped around him, placing the glass on the table and pouring from the bottle. Then she disappeared.

Grant led his visitor into the conference room and helped him settle into a chair at the near side of the table. Henry now faced away from the main room, allowing Larry and me to snoop with little fear of detection. Grant told him, "I was *so* sorry to hear of the trouble you and Arlene are having." His tone was sincere, despite the handsome commission he'd reap from the fallout.

"Bah." Henry wobbled his head. "It's my own damn fault."

Grant sat across from him, where he could keep an eye on me. He told Henry, "I'm not here to judge. I just hope I can help you straighten this out."

Henry sat back, studying Grant. "You're, uh . . . not married, are you?" He fingered the glass of water, then sipped from it.

Grant grinned. "No, Henry. I thought you've always understood— I'm not the 'marrying kind.' "

The old man laughed. "Yes, yes, I understand. I mean, you're not attached?"

Grant shook his head.

"Why not?"

"The usual excuse. The right person never came along." Grant's faraway look made me wonder if he was thinking of Kane, the pet car parker with whom he'd traded roses the night before.

Henry exhaled a long sigh; from the sound of it, it could have been his very last. But no. He told Grant, "I never thought I'd say this, but you may be better off alone." The comment was so unexpected, it was impossible to read his meaning. Was he saying, in effect, that Arlene was a shrew and he wished he'd never married her? Or did he mean that their breakup was so painful, their happy years together did not now seem worth the price?

Grant didn't pry. "Life can be a mystery, Henry."

Snort. "I *still* haven't figured it out." He didn't need to add that his time was nearly up. He did add, "So you've found a place that'll keep her happy?"

"It's a marvelous house," Grant assured him, "but only time will tell if Arlene will be happy there. Let me show you what I've got." Sliding the set of plans across the table, he shifted into his sales mode.

Larry and I backed away from the conference room. I asked, "Now what?"

He reminded me, *"You* set this up. Did you think he was going to conveniently let it slip, over chitchat, that he murdered his nurse?"

I didn't bother answering. If this meeting was to yield anything more productive than a real estate deal, a measure of confrontation was apparently in order. On the sideboard near the front door, I noticed the tray left there by Tracie. It held a pitcher of iced tea, another bottle of hotel water, and several of the short-stemmed water glasses. In the blast of sunlight from the door, I could see that the glasses were spotlessly clean. Nudging Larry, I said, "Bring that," meaning the tray.

Dutifully, the detective got the drinks, then followed me toward the doorway to the conference room. Pausing there, I heard Henry tell Grant, "You really don't need to sell *me* on the place. If Arlene wants it, that's that. You know my banker; he can handle the paperwork."

"I'll take care of it, then," said Grant. "We may need you here for the actual closing, but—"

"Fine, Grant. Whatever."

"Excuse me?" I said, inching in. "It sounded as if you'd finished your business, and I just wondered if anyone would care for some refreshment." Larry sidled in with the tray and set it on the table.

Grant watched us wide-eyed, like Ricky Ricardo wondering what Lucy and Ethel were up to.

From where Henry sat, he hadn't yet gotten a good look at us, so he doubtless assumed we were an extra pair of Nirvana staffers. "Sure," he said vacantly, "more water, please."

Seizing the moment, I reached from behind him, plucking up the glass he'd drunk from, being careful to handle only the stem. Examining it in the light that flooded the room from the rear wall of glass, I confirmed that the goblet was well smudged with Henry's fingerprints. I set the glass aside, on the credenza, before pouring the bottled water into a fresh glass and setting it on the table near Henry.

Following my movements with his eyes, Larry shook his head, amused that I was preparing to steal yet another piece of stemware. Then, as if remembering something, he checked his watch.

"Thank you," said Henry, reaching for the glass and drinking.

As he set it down, I moved around the table and sat near Grant. Larry took the chair nearest where he stood, at the far end of the oval table. Henry looked across the table at me, then at Larry, wondering what was going on. When he returned his gaze to me, he asked, "Didn't I, uh . . . weren't you at Jodie's memorial yesterday?"

Larry answered for me, "Yes, she was, Mr. Harris. So was I." He rose to shake Henry's hand. "No, please don't get up. My name's Larry Knoll and—"

Grant interjected, "He's my brother, Henry. Larry is a detective with the sheriff's department. He's in charge of the investigation of Jodie's death." Then Grant patted my hand, telling Henry, "You already know Claire Gray. I introduced you yesterday."

"Your brother?" Henry seemed far more intrigued by the siblings' relationship than by the murder. "Yes . . . ," he conceded, "there is indeed a resemblance."

Larry sat again, explaining forthright, "Though we've yet to pin down an exact motive, we now have reason to believe that Jodie died as the result of an extramarital relationship she was having."

Hearing this, Henry paused, then bowed his head. "Infidelity. It's a dangerous game."

I cleared my throat. "I'm sorry about your difficulties, Henry. I've heard the whole story. Grant and I had dinner with Arlene last night—"

"Then you *have* heard plenty!"

I allowed a slight laugh. "Yes. She told us about the letter she received from your mistress on Friday; in fact, she showed it to me. She said you were enraged when you learned about the letter on Friday night. And she said she didn't see you on Saturday morning because you had a golf game at Mission Palms."

Coldly, he repeated, "You *have* heard plenty."

I continued, "Yesterday, when I met you at Jodie's memorial, you were talking with Dr. Percy Blair. You said to him and to the rest of us, more than once, that you 'came to love Jodie' during your extended stay at Coachella Medical Center this past summer. Henry, has it not occurred to you that the timing of the letter from your mistress, coupled with the timing of Jodie's death on Saturday morning, suggests that your mistress may have been Jodie herself?"

Predictably, Henry reacted to my words with a mixture of shock and flustered indignation. He sputtered, "How *dare* you! If you . . . if you think . . ."

Larry leaned forward, raising a finger. "Before you say anything else, Mr. Harris, you should be aware that I've already talked to the pro shop at your club. You were *not* scheduled to play on Saturday morning, and in fact, you completely missed a tee time later that day."

Hearing this, Henry seemed to shrivel before our eyes. He looked old, sickly, and, now, cornered. He parted his lips to speak, but his tongue sounded pasty in his mouth, so he reached for the water and drank a swallow or two. Taking a moment to straighten his tie and square his shoulders, he then told us, "Yes, I was having an illicit affair with another woman. By its nature, of course, such a relationship is highly secretive, but when Arlene confronted me with it, I admitted it. There was no point in compounding my guilt with clumsy lies. Similarly, there is no point in denying it to you."

I clarified, "But you do deny that the other woman was Jodie Metz-Huron?"

"Certainly. I recall saying yesterday that I 'came to love' Jodie, and I still mean it. But surely, Miss Gray, your command of the language is sufficiently astute to understand that one may 'love' a person without carnal overtones. Jodie nursed and befriended me during my hospital stay, and for that, to this day, I do love her." He paused, drinking again.

I recalled, "Your wife said that when she confronted you with her knowledge of the affair, you were 'furious.' Is that true?"

He slapped the table. "Of *course* I was angry—mad as hell. Why wouldn't I be? I'd been betrayed." Realizing that this emotional display did not serve his best interests just now, he cleared his throat and composed himself. Choosing his words delicately, he continued, "My . . . paramour understood, from the time we met, that our relationship, while loving, would never replace my marriage; the logistical considerations of divorce simply outweighed my passion for the woman. She said she understood this, but apparently she was merely buying time."

Larry asked, "Buying time for what, Mr. Harris?" He had taken a pad from his coat pocket and was now scribbling notes.

"Buying time till I'd have a change of heart. As this was not forthcoming, she decided to take matters into her own hands. Hence the ploy to break up my marriage by sending that ridiculous letter to Arlene."

I reminded him, "The letter was far from literary, but it served its purpose. You and Arlene—"

"Yes," he interrupted, "Arlene and I are through, but now my paramour is also alone, which was *not* her purpose."

Larry asked, "You've told her so?"

"First thing Saturday. I would have confronted her on Friday night, when I first learned of her stunt, but I was so incensed, I thought I'd better try to cool off first—not for *her* sake, for *mine,* because of my heart. Yes, I probably did tell Arlene that I was going golfing Saturday morning. In truth, I don't remember *what* I told her, but golf would be a logical story. As you have already determined, I did not go golfing that morning; instead, I went to visit my ladyfriend for the last time. We had a heated fight—strictly verbal, mind you—ending our relationship. I have neither seen nor heard from her since." With a bitter smile, he summarized, "I've lost both my wife *and* my ladyfriend."

Larry looked him in the eye, asking, "Is your ex-mistress dead, Mr. Harris?"

He replied flippantly, "I really don't know, but I assume she's still alive and kicking; she was highly active the last time I saw her. I do know this, however: my secret love was *not* Jodie. I did *not* visit Jodie on Saturday, and I most certainly did *not* kill her." Pausing, he reminded us, "I loved her."

Larry put down his pen. "These circumstances are disturbingly suspicious, Mr. Harris. Surely you appreciate—"

"Are you arresting me?"

"No. Not yet. But as of this moment, I do consider you an active suspect. You could change my mind very quickly, though, by simply revealing the identity of your ex-mistress. If your story checks out, you're in the clear." Larry raised his brows, as if to ask, How 'bout it?

Henry rose with indignation, and a bit of difficulty. "My ladyfriend's indiscretion in writing the letter was of course inexcusable, but I have always held myself to a standard higher than that of those who fail me. Many might say that I now owe her nothing, which may be true, but I refuse to demean myself by sullying her name." And with that, Henry turned and left in a huff.

His display of pique lost its punch, though, during the full minute he needed to leave the table, hobble through the office, and reach the front doors. The rest of us sat in silence till we heard the door close behind him.

"Well, now," said Grant. It was the first time he'd spoken since his brother and I began questioning Henry. "I'd say that went *exceedingly* well." His tone was more sniggering than bitchy, which surprised me. After all, Larry and I had all but accused Grant's long-standing client of murder, and in the process, we'd probably dashed a multimillion-dollar real estate deal.

Larry rose, stood behind Grant, and placed his hands on his shoulders. "Sorry, Grant. I didn't expect the discussion to get so pointed, or testy. I thought we'd just sound the guy out."

Grant stood. "It's not your fault. I don't know whether Henry is obstinate or just old-fashioned. If he'd named his mistress, this meeting would have ended on a cheerier note."

"Unless," I said, also rising, "the mistress was Jodie." Stepping around the table to the credenza, I lifted the smudged water glass by its stem. "Here's one way to find out if Henry was ever in her bedroom."

"That reminds me"—Larry snapped his fingers—"I should be able to get a report on Dr. Blair's prints by now. I took the glass in this morning. The lab was backed up with something, but they said I could get results before twelve." It was now noonish.

"Need a phone?" Grant offered.

The detective reached into a pocket. "Thanks, but I'm fully connected these days—pager, phone, you name it." He punched a short, programmed number into his cell phone. A few seconds later, he identified himself and was transferred to the forensics lab in Riverside. Grant and I waited silently, straining to hear, but we could make little of Larry's end of the conversation.

Till we heard him say, *"They did?* No bull—a direct match? Thanks, Tania. I've got work to do." He snapped the phone shut. Shaking his head, he said with a laugh, "I'm stunned, Claire. I thought the whole business about the patchouli was far-fetched at best, but your instincts were dead-on when you snatched that wineglass at the memorial service. It was covered with good, clean prints, and the lab got a conclusive match with the set of mystery prints we found all over the crime scene."

Grant told his brother, "Don't encourage her. Next thing you know, she'll want a badge and a gun."

Rotely, Larry corrected, "We refer to it as a weapon."

Trying not to gloat, I mused, "It seems Dr. Percy Blair has some explaining to do." As an afterthought, I added, " 'Mentor,' indeed." Harrumph.

Larry nodded. "I want to act fast and confront Blair right at the scene, at the Huron house. He'll know we mean business. Where's Paul today, Claire? I need to let him know what's happened and try to set up a meeting at the house."

"He's got his hands full with the opening of the college, so he should be on campus all day. Shortly after ten, I noticed he wasn't in his office, but he may have been over in the sculpture studios. Try the main switchboard; maybe they can track him down." I told Larry the number.

He flipped open his phone and dialed. After several attempts and transfers, though, he was unsuccessful in reaching Paul.

I suggested, "Maybe he went home for lunch."

Larry nodded, checked his notes for the number, and phoned the Huron house. After several rings, Paul's answering machine switched on. Larry said into the phone, "Hi, Paul. Detective Knoll with the sheriff's department. Listen, good news. We've just had an important new development on the case, and I need to set up a meeting with someone—there at your house, and as soon as possible. You have my pager number, so please get back to me right away. Thanks, Paul." And he shut the phone.

"Hey," I said, recalling, "Oralia cleans the Huron house every Tuesday and Thursday afternoon. She should be there by one today. I'm sure she'll let us in."

"Good thinking." Larry got on the phone again, calling Coachella Medical Center and asking for Dr. Percy Blair's office. The doctor wasn't available just then, so Larry said, "Please give him this message. It relates to the police investigation of the death of one of his co-workers." Larry detailed who he was and where he wanted the doctor to meet him. "Please let him know that this is a matter of great urgency, and his cooperation will be appreciated. Yes, one o'clock sharp. Thank you."

Hanging up, Larry told us, "She seemed to know Blair's schedule, and she thought he'd be available. If not, I told her how to reach me."

Checking my watch, I realized that I was hungry. "Do we have time to grab something on the way over?" What I was really asking, of course, was whether he'd permit me to tag along for his questioning of Dr. Do-Good.

Larry grinned, finding my motive transparent. "I suppose so. Grant, care to join us?"

"Let's see," said Grant, pressing a finger to his cheek as he considered the offer, "burger, fries, and inquisition? No, thanks. I'll just tootle down to the Regal Palms for something light, like a salad and a cocktail. Besides, two's company, so you kids feel free to run along."

And we did.

20

Larry drove. I expected to get something of a rush, riding in an honest-to-God, souped-up, unmarked squad car, but in truth, the vehicle was unremarkable. Thoroughly quotidian, it simply struck me as a company car, one that could be switched at a moment's notice with any other in the fleet.

Equally quotidian was our lunch. Grant's burger-and-fries prediction was right on the mark, as neither Larry nor I was inclined to linger over a chic dining experience. We simply needed fuel, and Larry knew a dim but friendly joint along Highway 111, between Rancho Mirage and Palm Desert, where we could stoke up for the afternoon while conversing in reasonable privacy.

Grant's prediction that lunch would also include an inquisition wasn't far off base either. It was I, however, not the detective, who did most of the questioning, pumping him for any additional information on the case and quizzing him about how he planned to confront Dr. Do-Good.

"There *is* no plan," he told me, pausing to suck Diet Coke from a straw. "In cases like this, when I've got one good piece of evidence but not much else to go on, I play it by ear and let the conversation evolve. After all, this is merely an inquiry, not an official interrogation. I don't intend to *accuse* Blair of anything yet. Once I let him know about the fingerprints, I'll let *him* steer the course. And by the way, Claire, there are procedures in questioning that must be followed to the letter, so please, it's important that you stay strictly in the background."

I nodded, making a show of zipping my lips, then immediately opened them to savor a few more french fries. They were thin and crisp, just the way I like them. "Frankly," I said, "I was surprised you let me come at all."

He laughed softly. "What can I say? Your offbeat 'dramatic perspective' has proved helpful. Also, you delivered that wineglass, giving us a positive ID on the mystery prints from the crime scene, so let's just say I owe you one." His eyes fell to his fries, which he clearly enjoyed as much as I did.

Shortly before one, we were back on the road. Entering Palm Desert, we turned onto El Paseo, then turned again, climbing the hill that led to the outskirts of town. Soon we were on the quiet side street, edged by desert on one side, that took us into the developing neighborhood of new homes. Larry turned into the cul-de-sac, and the Huron house lay just ahead.

The garage door was open, and there was an older-model brown Toyota, nicely waxed, parked at the curb. "You were right," said Larry. "That's Oralia's car—she's here. No sign of the eminent cardiologist yet. Hope he's coming. This'll be a hell of lot easier on him if he cooperates." As Larry finished speaking, he parked behind the Toyota.

Getting out of the unmarked cruiser, I noticed that the day had turned hot. Not only that, but the high, wispy clouds I'd noted earlier had now thickened some, giving the sky a whitish cast. I felt sweat rise on my back as we walked the short distance from the curb, up the driveway to the garage.

Within the garage, in the deep, midday shadows, was parked the green Honda. The other space was empty, just as it had been on the prior weekend. Seeing the car in the garage, Larry said, "Paul must be home. I guess he got my message."

"No, that's Jodie's car. Paul's is blue. Everyone gets them mixed up."

Stepping to the kitchen door, Larry knocked, and we waited.

A few seconds later, Oralia answered, greeting us politely and admitting us without question. She'd been making a fresh pitcher of iced tea. Several glasses were set out with spoons, napkins, sugar, and lemon slices.

Not anticipating such hospitality, I laughed, commenting, "It seems you were *expecting* us, Oralia."

She explained, "When I arrived a few minutes ago, I checked the answering machine. Both Mr. Huron and Miss Jodie asked me to do that, in case they left instructions for me. Today I heard the detective's message for Mr. Huron about having a meeting here. I was not sure who was coming, or when, but I thought I should have something ready." She glanced at the pitcher of tea.

Larry said, "Very thoughtful, Oralia."

She gave a courteous nod, but seemed distracted and fretful.

"Is anything wrong?" I asked.

She wrung her hands. "The message," she told Larry. "You said there was a 'new development,' I think? I could not help wondering if there was some problem with the grocery bill that I told you about yesterday."

"Ohhh—" Larry smiled warmly. "Sorry if I alarmed you. No, there was no problem. The Warhaniks found the Vons receipt, and it clearly shows that you could not have been here in Palm Desert at the time of the murder. I hope you understand that it was never our intention to accuse you; we simply needed to explore every possibility."

"Of course," she said, returning his smile. "I was happy to help." On this point, I knew, she was more relieved than sincere.

After a lull, she offered, "Can I pour you some tea?" Both Larry and I accepted—the lemon would help cleanse the lingering taste of our greasy lunch. While pouring, Oralia asked, "So, then, will someone be meeting you here? Were you able to reach Mr. Huron?"

Larry said, "I left messages for Paul both here and at school, but it seems he hasn't gotten them yet. Meanwhile, yes, someone is supposed to meet me; he should arrive any minute. It's Dr. Percy Blair. Do you recall ever seeing him here?"

Oralia answered with a blank look.

I explained, "Dr. Blair was Jodie's boss at the hospital."

"Ah. She spoke of him, yes, but I have never met him."

Larry asked her, "Any idea where Paul might be today?"

She shook her head. "He is always at the college. He is not there?"

"He must be," I said through a thin laugh. "At breakfast this morning, he mentioned having 'tons of work' to do. With school opening next week, Glenn is really running him ragged. I imagine he hasn't had time to check messages."

Dingdong.

We all froze, as if caught in the act of something sinister. Larry grinned. "Must be Dr. Blair."

"I will get it," said Oralia, turning to leave the room.

We heard her pass through the living room and open the front door. I recognized the doctor's voice as he introduced himself, saying that a sheriff's detective had left a message—blah, blah, blah. Oralia cut him short, saying, "This way, Doctor." And a moment later they appeared in the kitchen.

Dr. Percy Blair was dressed elegantly, as the day before, in a chic suit of Italian cut, which struck me as more appropriate for evening wear than business dress. What's more, the whole look seemed too consciously youthful for his years. Though tall and lean, and by no means "old," fifty at most, his attire had been designed for a man twenty years younger; there was something sad and graceless in his attempt to project studliness instead of maturity. Was the name Percy, I wondered, short for Percival? That alone could account for a mountain of insecurity. As before, he wore far too much jewelry, most of it diamond-studded, including his massive cuff links. And he positively reeked of patchouli.

Oralia offered him tea—he declined—then Oralia disappeared into the house to resume whatever domestic duties we'd interrupted.

Larry introduced himself, handing the doctor a business card. Blair pocketed it without glancing at it, without offering his own in return.

I reintroduced myself, reminding him that we'd met at the memorial.

"Of course," he acknowledged coldly, sounding neither glad to see me nor surprised by my presence. I didn't exist. Which suited me fine—I'd have little trouble following Larry's admonition to stay in the background.

Larry told him, "Thank you, Doctor, for coming over on such short notice. Did you have any trouble finding the place?"

"None at all," he assured the detective.

"I thought not. I had to wonder, though—you were a few minutes late."

"Your directions were thorough and precise," said the doctor, sounding peeved. "I was late because I had a last-minute phone call from a patient, Henry Harris. He was extremely upset."

I couldn't help wondering: had this been strictly a doctor-patient conversation relating to heart problems? Or had Henry phoned to "report" to Blair? Were they possibly in league with regard to Jodie?

Larry said, "You know, then, that Mr. Harris and I met this morning."

"I *know* that you damn near sent him into cardiac arrest with your insane accusations—or were they merely insinuations? Henry deserves far better treatment, Detective. He's been through a lot lately."

"We *all* have," Larry reminded him. "We're dealing with murder."

Blair exhaled, sounding frustrated. "Yes, yes, yes," he clucked, "it was a horrible tragedy, of course. It's been difficult on everyone who knew Jodie—she was such a love. But isn't it time for all of us to move *beyond* this?" The tone of his question struck me as all too similar to Glenn Yeats's apparent eagerness to brush aside the murder.

Larry told him, "Maybe you're ready to 'move beyond it,' Doctor, but I *can't*—not until we've named the person responsible."

"I understand your duty," said Blair, his patience clearly stretched, "but at the same time, *you* must understand that I'm a busy man, with a busy schedule, and I happen to be in the business of saving lives, which I, for one, consider fairly important. So let me tell you succinctly: I'm terribly sorry about Jodie's death, but I simply have no useful information for you. And I really *can't* be bothered with all this cloak-and-dagger. Besides"—he let out a single, derisive snort of laughter—"why would you summon me *here*, of all places?"

Larry smiled. Moments like this, I imagined, were far too scarce in his profession. He answered the doctor, "I asked you *here,* of all places, to have you explain why your fingerprints were found all over the premises."

Predictably, the good doctor was stunned. He paused, speechless, then rattled his head, as if not believing what he'd heard. "I'm, uh . . . what did you? . . ."

Larry elaborated, "After Jodie was killed last Saturday, we found five sets of fingerprints in and around her bedroom. Four of those could be readily identified; they belonged to people we'd known to be in the bedroom. But the fifth set was a mystery. They *covered* the bedroom, the bath, even the bed frame itself, giving us the wild notion that Jodie had been, shall we say, 'entertaining' in there. A stray cuff link was also found near the bed, apparently a love token left by Jodie's visitor. Have you been searching for that 'missing link,' Doctor?" Larry added, fudging, "Your thumbprint was on it."

Blair parted his lips to speak again, but his tongue sounded sticky in his mouth. It reminded me of the reaction we'd gotten earlier from Henry Harris when he learned that we knew he hadn't spent Saturday morning on the golf course. Blair's current reaction, however, was all the more dramatic—he stuck a finger in his shirt collar and tugged, short of breath.

I offered, "Iced tea, Doctor?"

Turning, he looked at me and blinked, having forgotten I was there. "Uh, thank you," he mumbled, "yes, please."

I poured the tea and handed him the glass, from which he immediately took a gulp. Gesturing toward the breakfast table, I queried, "Do you need to sit down?"

Nodding, he stepped from the center island, where we all stood, to the table by the patio doors, then sat. He drank more of the cold tea before setting it down.

"Now, then," said Larry, pacing toward the table, "back to those fingerprints. Our tests are nothing fancy—this isn't DNA—but they're highly reliable. Any prosecutor worth his salt would have an easy time building a strong circumstantial case against you. Murder convictions have been won on far less compelling evidence. However, we needn't go down that road at all. I'm a reasonable man. And I recognize that you may have a perfectly reasonable explanation for the presence of your fingerprints in a murder victim's bedroom. If so, we can clear this up here and now. Then *you* can get back to the important business of saving lives, and *I* won't need to bother you with more of this cloak-and-dagger. Fair enough?"

Blair raised his gaze from the floor, but his eyes never met Larry's. "I'm sure there's been some mistake, Detective. You hear about these mix-ups all the time. I doubt if it's even possible to—"

"We'll double-check, if you like. We can take a quick drive down to the Indio jail, pull a fresh set of prints, and compare them against those found at the crime scene." Larry jangled the car keys in his pocket. "Ready?"

Blair waved his hands. "I'm sure that's not necessary. There's no reason—"

"Or maybe it would be helpful to refresh your memory. The bedroom's just down the hall. One quick look, and maybe something'll click. I can point out exactly where we found your prints—on the headboard, on both nightstands, and all *over* the wall. There were even a few footprints, one of them near the goddamn ceiling. It wasn't Jodie's; we checked." Larry jerked his head toward the hall. "Come on, Doc. I'll show you." With a laugh, he added, "When you think about it, it's really kinda funny."

Dr. Do-Good made no move to rise; in fact, his hands gripped the arms of the chair, as if hanging on for dear life. "No, wait," he said at last, "I can explain."

"Good," Larry said softly, "I thought so." He pulled out his pad and pen, sat across from Blair at the table, and asked, "What happened?"

Blair hesitated, drinking the last of his tea. I stepped to the table with the pitcher, poured more for him, then backed away. Finally, he told us, "Yes, I did love Jodie—intensely. How could you possibly think I would kill her?"

"Someone did," Larry reminded him. "Convince me that it wasn't you."

"God. Where to begin?"

Larry prompted, "Where and when did you meet?"

"This past summer, late June, at the medical center. It was shortly after Jodie began working there. She and her husband had just moved from the East Coast—Rhode Island, I guess. He's on the start-up faculty of that new college out here—well, you know all that.

"She caught my eye right away. She was beautiful, of course, but more than that, she went out of her way to endear herself to me. Even from afar, she had known of me by reputation, and she wasted no time telling me that it had been because of me that she'd agreed to her husband's plan to move cross-country to the desert. I don't mean to sound vain, but she seemed to idolize me.

"What's more, I quickly determined that she was both talented and dedicated to her profession. So it was only natural that I took on something of a mentor's role for her at Coachella. She trained with me, learning new techniques, quickly mastering them. She became as valuable to me as I was to her. Neither one of us was willing to draw the line there, however, and before long, we were involved intimately as well as professionally." Having reached the stickier part of his story, Blair paused to drink.

Larry asked him, "Was your affair widely known at the medical center?"

He shook his head. "Maybe I'm kidding myself, but I don't think so. I sure as hell hope not. Jodie was new here, so she didn't have many friends; as far as I know, I was her only confidant. As for me, the relationship was totally clandestine—I told *no one*—I certainly didn't go around bragging to 'the boys.' If word got out, it would seriously jeopardize my professional standing, to say nothing of my marriage."

Larry checked his notes. "So this went on—how long—two or three months?"

"We were intimately involved for the last six or eight weeks. Because of our odd schedules—it's the nature of medicine—we found it easy to contrive meeting times, usually at a hotel, a small resort, out of the way in La Quinta. That routine was starting to get old, though, and when I saw Jodie at work last Thursday, a week ago today, she told me that Paul was being sent out of town on business. We'd been itching to 'play house,' as it were, and this was the opportunity we'd been waiting for. So we told our respective spouses that we were working the Friday-night/Saturday-morning shift that weekend. In reality, of course, we spent the night here, mostly in the bedroom.

"Not only was Paul's trip fortuitous, but even the timing of his car repairs proved accommodating. His car was in the shop for some reason that weekend, which meant there was an extra garage space I could use overnight, hiding my own car from the eyes of any curious neighbors.

"Jodie and I made love repeatedly that night, then showered together in the morning, keeping an eye on the clock. As I recall, Paul's flight was due in at nine-twenty. A friend, a fellow faculty member, I believe, had volunteered to drive him from the airport, since Jodie was supposedly working. We figured that by the time he got his bags and made the trip from Palm Springs, he'd arrive back at the house around ten."

As Dr. Blair recounted this, I recalled the particulars of my airport excursion on Saturday. Paul and I drove up to the house at 9:50 that morning, within ten minutes of the time estimated by his scheming wife. Close enough.

Blair continued, "There was an element of risk in all this, which only heightened its erotic allure. Still, we were both nervous about the timing and wanted to be sure there were no slipups. So we got up early that morning, had our shower, then shared a pot of coffee before I left the house at a few minutes after eight. That would give Jodie nearly two hours to clean up any evidence of our lovemaking, put herself together, and get out of the house before Paul's return."

Larry looked up from his notes. "And that was the last you saw of Jodie?"

"Yes." Blair sighed. "When I left the house at eight that morning, we parted with a kiss. I had no idea that I would never see or touch her again. She was perfectly healthy *then,* Detective. I understand from the news media that you've fixed Jodie's time of death between eight-thirty and nine that morning. I was long gone by then." He emphasized, "I did *not* kill her. Why would I? I loved her."

"Can you account for your whereabouts between eight-thirty and nine?"

The doctor puckered a silent whistle. "Yes, indeed. I was with Candy."

I blurted, *"Candy?* Who's Candy?"

Larry suppressed a laugh.

Blair explained, "Candy—Candace—is my wife. I'd told her that my hospital shift was ending at eight, so I went directly home from here, arriving before eight-thirty. I had a bit of breakfast with her, then, claiming exhaustion from a rough night on the job, went to bed for a few hours." With a licentious smirk, he added, "The exhaustion was genuine enough, though its cause was a fabrication."

"What's your home address and phone number, Doctor?"

Blair recited them.

Larry jotted them down, saying, "I'm sure you understand that I'll have to check this story with Mrs. Blair. If she corroborates it, you're probably off the hook." He closed his notebook. "There, now. Aren't you glad you've explained yourself and cleared the air?"

"Thrilled." Blair rose from his chair. "My wife is about to learn that I've been guilty of a major transgression of vows that she has always held sacred. She's suspected me of past flings, I could tell, but she's never said a word—I've always admired her fortitude. Now, who knows? I presume the floodgates are about to be thrown open. What's more, I fear she may actually spite me by refuting my alibi."

I couldn't resist interjecting, "Can't say I'd blame her."

He looked at me. "To tell the truth, neither would I." He tossed his hands with a pathetic laugh. "Either way, I seem to be in one hell of a mess."

I wanted to add, It's a mess of your own making. But why bother? He was already a dead horse, hardly worth kicking.

Larry said, "One more question. You don't happen to be in possession of Jodie's wedding ring, do you?"

"Of course not."

"But I assume you can recall seeing it."

"Many times. Jodie was very fond of it. She often showed it off. It was quite pretty, in it's own way, I suppose. To be honest, I've never much cared for pearls." Blair didn't need to explain that his own taste ran more toward diamonds.

"Was she wearing it Saturday morning?"

"When I *left,* yes. She made a point of putting it on, so she wouldn't forget it. But she *never* wore it to bed."

I asked, "Really?" Puzzled, I reminded Larry, "Paul told us that Jodie *always* wore the ring. Earlier, when we found the body, he told me that she'd never once taken it off during the years they were married."

Blair tisked. "That's ridiculous. I often saw Jodie without the ring. She rarely wore it at work." He laughed, asking me, "How could she get a latex glove over *that* thing?" Then he turned to Larry, who still sat at the breakfast table, rubbing his chin, thinking. "May I leave now, Detective? I need to begin some preemptive damage control."

Larry stood. "So much for your busy life-or-death schedule, eh?"

"It's still life-or-death; now it's a question of *whose.* One's priorities can shift rather quickly."

"Mm-hm." Larry could barely contain his disdain for the man. "Certainly, Doctor, you're free to go now. However, I'll have to ask you not to leave the valley till further notice. You'll need to be available for further questioning. And you should probably call your lawyer."

"Now, *that's* a no-brainer." Blair glanced about the kitchen, looking lost, as if the unsettling conversation had blotted out his memory of arriving.

Larry told him, "Just use the garage door. It's the quickest way to the street."

The doctor shook his head. "Sorry, an old superstition: always leave a building by the same door through which you entered. No point in tempting fate. Not now."

I stepped to the living room and pointed to the front door, telling him, "This way out, then."

Percival Blair nodded, passed by me, and left through the front door, pulling it closed behind him.

Returning to the kitchen, I asked Larry, "What do you think?"

"I think he's a prick. Oh, excuse me."

"I think he's a prick too. But do you think he killed Jodie?"

"Maybe. We'll see what his wife has to say. Unfortunately, regardless of whether she corroborates his alibi or refutes it, I doubt if we can simply accept her story at face value."

I wrinkled my nose. "You're one step ahead of me."

He explained, "On the one hand, she's his wife. If she says he *was* home by eight-thirty on Saturday morning, she's either telling the truth or trying to protect him. On the other hand, she's his *wronged* wife. If she says he was *not* home by eight-thirty, she's either telling the truth or trying to screw him."

"Tit for tat," I mused. "Did you believe him, about not having the ring?"

"I don't know what would motivate him to take the ring, unless, as you've suggested, the theft was meant to have symbolic value. Clearly, he had no affection for the ring itself, and he hardly fits the profile of someone needing to make a few quick bucks from the sale of stolen jewelry. Actually, I hope he *doesn't* have it."

I guessed, "Because you'd have a rough time finding it?"

"Right. It's a *ring,* for God's sake. He could hide it anywhere, absolutely anywhere, or simply dispose of it. I could devise search warrants from now till Christmas, but they'd never lead me to that ring if Blair took it. So I'm hoping he *doesn't* have the ring. If it's out there in circulation somewhere, there's a chance that someone will identify it from the story in the paper, which could provide a connection back to the killer, whether it's Blair or someone else."

Pondering this, I took the doctor's empty glass from the table and put it in the sink. Instinctively, I carried the glass by its base, so as not to sully any fingerprints on it, when I realized that my penchant for smudged glassware had turned a tad obsessive. Besides, I'd already nailed Dr. Do-Good.

"Hey," said Larry, "who's this?" I couldn't imagine what he meant till I saw him unclip the pager from his belt. Glancing at the number on its readout, he said, "Paul must be back in his office." He showed me the number, and I confirmed that it was a campus phone.

Larry took out his cell phone and began to place the call, but I stopped him, asking, "What are you planning to tell him?"

"*Everything*, I guess. There's plenty to report."

I bit my lip.

"What's wrong?"

I sighed. "It's just that Paul's been into this denial thing since the morning when he found Jodie's body. He's been pushing the bungled-burglary angle because it allows him to avoid the possibility of Jodie's involvement with another man. He's wistfully described his relationship with Jodie as 'perfect.' In other words, he has *no* grip on the realities of his marriage or of his wife's death."

Larry nodded. "Bad move, then, to spill it through the phone."

"I just don't know how he's going to handle this news—our incontrovertible evidence that Jodie had taken advantage of Paul's absence last weekend, seizing the opportunity to host a sex romp in their wedding bed."

Larry assured me, "I hadn't planned to phrase it in quite those terms."

I grinned. "Of course not. But the upshot is, I think we need to be with him when he hears this."

Larry mulled the situation for a moment, then suggested, "Your car is back at the sales office, so I need to take you up to Nirvana anyway. Why don't I ask Paul to meet us there? It's quiet, it's out of the way, and it's neutral territory."

"Perfect."

Larry flipped open his phone and dialed Paul's number.

21

Paul was heartened to hear from Larry that there'd been an important breakthrough on the case, but understandably, he was baffled by Larry's reluctance to tell him what it was. Further, Larry's suggestion that Paul meet us at the Nirvana sales office must have seemed downright nonsensical, since the logistics of my car, to say nothing of that morning's setup of Henry Harris, now seemed beyond coherent explanation. Nonetheless, Paul's curiosity was far stronger than his confusion, and he readily agreed to Larry's proposal, saying he'd drive over as soon as he'd caught up with his other phone messages.

So Larry and I thanked Oralia for being so accommodating, then left the Huron house, driving back to Rancho Mirage in the anonymous white sedan with county plates. We didn't talk much in the car. Larry was occupied with driving, while I tried to digest the meaning of what we'd learned from Dr. Blair.

Who, I wondered, had been at the Huron house on Saturday morning between Blair's claimed departure at eight and Paul's arrival shortly before ten? Who killed Jodie?

It could have been Dr. Blair, who may simply have lied regarding the time he left the house that day. If so, I saw no apparent motive for the murder; I could only speculate that their love had somehow soured. Another point suggesting Blair's guilt was that a cardiologist would be familiar with the freakish *commotio cordis* phenomenon and would know precisely how to deliver the fatal blow.

If it was not Dr. Blair, then someone *else* had come to the house, within a half hour of Blair's departure, and killed Jodie. Again there was no apparent motive. Theft no longer seemed likely; I was convinced that we were dealing with a crime of passion. What sort of passion, though? Did Jodie have a *second* lover, a jealous paramour who'd turned murderous after discovering her overnight gymnastics with Dr. Do-Good?

Was it Henry Harris after all? He'd already admitted to a secret visit to his unnamed mistress on Saturday morning. And even frail Henry could have summoned sufficient strength to deliver the deadly blow. What's more, I knew that he and Blair were frequently in touch—they'd both attended Wednesday's memorial service, and they'd spoken again by phone today.

Or was it Tanner Griffin? Though I was loath even to consider the possibility of his complicity in Jodie's death, I now knew firsthand that Tanner was a man of intense passions. Further, I knew that he and Jodie had shared a mutual attraction, and I knew that they'd spoken by phone on Friday regarding the rework of Paul's car repairs. Tanner had told me that their conversation touched on Paul's unexpected business trip. Had one thing led to another?

Or was it someone else entirely, someone whose name had never been raised in the context of Jodie's death, someone with a powerful motive that was not yet apparent to me?

"You're awfully quiet," Larry turned to tell me as we pulled up to the gatehouse below Nirvana.

"You've been less than gabby yourself. Seems we have plenty to think about."

The security guard leaned to the car window and, recognizing Larry, gave a little salute while triggering the gate open. As we drove through, Larry wondered aloud, "How's Paul going to react to the news about Blair? His emotions were pretty fragile last weekend. This won't send him over the edge, will it?"

"Hope not." It was a lame answer to a good question. Though Paul's disposition had improved steadily all week, I could well recall his mental state on Saturday, when the shock of his discovery was fresh. Alternating between sobbing, rage, and frenzy, he'd been the very picture of raw grief in the face of sudden, unexpected death. During the intervening days, he'd begun to cope, to put his life back together, and to focus on the world around him, the world of the living. He had not yet, however, shown any signs of emerging from his state of denial, from his fantasy of the perfect marriage to the perfect wife. His delicately revised memory of their relationship was about to hit the hard wall of reality. Would the loss of his delusion prove even more debilitating than the loss of his wife?

Larry passed the hotel on the way up the mountainside; a knot gripped my stomach as we approached the sales office. Turning into the parking court, I noted with relief that Paul had not yet arrived—I knew his blue Honda only too well by now, and it wasn't there. Neither, for that matter, was Grant's Mercedes. He could have been out on a sales call or perhaps still at lunch. It was about two o'clock.

Getting out of the car and crossing the entry court with Larry, I broke into a sweat, due partly to nerves, partly to the weather. Even at this higher elevation, the afternoon felt torrid, even muggy. I'd known nothing but sunshine and blue skies since moving to the desert, but today the sky had steadily clouded over, turning not gray but hot white, as if sprayed with steam.

The rush of chilled air from the office felt clean, dry, and welcoming as Larry tugged open the glass door and we stepped inside. Tracie popped out from somewhere, hearing the door. "Oh"—nice smile— "welcome back. Your brother took a late lunch, Detective Knoll. If you need to reach him, I can phone the hotel dining room."

"Thanks," said Larry, dabbing his forehead and the back of his neck with a handkerchief, "but let him take his time. I just drove Claire up to get her car. Someone else will be meeting us as well. Okay if we use the conference room for a few minutes?"

"Certainly. I'll set out some water."

I said, "If you don't mind, Tracie, could you phone the gatehouse and let them know we're expecting Mr. Huron? He drives a blue Honda."

"Happy to." She blinked and disappeared.

As Larry and I walked through the main room, I paused to take another look at the model of the proposed golf course, wondering aloud, "How would it endanger the bighorns?"

"Beats me. I've never heard of a sheep being killed by a golf ball. Sure, you might *daze* a few, but . . ."

I gave him a skeptical grin.

"It has something to do with grazing or lambing or whatever."

"Ah." I still didn't get it. Turning from the model, I followed Larry into the conference room.

Considering the logistics of the room, we decided to sit at the far curve of the oval table, on either side, saving the end seat for Paul. In effect, we could huddle there, with Paul between us, should the need arise to comfort or (God forbid) restrain him.

Tracie bumped open the kitchen door with her hip, bearing a tray of glasses and bottled water. Setting it on the granite-topped table, she said, "Your guest is on his way up. He arrived while I was on the phone."

"Thanks, Tracie," said Larry. "We'll stay here. Could you send him back?"

Blinking again, she was gone.

With elbows on the table, Larry leaned toward me, saying quietly, "I'll give him the news, but feel free to jump in anytime. You know him better than I do, and besides, he may need a bit of mothering."

I understood what he meant, but I flinched at the notion of mothering Paul. Twenty-two years his senior, I was indeed old enough to be his mother, but I thought of him as a friend, a co-worker, and a contemporary. At times, I had even felt the twinge of physical attraction to him.

"They're right in here," Tracie told Paul as they appeared in the wide doorway. "I thought you might like some cold water," she added, indicating the tray.

"Yeah, I could use some. Thanks." He wore the same black T-shirt and jeans that he'd worn at breakfast, but the six intervening hours had taken their toll. That morning he'd looked fresh, vigorous, and ready to take on the world; now he looked hot, sweaty, and haggard.

Tracie bowed out. Larry and I stood. Paul poured himself a glass of water. Larry thanked him for coming. I made some comment about the weather.

Paul mopped his brow with one hand, lifted the glass with his other, and drank. "God," he said between gulps, "what a day."

I assumed it was more than the heat that had gotten to him. With an understanding nod, I asked, "Problems with the kiln?"

"Hm? Oh, yeah. That . . . and everything. I've been putting out fires."

"Sit down," Larry and I told him. "Have a chair."

When Paul had settled between us, I said, "This morning you seemed so confident that everything would pull together for the opening of school. Trouble?"

He shook his head. "Nothing in particular. Guess I'm just feeling overwhelmed. And pressured." He turned to Larry. "Anyway, I could use some good news, so I was glad to get your call. But, uh . . . why all the mystery?"

"Sorry," said Larry through a quiet laugh, "didn't mean to alarm you. Truth is, we did have an important breakthrough on your wife's case today. Claire was an enormous help, by the way."

Paul turned to me with a smile of thanks.

Larry continued, "We're much closer to understanding what happened at the house on Saturday morning. But both Claire and I thought you deserved to hear about this in person, face-to-face."

Paul's features twisted. *"That* sounds ominous."

Larry conceded, "I'm not at all sure you'll welcome this news. We're now fairly convinced that Jodie's death had nothing to do with a burglary, botched or otherwise."

"But the ring, the Rolex, the other stuff that's missing—"

"Paul, more and more, Jodie's murder appears to have been a crime of passion. We have good reason to believe that she'd been involved with another man." Larry paused. "In fact, we know it."

Paul sat stiff, with a wary expression, not wanting to hear this, but needing to know more. He demanded flatly, "Who?"

"We just met with Dr. Percy Blair, and he admitted—"

"Blair?" Paul tried to claw the table with both of his strong, sculptor's hands, but his fingertips squeaked on the granite, failing, of course, to penetrate it. "Blair was her *idol*, her goddamn *mentor*. She'd been depressed about moving here, but when Blair took her under his wing, that's when she—" He broke off, sensing the obvious. Then he planted his elbows on the table, held his head in his hands, and inhaled loudly.

I thought he was preparing to scream. Reflexively, I tensed.

Instead, his shoulders arched, and then he sobbed. "Oh, Jesus . . . ," he whined through the tears that suddenly soaked his hands and dripped to the stone surface of the table. After a few moments, he looked up with gaunt, wild eyes, turning from Larry to me and back to Larry. He demanded, "Blair killed Jodie?"

Larry tried explaining, "We don't know. I don't think so. He claims to have an alibi, which I haven't been able to check yet. He claims he left the house before—"

"If he didn't *kill* Jodie," Paul interrupted, "what exactly *did* he do?"

Larry hesitated, then looked to me—for motherly help.

I touched Paul's arm. He'd asked a direct question, and I saw no point in clouding the answer with euphemisms. "Dr. Blair and Jodie were sexually involved. They were having an affair that went back six or eight weeks. Last Friday night, while you were in Dallas, they slept together—at the house. He claims that Jodie was alive and well when he left her at eight on Saturday morning."

Paul inhaled deeply again, using his hand to wipe a trickle of snot from his upper lip. Struggling to compose himself, he asked, "You believe him?"

"As Larry was saying, it's a tough call. As far as we know, he had no *reason* to kill Jodie."

"No one did," Paul said in a pleading tone, as if we hadn't yet considered the frustrating conundrum of a motive. Paul's shoulders began to jerk, and he again broke into tears, covering his face with one of his huge hands—a lame attempt to prevent us from witnessing his pain.

Larry told him, "I know how awful it is for you to hear these things. But Blair's admission of his involvement with Jodie opens a promising new avenue of investigation. I don't have all the answers yet, but now, at least, I know what questions need to be asked."

"Where's the paaarty?" lilted Grant's voice from the front of the office. He'd just arrived back from lunch and apparently noticed the extra cars parked outside. "Who's *here?*" he gabbed maniacally while whisking through the main room, past the model of the golf course, then appearing in the doorway to the conference room. "Well, *there* you are!"

"Hi, Grant," Larry and I greeted him quietly. "Nice lunch?"

"The service was a bit slow, but the—" He stopped short, getting a good luck at Paul in his misery. "Good *Lord,* you poor *lamb.* What *have* they done to you?" He dashed around the table, positioning himself behind Paul to pat his shoulders while cooing there-theres and now-nows.

Paul screwed his head to look up at Grant with puffy eyes and tear-smeared cheeks. "Your brother brought good news. He thinks the case is now on the right track." Then Paul turned away, raising a hand to his mouth to suppress a sob.

Grant eyed us accusingly. "I might have guessed."

I told him, "We're *trying* to solve this."

"I *know* that, doll. And I'm sure Paul appreciates your efforts. But delicate matters must be handled with a measure of *delicacy.*" He rolled a chair up to the table and sat next to Paul, displacing me by several inches. Slinging an arm around Paul's shoulders, he rocked him like a baby.

Larry told Grant, "We talked to Dr. Blair."

"And I assume the inquisition was productive?"

Larry and I filled him in, which forced Paul to hear, once more, the litany of his wife's infidelities.

"This went on for *six weeks*?" repeated Grant, aghast.

"Maybe eight," I told him, purely in the interest of precision.

Grant tisked. "Well, *that* tramp."

Paul heaved a loud sob.

"Oops. Sorry, love."

Paul shook his head. With a sigh, he told Grant, "There's no need to apologize. You're probably right. I should have known."

I asked, "You never had an inkling?"

He paused, not out of reticence but seemingly intrigued by the question, as if he'd never considered it. "Over the years, from time to time, yes, I'd had suspicions that Jodie may have been seeing someone. But I just didn't *want* to believe it, so I never confronted her with it. The iffy periods always passed, and we were as good as ever."

"What about this past summer?"

He mustered a laugh. "That's the irony. The move depressed her, and when she finally perked up, I was *grateful.* I was *glad* her mood had improved, so I wasn't about to question her, or myself, about the source of her happiness. Maybe, deep inside, I saw danger signs, but I chose to ignore them. I mean, I didn't 'know' she was being unfaithful, so the problem didn't exist. I guess I preferred ignorance to the truth. It was . . . easier."

I told him softly, "Denial always takes its toll, eventually."

He nodded, sitting back in his chair. "Now that I 'know' about Jodie, I can't honestly say how I feel. There's a sense of resolution—there's no need to keep wondering—but how do I rewrite the last five years? And now that she's gone, how do I remember her?"

Grant jumped in, doing his best to console Paul, reassuring him that nothing had really changed, reminding him that the love he and Jodie shared was still real in spite of her occasional forays into other men's affections. Grant's words were predictable, intended to soothe and reconcile, but I didn't entirely buy them, and neither did Paul. Despite Grant's platitudes to the contrary, a great deal had suddenly changed for Paul, shattering the image he had cherished of his late wife, and worse, confirming his worst fears, those of his own inadequacy.

Even as Grant spoke, Paul squirmed in his chair, clutched his legs together, and chewed the knuckle of his index finger. Before my eyes, he seemed to grow smaller, to shrivel within himself. The bitter reality of his wife's infidelity was far from enlightening or liberating. No, he found it, in a word, emasculating. In truth, I felt he was blowing out of proportion the wounded-male-ego overtones of Jodie's philandering, but his torment was genuine, and I could not help but pity him.

Though well-intended, Grant's gentle reassurances had dragged Paul's emotions even lower, so I decided to try another tack. Since the ephemera of love, longing, and betrayal inhabited a mental territory that was slippery at best, the antidote, I reasoned, lay not in feel-good psychology but in the nuts and bolts of the investigation.

When Grant paused long enough to breathe during his buck-up monologue, I asked Larry, "Now that you have a clear picture of events at the house prior to Jodie's death, how do you intend to proceed?"

The detective sat back in his chair, glad to return to the realm of the objective. "The first order of business, of course, is to check Dr. Blair's alibi with his wife. He claims she knew nothing of what he was up to, so I'm not looking forward to my conversation with her." Larry didn't need to add that what he dreaded from Mrs. Blair was a breakdown similar to Paul's.

Grant asked him, "You've abandoned the theft angle entirely?"

"I've abandoned the notion that Jodie's ring disappeared in the course of a burglary, but I'm more convinced than ever that Jodie's ring is the key to this case."

Intrigued, Paul rose from his miasma of woe to ask, "Why?"

Larry smiled at me. "The ring has considerable monetary value, which would be of interest to a thief, certainly. But Claire also pointed out that a wedding ring carries heavy *symbolic* value, suggesting a crime of passion."

Paul conceded, "Makes sense." Turning to me, he asked, "When did you start to think along those lines?"

"Practically from the moment we discovered the body. It struck me as odd enough that a ring had been taken from a dead woman's finger, but when I witnessed *your* reaction to the missing ring—you may not remember, Paul, but you were nearly hysterical—that's when I realized that the ring wasn't just 'stolen.' It was taken to leave a message."

Paul blinked. "A message to *me*?"

"Maybe. I honestly don't know. But from the moment you pointed out that Jodie's ring was missing, I was fairly convinced that she had *not* died because she'd startled a burglar." Pausing, I added, "This was just a hunch, of course. The patchouli compounded my suspicions."

Grant laughed. "Here we go again: Madam Sleuth, 'the nose that knows.' "

"Oh, shush." I smacked his arm with the back of my hand.

Larry said. "Give her some credit, Grant. It was the patchouli that led her to Dr. Blair. He may not be the killer—or maybe he is—but we know a *whole* lot more than we did before Claire sniffed him out at the funeral."

Paul signaled time-out. "I seem to be *way* behind here. Patchouli?"

I stood, needing to stretch. Circling the table, I explained, "At the crime scene on Saturday, I noticed a heavy fragrance hanging in the room. I presumed it was perfume, but glancing around Jodie's things, I couldn't see that she *had* any perfume. So naturally, I wondered if there had been someone else in the room."

Paul told me, "I was so distraught, I didn't notice the smell. But you're right—if someone's perfume lingered there, it wouldn't have been Jodie's. I'm allergic to fragrances, so she never wore perfume."

This, I noted, was consistent with the information on Paul's health records that Glenn Yeats had pulled up on his computer for me. I also recalled that Paul was sneezing through his tears at the crime scene, doubtless a reaction to the heavy fragrance.

I explained to him, "The scent was familiar to me, but I couldn't identify it. Then, at Jodie's memorial service yesterday, Kiki got a whiff of it and told me it was patchouli, a classic, heavy scent worn by men as well as women. Dr. Blair had splashed it on so heavy, we eventually picked him out of the crowd. His fingerprints on a wineglass confirmed that he had been in your bedroom."

Paul clenched his two fists on the table, lowering his head.

Larry reminded him, "Blair admits that he wronged you, Paul, but he insists that he never hurt Jodie." He stood. "Look, I need to get going on that alibi. With any luck, I can still track down Mrs. Blair this afternoon." He moved toward the doorway.

Paul looked up. "Let me know, okay?"

I gingerly raised a hand. "Me, too?"

Larry paused. "Sure—both of you." Stepping out to the main room, he turned back to tell Paul, "Sorry this has been such a rough day for you." Then he said good-bye to his brother and left the sales office.

Paul and Grant rose from their chairs. Paul looked a bit wobbly, standing with his hands braced on the table, still shaken by all he'd learned.

I offered, "Can I drive you home, Paul? If you'd like, maybe we could have dinner later."

He straightened up, squaring his shoulders. "Thanks, Claire, but I'll be fine. Besides, I still have some fires to put out. There's plenty to keep me busy on campus."

I nodded, glad to hear he was trying to focus on fires other than Jodie.

22

Friday morning dawned late through heavy clouds. The sky was no longer white and hot, as on Thursday afternoon, but gray and cold. It looked as if it could rain, a phenomenon I'd yet to experience in the desert.

Thursday evening, Grant had phoned me at home from his condo across the courtyard. "I just ran into Kiki," he told me, "parking in the garage. On an impulse, I invited her over for breakfast tomorrow morning. Care to join us?"

"Love to. What are you doing tonight? No, let me guess—dinner at Fusión, or at least a quick drive-by?"

"You she-devil!" He howled. "I'm tempted, doll, but I'm shot. It was a hellish afternoon, wasn't it? And I think there's a low-pressure system rolling in, which doesn't help. Early to bed for me tonight."

We compared a few notes on our meeting with Paul at the sales office, agreeing that he was better off living with the truth—the pain would pass. It seemed that the healing process had already begun. By the time we had left Nirvana, driving off separately from the bottom of the mountain, he'd gotten a new grip on reality, heading toward campus to put out his fires.

I asked Grant, "Any word from your brother?"

"I just called Larry from the car. He hasn't been able to meet the doctor's wife yet. She was on a day trip to L.A., a Getty tour, I think. So she'll have quite the surprise waiting for her tomorrow morning, unless the revered Dr. Blair pours out his two-timing heart to her later tonight."

I snorted a rude laugh. "Don't count on it. Dr. Do-Good is a weasel."

"Possibly a murderous weasel," Grant reminded me.

We gabbed a bit more in this vein before hanging up. Not much later, I went to bed. Though it was a ridiculously early hour to retire, it had been a long, eventful, and trying day, so I slept like a drugged baby that night.

By morning, I was fully rested, ready to begin again. I rose later than usual, needing only to put myself together; today I wasn't hosting breakfast, but attending one. While I had barely managed, the day before, to slop yogurt into a dish for Paul, I had a hunch that Grant's morning repast would involve a bit more fussing.

Stepping outside my front door, I picked up the rolled copy of the *Desert Sun.* Heading across the courtyard, I smelled bacon and cornmeal and butter and syrup—"the nose that knows." Passing the fountain, I noted that its trickle was not accompanied by the usual chorus and chattering of birds; even they, it seemed, were sleeping late on this cloudy morning. Then I opened Grant's iron gate and stepped into his entry court. The front door was wide open; the smells of breakfast intensified. I poked my head inside and yoo-hooed.

"Mornin', doll," Grant called to me. "Come on in—got my hands full."

Passing through the front hall, I found him hard at work in the kitchen. The exhaust fan whirred, bacon crackled, and gurgling water rinsed something in the sink as the oven door closed with a clunk, all of these sounds underlaid by the sprightly strains of Mozart from the living room. Grant wore an apron over his elegant but understated office clothes, basic gray today, doubtless chosen to coordinate with the dim weather. Slipping off a pair of big, goofy oven mitts, he greeted me with a hug and a kiss. "I don't usually bother with breakfast, but what are friends for?"

I laughed. "It looks as if you've been at it for *hours.*"

"Nah," he assured me, "everything's under control. You're first to arrive."

"Kiki takes longer than I do getting her act together."

He turned off the water, took the bacon off the stove. "Juice? Coffee?"

Opting for the latter—Grant, the former—I followed him into the living room, where we settled by the fireplace to wait for Kiki. As the morning appeared too risky for an outdoor meal, Grant had set the dining table for our breakfast. At the far side of the room, in the light from the French doors, the table looked ready for a magazine photo shoot, replete with a huge, wild arrangement of fresh flowers, colorful crockery, and starched, folded napery that could pass for origami. No one, even Grant, could have thrown this together on the spur of the moment—while cooking breakfast, no less—so I suspected he had tinkered with the table into the night. As I still carried the rolled newspaper under my arm, I set it on the coffee table next to Grant's paper, which had already been read, as evidenced by its slight but telling disarray. Herr Mozart continued to grind away melodiously in the background.

Grant asked idly, "Busy day today?"

"*I'll* say. I have plenty of catching up to do at the office. The last few days, I've been . . . distracted."

He eyed me knowingly. "Police work?"

"That," I admitted, "plus, I've been pulling a few strings for a new student."

"I thought they were *all* new."

"This one's newer. We met just last Monday, and we didn't seriously discuss the possibility of his enrollment until yesterday."

Grant looked at me over the rim of his juice glass. "*His* enrollment? This student is a 'he,' then? He must be good."

There was no point in protracting this. Though Grant had merely narrowed my student's identity to half the population of the world, he would eventually piece together what I'd done, so I decided to be frank with him. I realized, as well, that I was itching to confide my exploits to *someone,* and I doubted that Grant would be harshly judgmental. "Yes," I answered, "he *is* good. In fact, he gave one of the finest auditions I've ever seen." My mind reeled at the memory of Tanner's finale.

"My. That's high praise, coming from you. Where'd you find him?"

I hesitated. "Desert Detail. Jodie's body shop."

Grant rolled his eyes. "A grease monkey?"

"Hardly. He manages the place—that's where I'm having my car windows tinted." I didn't mention that I had originally driven out there due to my suspicion that Jodie's "marvelous mechanic" might have been the man who killed her. Now I felt comfortable laughing at these suspicions. With a chortle, I told Grant, "You'll have to get a look at him sometime."

That caught his interest. "Oh? Easy on the eyes?"

I nodded. "You have *no* idea."

He ticked off the next item: "Age?"

"Twenty-uh-six, I think."

"Height?"

"Hello-o-o . . . ," lilted Kiki's voice just before she popped into the hall through the open door. "I hope I'm not *terribly* late." She wore tight black capri pants and an odd top, sort of a white, lacy smock, loose-fitting, hip-length. I blinked away the bizarre image of an altar boy on estrogen.

Grant rose, whooshing toward her. "Just in time for breakfast," he told her, pausing to peck her lips, "but you nearly missed Claire's story about the remarkable audition she—"

"Later," I cut him off quietly but firmly.

Kiki eyed my cup of coffee, Grant's glass of juice. "Juice would be lovely," she told him, smiling her thanks for his anticipated hospitality.

"Of course, milady." He curtsied, then tiptoed backward into the kitchen.

Kiki strutted toward me on four-inch heels, leaned, and we kissed cheeks, exchanging good-mornings. Sitting next to me on the sofa, she patted my hand. "What *have* you been up to, dear?"

"Me?" I asked guiltily, assuming she was quizzing me about Grant's reference to the audition. "Just . . . keeping busy."

"I should *say*. I stopped by your office several times yesterday, but you were never in. We need to discuss future staffing of the—"

I laughed, interrupting, "Don't even *ask* about yesterday. It was mayhem. I don't think I spent two hours at my desk."

"Actually," said Grant from the kitchen, "*I* saw quite a bit of Claire yesterday." Reappearing with Kiki's orange juice, he explained, "I witnessed not one but two police interrogations that she *ruthlessly* commandeered." He sat across from us.

"That's hardly true," I corrected him.

Kiki swallowed her first sip of juice. She asked me flatly, "Still at it, eh?"

"I guess I *have* gotten more wrapped up in the investigation than I'd intended."

Grant laughed. "My brother's not complaining. The way I hear it, Claire's been quite helpful." He winked at me.

Kiki turned to me with raised brows. "So—any news?"

"If you're asking who killed Jodie, I'm afraid we haven't figured that out yet."

"But," said Grant, raising a finger, "thanks to Claire's instincts, they've determined that Dr. Percy Blair, the victim's boss, had *slept* with the victim the night before she was killed. He's admitted it."

Kiki sipped more juice. "How *delicious.*" She was apparently referring to the story, not the juice, because she added, "Tell me more."

Since she'd been at Wednesday's memorial service with me, she already knew the background of the patchouli and the fingerprints on the wineglass. Grant brought her up to date on the results of Thursday's meetings with Henry Harris, Dr. Blair, and Paul Huron.

As he told this story, liberally embellishing it with dramatic detail, I rose and snooped about the room, appreciating once more the many decorating touches that made the space so distinctly Grant's. Eventually I made my way to the dining table, and while perusing its setting, my eye wandered to the French doors. *"Rain,"* I said, astonished. "It's raining." In truth, it was barely drizzling, spitting a few drops here and there.

Grant said, "It *does* happen, even in the desert."

"Does it ever amount to anything."

"Rarely. Maybe three inches per year."

"Will it last? I don't think I like this." I was already spoiled.

"It should blow over fast. Check the paper. Weather is always a hot topic here—no pun intended." He smiled cleverly. Kiki laughed. I groaned.

As Grant resumed telling Kiki of my contributions to the Huron case, he lifted the front section of the *Desert Sun* from the coffee table and held it in my direction. Strolling back across the room, I took it from him, glanced at the weather box near the masthead, and saw that he was right. Blue skies would return that afternoon, it said.

Satisfied, I skimmed the rest of page one, thinking there might be some follow-up on the previous day's ring story. But no. The headline story related to a hit-and-run accident; a young man was dead. There was an ongoing series about a school-budget referendum that I hadn't been paying attention to. More trouble in Eastern Europe. Scandal in Washington. Ho hum.

As I reached to set the paper down, a mug shot near the fold caught my eye. Pictured was the smiling face of the young man who'd been killed in the accident, and for some reason, he looked familiar to me; he had a fetching mole on one cheek. The caption identified him as Sarad Patel, twenty-three years old. Was he perhaps a waiter whom I'd encountered somewhere during my brief time in the valley? There was another photo, larger—the main photo on the page—of the victim's young widow, Rajni Patel, holding their baby, now fatherless. Though the mother was in tears, the baby smiled in toothless ignorance at the camera. Pretty baby. Handsome father. Mom looked like hell, but that was doubtless the result of her emotions, not her genes.

It was one of those stories that, once you were pulled into its gut-wrenching circumstances, begged to be read. So I started from the top. Patel was killed by a hit-and-run driver at eight-o'clock Thursday night. He was on foot, walking to his home on a quiet side street in Cathedral City, shortly after getting off a bus. He was found by neighbors who rushed to the street, responding to the sound of squealing tires. No one saw the vehicle that hit Patel. He sustained massive injuries and was declared dead at the scene. Because he was killed near the sidewalk, where he was crushed, not thrown, police concluded that he was the victim of either drunk driving or homicide. A full-scale investigation was being launched.

Lower in the story, a paragraph jumped off the page at me: "Patel was returning from the airport, where he was employed as a clerk by RideRite Rent-a-Car. Fellow employees at the rental agency described him as an affable young man, exceptionally courteous, always ready with a smile for customers and friends alike. He joined the company—"

"My *God*," I said, holding out the paper to Grant and Kiki, "I *knew* this kid, the one who was killed."

"What?" they asked, rising. "Who, Claire?"

I tapped the photo on the newsprint, explaining, "I didn't really *know* him, but he smiled at me—at the airport, where he works. Worked. We had this little . . . exchange. He was so *nice,* just like the Asian lady." I dropped the paper.

Grant asked, "What Asian lady?" He helped me sit down.

"Claire, dear," said Kiki, "whatever are you talking about?" She and Grant were now sitting with me, flanking me, on the sofa.

Realizing that my emotional reaction to the story must have sounded incoherent, I paused, then told them calmly, "Saturday morning at the airport, I was amazed by how *friendly* Californians are. An Asian lady, who was in a hurry, stopped to give me directions, simply because I looked confused. Then, as I was leaving, the young man at the car-rental counter gave me the nicest smile. So I sort of flirted with him, making him blush. He was a sweetheart." I sighed, "Oh, the poor kid. And his family . . ."

Grant patted my hand. "I'm sorry, love. Sometimes bad things happen to good people. For the rest of us, life goes on."

Kiki took my other hand. "Maybe you could send flowers. Or a small check."

I nodded, downcast. "Thanks, Kiki. That's a good idea." It helped to think there was something I could do. Still, I was troubled. The boy and I hadn't even spoken, but our lives had brushed, and for a moment, they'd touched—purely in a spirit of friendship, with respect for each other's humanity, giving no thought whatever to our relative stations in life. His smile had enlightened me.

Thoughts of his untimely death naturally led me back to Jodie. Her too I had barely known, and she too had died under mysterious circumstances, a victim, a sad statistic. In all my years living in New York, seen by many as a crime capital, I had never known a victim of serious crime. Maybe I'd simply run in the right circles. But now, here in the blissful Coachella Valley, two acquaintances had been killed, in the prime of life, within six days of each other. Not that I put any faith in omens, but clearly, this did not bode well.

"Happier thoughts now," Grant insisted, rising. Stepping toward the kitchen, he told us, "If I don't get breakfast served, it won't be worth eating." He turned back, adding, "And believe me, you *don't* want me to start over."

"Can I help?" Kiki and I rose. "What can we do?"

"Just get yourselves settled at the table," he called from the kitchen, rattling God knows what. "This'll only take a minute."

The music had segued to something even brighter than the Mozart—Vivaldi, if I'm not mistaken—and my spirits quickly lifted from the passing funk generated by the story about Sarad Patel. Grant was right; life goes on.

Within minutes, Grant joined us at the table, delivering a bountiful breakfast that could have sated a threshing crew. He'd baked. He'd grilled. He'd buttered and browned. And he'd opened a bottle of champagne, *good* stuff, ice cold. I wouldn't normally indulge at that early hour, particularly on a weekday, a workday, but the sparkling wine suited both the music and the company, so I enjoyed a glass with my amiable companions, taking sips between bites of gorgeous strawberries as big as toddlers' fists.

We gabbed about everything. Grant hadn't heard back from Henry Harris and didn't know whether to proceed with the purchase of the house for Arlene. Kiki was interviewing a prospective staff member that morning, hoping she'd commit and be on board by Monday. I was eager to drive over to campus and check progress on the theater, due to be completed that day. And we discovered that all three of us had been invited to Glenn Yeats's party that night, agreeing that the whole premise—helping Paul "get beyond this"—seemed indecorously self-serving on Glenn's part. "But he throws a great party," Grant reminded us, and we all agreed we wouldn't think of missing it.

At a lull in our conversation, Kiki asked me, "What was Grant saying earlier—you have a story about a 'remarkable audition'?"

My eyes bulged as a fizzy swallow of champagne stuck in my throat.

"Yes," Grant chimed in, "that story hadn't quite reached its climax, as I recall."

After managing to swallow, and flashing Grant a menacing look, I told Kiki, "I'm admitting a last-minute applicant to the program, someone I found locally. He's a natural, an extraordinary talent." I suppressed a petite champagne belch.

Grant told Kiki, "It sounds to me as if Claire *recruited* this young man."

"Perhaps I did; that's part of my job. In truth, the decision for him to enroll was a shared one. He stands to benefit from DAC's program, and vice versa."

Grant told Kiki, "If I understand correctly, he's the leading-man type."

"Oh?" Kiki turned to me. "Who is he?"

"Not that you'd know him, but his name is Tanner Griffin."

"Sounds dreamy," Grant purred. "You *must* introduce us."

"Rest assured, Tanner is indeed 'dreamy,' though I prefer to think of him as 'solid.' Everything about him—voice, body, personality, the works. But don't get your hopes up, Grant. He wouldn't be interested."

Grant singsonged, "Never can tell . . ."

Through a low chortle, I told him, "Trust me on this one."

With a loud, exaggerated gasp, Grant stood. A fork clattered off his plate as he raised both hands to his cheeks. "Good *Lord,*" he yelped, wide-eyed, "milady is fucking her protégé!"

"Don't be ridiculous," I told him, grateful that his wording allowed me to escape on a technicality. If, however, he had switched the subject and the object of his accusation, he'd have left me no room to wriggle.

Grant sat again. Glibly, he said, "Just checking, doll."

I dabbed my lips with the big linen napkin, then set it on the table. "To be perfectly honest"—even as I spoke, I wasn't certain how far to go with this admission—"I don't think of Tanner as just 'any student.' "

Grant stage-whispered to Kiki, "He's twenty-six."

I continued, "Tanner has a special talent, and at some level, yes, it seems we've sort of . . . connected. I'll be the first to acknowledge that this relationship raises some sticky issues of propriety, but I need to explore this my own way, in my own good time. Kiki, you're my oldest friend. Grant, you're my newest friend, but I already consider you one of my best. Both of you, I need your support. Which is to say, I need your understanding *and* your tight-lipped discretion."

They looked at each other soberly, unprepared for my serious tone.

Kiki turned to me. "Claire, dear, you *know* you can depend on me."

With a little laugh, she added, "We've seen each other through quite a bit over the last four decades."

Grant said, "I didn't mean to razz you—I had no idea I was hitting so close to home. You can confide in me anytime, Claire. I'm honored." He paused, grinned. "But I *would* like to get a look at this hunk."

"Me *too*," added Kiki.

Grant blinked, having overlooked something that now seemed obvious. "You're bringing him to the party tonight, aren't you?"

I laughed. "Of course not. It's not as if we're 'dating.' " The thought of bringing Tanner to the party hadn't even occurred to me.

But now that Grant had suggested it, the idea had a certain appeal.

23

Lunch on Friday consisted of a rubbery vending-machine sand-wich at my desk. I wasn't even hungry, having enjoyed myself without restraint that morning at breakfast with Grant and Kiki, but I thought I'd better eat something. Dinner would be a late buffet on Glenn Yeats's terrace, following an evening of cocktails. The decision to lunch in my office had nothing to do with my affection for the scenery but was motivated by raw efficiency. I'd been busy all morning preparing for Monday's start of classes, and I hadn't quite finished by noon.

Part of the last-minute rush had been the processing of documents that would admit Tanner Griffin to the college. It was now early after-noon, and this task was essentially complete. Though I still had misgivings about the wisdom of entering into a teacher-student rela-tionship with someone I found so physically attractive, these qualms were conquered by my eagerness to get on with it—the job, that is.

By two o'clock, I grew tired of my desk and curious about the the-ater. Had Morgan and his helper finished with the last few items on my punch list? What's more, I now found it difficult to concentrate on the stray bits of paperwork that still needed my attention; they could wait. The reason for this lack of focus was not fatigue. No, all morning, since breakfast, my mind kept bouncing back to Grant's suggestion that I bring Tanner to the party with me that night.

The more I thought about it, the more I liked the idea. First, I enjoyed Tanner's company and would welcome the opportunity to get to know him better in a purely social setting; so far, we had seen each other only at Desert Detail and on campus. Second, I assumed that Tanner would enjoy my company as well; though I could not be sure *why* he found me attractive, he clearly did, as evidenced by Thursday's matinee. And third, well . . . hell, I'd be the envy of every woman at the party (and many of the men) if I strutted through the door with Tanner Griffin on my arm.

Hmm. Editing this imaginary script, I decided that if I did bring him, it would be prudent *not* to appear romantically involved; indeed, I wasn't even sure that "romantically involved" applied to us. We'd had some impromptu sex. Perhaps it had merely been the equivalent of a hand-shake between soul mates, a greeting of recognition. I had no idea whether more might follow. In any case, if Tanner were to accompany me to the party that night, it made sense that we should be discreet about the depth of our interest in each other. We would simply be "together." I would introduce him as a new student, an important ad-dition to the theater program—all true enough—if, in fact, I decided that I wanted him to accompany me.

Of *course* I wanted to be with him that night. Why not?

For one thing, Glenn Yeats had not invited me to bring a guest. I doubted that he would mind, but it would be presumptuous of me to show up with someone not expected. I reasoned that Glenn had invited me solo because he was aware that I was new in town and unattached. He hadn't wanted to put me in the embarrassing position of needing to scrounge up an escort. Surely, he'd be delighted to welcome anyone I wanted to bring. In fact, he'd already met Tanner, in the hallway on Thursday, and seemed to like the guy. Who wouldn't?

The solution to this dilemma was a matter of common sense: I would walk down to Glenn's office and talk to him about it, letting him know that I wouldn't dream of imposing on his hospitality, while giving him the opportunity to suggest that I bring Tanner. Simple.

I stood, stretched a kink from my shoulders, and switched off my desk lamp. I had my plan: I'd visit Glenn, check the theater, come back to my office to finish up the last of my desk work, phone Tanner about tonight (if my visit with Glenn went as expected), then head home.

Leaving my office, I closed the door behind me and started down the curved hall. The fourth door I passed was open, and glancing inside, I saw Paul Huron at his desk, talking on the phone. He must have heard my steps, as he turned just then and saw me. Waving me in, he continued with his conversation, sounding both earnest and upbeat. I quickly surmised that he was talking to Detective Knoll.

"So I'll get it back—I mean, eventually?"

Good Lord, I wondered, had they found the ring?

"That's wonderful news, Larry. Thanks so much. And let me know what happens with Dr. Blair, okay?"

This was sounding more and more intriguing. Glad I stopped by.

"As a matter of fact, she just walked in. Sure, I'll bring her up to date." Then he said good-bye and hung up the phone.

"Well, now." I arched my brows. "Promising developments?"

He motioned for me to sit in the extra chair near his desk. "Developments, yes, but I'd call them mixed."

Settling in, I said, "Let's start with the ring. It turned up?"

"It certainly did, thanks to that photo in yesterday's paper. Get this: a groundskeeper recognized it after finding it in some shrubs near the gatehouse that leads up to Nirvana from Highway One-Eleven." He crossed his arms.

"*Huh?*" I asked stupidly while trying to fathom the meaning of this discovery. Had the killer—or thief, or someone else—simply tossed it there while passing on the busy highway? And why there, of all places?

Paul continued, "It's being held in evidence, of course, but I'll eventually get it back; that's the main thing. I can never bring Jodie back, but I think she'd be happy to know I'd at least gotten her ring back. The figures represented *us*, you know." He paused in thought, looking blissfully nostalgic. Had he already managed to repress the facts about his wife that he'd learned just yesterday? Was he again indulging in his fantasies of the perfect marriage?

Jerking him back to reality, I asked, "What about Dr. Blair?"

He frowned. "That's where the news gets mixed. Larry spoke to Candace Blair, the doctor's wife, this morning, and she was stunned by the news that her husband had been involved with Jodie—though I doubt if she was any more stunned than I was." He shook his head. So much for the fantasy of his perfect wife.

"Such news is never easy," I commiserated. "You'd think Dr. Do-Good would have at least tried to prepare her for the shockeroo."

"If he did, he did a lousy job of coaching her."

"Oh? Don't tell me she had a problem corroborating his alibi. Not that it wouldn't serve him right, the weasel."

Paul nodded, "According to Larry, her recollection of Blair's return home on Saturday morning seemed to be clouded by her shock, and possibly by rage. The bottom line is that she claims not to remember whether he returned shortly after eight that morning, as he claimed, or shortly after nine."

I thought aloud, "If he went home at eight, he's clear. If he went home at nine, that would leave him at the crime scene at the time of the murder."

"Exactly. So Larry has called the doctor in for questioning later this afternoon. This time it's an official interrogation—lawyers, tapes, the whole bit."

"Poor Percival," I lamented falsely.

Paul seconded, "He gets no sympathy from *me*."

The two of us continued to deride Blair, finding him an easy target while venting our frustrations over the case.

As we spoke, I tried to weigh the two developments Larry had just reported to Paul. While both nuggets of news offered promise, taken together they were perplexing. Blair's now-shaky alibi pointed suspicion solidly toward the love-gone-sour theory, while the ditched ring seemed to support the original notion of a bungled theft. If Blair was in fact the killer, had he taken the ring to create a false lead? Not a bad idea. But why would he then ditch the ring at Nirvana? At first blush, this struck me as a clumsy attempt to cast suspicion on Glenn Yeats. But why? Glenn had no motive whatever to want Jodie dead.

Thoughts of Glenn led to thoughts of his party that night, reminding me of my intention to visit his office. As Paul and I had lambasted Dr. Blair sufficiently for the moment, I rose, preparing to leave. I told Paul, "I'd better be going. I need to discuss something with Glenn, then check out the tech installation in the theater. If you hear anything else from Larry, we can talk about it at the party tonight. It starts at seven, right?"

He stood. "That's what I hear. I'll probably be there."

I laughed. "I *hope* so."

"I mean, depending on how I feel. This may be a rough weekend."

I got the sudden impression he didn't understand that he was the party's guest of honor, that it was being thrown specifically to help him cope with his rough weekend. Though tempted to clue him in, I thought I'd better not. Glenn might have deliberately been vague on this point to Paul, letting him think that the party's timing, which marked the eve of one week since Jodie's death, was coincidental.

I simply told him, "We'd all miss you. Do try to make it."

"Thanks, Claire. You, Glenn, *everyone's* been so helpful."

He stepped toward me and gave me a parting hug, we said good-bye, and I left his office.

Out in the hall, I continued walking the circular concourse that would take me to Glenn's office suite. With my head lowered in thought, I wondered how they had cut the carpeting for the curved hallway, judging the design to be highly wasteful. I also wondered how receptive Glenn would be to my notion of bringing a guest to his party that night. And I wondered if he'd heard yet about Jodie's ring being found at the entrance to Nirvana.

Glancing up, I saw that I had arrived at the twin mahogany doors that separated Glenn's private domain from the rest of the world. I twisted one of the knobs, swung the door open, and stepped inside the waiting room. There was no one there; all was quiet; it was Friday afternoon.

"May I help you?" asked a soft voice from the next room, Tide Arden's office, before Tide herself appeared in the doorway. "Oh," she said with a pleasant smile, "good afternoon, Ms. Gray." In calf-high boots, a leather halter, and a heavy chain necklace made of two-inch chromed links, she looked as fearsome as ever. I'd come to understand, though, that her sense of fashion was not an accurate projection of the person within.

"Hello, Tide. I know how busy Glenn is, but I wonder if he could spare me a minute or two."

"Sorry, Ms. Gray. He left for the day, just a few minutes ago. He asked me to remind you about the final checklist for the theater."

Marveling at the tycoon's mother-henning, I told Tide, "I was just on my way over there."

"Excellent."

"Do you know if he went home?"

"I think he's checking on preparations for tonight's party. If you need to speak to him, I could try to reach him in his car."

"No, please, I wouldn't want to disturb him."

She paced a single step toward me on muscular legs the color of rich cocoa. "Is it important? May I be of help?"

I hesitated. "Perhaps you can. It's about the party. Glenn caught me on the fly yesterday when he invited me, and it wasn't clear if the invitation was meant for me alone or if I was welcome to bring someone."

"Ahhh." She laughed knowingly. "I apologize on behalf of Mr. Yeats. It *was* something of a last-minute idea, the party, and there wasn't time for written invitations, so he and I got the word out verbally—as you know." After a brief pause, she asked, "Would you like to bring someone?"

I exhaled. "Do you think he'd mind? I wouldn't want to throw off any plans—"

"No *problem,*" Tide assured me with a flick of her long, slender hands. "I'm keeper of the guest list, and I doubt if Mr. Yeats has even glanced at it since we first discussed it yesterday morning. I was just getting ready to phone the final number to the caterer." Curling a finger, she bade me to follow her through her office.

"Then it's not too late to squeeze in one more guest?"

"For you, Miss Gray, I'm sure he'd happily accommodate a last-minute *invasion.*" And she swung open the door to Glenn's inner sanctum, strutting forward to his semicircular desk. The bank of computer monitors flickered in the background.

Following, I assured her with a chortle, "I have no intention of bringing a platoon, just one young man."

"Well, then," she said, plucking a mercurochrome-colored acrylic clipboard from the tycoon's black granite desk, "let's put him on the list." She turned, smiling. "Name?"

"Uh, Griffin. Tanner Griffin."

Tide squinted. "Hmm." She wrote the name on the list. "Seems familiar."

"Some paperwork may have crossed your desk today with Tanner's name on it. He's a last-minute enrollee in the theater program."

"Of course, that's it." Her words conveyed simple recognition, with no raised brows, no overtones of surprise or disapprobation. She ran her finger down the list, moving her lips as she counted silently. Then she clicked her ballpoint and wrote a number near the bottom of the page, circling it with a flourish.

As she did this, I glanced about the room, marveling at the exactitude with which Glenn's home office had been replicated here. The effect was more than striking; it was downright eerie.

Idly, I asked, "Will you be there tonight?"

She smiled faintly. "Of course. Mr. Yeats seems to find me indispensable."

I knew by her tone that she wasn't bragging; she was talking about Glenn, not herself. "Come to think of it," I told her, "since the faculty party last week, I can barely recall seeing Glenn without you in the background."

She acknowledged this with a nod, then asked, "Do you have a free moment, Ms. Gray? Please make yourself comfortable." She gestured toward one of the buttery tan leather armchairs grouped in front of the desk. Clearly, she had no qualms about making herself at home in the boss's office.

Just as clearly, she wanted to talk. By my count, this was my fourth encounter with the woman, but we had never exchanged more than perfunctory greetings, if that. Perhaps it was the quiet Friday afternoon, perhaps it was our growing familiarity, but she now seemed inclined to open up to me. With my curiosity piqued, I followed her suggestion and sat.

She sat across from me on a matching leather sofa. Her high boots and skimpy halter squeaked as she settled in, hide against hide. The oversize chain links around her neck clacked as they slid through the cleavage of her ample breasts. She gave me a quiet smile that seemed almost bashful. "I'm sure you're aware, Ms. Gray, that Mr. Yeats has a great deal of respect for you."

I returned her smile. "Thank you for saying so, Tide, but I do wish you'd call me Claire."

"I'd be honored, of course. I've always held you in such high esteem, Claire—just as Mr. Yeats does."

Though flattered by her words, I felt they struck the wrong notes. Her references to "respect" and "esteem" seemed so stuffy and formal. Why hadn't she simply said that Glenn liked me or that she herself had enjoyed my work?

As if attuned to my thoughts, she continued, "Mr. Yeats has always said that respect is everything. It's the only thing that really matters, in life or in business."

"It's important," I granted, not quite catching her drift, or Glenn's. "Every human being deserves respect, at least out of the gate. But it's easily lost by one's own actions, and it needs to be earned again every day."

Her look of dismay suggested that my statement was tantamount to blasphemy. "Mr. Yeats considers respect to be the due reward for a lifetime of achievement, such as yours." She hardly needed to add, "Or his own, for that matter."

I sensed that the concept she was driving at was not respect but adulation—or, in the vernacular, ass kissing. Shaking my head skeptically, I said, "I'm grateful that both you and he find my career so exemplary, but a person, a whole person, is more than the sum of his or her achievements. Plaques on a wall or trophies on a shelf represent a very narrow dimension of human worth. I've known some brilliant people who've made remarkable contributions to a particular field of endeavor, only to prove themselves real shits in other aspects of life. I don't respect them. And the ones who feel they can demand it only magnify their shortcomings with their buffoonery."

Tide laughed nervously. "Thank God neither you nor Mr. Yeats has such shortcomings. The esteem of the college rests upon people like you. Truly, I'm humbled to know both of you."

I simply thanked her and let the topic pass, though her deferential attitude seemed uncomfortably over the top.

After a pause, I asked, "How long have you been with Glenn?"

She thought a moment. "Eight years. During my senior year of college, I served an internship at his San Jose headquarters. I was a programmer, and there was—"

I interrupted, "A computer programmer? I'm impressed, Tide. I know how difficult it can be for a woman to get *anywhere* in a male-dominated field." With a low chortle, I added, "Trust me, I've been there."

"Back then," she said, bending forward a few inches, as if to impart a secret, "I was still Timmy."

I don't know whether time stood still, my heart skipped a beat, or the planet stopped spinning, but I was momentarily at a loss for words. Her statement was unequivocal, its meaning perfectly clear. The first time I'd seen her, the word *mannish* had leaped to mind, but just now, the revelation that Tide was née Timmy came as a bombshell. I was stunned, literally unable to move. Staring at her, I found her masculine qualities as plain as ever—the height, the muscles, the broad, square shoulders—but try as I would, I could *not* visualize her as a man. Tide was every inch a woman.

"Ah!" I said nonchalantly, without flinching, "I hadn't realized."

"*Thank* you, Claire," she gushed. Apparently I'd paid her the highest of compliments. "It's hardly a secret, but I don't broadcast it either. It's been four years now, and even *I'm* still getting used to it. The fact is, plain and simple, for most of my life, I was someone else. Moving here to the desert, that's helped. It's like starting over."

With a quiet laugh, I mused, "I'd had that very thought myself." Then, genuinely curious, I said, "Pardon my ignorance, Tide, but I assume you're not talking about . . . just the clothes."

"*No,* ma'am," she assured me with a shake of her head. "I'm not playing dress-up." Straightening her posture, she said with exaggerated pride and dignity, "I am *fully* transgendered."

Now that I had the whole picture, as it were, I told her softly, "I admire your bravery, adapting to everything."

She shook her head again, dismissing my compliment. "This part's easy, Claire. The hard part was before. My whole life was screwed up; it was *backwards* somehow. I was always good in school, since my studies gave me something to focus on—other than 'the woman trapped inside.' So when I first went to work for the software conglomerate, while I was still a college senior, I readily proved myself to be smart and efficient." She wasn't bragging; her tone was matter-of-fact.

She leaned back, crossing her legs at the knees. "Mr. Yeats has always taken a hands-on approach to the company, and even though it's huge, he made a point of spending time in every department. And he noticed me. Before long, I was working on special assignments for him, and by the time I graduated and joined the company on a permanent basis, he'd moved me into his office. When he moved out here to the desert and decided to build the college, he brought me with him. He calls me indispensable, and I feel honored to work for him, even though I'm not pursuing my intended career. Hell, I'm a special assistant, a glorified secretary."

"There's no shame in that. Your assistance *is* valuable. It seems you find the position challenging and fulfilling and—"

"And *rewarding,*" she finished my thought, nodding her agreement. "The acceptance I've found, since the first day I went to work for his company, was overwhelming. I felt as if I'd come home. My own personal mess didn't matter at all; I was valued for what I could contribute. Still, the mess was always there, deep inside. Eventually, the whole gender thing became so psychologically crippling, I could barely work. He was *so* understanding when I finally spoke to him about resolving the crisis and making the switch. He not only encouraged me; he paid for everything—hormone and depilatory treatments, counseling, and the surgery itself. He's been like a father to me. I owe D. Glenn Yeats *everything.*"

Sitting there, listening, watching Tide Arden speak, I marveled at the passion in her voice, in her face, and in her movements. I also marveled at Glenn's ability to inspire such fierce loyalty among his staff.

Tide paused, then concluded her story, stating flatly, "I'll be with him for life."

Clouds parted that afternoon, as predicted, and drier air moved into the valley from the west. I noted the difference the moment I stepped outdoors, crossing Campus Circle to check the progress on my theater. High trails of vapor, now white, not gray, streaked the blue background of the sky, moving fast to the east. The sun had returned, and heat rose from the plaza's pavement, a comforting reminder that darker days are few in the desert.

Entering the theater with my key, crossing the lobby, then stepping through the double doors to the auditorium, I saw at a glance that the technical installation was complete. Morgan and his helper were gone; no one else was present; the building was empty, except for me. A few work lights had been left on backstage, so I had no trouble making my way down the aisle toward the rehearsal stairs, which had been moved from stage right to stage left. Approaching the stairs, I intended to mount the stage and cross to the control panel in the right wing, where I could flick on the houselights and the full complement of stage lights, the better to inspect the work that had been done.

As I climbed the first few stairs, though, the work lights blinked out.

"*Hey*," I shouted, blinded by darkness, catching my balance, "anybody here?"

I stood motionless for a few seconds, listening to the room's utter silence. I heard the blood pumping behind my ears, nothing more, till the stillness was broken by a soft thud. I recognized the sound as a distant stage door.

"It's *me*," I said, "Claire Gray," uncertain whether the sound of the door had signaled someone's arrival or departure—or simply my own imagination. There was no response.

Teetering on the open stairs, I clutched the folder I carried in one hand and reached out with my other hand to feel the steps in front of me. Then I climbed like a baby to the stage apron, where I turned and sat. Closing my eyes, I calmed myself, wondering what to do.

When I opened my eyes, they were better adjusted to the darkness, and in the faint ambient light of the auditorium, I saw exit signs glowing above the distant doors at the top of the aisles. Looking to stage right, I also saw rows of tiny red pilot lights on the rehearsal panel in the far wing. Weighing my options, I decided it would be easier to cross the flat stage than to find my way through the raked auditorium. What's more, by crossing the stage, I could switch the lights on and complete my inspection.

So I stood, moving upstage a few feet to steer clear of the apron's curved front edge as I crossed to the right wing. Focusing on the pilot lights, I placed one foot in front of the other, gaining confidence that there were no obstructions between me and my goal, when—I had not yet reached center stage—something in my peripheral vision seemed to move. Glancing upstage, I froze, gasping at the sight of a dark, murky figure, barely discernible in the dimness, who swayed where he stood, making silent, menacing gestures.

"Who *are* you?" I demanded. "If this is your idea of a joke—"

But there was no answer.

His silence, I was certain, was meant to taunt me, which allowed my instinctive fear to be outweighed by anger. Marching upstage to confront the prankster, I gambled that my aggressive reaction would be sufficiently unexpected to throw him off guard. If he meant to do me harm, my chances of thwarting him would only worsen if I screamed, turned, and attempted to escape, tumbling from the stage apron to the auditorium floor. So I stepped forward, brazenly approaching my tormentor. When mere inches separated us, I stopped dead in my tracks, raised a hand to my mouth, and broke into laughter.

There, upstage center, stood the potted fern and shabby stuffed parrot that decorated our homely Chekhovian parlor. In the darkness, the perched bird took on the appearance of a head and shoulders, while the fern, wobbled by a draft, gave form to the rest of its body.

"*Ughhh . . . ,*" I groaned loudly, pleased beyond measure to hear my guttural utterance reverberate in the perfect acoustics. Now that I had my bearings, I had no trouble locating the dainty desk near the lolling couch. I set my folder of checklists on the desk, then turned downstage right, crossing on a diagonal toward the control panel in the wing.

With the pilot lights to guide me, I arrived without further incident, chiding myself for jousting with boogeymen in the dark. A moment later, I was flicking switches, and the black chasm of the theater was transformed into a radiant, roiling sea of scarlet velvet. Next, I switched on the stage circuits, which delivered, with a hum, a flood of focused, brilliant light.

Crossing upstage center to the desk, I spun in a complete circle and soaked it all in. The state-of-the-art theater was now finished, and for all intents and purposes, it was mine. I quickly surveyed the work Morgan had wrapped up that morning, and since everything seemed in order, I opened the folder and signed the various checklists. I sighed. A big, deep sound from the lungs and diaphragm, my sigh filled the space, signaling my relief and my contentment and my eagerness to bring a script to life, to fill those hundreds of red seats with their first audience, a many-headed mistress to be wooed and cajoled and transported to a new world, a new reality that would be created before their very eyes.

I could have stood there for hours; just *being* there was its own nourishment and reward. But as I turned again to appreciate all the efforts, knowledge, and commitment represented by the new structure, my eyes fell upon the lolling couch, and memories welled within me of tangling there with Tanner Griffin the day before.

I realized that I shouldn't tarry in the theater with my thoughts. The afternoon was slipping away, and I had yet to speak to Tanner about the party that night. After resolving all my angst about whether or not to invite him, what if he wasn't even available? It was Friday, after all, and an attractive guy like Tanner would—

Enough speculation, I told myself. Shut down the lights, lock up the theater, get back to your office, and phone him.

Crossing again to the control panel, I was about to switch off the stage circuits, but paused, turning back for one more look. And that's when I finally saw it.

There, downstage center, a sizable section of the floor was missing;

I hadn't noticed it earlier, as the black flooring seemed to match the darkness beneath. I crossed the stage apron to center, stopped with my toes at the edge of the trap opening, and peered down. The hydraulic lift had been fully lowered, some thirty feet to the concrete bottom of the pit beneath the stage. Dismayed, I realized that the gaping hole lay directly in the path I had been walking, in the dark, from the stage-left stairs to the stage-right wing. It was only my confrontation with a stuffed bird, causing me to veer upstage from my intended path, that had saved me from a serious, and probably deadly, fall.

My mind raced to weigh the possibilities. There were but two. If I had fallen, it would have been the result of either scheming or accident.

Had someone planned this? A section of the stage floor had been lowered, and the rehearsal stairs had been moved to stage left. As I climbed the stairs from the auditorium, the work lights went out. Then I heard the thud of a door, suggesting that someone had waited for me, leaving me in darkness, prompting me to cross the stage toward the control panel, setting me up for a thirty-foot plunge.

Or was this merely a chain of circumstantial events? The stage hydraulics could have been left fully lowered, needing some final tweaking. The work lights could have been turned off by a timer, or perhaps they'd simply failed. The thud of a door could have been imaginary, concocted by my frightened brain in exactly the same manner as the stuffed parrot had been transformed into a menacing figure in a trench coat.

Clearly, I reasoned, the latter possibility was more likely, as I could think of no possible motive for treachery against me, save one—my involvement with the investigation of Jodie Metz-Huron's death. Had I made someone nervous? Did the killer now fear that I was getting too close to unraveling the particulars of the crime? Had I been far too glib in dismissing warnings of danger from Larry and others? Was I to be the second victim?

This fretting was ridiculous, I assured myself. There was no shortage of suspects as Jodie's killer, but none of them would have sufficient technical savvy or theatrical background to pull the stunt that might have killed me. Even as I thought these words, I realized that Tanner Griffin fit these criteria, but I had already been satisfied that he had no complicity in Jodie's death. He'd told me that he was at Desert Detail, working, on Saturday morning when Jodie was killed; right now, surely, he was also at the shop in Palm Springs, working, which meant that he could not possibly have been responsible for the thud I'd heard.

There was one way to find out. And I needed to phone him about tonight's party anyway.

At the desk, I opened my folder and retrieved the checklists. The parrot watched over my shoulder with a lifeless, glassy eye as I amended the forms, asking Morgan to double-check the stage hydraulics and the circuit controlling the work lights.

Closing the folder, I returned to the control panel and shut down everything but the work lights. Then I left the theater, locked it behind me, and returned to my office.

"Good afternoon. Desert Detail." The voice had an accent; it wasn't Tanner.

"Tanner Griffin, please?"

"Sorry. Not here right now."

Hmm. "It's really quite important. Do you know where I might reach him?"

"Try his cell phone." He gave me the number.

I hung up, hesitated, then picked up the receiver again and dialed. Listening to the other phone ring, I wondered where he was, trying to convince myself that it was logistically impossible for him to have been at the theater mere minutes ago.

"This is Griffin." It certainly was; I'd know that voice anywhere. And from the blustery racket in the background, I assumed he was out in his Jeep.

"Hello, Tanner. It's Claire."

There was the slightest pause. "Claire. Great to hear from you." After another short pause, he added, "Where are you?"

"At my office." Was I imagining things, or did his question carry a subtext? "You seem, uh . . . surprised to hear from me."

"I am, sort of. I wasn't sure how you'd feel about everything. I mean . . . after yesterday. So I'm glad you called."

Through a soft laugh, I reminded him, "The phone works both ways."

"I know. I could have called—I should have. The day sort of got away from me, and I've been out running errands most of the afternoon. But I couldn't help wondering if you had any regrets about what happened."

"*Hardly*. And you?" Holding my breath, I felt my heart race as I waited for him to answer.

Quietly, he told me, "No regrets whatever. I was afraid, though, that you might think I'd been too aggressive, and—"

Surely, these were not the words of a man who meant me harm. I dismissed as delusional the notion that he, or anyone, had lain in wait for me at the theater. The gaping pit represented a potentially tragic accident, not a murder plot.

"Tut-tut," I cut him off, "none of that. We're adults. We were both willing partners." We spoke in this vein for some minutes, each assuring the other that we harbored no festering suspicions that our coupling had been motivated by casting-couch dynamics rather than attraction or passion. Far older than he, I could easily have concluded that his love-making was a means to an end, as I held control over both the theater program and the scholarship he sought; far younger than I, he could easily have concluded that I'd thrown myself at him, expecting his services in payment for the favors I could bestow. But our words made it plain that neither of us had been that conniving. We had simply reacted to the instincts of the moment, and neither one of us now felt scarred or used. To the contrary, we were both still enjoying some woozy afterglow.

"So," he asked with a measure of embarrassment, "everything's still set for Monday?"

"Of course. I've spent much of the day 'processing' you. We can finish up Monday morning. Be in my office by eight, and be sure to bring your transcripts, résumé, and completed applications."

"Without fail. I'll be spending the whole weekend on it."

As he'd opened the door to the underlying purpose of my call, I asked, "Do you happen to be busy tonight?"

"Well, *yeah.*" He laughed. "Those applications."

"I'm sure they're not *that* daunting. I know this is terribly short notice, but would you care to attend Glenn Yeats's party with me?"

Tanner had been in the hall with me on Thursday when Glenn had invited me, so he was already aware of the particulars. He said, "Do you think it would be okay? I'd love to see the place—*and* spend the evening with you—but . . ."

We talked it through, and before long, we were on the same page. I would introduce him as a promising new enrollee in the theater program, and though we would clearly be together, he understood that we should be discreet with regard to our feelings toward each other.

"When can I pick you up?" he asked. Such a gentleman.

I immediately began rethinking my outfit—what to wear in an open Jeep? Even as we spoke, I could hear the roar of the wind over his phone.

We soon determined that we would face a time crunch. The party would begin at seven, but Tanner wouldn't be able to leave Desert Detail till six. He would need to go home, shower, and change. Since he lived in Palm Springs, and I lived in Palm Desert, and the party was midway between, in Rancho Mirage, he wouldn't have time to fetch me. We would simply meet at Nirvana.

He said, "I may be a few minutes late, but I'll get there as fast as I can."

"Take your time, and drive safely. As for me, I need to be there promptly at seven." Laughing, I explained, "Glenn Yeats lives his life by the clock, even his 'relaxed' social life, and I want to measure up to his expectations—at least for a while. So I'll be waiting for you, Tanner."

"Thanks, Claire. This ought to be quite an evening."

Indeed. I finished at the office around four and went straight home to Villa Paseo. Phoning both Grant and Kiki, I informed them that I'd followed through on Grant's suggestion to invite Tanner to the party. They would be the only ones there who understood that Tanner was more than "just a student," so I wanted to get their joking and gibes out of the way *before* the party, while securing their promises of discretion. I preferred to drive alone that night, keeping open my options for afterward, so Grant offered Kiki a ride, which she accepted.

Sometime after five, I began spiffing for the evening. Finishing with the shower and my hair, I had just stepped into my closet to tackle the issue of clothes when the phone rang. Throwing on one of my silk robes (a red one, since I knew I'd be wearing red that night and I was getting in the mood), I trotted down the half-flight of stairs and took the call in the kitchen. "Yes?" I asked cheerily.

"Well, well. What's got into *you?*"

Somehow, I'd managed not to recognize my mother's ring. I told her, "It's Friday night," which struck me as sufficient explanation for my upbeat tone.

"So? Are you going out?"

I snorted. "I *am*. God, Gwyn, you sound disappointed to catch me in a decent state of mind. Would you prefer a slump?"

"Of course not." She laughed with grim humor. "Now, back up. Tell me about tonight."

I affected the drone of a weary socialite: "Just another soirée at the Yeats estate."

"Hngh. Going *with* anyone?"

I glanced at the wall clock; it was nearly 8:30 in New York. "Shouldn't you be eating dinner or something?"

"I *ate* dear. Long ago." She paused before hammering, "Going alone, eh?"

Miffed, I considered my options. I could tell her that I was going alone, which would be simplest, but then I would endure another lecture about spinsterhood. I could tell her that my neighbor Grant was taking me, which sounded less pathetic, but then I'd hear the old admonitions against keeping company with gay men. Or I could tell her that I did in fact have a straight, attractive, male escort that evening, which was precisely what she'd been longing to hear, but then the *real* grilling would begin, and I had no intention of explaining who Tanner was.

Why not? Nearly any woman of my age would be eager to *brag* that a man of Tanner's youth had found her both sexually and socially appealing. Why should I be reluctant to confide this to my own mother, a woman who'd been fretting over my lack of relationships for three decades? Was it because I didn't want to give her the satisfaction of thinking that, at long last, I'd understood her wisdom and followed her advice? Or was it because I feared she would disapprove of Tanner when she learned he was less than half my age? If she didn't approve, so what? Her opinions had meant little to me in the past. Or did I fear her disapproval of Tanner because it reflected my own misgivings about intimacy with a young man who was soon to become my student?

No. None of the above. What galled me about Gwyn's questions was the underlying assumption that she had the right to ask them, the right to know, and the right to judge. In her eyes, I was still accountable to her—for my own good, of course—like a child who couldn't possibly survive without her wise and protective mothering.

"Yes," I lied, "I'm going alone tonight."

"Oh, no, Claire honey, not again."

"Actually," I said truthfully, "it's not 'that' kind of a party. It's a party with a purpose."

She paused. "What in God's name is 'a party with a purpose'?"

I laughed, hearing the absurdity of my own words. "Glenn Yeats is throwing the party for Paul Huron, the man whose wife was killed. Tomorrow morning marks one week since the murder, and Glenn is afraid that the 'anniversary' may trigger another emotional crisis for Paul. The purpose of the party is simply to surround Paul with fellowship and help him glide through the shaky weekend."

Gwyn cracked, "Hope there'll be plenty of liquor!"

"Count on it." I laughed with her.

"I didn't realize Glenn Yeats was so kindhearted. It's nice to know he's taken such an interest in this man."

"Glenn is a complicated person. The more I get to know him, the more he surprises me. He truly *has* tried to help Paul get through the tragedy of his wife's death. But don't kid yourself—his motives have *not* been entirely altruistic."

"Really? How so, sweetie?"

As we spoke, it dawned on me that our conversation had become entirely civil, even pleasant. We were communicating for a change, not sparring, and for once, I felt no impulse to hang up on the woman. Checking the clock, I saw that I had plenty of time—I needed only to get dressed—so I explained, "Paul is a sculptor; that's why Glenn recruited him for the college faculty. But over the summer, Paul has become more and more involved with administrative matters at the school, and Glenn has depended on him to honcho the final preparations for the big opening next week."

Mother surmised, "Meaning, even though Glenn Yeats cares about Paul's loss, he cares more about keeping Paul in shape for the job."

" 'Fraid so. I don't mean to imply that Glenn has been in any way underhanded or duplicitous. In fact, he's been almost embarrassingly transparent in his campaign to 'help Paul get beyond this.' He's used those very words, repeatedly. What's more, he never misses an opportunity to tell people that he finds Paul 'indispensable.' "

"Oh, Lordy, I know the type. They're always . . ."

As Gwyn gabbed agreeably onward, my mind was still stuck on the word "indispensable." That very afternoon, Tide Arden had used it to describe her own relationship to Glenn Yeats. What's more, I could recall Glenn using the word when he first introduced Tide to me. Thoughts of Tide naturally led me to ponder that afternoon's revelations of her past, of the changes she'd undergone in her search for the woman within.

"Are you still there, Claire?"

"Sorry, Mother. My thoughts drifted." I was tempted to share with her the story of Tide's transformation, but I hesitated, wondering if my sole intention was to shock her straightlaced sensibilities. No, I realized, that wasn't the point. I told her, "I was thinking of another example of the intense loyalty Glenn can inspire in the people he depends on. It's a funny kind of symbiosis."

"Funny kind of *what?*"

"Symbiosis, or mutual dependency. Glenn's executive secretary is a perfect example. Tide Arden—she's a black woman in her late twenties, *but*"—I paused for effect—"she's a woman with a past."

"Oh, my."

I laughed. "It's not what you're thinking, Gwyn, not by a long shot. This afternoon, during a quiet conversation, Tide took me into her confidence and told me that eight years ago, when she first went to work for Glenn's company, she wasn't a 'she.' Back then, her name was Timmy."

"Ahhh," said Mother, unfazed, "she was transgendered."

Her blasé reaction was not what I'd expected. I asked, "You're aware of this . . . condition?"

"Well, of *course*. I have plenty of time for daytime TV these days.

Besides, Dr. Paxton has a nurse in his office who did it. Karmin, with a *K*, used to be Kevin. Not a pretty woman, but she seems happy now. The drag queens tend to be much more beautiful—just dress-up, no surgery. Oprah did a show on it."

"More than once, I'll bet. I'm delighted to hear you're so well informed."

"It's . . . interesting," she conceded.

"True enough, but in Tide's case, I found Glenn's role to be all the *more* interesting. You see, Tide—then Timmy—had gone to work in Glenn's office as a personal assistant, proving himself indispensable. But his struggle over 'the woman within' became so psychologically crippling, he opened up to Glenn about it."

"Uh-oh. I'll bet *that* didn't set well. You know those corporate types."

"That's what *I'd* have thought. But au contraire, Glenn not only proved to be understanding; he also paid the bills. Now Tide's *so* grateful, she told me, 'I'll be with him for life.' "

Mother sighed. "How touching. But you seem to be questioning Glenn's motive for helping."

"Exactly. Glenn *knew* he'd be buying her lifelong loyalty; *that's* why he did it. He's a man who's used to getting what he wants, and in this case, a valued employee came to him asking—literally—to be castrated. Glenn readily offered words of sympathy and wrote a check. Good Lord, he all but stropped the scalpel and made the emasculating cut."

"People like that . . . ," Mother clucked. "It sounds as if he needs to 'own' people." She prattled on, decrying such selfishness.

But I wasn't listening. My mind was in a spin.

Yes, Glenn did indeed need to "own" people, just as Mother had said. And I suddenly saw a shocking parallel between Tide's castration, which had effectively enslaved her to Glenn, and Jodie's murder, which had exposed her infidelities, emasculating Paul. Did Glenn take the whole control thing so far that he needed to surround himself with eunuchs?

Everything started to add up. First, at the faculty party on the Wednesday before Jodie was killed, I'd discovered that Glenn preferred to hire single people because they could focus on his objectives and dedicate themselves to their jobs. Tide Arden, the transsexual secretary, was an extreme example, and Glenn had described both Tide and Paul as "indispensable" to achieving his goals at the college. At that same faculty party, I'd heard Glenn tell Paul that he wanted to see him "rise to his full potential." Moments later, he asked Paul to travel to Texas, a trip that Paul later characterized as a wild-goose chase. It was during that trip that Jodie was killed, and afterward, Glenn had been all too eager to help Paul "get beyond this." And finally, good God, Jodie's wedding ring had been found near the Nirvana gatehouse. My first reaction had been that the killer must have thrown the ring there in a clumsy attempt to cast suspicion on Glenn, creating a false lead that would disrupt the investigation. Now I understood that there could be a far simpler explanation for the ring's presence at Nirvana: it could have fallen from Glenn's car as he stopped to greet the guard.

"People like that . . . ," Mother said again. "You don't want to get in the way of people like that."

Had Jodie gotten in the way of D. Glenn Yeats's master plan to create, overnight, a first-class arts college with a staff of selfless, blindly dedicated professionals, wed solely to their careers?

"Mother," I interrupted, "I don't mean to sound rude, but—"

"But there's someone at the door?" she asked coyly, having heard my ruse more than once.

"No, honest, I'm sorry, but something's just come up, something important. I really do need to go now." I paused for a breath, then told her sincerely, "I've enjoyed our conversation. I'm really glad you called."

"The phone works both ways, you know." She laughed.

So did I. "You're right. I'll do better, Gwyn. Promise. 'Bye now, love."

"Good night, Claire. Have fun tonight." And the line clicked off.

I needed to think. I needed to get dressed. I needed to decide whether to phone Larry Knoll with details of my castration theory. God, I could hear his skeptical laughter already. But first, I realized with a scatterbrained laugh, I needed to hang up the receiver I still held in my hand.

No sooner had I placed the receiver in the cradle—I was still touching it—when the phone rang, snapping back at me. Reflexively, I withdrew my hand, startled by the sound and upset by my thoughts. On the second ring, I took a deep breath and composed myself. On the third, I reached for the phone, answering, "Yes?"

"Hello, Claire? Glenn Yeats."

Huh? Had he somehow been listening to my conversation? Had he been reading my mind?

"Yes, Glenn. Good evening. What can I do for you?"

He hesitated. In a tone more meek than menacing, he said, "The party, as you know, doesn't begin until seven. But I was wondering if you'd care to arrive early, before the others get here. We could . . . talk. There's something I've been meaning to ask you about."

I wasn't sure how to interpret his request. Naturally, I was wary. Was I being lured into a dangerous situation? My experience in the theater that afternoon had already provided a goodly brush with fright, more than enough for any given day.

Then it dawned on me. Glenn Yeats had total access to the theater and complete knowledge of its technical workings; I'd seen the blueprints on his desk. That afternoon, he'd left his office, instructing his secretary to remind me to give the theater a final inspection. When the lights went out, I heard the thud of a door. And now here he was, on the phone, inviting me to come early to his party, before the arrival of other guests, claiming he wanted to "talk."

I should probably have shown greater caution, heeding the many warnings I'd heard over the past week, but my reticence was easily overcome by curiosity. I told Glenn with resolve, "There's something I'd like to ask *you* about as well." I checked the wall clock; it was nearly six. I'd need a few minutes to dress and about fifteen minutes for the drive. "I'll be there by six-thirty."

"Splendid. I'll be waiting for you."

And the line went dead.

Driving up the mountain road from the Nirvana gatehouse, I checked the Beetle's clock. With a minute to spare, I'd be on time, arriving at 6:30 on the dot. At least *that* aspect of the evening was certain. The rest was anyone's guess.

Back at my condo, after hanging up the phone, I'd stood motionless for a moment, pondering the meaning of Glenn's cryptic call. I knew only that there was something he wanted to discuss with me. It could relate to school, Paul, Jodie, anything. Was he chafing over the role I'd taken in the investigation? Had he somehow fathomed my new suspicions? If so, did he intend to plead his case and convince me otherwise? Or did he simply mean to muzzle me, one way or the other?

Telling myself that these frets served no useful purpose, I had then trotted upstairs to choose the outfit I'd wear that evening. No question, the night called for red, and I picked a dressy suit in nubby crimson silk with gold buttons. Black pumps, black bag, black kerchief knotted at my neck. A touch of makeup, a dab of Chanel. I was as ready as I'd get.

Driving away from Villa Paseo, I berated myself for not having told anyone that I'd gone to the party early, summoned for a private chat with the computer genius. I should have phoned Kiki or Grant or, better yet, Grant's brother. What's more, no one knew what had happened in the theater that afternoon—except, perhaps, the computer genius himself. Addled by curiosity, however, and rushed by the clock, I'd barely managed to dress in time, let alone pause to take precautions that were inspired, surely, by little more than paranoia.

Now, driving up the hill toward the Yeats estate, I brushed these concerns aside, distracted by the sheer magnificence of the setting. The clouds that had rolled through earlier that day had completely disappeared, leaving an indigo sky. A dazzling sun hung between the western peaks of the San Jacintos, spreading purple shadows across the golden slopes. Nearer, at the roadside, quail scampered at the sound of my car, disappearing in the undergrowth of sage. Overhead, a plane glided low on its approach to the airport. I could glimpse the distant runway on the valley floor, some thousand feet below, through the slit of a rocky arroyo.

Ahead, at the top of the roadway, rose Glenn Yeats's home. Again I marveled at its high drama, the striking contrast of its design, so manmade and sculptural, against the random, brutal formations of nature that surrounded it. Driving through its cold blue shadow, I made the final turn up to its entry court.

On my two previous visits, parking valets had awaited, but tonight I was early, and there was no one present. There in the driveway, the only other vehicle was a caterer's truck. I pulled in, cut my engine, and got out of the car.

"Perfectly punctual. I like that."

Turning toward the front doorway of the house, I saw Glenn standing, waiting for me, tapping the watch on his wrist. It was a Rolex (of course—in Rancho Mirage, the brand is more common than Timex), and though tempted, I didn't take seriously the notion that this might be the very watch Paul Huron had claimed to be missing from his home. As usual, Glenn wore a dressy long-sleeved shirt, French cuffed, replete with heavy links that had the glint of silver but were probably platinum. Though Dr. Percy Blair also wore heavy cuff links and had admitted to being with Jodie on the morning she was killed, we had no proof that the stray link found beneath her bed had belonged to the doctor. Might Glenn have made a house call of his own that Saturday morning?

"Just leave the keys in the car," he told me. "They'll take care of it."

Walking across the courtyard toward him, I greeted him through a smile. "It seems you've arranged for another perfect evening."

"I have my share of clout," he allowed while stepping forward and offering a hug. "Welcome, Claire."

Returning his embrace, I found him tense—I could feel it in his body through his shirt. Though the evening was comfortable, he was sweating. True to his style, he was dressed casually in expensive clothes, including stylish loafers with no socks. Once again, though, I felt that his "California look" seemed forced and unnatural—he couldn't quite pull it off. He was a computer genius, I reminded myself, a techie who'd turned a good idea into billions. Now he led a lavish life. Money wasn't an issue, not to one of the nation's wealthiest men, but there were still those things that money couldn't buy. Try as he may to look otherwise, his roots were showing.

Fair enough; he was who he was. So *what* if he was a dweeb? No harm done. But, I wondered, was he also something more sinister?

I glanced about the courtyard. "Seems I'm the first to arrive." I quipped, "How unstylish of me."

He looked me in the eye, grinning. "You have all the style, charm, and talent that any man or woman could ever hope to attain."

I smirked. "That's a bit thick, Glenn."

"Perhaps, but then, you already know I'm an ardent admirer. What's more, there's something I've been meaning to discuss with you. Shall we go inside?"

Stepping into the sprawling front hall (it could dwarf many hotel lobbies), we encountered the last-minute panic of caterers and other party staffers who scurried and fussed, having gotten word that guests (i.e., I) had begun to arrive. Tide Arden was there, at the other end of the hall, near the kitchen, checking her clipboard, barking her sweet-voiced commands. In the living room, someone was tuning the piano, filling the space with annoying, repetitive twangs.

"Let's seek refuge from this madness," Glenn told me with mock melodrama, escorting me down a side hall toward the double doors to his den.

As we stepped inside, he closed the doors behind us, shutting out the noise. The space seemed eerily quiet, and the air felt cool and artificial, like the dim lighting that seemed to emanate from nowhere. I now noticed that the room had no windows. Was it the lack of natural light, the lack of an exterior view, that had allowed him to duplicate the office so faithfully on campus? The curved wall of computer screens flickered behind his high-backed chair, reflected in the polished black granite of the desktop.

"Won't you sit down?" he offered, gesturing toward one of the leather armchairs arranged in front of his desk. It was the chair in the same position as the one Tide had invited me to sit in earlier that day in Glenn's campus office.

As I sat, Glenn settled on the sofa across from me, just as Tide had done that afternoon. The replicated room, the identical chair, the same sensations of sinking into the supple leather cushions, all these impressions combined to create the feeling of entering a flashback, as if time had warped and history was about to repeat itself. Was Glenn, I wondered, about to divulge that he'd been born a woman?

"What's so funny?" he asked.

"Nothing," I assured him with a laugh. "Just a passing thought."

After an awkward pause, he offered, "Would you like something to drink?"

"No, thanks. I'm fine." In truth, I would have enjoyed the first sip of a cocktail at that moment, but as we'd just gotten comfortable, I assumed the request would prove disruptive to the conversation he was trying to broach.

Spreading an arm across the back of the sofa, he told me, "With the college about to open, I feel that I've been living in a dream lately. I've wanted this badly, you know. Now that DAC is finally to become a reality, I can't quite believe it's happening."

"You've always been a man of grand plans, Glenn." I thought of the architect Daniel Burnham. "And your plans have never failed. Things always work out for you."

He shook his head pensively. "No, not always. It's a matter of . . . focus."

Eyeing him skeptically, I asked, "When have you ever failed?"

"Most notably, twice—two failed marriages. Lack of focus."

"You must have had other things on your mind."

"*Sure* I did." He laughed. "I was building an empire, as they say. Back then, maybe I married for the wrong reasons; I don't know. But I do know that those marriages *ended* for the wrong reasons."

"You've always been wed to your work," I reminded him, "and you expect the same of those who work for you. Don't tell me you're having second thoughts."

"Not at all. But a whole person, a complete person, ought to be able to juggle both—a job and a family. Lots of people manage to do it. I not only lost two wives, along with two staggering financial settlements, but two children as well, a son and a daughter. They're grown now, and I hardly know them."

"Have you been pondering your heir to the empire? You're only fifty-one."

"It's not that. The company has its own momentum; it'll survive me. In a sense, it already has. I've been *here*, doing *this* for the last few years."

"And from all accounts, the construction of Desert Arts College has been a model of efficiency. The whole project has moved along smoothly."

He frowned. "Until last Saturday, when we hit our little, uh . . . wrinkle."

Jolted by his callous word choice, I asked, "Are you referring to Jodie's murder?"

He leaned forward, explaining, "That came out wrong—I apologize. I don't mean to trivialize Jodie's death or its emotional aftermath for Paul, but the bottom line is, this tragedy has been a serious wrinkle for all of us. We've lost our focus at the time we need it most. It's even had an effect on *you*, Claire."

"Of course it has. Paul's still grieving. He needs our support."

"He *needs* to get beyond this. He *needs* to focus on the school. And *you* need to leave police work to the police."

Aarghh. I stood. "Why? So I can focus on the school? How *dare* you?" I spun around and began marching toward the door, positive that he harbored deeper reasons to discourage my sleuthing.

"No." He stood, pleading through an exasperated laugh, "I'd prefer that you stay clear of the investigation because it's *dangerous*. I respect your intelligence, but I'm trying to protect you."

I turned back, telling him calmly but firmly, "I'll decide for myself if and when I'm in danger, Glenn. Don't treat me like a child. I already have *one* mother; she's plenty. I don't *want* your protection."

He raised his hands in meek surrender. "Sorry. I guess I've overstepped my bounds. You're a fiercely independent woman, Claire, and I respect that."

Again the word "respect." What did he mean by it? "May I ask you a question?"

He smiled, taking a step toward me. "Certainly, Claire. Anything."

My intention was to engage him in an earnest debate on the semantic overtones of respect, but considering that he was now so humbled and accommodating, I seized the opportunity to quiz him on another topic entirely, a topic not nebulous but concrete. "Are you aware that Jodie's missing wedding ring was found earlier today?"

"Yeah." He scratched behind an ear. "That's the damnedest thing, isn't it? Detective Knoll phoned and told me that one of our gardeners had found it down at the gatehouse. He wondered if I had any idea how it got there."

"Do you?"

"Well, sure. As I told the detective, there are only two possibilities: the killer, someone from outside the development, either dropped it there by accident or put it there deliberately."

I could think of a third possibility, which focused on someone from within Nirvana. "What did Larry say?"

"He agreed. He also pointed out that the killer may have been trying to implicate *me*, in that I'm connected to the Hurons. He wondered if I had any notions as to who that might be. I didn't—and still don't. He asked me to give it further thought, and he suggested that I stay alert."

Hmm. The ring's appearance at Nirvana had raised the same possibilities to Larry as it had raised to me. It seemed, however, that he was more willing than I was to dismiss the likelihood of Glenn's complicity. But then, Larry hadn't yet heard my castration theory.

"Now," said Glenn, "there's something I need to ask *you* about." His tone was both menacing and playful.

I crossed my arms. "I thought we'd already covered that. You want me to steer clear of the murder investigation, right?"

"No—well, yes, I do—but that's not why I asked you to arrive before the others tonight. Claire, please, sit down again. This is important."

Intrigued, I nodded, returning to the chair I'd vacated. As I sat, Glenn clasped his hands behind his back and, without looking at me, began to speak as he paced around the room, circling behind his desk.

"There's no easy way to raise such a concern, and I'm not that smooth a talker, as you've already determined, so I'll try to be direct." He cleared his throat. "I've come to take significant pride in my ability to attain things that other men have not. It started as an idea, a technological concept that was right for its time. The idea itself was sheer luck; who knows the source of inspiration? But the rest, the 'empire,' was a matter of skill, determination, and the willingness to take enormous risks. History has already proven that I was up to the task; I rose to it and succeeded. As a result, the world is a better place. Even my rivals admit to that. But despite all appearances, this hasn't been easy. My accomplishments have taught me the necessity of control, absolute control, which must extend to every facet of the organization. Unfortunately, I've also learned that there's a stubborn variable within any organization, one that, by its nature, resists control. That variable, in a word, is people."

I was listening without reacting, wondering when he would get to the point. He'd said he would "be direct," but I couldn't imagine the object of this self-congratulatory preamble. While lecturing, he had sauntered through the room in a sweeping arc, passing the wall of computer screens, ending directly behind the chair where I sat.

My musing was interrupted by the touch of his hand on my shoulder. It jolted through me like an electric shock. I don't mean to suggest that he grabbed me or hurt me; in fact, his manner was gentle. Rather, it was the element of surprise that produced such a visceral reaction. When his other hand touched my other shoulder, I stiffened.

He continued, "I don't mean to be overweening, but am I correct is presuming that your childbearing years have passed?"

Huh? Had he asked if I'd had a pleasurable bowel movement that day, I could not have been more stunned. What was this, a test? As proof of my loyalty and commitment to the DAC project, did he need for me to be spayed and barren, as Tide had been castrated and Paul emasculated? Even as I asked myself these questions, his hands slid across the shoulders of my red dress to my neck, where he hooked his thumbs under my knotted black kerchief. Suddenly frightened and feeling utterly powerless, I resisted the urge to struggle or scream, certain that any call for help would not be heard beyond the walls of Glenn's soundproof bunker.

"The reason I ask—"

"Yes," I managed to gasp, "I can no longer have children."

He removed his hands. "Good heavens, Claire, you're shaking." He stepped around the chair and crouched in front of me. "Is something wrong?" Since beginning his odd monologue, his eyes had not met mine, but now he peered intently at me with a look of real concern.

"I, uh, guess," I stammered, "your question took me unawares."

He reached for my hands and patted them with his own. "I'm an oaf." He shook his head. "I warned you that I'm not a smooth talker. I didn't mean to sound indelicate, but I wanted to make the point that I too am beyond my parenting years. My fathering days are long behind me."

I grinned. "Don't be ridiculous. Men can procreate into their eighties. It's not—" I stopped short. Was he telling me that he'd had *himself* fixed?

He laughed quietly. "I'm not talking about the *ability* to reproduce. I'm talking about the desire."

I withdrew my hands from his, perplexed. "What on *earth* are you driving at?"

With a sigh of resignation, he said, "My 'direct' approach to this awkward topic has been lame, I admit. Let me try again." As he rose from his squatting position, his knees cracked. Shaking one leg, satisfied that he'd restored circulation, he sat on the broad, upholstered arm of my chair. Looking me in the eye, he smiled, then said, "Claire, I love you."

Even more stunned now than by his previous remark, I felt my jaw sag.

"Don't say anything." He raised a finger to my lips, then lowered his hands to his lap. "Let me explain. You already know that I'm not the romantic type; my abysmal achievements in the realm of relationships are a matter of public record. What's more, I am not, by any stretch, an artistic person. I have always, though, had the deepest admiration for artists, hence my commitment to the arts college. While writing checks is not in itself 'creative,' the funding is my way of contributing to the arts. Why? Because the arts contribute so much to *me*. It's a left-brain/right-brain kind of thing. People of sensitivity complement my mathematical, analytical nature. In short, artists make me whole.

"And my favorite art form has long been theater. You, Claire, are one of American theater's brightest lights. I am utterly awed to have you on my faculty, and that alone is enough to convince me that the DAC project will succeed. Still, *my* life would be immeasurably fuller if you were to enter it and—at some level—share it with me.

"Which brings me back to a statement that's both childishly simple and profoundly complex: Claire, I love you. At least, I think I do. And I wonder if perhaps you could ever love me. Might we try? Might we see if romance is possible? The experiment could begin here, this evening." He cleared his throat and stood. "Miss Gray, might I escort you to my own party tonight?"

I was astounded. First, I'd never entertained overtures from a billionaire before, which was plenty to ponder. Second, my doting billionaire was apparently unaware that I already *had* an escort for the evening, a hunky twenty-six-year-old who would be arriving any minute. And third, though Glenn's speech sounded sincere enough, I didn't know what to make of it in light of my new suspicions linking him to Jodie's murder. With so much to weigh, it was impossible for me to give him a direct, immediate answer.

I stood. "Glenn, I know this sounds horribly cliché, but this is all so sudden—"

"I had a feeling I was about to hear those words." He grinned.

I nodded. "Sorry. But you must admit, the questions you've asked me—out of the blue—require mindful consideration. I can't react that quickly, and for your own sake, you shouldn't want me to. Even if I hadn't been surprised to learn of your feelings, even if I myself had entertained these same notions, I doubt that I could find the frame of mind to weigh romance tonight." Obliquely, I explained, "The murder investigation has produced some confusing developments, and frankly, I'm distracted."

He crossed his arms. "There you go again. I knew it—your growing involvement with the investigation has you all in a dither. And to what end? Not only are you losing your focus on the school—and on me— but far worse, you're placing yourself at needless risk with a dangerous, amateur foray into police work."

Sternly, I reminded him, "We've already covered that." I was now truly irked, for a number of good reasons. There was something in his tone and his wording that revealed an assumption that my interest in the case was worthless and ineffectual; he seemed to characterize my efforts as the mere meddling of a nosy woman. What's more, it occurred to me that he was sounding more and more like my mother with his hand-wringing and my need to be protected by the strength and wisdom of others. Good God—Glenn and Gwyn—even their names were alike. Worse yet, Glenn's needling about the investigation rankled me because I suspected that his professed concern was no more than a ploy to get me off the trail and lose the scent of his own guilt.

In a display of remorse both dramatic and comic, he genuflected before me, bowed his head, and flourished an arm. "I beg your forgiveness, dear lady. If I promise never again to deride your sleuthing and bravery, could you find it in your heart to overlook my past transgressions and skepticism?" He looked up at me, twitching a brow.

I paused in thought, enjoying his scrape and bow. Then I allowed a smile and a nod. "Get up, Glenn. Fair enough. Even trade. You are forgiven."

He stood, taking my hands into his. "Then I haven't blown it? Will you at least consider the possibilities I've raised—regarding 'us'?"

"Well . . ." I laughed softly. One of the nation's wealthiest men had just professed his love for me, and though I had never been driven by mercenary motives, I also understood that his overture could conceivably lead to a union governed by California's community-property laws. "Of course."

He smiled. "That's all I ask, Claire, at least for tonight."

"Good. Give me some time to deal with this." Awkwardly, I added, "I think it would be best if we not stroll arm-in-arm among your guests this evening."

"Certainly. I understand." Actually, he didn't.

"Do you remember Tanner Griffin, the prospective student I introduced to you yesterday on campus?"

"Ah . . . good-looking young man, if I recall correctly."

Deadpan, I affirmed, "That's the one."

"Did you convince him to sign on with the program?"

"I did. The paperwork crossed your desk this afternoon. I talked to Tide about it; you were out. I also asked Tide if you'd mind if I brought Tanner to the party. She added him to the list. He'll be meeting me here shortly. Hope this wasn't a faux pas."

He chuckled. "Not at all. *Mi casa es su casa.*"

Hmm. In light of Glenn's overture, I didn't know whether to interpret the aphorism figuratively or literally.

He began strolling me toward the double doors, suggesting, "Would you care to enjoy a drink and perhaps wait on the terrace while the other guests arrive? I have some last-minute business to tend to here in the office."

"That sounds wonderful." I needed a drink. What's more, I didn't want Glenn hanging on me when Tanner arrived. Most important, a few minutes alone would allow me to sort through Glenn's words and my own thoughts.

He opened one of the doors. "I'll try to join you by the time things get rolling."

I touched his arm. "Don't be too long—you'll be missed. It's *your* party."

"It's *Paul's* party," he reminded me. "We're doing this for him."

I smiled. "That's so thoughtful of you, Glenn." But was it? I still questioned the reason behind his relentless campaign to breeze Paul through his mourning.

"Claire." He paused, taking my fingers into his hand. "I hope you appreciate the depth of my feelings for you, in spite of my poor job of articulating them. Please take my words to heart. I don't mean to sound presumptuous, but as you get to know me better, you'll come to understand that I'm not what I seem."

Ending on that ambiguous note, he inched his face nearer mine, signaling that he would welcome a kiss. Though we had previously exchanged casual acts of affection—a hug or a peck upon greeting, a touch on the arm or the back during conversation—those were social courtesies in the realm of friendship between colleagues. Now, though, due to Glenn's brief statement, "I love you," the dynamics between us had forever shifted. Henceforth, no kiss between us could be casual. Rather, the kiss he now offered was deliberate, carrying overtones of foreplay, commitment, and God only knows what other emotional baggage.

Though I wanted to slip away, I had told him that I would consider the possibilities he'd raised. Though he kindled no spark, he had assets, beyond the obvious financial ones, that I found highly attractive—he was intelligent, ambitious, accomplished, generous, and seemingly kind.

So I kissed him.

It wasn't passionate—the moment was wrong for passion, which neither of us expected—but the kiss was sincere. It didn't stir or dazzle me, but his kiss conveyed both longing and patience; he was willing to let me set the pace and lead the way. I didn't swoon, but I felt something well up within me, something peculiar and difficult to define. But it closely resembled . . . well, pride. Or a sense of conquest. After all, I told myself, any woman would feel privileged to command the affections of D. Glenn Yeats.

Unless, of course, he was ultimately exposed as Jodie Metz-Huron's killer.

Stepping outside the den, as the door closed behind me, I could hear the merry racket of party preparations. The piano had been tuned, and the pianist was now warming up with a few scales and jazzy riffs. Just-polished glassware clinked and clattered while being arranged in rows at the bar. Voices rose in greeting as the first guests arrived.

When I appeared in the main hall, Tide Arden spotted me and, snapping her fingers, summoned a tuxedoed waiter with a tray, who offered to get me a drink. I had a distinct taste for a martini—anything pure and strong—but as the evening was young and its course uncertain, I judiciously opted for a kir, telling the waiter he could find me on the terrace.

It was shortly after seven o'clock when I ambled outdoors through the living room's missing wall. The sun had just set, and with it, the day's heat had quickly dissipated. Strolling across the terrace past the pool, I noted the warm palette of the evening sky reflected in the still water. Looking up, to the east, I saw a wedge of moon, orange and huge, creeping skyward like a crag-toothed smile from behind the peaks that backdropped the house. Directly overhead, a jet rumbled toward the airport.

I had noticed planes landing before—often, in fact. The Palm Springs area didn't seem large enough to support so many flights. Then again, I reasoned, the valley was isolated and its population inordinately affluent; most people who came here, at least those from any distance, flew.

Sitting on the stone parapet at the far end of the terrace, I gazed down through the jagged arroyo, which afforded me a view of the airport and the road winding up the moutainside from the gatehouse. Several cars snaked up the steep incline, banking back and forth with the curves, passing the hotel. The last stretch of road to the private mesa normally bore little traffic, but tonight was different. These cars brought invited guests, arriving for a party.

"Your kir, Miss Gray." The man in the tux lifted my glass from his tray.

"Thank you."

As he nodded and disappeared, I sipped the chilled Chardonnay, tinted inky pink by a teaspoon of cassis. The slightest sliver of curled lemon peel floated on top, lending its perfume to the other flavors. The proportions were perfect, the presentation was pristine, and the overall setting was, well . . . nirvana. It was almost enough—almost—to make me forget the dueling perplexities that still tugged for my attention: Jodie's murder, which had preyed on me for nearly a week, and Glenn Yeats's declaration of love, which had jolted me mere minutes ago.

Glancing again past the parapet, I saw the arriving cars at closer range as they made the final turn near the house, engines whirring, climbing the drive to Glenn's entry court. The dusky sky still shone with enough light that I could recognize some of the cars as they swerved into view beneath me.

First I saw Paul Huron, our unwitting guest of honor, arriving in his Honda, the dusty-metallic blue one. Or was it? The evening sky gave colors an off cast. On second look, I realized that Paul was driving the other car, the dusty-metallic green one. No question, it was Paul; I could see him through the windshield. Having driven his blue car most of the week, perhaps he'd found it low on gas tonight.

Then I saw Grant Knoll's long, white Mercedes glide into view. Stately and serene, it cruised past with authority, taking the steep upgrade without so much as a grumble. Through the reflections in the tinted passenger's window, I could glimpse Kiki gesturing in animated discussion beneath the brim of her hat.

Several cars and a minute or two later, a black, spotless Jeep muscled up the roadway and popped into view beneath me. Even from my high vantage point, I had no trouble discerning the Desert Detail logo on its door, catching the day's last glint of light. I didn't need a gold-leafed sign, though, to spell out the arrival of Tanner Griffin, for there he was, plainly visible behind the wheel of the open Jeep, his thick, sandy hair tousled by the wind. The mere sight of him, the knowledge that he would, any moment, step into the house, sent a wave of raw emotion through me that words cannot precisely describe, though *lust* comes close.

During the several seconds while Tanner passed within my view, I pondered the sight quizzically, as something looked different about him. Then it clicked: I couldn't see his knees. Till now, I had seen him only in shorts, but tonight he was wearing black dress pants. I laughed aloud at the impossibility of our mutual attraction, at our defiance of the odds and conventions and proprieties that should rightfully have kept us apart.

Just as Tanner's Jeep slipped out of view, another plane rumbled overhead, reminding me of the night when I'd met Jodie, talking late on this same terrace. Now she was dead, and her wedding ring, taken by her killer, had been found near the bottom of the road, in some bushes near the—

"Good God," I mumbled, standing. My lips quavered as I struggled against my own disbelief, but suddenly I knew, with complete insight and irrefutable certainty, the secret to Jodie's murder. I paused to recall the entire sequence of events, checking every detail, and the pieces fit together like clockwork. All at once, I felt used, old, gullible, foolish— and angry.

I took a last, stiff swallow of the kir, set down the glass, and marched indoors.

Guests were arriving quickly now, their cars whisked away by a small battalion of uniformed parking valets. Most of the partygoers still mingled in the expansive entrance hall, gabbing giddily about the house, the opening of the college, and of course, the still-unsolved murder. Waiters plied the crowd, angling between the guests with their trays, delivering drinks to some, taking orders from others. A huge chandelier, modern and asymmetrical in design, adorned with long, irregular shards of faceted crystal, hung high over the heads of all, flashing random splinters of light as diverse as the people and conversations below.

Stepping into the fray from the living room, where the pianist plunked away at a medley of show tunes, entertaining only himself, I spotted Grant talking to Paul near the far end of the hall, away from the crowd. Grant, as usual, had dressed impeccably for the occasion, choosing a jacket and slacks of slightly different desert hues, suggesting sand and sage; Paul, as usual, wore basic black. Even at a distance, I could tell from Grant's facial expressions and gentle gestures that he had seized the first possible moment to take Paul aside and offer words of comfort and reassurance. Paul listened quietly, nodding his appreciation of Grant's thoughtfulness. As I approached them, both turned and smiled.

"Evening, Claire," said Paul.

"Great outfit," said Grant, winking his approval. "Red does become you."

"Gentlemen," I greeted them. "Hope I'm not interrupting."

"Nah," Grant assured me with a soft laugh. "I understand from Glenn's secretary that you arrived early for a 'private meeting.' So tell us. What did—?"

"That can wait," I cut him off. "I need to talk to your brother. Do you know if he's on duty tonight?"

Grant and Paul exchanged a look of guarded surprise. Paul asked me, "You need to talk to Detective Knoll—now? Why?"

Tanner Griffin had just stepped indoors from the parking court, causing heads to turn. He was easily the youngest of the guests that evening and unquestionably the most handsome man on the premises. Watching him, I realized that I had previously seen him wearing not only shorts but heavy work shoes as well. Tonight he presented another image entirely, wearing black slacks and classic, dressy bluchers with a white linen shirt—pure and timeless, both easy and sophisticated. The pants nicely displayed the bottom half of his jaw-dropping physique; the shirt hung matter-of-factly from broad, square shoulders, setting off his deep, perfect tan and his mop of sandy hair. He looked about, searching for me, returning the smiles of nearby guests who couldn't take their eyes off him. Exchanging a few brief greetings, he introduced himself here and there, shaking hands. Kiki, who was standing near the doorway when he entered, had deduced his identity from my description and now hustled toward him, bracelets jangling through the din, eager to make his acquaintance.

Standing down the hall with Grant and Paul, I had observed all this in silence. From where he stood, Paul could see the door, and it was apparent from his expression that he couldn't quite place Tanner, whom he'd met on campus three days earlier. Then, with a flash of recognition, he asked, "Isn't that—?"

"Yes," I answered without elaboration.

Grant, with his back to the door, had seen none of the hoo-ha surrounding Tanner's entrance. He patiently reminded me, "You haven't answered Paul's question. Why do you need to talk to my brother Larry?"

I stepped close to both of them, tightening our circle and hiding me from Tanner's view. "I won't beat around the bush; there isn't time." Pausing briefly, I announced, "I know who killed Jodie."

Both Grant and Paul were momentarily stunned, unprepared for my flat declaration. "Well, who—?" they asked with a confused mixture of relief and skepticism. "Are you sure?"

"All in due time. I had my doubts, but now I'm sure."

As we spoke, Tanner had begun to cut through the crowd, making his way farther into the hall, still glancing about in search of me. Grasping Grant's and Paul's forearms, I turned our threesome at an angle that better hid me.

Standing in this new position, I could tell by the blank astonishment on Grant's face that he'd just gotten a good look at Tanner. "Merciful heavens . . . ," he mumbled, staring at Tanner with wide, intent eyes, unwavering and catlike. He looked ready to drool—or pounce.

Leaning close to Grant's ear, I told him, meaningfully, "Yes, that's the mechanic Jodie hired to work on Paul's car."

Paul placed his hand on my shoulder, asking, "Is he . . . dangerous?"

I assured him, "There's nothing to fear—not yet." I turned back to Grant, asking again, "Is Larry on duty tonight?"

"I'm not sure, but you can always reach him through his pager." Grant slipped his hand inside the breast pocket of his jacket. "Here, use my cell phone." Handing it to me, he told me the programmed code that would beep his brother anytime, anywhere.

Nodding my thanks, I stepped away in search of privacy to make the call, but then I turned back to watch Grant and Paul, who were huddled in conversation, already comparing notes on the evening's developments. Returning to them, I gathered them near.

"Keep this quiet," I told them. "Don't cause a stir. Things will heat up fast enough when Larry gets here."

Then, with phone in hand, I sidled out of the hall.

Fifteen minutes later, I was waiting outside the house in the parking court when Larry Knoll pulled in. Opening the door of the unmarked white sedan, he stepped out and showed the valet his badge. "Leave it here in front," he told the kid. "I shouldn't be long."

Stepping toward each other, we met on the pavement and clasped hands. Dispensing with other greetings, he simply asked, "You're sure?"

"Absolutely. It all adds up."

Walking me toward the house, he said, "I have to admit, Claire, I'm impressed by your past diligence, *and* your current confidence. Tell you what. The house looks crowded, and you know the lay of the place better than I do. I want *you* to choreograph the unmasking tonight."

Stopping in my tracks, I blurted, *"Me?"*

He laughed, tugging me onward. "I'll be there to back you up."

When we entered the house, it was indeed crowded. All the guests had arrived, and the party was in full swing. Noise, music, and laughter shot through the air, as did random flashes of light, refracted by the long, daggerlike crystals of the chandelier.

Standing beneath it, in the center of the hall, was Tide Arden, craning her sinewy neck as she surveyed the party's to and fro. As I shepherded Larry through the mob to the side hall that led to Glenn's office, I caught Tide's eye, bidding her to follow us. As it happened, Grant and Paul were huddled where I'd left them, doubtless still engrossed in speculating on where the evening was headed. Seeing me with the detective, both Paul and Grant instinctively dropped their discussion and joined Tide, following us down the side hall.

Arriving at the double mahogany doors, where the party's din was sufficiently distant to allow normal conversation, I asked Tide, "Is Glenn still in his study?"

"Yes, but he should *never* be disturbed."

"Claire!" said Tanner, rushing down the hall toward us. *"There* you are. I've been looking all over for you." He stopped inches in front of me, achingly gorgeous as ever. Now at close range, Grant looked him up and down, not once but twice, unable to conceal his hungry fascination.

"Ah! Tanner! I guess I missed you in the crowd," I fibbed, taking his hand, but offering no other sign of affection, as planned. "I'd heard you were here, but I couldn't find you." Dropping his hand, I quickly introduced him to Tide, Larry, and Grant. He already knew Paul, who warily said hello.

"Gosh," said Tanner, bright-eyed, looking about, "what a fantastic place. Thanks so much for including—"

"Tanner," I interrupted him, hooking my arm around his, "let's find a quieter place to talk." As if just then noticing the mahogany doors, I suggested, "How about in here?"

Tide stepped forward to deter me, but she was too late—I'd already turned the knob, opened one of the doors, and stuck my head inside.

The room was dimly lit, as before. Glenn sat in his high-backed chair, behind his desk, silhouetted by the bank of computers on the far wall. I said, "Excuse me?"

Glenn had already looked up, hearing the door open. "Oh, it's you, Claire." He smiled. "What can I do for you?"

I stepped inside with Tanner in tow. "Sorry to disturb you, but your guests have been wondering where you are."

He waved me in, explaining, "I was just finishing up."

Tide opened the door wide as she rushed in. "I'm so sorry, Mr. Yeats. I told Ms. Gray that you shouldn't be disturbed, but—" She stopped, frustrated, watching Larry, Grant, and Paul file into the room as well.

Glenn laughed, standing at his desk. "It's perfectly all right, Tide. Any friends of Claire's are friends of mine." He'd already met everyone in the room, so there was no need for introductions. "Come on in, everyone. Get comfortable," he offered, volleying fragments of small talk with his guests as we settled into the room. He made a point of telling Tanner, "I understand that Claire has convinced you to enroll in her program at DAC. Welcome aboard."

Paul had been in Glenn's identical office on campus, but this was new turf for Grant, Larry, and Tanner, who were duly wowed by the luxe appointments and technical wizardry of the billionaire's inner sanctum. Glenn sat again at his granite-topped desk with the grid of computer monitors glowing blue behind him. When he tapped a button on his desk, the room's ambient lighting ramped up to a homey level conducive to conversation. I stood aside, listening to the chitchat and watching with interest as the others took seats within the grouping of leather furniture arranged in front of Glenn's desk.

Perpendicular to the left side of the desk were two armchairs. Tide immediately chose the chair nearest the desk, where I had sat earlier that evening; I reasoned that this was where she normally sat during working hours if summoned to take notes or dictation. Tanner sat in the chair next to her, away from the desk. Across from these two chairs, perpendicular to the right side of the desk, was a small sofa. As Grant had kept Paul company since their arrival that evening, they now sat together on the sofa, Paul near the desk, across from Tide, and Grant away from the desk, directly across from Tanner, affording himself a fine view. One remaining armchair faced the desk squarely, closing the arrangement of furniture. Further behind this last chair, also facing the desk, were the room's double doors. Larry motioned that I should take the last seat, which I did, with Tanner to my left, Grant to my right. Larry had been ambling about the room, but now stationed himself near the doors, closing them, literally "backing me up," as promised.

Paul, sitting near Glenn, spoke to him over the desk about various details of the school's opening on Monday. Tide magically produced a steno pad from somewhere and began making a "to do" list for Glenn, adding a few items of her own. Grant wasted no time getting to know Tanner, leaning forward, elbows to knees, entranced by every word the young man uttered. During all of this interplay, neither Larry nor I spoke.

At a lull in the conversation, I stood, clearing my throat. With a soft laugh, I stepped to the center of the group, telling them, "I suppose you're all wondering why I've gathered you here this evening." It was a stock line from nearly every drawing-room mystery I'd ever directed, but the humor was lost on my little audience, who gazed at me with blank stares, wondering why, in fact, I *had* gathered them there.

I continued, "There's a cloud hanging over tonight's merriment—

the tragedy that darkened our lives nearly a week ago."

Reminded of his loss, Paul bowed his head, covering his brow with one hand. Grant patted the widower's shoulder. Glenn stiffened in his chair, sitting back from his desk. Tide scratched a few notes, frowning her disapproval of my topic.

"The untimely death of Jodie Metz-Huron has not only shaken the life of her loving husband, but it has also inconvenienced our esteemed employer, D. Glenn Yeats, by jeopardizing the efficient and timely open-ing of Desert Arts College, a project he has pursued with a particular passion."

Glenn eyed me through a leery squint, wondering where I was headed.

Turning away from him, I told the others, "There's nothing to be gained by protracting the suspense, or the inconvenience, of Jodie's death. I've gathered you here to inform you that the riddle of her mur-der has been solved."

My listeners reacted with cautious surprise, subdued chatter, and nat-urally, extreme curiosity. Hoping to nudge me toward my revelation, Grant asked, "Does the solution to the riddle relate to the wedding ring, which was found at Nirvana yesterday?"

"Certainly. The killer took the ring. But this wasn't simply a matter of theft, as it first appeared, nor was the ring taken to 'send a message,' as I later theorized. No." I turned to Tanner, crossing my arms. "The clue to the identity of Jodie's killer rests with Jodie's green car and with the timing of repairs."

As everyone paused to consider this, Tanner looked at me with wide, astonished eyes. Glenn mumbled something to Tide, whose pen began scratching. Grant said something quietly soothing to Paul. With ex-pressionless features, I stared at Tanner. Then, from behind me, Paul said, "Wait a minute, Claire. One small detail. Jodie's car wasn't repaired; mine was."

I grinned at Tanner. "Exactly, Paul. And that's what makes it so clear to me"—slowly I turned—"that *you* killed Jodie."

After a moment of hushed dismay, the group erupted into animated discussion, gabbing among each other and firing questions at me. The gist of their hubbub was that they didn't believe my accusation. Paul flatly denied it, telling me, "I'm not only insulted, Claire, but dumb-founded. I could *never* have killed Jodie; I *loved* her. But more to the point, I was on a plane when she died, as *you* well know. You picked me up at the airport and drove me home."

His statement quelled the rest of the group, as he'd succinctly stated the alibi that had held him above suspicion from the start.

"Hear me out," I ordered him, and everyone. "Let's start at the beginning. We know that Jodie had been having an intimate affair with Dr. Percy Blair for some weeks; the sainted Dr. Do-Good himself has admitted to it. When Paul was sent to Dallas last weekend by Glenn to recruit the glass sculptor Dane Carmichael for the DAC faculty, Jodie and the doctor seized the opportunity to 'play house' in the Hurons' home—and bed—overnight on Friday, claiming to their respective spouses that they were working an odd shift at the medical center. Paul's plane was due into Palm Springs at nine-twenty on Saturday morning, and Dr. Blair left the Hurons' house shortly after eight, leaving behind both a cuff link and the strong, lingering scent of his patchouli. Jodie was alive and well when he last saw her, exactly as he has claimed.

"For some reason, either planned or accidental, Paul ended up on an earlier flight home that morning. The frequency of planes gliding over the terrace this evening triggered the idea, and I recalled Glenn telling us that there are *lots* of flights between here and Dallas—it's an AirWest commuter route. So Paul ended up on an earlier plane, arriving, let's say, around eight. This is where the whole business of the car repairs comes into play, and it's crucial.

"Jodie had taken Paul's blue Honda to Desert Detail for repairs of a fender bender. It was originally supposed to be returned to the Hurons on Friday, while Paul was still in Dallas, but because it needed repainting, de-livery would be delayed till after the weekend. Jodie learned this from Tanner on Friday and informed Paul by phone. It would have no effect on my plans to pick up Paul on Saturday morning, as arranged before he left.

"Paul arrived at the airport earlier than planned, so I wasn't there to pick him up. Since he now knew that he'd be without a car for a few days, he decided to rent one at the airport, drive himself home, then phone me to explain that he didn't need a ride that morning. He prob-ably rented the car through Monday.

"The drive from the airport takes twenty-five minutes, so let's say Paul arrived home around eight-thirty. He was surprised, of course, to find Jodie and her green car there, since she was supposed to be working a nursing shift, but he was *enraged* to smell the lingering scent of patchouli. Allergic to fragrances, he knew that he wasn't smelling perfume of Jodie's (she never wore any) but the scent of a man who had just slept there, confirming a suspicion they had lately fought over. They fought again, but this time Paul got physical, imparting the lethal blow to Jodie's chest at, say, eight-forty. The patchouli had by now triggered his sneezing and splotchy eyes. He took Jodie's ring (perhaps because he was sentimental, or to underscore his anger at being cuckolded, or to suggest theft, or to later frame another suspect—there are plenty of possible motives); then he got back into his rental car and tore back to the airport with his baggage. Little more than an hour after renting the car, he returned it to a surprised clerk, Sarad Patel, at the RideRite Rent-a-Car counter.

"A few minutes later, I arrived in the nick of time to meet his nine-twenty flight. Paul was waiting at the baggage carousel, which had just started to turn, and I found it strange that he had his bags before anyone else—"

Paul interrupted, "I carried them on, for Christ's sake." His voice, to say nothing of its testy tone, took everyone by surprise.

I shook my head, asking, "Then why were you waiting at the carousel? If you already had your bags, and I wasn't waiting at the gate, why wouldn't you just go out to the curb to look for me?"

He didn't answer. He didn't need to. He'd gone to the carousel to reinforce the appearance that he'd been on the nine-twenty flight.

I continued, "While we were at the carousel, I noted Paul's sneezing and runny eyes, which he attributed to hay fever. I later learned from Glenn that Paul has no medical record of allergy to pollens."

Glenn crossed his arms, grinning, as if to say that I should never have doubted his computerized records.

"Then, as Paul and I left the airport together, Sarad Patel waved at us from the RideRite counter. I mistook this gesture for random friendliness, when in fact, it signaled recognition of the customer he'd dealt with twice that morning—Paul Huron. Moments later, out at the curb, while Paul was loading his bags into my car, he ripped off the airline tags, which were taken away by the wind, removing any immediate evidence of which flight he was on—he would depend on his printed itinerary as 'soft proof' of his arrival time that morning, allowing me to corroborate it.

"Driving home to Palm Desert, we stopped along the way at a traffic light in Rancho Mirage near the Nirvana gatehouse. Paul could have tossed Jodie's ring into the bushes from my open car as we waited there, or he could have planted it there anytime during the following week, attempting to muddle the investigation while casting suspicion on Glenn."

Looking genuinely hurt and betrayed, the billionaire turned to Paul, hoping for a denial, but Paul refused to make eye contact with him.

"Finally, we arrived at the house. It was now nine-fifty. Entering the kitchen through the garage, I noticed the green car parked there, thinking nothing of it, assuming that it was Paul's car returned from the shop and that Jodie's was at the hospital. It was an easy mistake for *me* to make, but"—I paused for effect, stressing the importance of this point as I turned in a circle for everyone's benefit—"but *Paul would have instantly known otherwise.* He should have reacted to finding his wife's car at home. Instead, he waited till he got indoors to react, when he 'found' Jodie's body. Think about it:

"First, the only reason for Paul to pretend that he didn't recognize the car was to foster the illusion that he still assumed Jodie was at the hospital. Second, the only reason to create such an illusion was to conceal his knowledge that Jodie was not only inside the house, but dead. And third, the only reason he could *have* such knowledge was that he'd already been there, an hour earlier, when he killed her."

As my words sank in, the group recognized the strength of my logic. All heads turned to Paul, who stared at me, unflinching. Next to him on the leather sofa, Grant shifted the weight of his body. The cushions squeaked in the silence as he moved away from Paul by perhaps an inch. It might as well have been a mile.

I told everyone, "Paul readily convinced me that Jodie's death was a shocking surprise to him. With that accomplished, his act continued. Crazed by 'grief,' he did a good job of trashing the crime scene, seriously wrenching the initial investigation. He also did a good job of sobbing and blubbering, helped along by his retriggered reaction to the scent of patchouli. Later that day, he reported to police that he'd discovered other items of value missing from the house, a gold watch and some silver tableware, but these items probably never existed. He was simply trying to bolster the bungled-burglary theory and to cast further suspicion on his housekeeper, Oralia Alvarez, a hardworking woman who exhibited far greater loyalty to her employer than he did to her."

Tide Arden, finding this detail particularly damning, could not conceal her disgust, slapping her steno pad on the nearby desktop with such vigor that the noise made me jolt. Others gasped. "Sorry," she said demurely.

Paul crossed his arms and turned to Glenn. Looking his benefactor in the eye, he said, "This is pure speculation, all of it. She's gone off the deep end with these accusations. Seriously, Glenn, the woman is dangerous. She needs help."

I stepped in front of him, planting my butt on the edge of Glenn's desk. "I'm not finished, Paul. It gets far worse. And once again, the key rests in people's confusion over your two cars, the nearly identical Hondas."

He snorted a derisive laugh. "Here she goes again."

I told the others, "On Monday, I learned from Tanner that Paul's blue car was still in the shop, and I later reported to Paul that arrangements needed to be made for its return. Paul mentioned that he didn't need two cars, but at the same time, he was eager to get the other one back, as driving Jodie's was a grim reminder of the murder. After his blue car was returned on Tuesday, Paul *always* drove that one—until tonight, when he arrived in the green car." I flipped my hands, asking anyone, "Why?"

Paul mimicked my gesture while answering in an exasperated tone, "Because my own car was nearly out of gas. I didn't notice till I was ready to leave tonight. I was running late and didn't want to take the time to fill it, so I drove the green car instead. Big deal."

I rose from the desk and stepped to the center of the group, telling them, "A reasonable explanation. But I have a better one. On Thursday morning, when the photo of the wedding ring appeared on the front page of the *Desert Sun,* Paul was upset that they'd run his own head shot with the story, claiming that he wanted no sympathy. In fact, he was upset because someone might recognize him, someone who might recall an unusual incident involving Paul at the time of the murder: Sarad Patel, the clerk at the airport car-rental counter, who knew that Paul had arrived on Saturday morning, rented a car for a few days, then returned it within an hour. Seeing Paul's face on the front page of the paper, Patel might begin to connect the dots very quickly."

Turning squarely to Paul, I addressed the others, continuing, "So Paul was on a mission on Thursday, a mission to save himself. Though he claimed that morning to have 'tons of work' to do on campus, his whereabouts were a mystery most of the day. Why? He was stalking Patel, and finally, that evening, managed to kill the clerk—a pleasant young man, a husband and father, the victim of a hit-and-run 'accident.' The car that killed him jumped the curb and crushed him near the sidewalk, doubtless sustaining some damage in the process. The damaged car, a dusty-metallic blue Honda, is now hidden at home in Paul's garage. And *that's* why he drove the other car tonight."

I moved one step nearer the sculptor and paused before accusing him. "Paul, you murdered not one victim but two. And this afternoon, you very nearly added a third victim to your list—me."

"Good God," said Glenn weakly from behind his desk, sounding sickened. "What are you talking about, Claire?"

I recounted for everyone the incident in the theater, concluding, "When the lights went out, I thought I heard a thud, someone leaving by the stage door. It was Paul. Not an hour earlier, we'd been talking in his office, and I mentioned that I'd soon be checking the tech installation. Paul was 'Mr. Indispensable' on campus, so he had access to every building and a working knowledge of the stage hydraulics. He set me up for an 'accident'—and damn near killed me."

No one spoke. No one moved. For all I could tell, no one breathed. Larry Knoll remained standing near the door, where he'd listened to my entire discourse without comment. Paul's eyes were locked on mine.

Then he smiled gently. When he spoke, his cocky manner was replaced by an ameliorating tone. "Claire," he tried to reason, "I can understand how the situation, taken as a whole, might give rise to your suspicions, but really, you've got it all wrong. I'm sure if you—"

"Glenn," I interrupted Paul, having no interest in his squirming, "does your computer have access to flight schedules?"

"Piece of cake," he said, leaning over the keyboard at his desk. "I assume you're interested in AirWest flights, Dallas to Palm Springs, last Saturday, right?"

I didn't need to answer. As he tapped the keys, one of the monitors behind him flashed various pages of information, then settled on the timetable in question. He scrolled to the arrivals, then stopped. "There's Paul's scheduled flight," he told me, highlighting it, "arriving at nine-twenty." He scrolled up a line. "Here we are. The flight before it arrived at five minutes till eight, which neatly fits the scenario you suggested. Very good, Claire. I'm impressed."

Though I appreciated the compliment, I couldn't help noting the irony that it was I myself who had originally placed Paul above suspicion by confirming his scheduled arrival, even producing the printed itinerary from his jacket for Larry Knoll at the crime scene. There was no point, though, in chiding myself for past shortcomings. Onward.

I told Paul, "Before you continue with your denials, you should be aware that three things can now be easily accomplished. First, Glenn can keep typing, and we can check passenger manifests of the two flights, confirming when you really arrived. Second, we can check RideRite's records, confirming that you dealt with Sarad Patel last Saturday, renting a car before Jodie's murder and returning it immediately afterwards. And third"—I glanced toward Larry—"Detective Knoll can get a warrant to enter your garage and check the blue Honda for evidence that it's the vehicle that killed Patel."

Larry nodded. His expression told me that he'd gotten the warrant in motion before arriving at Nirvana that night. No doubt about it, Paul was sunk. Turning back to him, I saw that he knew it, too.

His shoulders had slumped; his head had fallen. When he looked up, a tear slid down his face. There was no patchouli in the room—this was a tear of genuine grief. Quietly, he told me, "I didn't plan to surprise anyone."

"What do you mean, Paul?"

He took a deep breath, then exhaled an agonized sigh. "The early flight—I didn't plan it. I didn't mean to 'catch' Jodie. The recruiting trip was such a washout, I went to bed early on Friday night, got up early on Saturday, and having nothing better to do, headed out to the airport. When I arrived, they said I could just make the earlier flight, so I took it.

"The rest, well . . . it happened essentially as Claire described it. Except, I swear to God, I never meant to kill Jodie. Yes, I was surprised to find her at home when I got there, and yes, I was furious when I smelled the cologne. Suddenly I knew that everything I'd feared, everything we'd fought about, was true—there had indeed been another man. So we fought again that morning. It was verbal; well, it was shouting, and we both said some awful things. As it escalated, it turned into sort of a shoving match. For whatever it's worth, Jodie started the physical stuff, and I began pushing back. It didn't last long, though, and I still don't understand what happened. I hit her in the chest with my palms— not meaning to really hurt her, much less kill her—when she suddenly just dropped to the floor, gasping for breath. Within seconds, it seemed, she was dead."

While Paul was telling his story, I had returned to my chair and perched on the arm near Tanner, who reached over to pat my hand.

Paul continued, "In a panic, I hatched the scheme to return to the airport and fudge my arrival. Before I left the house, I took Jodie's ring, thinking it might be useful in building a story; there was no plan for it at that point. So I let the ring angle evolve as the investigation proceeded, and it wasn't until yesterday, when Detective Knoll called me to meet him at the Nirvana sales office, that I pitched the ring into the bushes near the gatehouse. I was afraid of what might develop if that kid at the car-rental agency recognized my picture in the paper. The ring in the bushes was simply meant to perplex the police and send them down the wrong trail again." He paused, shaking his head, dragging a weary hand across his sweaty brow.

I asked, "Yesterday, as the hours passed, didn't you begin to feel relieved that nothing had come of your photo in the morning paper? Chances are, Sarad Patel never even saw it."

Without hesitation or emotion, Paul said, "I couldn't take that chance. All day long, I was sure he would read the paper at the airport, and I went there to watch, but as far as I could tell, he never got around to it. So I figured, maybe he reads the paper at home, saving the morning paper till evening. Lots of people do that. Poor kid, he gave me one clean chance to make sure he wouldn't see the paper that night, and I took it."

Lest there be any ambiguity to Paul's statement, I prompted, "Meaning, you ran him down in your car, killing him as he walked from the bus to his home last night."

"Yes. I had to."

Having a roomful of fellow witnesses to these admissions, Larry Knoll left his position at the door and stepped among us. Paul stood, knowing what would follow. He offered no resistance as Larry handcuffed him, recited his rights, and led him toward the double doors.

The rest of us sat speechless as they crossed the room. Larry opened one of the doors, admitting the thump and babble of party noises from the hall. He turned to tell me, "Thanks, Claire. Stay in touch." Then he led Paul out into the fray, closing the door behind them.

I got up from the arm of the chair and stepped a single pace toward the door, wanting to respond. But Larry was gone, of course, as was the killer who had lived among us. The mystery was now solved. The drama had ended.

There was a moment's silence.

"Whew!" said Glenn from behind me. "I could sure use a drink." I heard the scrape of his chair as he pushed it back from his desk and stood.

In the next moment, everyone had risen, and as I turned, they gathered around me—Glenn, Tide, Tanner, and Grant—raising their voices in a chorus of congratulations while clucking their dismay over Paul's desperate actions and the hellish future he now faced.

Standing among them, listening, I felt a smile bend my lips as I considered the broader implications of this bittersweet evening.

I hadn't lost a friend and colleague.

I'd gained a housekeeper.

Glenn wasn't the only one who needed a drink. The night was still young, the party was at full tilt, and it was time for a martini.

I didn't even need to ask for it. As we filed out of the study and joined the crowd, Grant offered, "Can I get milady a little something?"

"Thank you, dear." I squeezed his arm. "You know *just* how I like it."

"Right, doll—flecks of ice on the surface." And he pattered off to the bar.

Predictably, Larry's dramatic exit through the house with Paul in shackles had caused a stir among the guests, all of whom knew Paul. Word quickly spread that two nasty local murders had been solved right there on the premises, and while there was naturally some dismay in learning the truth about Paul, there was a general consensus that the arrest had afforded a marvelous entertainment—it would be an evening long remembered.

Glenn's motive for hosting the bash had been to surround Paul with fellowship and merriment while easing him into a difficult weekend, so the party had now lost both its purpose and its guest of honor. The plan had been to serve dinner late, but Paul's arrest had provided such a stunning, early focal point that the rest of the evening began to feel anticlimactic, so Glenn asked the caterers to serve dinner as quickly as possible.

The poolside buffet was simple but elegant, and the terrace offered a spectacular setting under the night sky. The crescent moon had risen high from the horizon, looking smaller, bluer, and brighter. A riot of stars arched from the nearby Santa Rosas to the distant peaks of the San

Bernardinos. A warm breeze drifted through the cool night, carrying with it the howl of a lone coyote, calling from the depths of an arroyo.

People sat in clusters, talking while they ate. Running through the chitchat was a common theme of crime and punishment, hardly the lighthearted banter of revelry. The mood of the party had grown serious, and in doing so, the party died.

When the meal was finished and its remains had been cleared, most of the guests opted for one more drink, then said their good-byes, thanking Glenn, lauding me, and lamenting Paul's fate. Glenn dismissed the pianist and most of the staff, but kept the bartender, who eventually had only five of us to serve—Glenn, Grant, Kiki, Tanner, and me. It was not very late, barely past ten o'clock.

Lingering on the terrace, we settled comfortably on a cluster of furniture near the pool's edge. As hero of the evening, I was allotted the chaise longue—a recumbent throne, as it were. I stretched out on its ample cushions with a martini at hand and Tanner sitting at my feet—the perfect setup. Glenn sat near me on an ottoman. Grant and Kiki lolled in armchairs. The lone coyote had found a friend, and they both serenaded us from the distance.

"A crime . . . of *passion,*" Grant intoned theatrically, addressing the heavens. Then he turned to me. "You were right, doll, right from the start. Jodie's death had nothing to do with greed. It was a crime of passion, pure and simple."

I nodded. "And it was the basest of passions that killed her: rage."

Tanner nodded. "But was it murder? The way she died was sort of a medical fluke, and Paul said he never meant to kill her."

"I believe him," said Glenn.

"So do I," Kiki seconded, then drank from whatever concoction had caught her fancy that night. Though she hadn't been in the study to hear anything Paul had said, she was generous with her friendship and had no qualms about extending to Paul the benefit of her doubt.

I told them, "The prosecutor, judge, and jury can wrangle over the particulars of Jodie's death, but Sarad Patel is another matter altogether."

Glenn shook his head. "Open and shut, I'm afraid."

Grant concurred. "Calculated, premeditated, cold-blooded, willful, ruthless, blackest murder most foul." He smiled, adding, "The prose-cution rests."

"Even so," said Glenn, "I pity Paul. What he did was horrible, but he was not, at his core, an evil man, a born killer."

"Hold on a minute." I reminded everyone, "Paul tried to kill *me* this very afternoon. I have no lingering sympathy for the man."

"That was truly unconscionable of him," Glenn admitted. "Still, cir-cumstances spun out of control for him, and one thing led to another. I wish I could have helped him."

"You called him 'indispensable.' Now what?"

"I'll adjust. Always have." Glenn took a hefty swallow from his glass. Tanner stifled a laugh.

I nudged him with my foot. "What's so funny, young man?"

"I was just thinking—back in the study, when you stood up and announced that you'd solved the riddle of Jodie's death, you seemed to be hinting that *I* was responsible."

Grant said, "That's certainly the impression she gave *me* out in the hall, while talking to Paul." Under his breath, he added, to Tanner, "I was *sure* she was mistaken, of course."

I explained, "I *meant* to give the impression that I suspected Tanner."

"Thanks," he said with a snort.

"It was merely a temporary ploy," I assured him. "Grant and Paul were schmoozing, and I needed to get in touch with Grant's brother. The nature of my urgent police business was obvious enough—I'd fig-ured out who killed Jodie—but I couldn't let Paul know that I suspected *him* until after we'd lured him safely into Glenn's study, with a cop stationed at the door."

Glenn leaned forward, laughing. "For a moment there, I thought she was trying to pin it on *me.*"

I now felt foolish for having concocted my exaggerated "castration theory," and I was grateful that I'd never had the chance to share it with Larry. With the mystery solved, Glenn's sinister edge seemed to evap-orate. I admitted to him, "There were moments when I had doubts about *both* you and Tanner, but by the time we all piled into your office, I knew exactly who the guilty party was."

With good-natured sarcasm, Grant told me, "I'm sure Henry Harris will be relieved to hear that. Maybe Arlene's house deal will happen after all."

Tanner asked, "Who?"

I explained, "Henry Harris was one of my *other* two suspects. He had heart surgery this past summer, and Jodie helped nurse him through a long recovery. At her memorial service, both Henry and his doctor said that they had loved Jodie, raising my suspicions. But it turns out that Jodie couldn't have been Henry's 'other woman' because Jodie's 'other man' was none other than Henry's doctor, Jodie's boss—Dr. Percival Do-Good Blair."

Kiki gasped. "What a horrible name. Who'd *do* that to a child?"

Grant told her, "Claire made up the 'Do-Good' part."

"No," said Kiki, "I mean, *Percival?*"

I told them, "Percy-poo may be off the hook for murder, but he's in deep trouble with his wife, and Lord only knows how this'll affect his career."

"Other people's problems . . . ," said Kiki, dismissing Blair's plight. "Tonight is no time to fret over misfortune. Tonight we celebrate Claire's triumph." And she downed the last of her drink.

To a chorus of cheers and hear-hears, the others did likewise.

Glenn gave me a sidelong glance. "All's well that ends well, Claire. But honestly, it worries me to think of the dangers you faced."

I bristled, then let his comment pass. Though tempted, I saw no point in rebutting him. The issue, after all, was now moot. My sleuthing days were over—weren't they? With a laugh, I assured Glenn, as well as the others, "I'll make every effort to restrict my future triumphs to the theatrical variety."

As the others joined me with their laughter, though, I couldn't help thinking of Larry Knoll's parting words—"Stay in touch."

Glenn stood, displaying his empty glass. "One more round?"

My martini glass was still half-full, but had lost its chill. "I could use a refresher. We'll call it a nightcap."

Tanner rose from where he sat at the foot of my chaise. Taking our glasses, he offered, "I'll get them, Glenn." They were by now on a first-name basis, but neither man yet had an inkling that the other's interest in me was intimate as well as professional.

As Tanner reached for the remaining glasses, Grant and Kiki exchanged a glance that asked, Should we? This would be a mutual decision, as they'd ridden together in Grant's car. Then Kiki told us, "If you don't mind, I'd prefer to call it a night." She set down her glass and checked her purse.

"Me too," said Grant, rising. "Saturday's a busy day for me."

Kiki stood. "It was wonderful, Glenn, as always. And Claire, I couldn't be prouder of you." Her expansive smile reminded me of the girl I'd befriended some thirty-five years earlier at college.

Swinging my feet from the chaise, I stood, straightened my skirt, and offered her a parting hug.

Tanner headed indoors to the bar to get our fresh drinks.

Glenn said his farewells to Kiki and Grant, then checked his watch, saying, "I'll see you out to your car. My European offices are just opening, and I need to phone in." Turning to me, he asked, "Will you be okay on your own out here? This won't take five minutes."

"Take your time. The night couldn't be lovelier."

So Glenn escorted Kiki inside, followed by Grant. As Grant was about to step through the invisible wall to the living room, he turned and offered me a jaunty wave.

With a finger wag, I summoned him back. Stepping alongside the pool to meet him halfway, I told him wryly, "Straight to bed tonight. Busy day tomorrow."

"Actually, after I drop Kiki at Villa Paseo, I thought it might be a nice night for a spin up to the Springs."

"You wouldn't be headed in the vicinity of Fusión, would you?"

"Now, *there's* an idea," he joshed, as if the thought hadn't occurred to him. "I'll bet the late seating will just be getting out."

"What was the kid's name?"

"Kane." Grant looked momentarily lost in the memory of his pet car parker.

I gave him a hug, kissed his cheek. "Good luck."

"You too, with Tanner. Lord, Claire, he's drop-dead." With a twitch of his brow, Grant added, "Would that he liked boys . . ."

I shrugged. "Sorry."

"Hey"—he snapped his fingers—"I've been dying to ask: Why did Glenn ask you to come early to the party tonight?"

With a little groan, I told him, "You *won't* believe it. It's a long story, so it'll have to wait."

"I'd suggest breakfast tomorrow, but my overnight plans are still iffy—"

"So are mine."

"—so how about dinner tomorrow night?"

"I'd love to. Call me at home."

He squeezed my arm. "Good night, doll." And he walked inside the house, leaving me alone.

Strolling past the pool toward the dark edge of the terrace, I sat on the stone parapet and looked out into the night. The vast sky, the mountains tinged by moonlight, the warm breeze that carried the slightest scent of oleander, filled me with a deep but ambiguous peace colored with pleasant ironies.

The most apparent of these agreeable inconsistencies were the ironies of my new life. The setting, career, and fresh challenges I faced in California seemed light-years removed from New York, where I'd lived and worked for decades. Only three weeks since moving, I had already entangled myself in a murder investigation, handily wrapping it up before the start of classes at the college. Oddly, with the murder puzzle solved, I felt a sense of loss as well as closure.

Other ironies, equally benign, were more cerebral. Though still struggling with lifelong insecurities, I had made some important, unexpected progress during a week when I had focused not on solving ephemeral issues of psychology but on the nuts-and-bolts issues of a crime. For the first time, I dared to wonder if there might be resolution ahead for my strained relationship with my mother. I decided to give Gwyn a call the next day. We needed to talk.

Even more mind-boggling were the new possibilities that faced me on the romantic front, where things had perked up considerably. Having fretted over the middle-age vexations of inadequacy and loneliness, I was suddenly found desirable by not one younger man but two.

Looking back at the lavish mountainside estate and all that it represented, I understood exactly what Glenn Yeats had to offer. Looking inside the house, I could see Tanner Griffin standing at the bar, chatting with the bartender while waiting for our drinks. Tanner's solid poise, his youth, his dreams, and his sheer magnetism were apparent at a glance, and I understood exactly what *he* had to offer.

Decisions, decisions . . .

A smile stretched my lips as I sat on the parapet, alone with the universe for a few moments. Then the profound but pleasant ironies of nature itself rose to the surface of my thoughts, and I was awed by the strange, mystic beauty of the Sonoran Desert. At first blush, its heat and barren sands might strike anyone as a hostile wasteland, but now, iron-ically, it felt very much like home.

Once again, I heard the distant howl of a coyote, drifting on the breeze from the crags of an arroyo.

Was he singing to the moon?

Or was he spooked by a dust devil—a dust devil dancing through the warm autumn night?